About the Author

Georgia Nix found a love for writing as soon as she picked up a pen. She fondly remembers being in junior school and taking a story home with her due to there being no class time left to finish it. From then on, she loved to write. She always seemed to have her head in the clouds! Georgia also adores animals. The idea for *Silent Delusion* first came to her when she was seventeen and feeding the rabbits at an animal sanctuary. From then on, the idea grew.

Silent Delusion

Georgia Erica Nix

Silent Delusion

Olympia Publishers
London

www.olympiapublishers.com
OLYMPIA PAPERBACK EDITION

Copyright © Georgia Erica Nix 2023

The right of Georgia Erica Nix to be identified as author of
this work has been asserted in accordance with sections 77 and 78 of the
Copyright, Designs and Patents Act 1988.

All Rights Reserved

No reproduction, copy or transmission of this publication
may be made without written permission.
No paragraph of this publication may be reproduced,
copied or transmitted save with the written permission of the publisher, or in
accordance with the provisions
of the Copyright Act 1956 (as amended).

Any person who commits any unauthorised act in relation to
this publication may be liable to criminal
prosecution and civil claims for damage.

A CIP catalogue record for this title is
available from the British Library.

ISBN: 978-1-80074-650-3

This is a work of fiction.
Names, characters, places and incidents originate from the writer's imagination.
Any resemblance to actual persons, living or dead, is purely coincidental.

First Published in 2023

Olympia Publishers
Tallis House
2 Tallis Street
London
EC4Y 0AB

Printed in Great Britain

Dedication

I dedicate this book to my wonderful mother, Karen. Karen, thank you for always supporting me.

Acknowledgements

Thank you once again to my mother, Karen, who encouraged me from day one. Thank you to my partner, Paul, for supporting me all the way in my publishing journey. Thank you to my friends, Melissa, Jean Sammy, Ray, Mo, Cameron and many others for supporting me also!

Chapter One

Melinda groaned and faced away from the offending TV. Her dark, almost black, eyes bored into the magazine she was reading.

"Ashley, for goodness' sake." Melinda threw the magazine down. "Turn that crap off!"

As always, the little girl was sitting cross-legged in front of the TV, gazing adoringly at the band that paraded onscreen. Through bites of cereal, Ashley sang the horrendous lyrics:

"Stay with me, let me in…"

"Ashley!"

"Because together, we will win…"

"All right all right, just turn the volume down, before my ears start bleeding."

God, the band was terrible, cheesier than the crisps she'd eaten for breakfast! And yet, Ashley watched their stupid TV show every morning like some demented robot, and Kenzie, Tom, and Callum sang to who she presumed was her.

Melinda jeered:

"This is a load of shit, a load of shit, a load of shit—"

"You're a load of shit," Ashley retorted. "Shush!"

Melinda smirked to herself. Her hair, constantly varying between straight and wavy, fell over her pale face in breast-length wisps. The blonde streak down the right front strands needed bleaching again, not that it mattered. No amount of hair was enough to shield her from how the band sauntered across the TV as if they owned it.

Ashley couldn't help it. She was seven. She was impressionable, naïve, and the band was the latest craze at school. Ashley was adorable, with her wavy brown hair, dainty figure, and lightly-tanned face patterned with freckles. Caramel, her eyes had a permanent sparkle.

"Aw, Kenzie," Melinda mocked. "My name's Tom and I'm your *best fwend*. Gimmie a hug will you, my best ever fwend—"

"Mel!"

Melinda rolled her eyes. She didn't fancy looking at the models in the magazine again. Curse her thighs for making her so disproportionate! Her breasts were too small, her hips too narrow. Taunting Ashley was much better entertainment:

"Oh look, we're all together now, a bunch of wusses eating cookies and drinking glasses of milk—"

"Mel, stop it!"

Melinda pulled a face. "Hi I'm Kenzie, and I'm a twat who thinks he's stunning but really I look like dog sick—"

Ashley turned the volume up.

"Oh no, no, no," protested Melinda, getting up. "I told you to keep it turned down."

"But I can't hear it. You keep talking."

"Ashley!"

Beaming, Ashley turned to her. "Stay with me, let me in—"

"Right, that's *it*!" Melinda headed for the TV. "It's going off."

"No!" The empty cereal bowl in Ashley's lap was sent soaring across the floor as she scurried across the carpet to the TV. "No, I'll turn it down, I will!"

Melinda sniggered. Placing her hands on her hips, she looked down at the girl as she sat there in her school uniform. "Why do you even like them anyway? Look at them!" She almost screeched with laughter as the mixed-race Callum twirled around in his vile costume, seeming more obscene than ever. "They can't even sing, *especially* Kenzie! And don't even get me started on their outfits—"

"Leave Kenzie alone! He *can* sing! He's the leader of the band. And they're called *Three Beams*!" Ashley whinged pathetically. "Of course they're gonna have three beams on their shirts and colourful trousers and colourful shoes and—"

"Yeah, well they look like prats."

"But—"

"And what's all that rubbish about 'life lessons? Are people your age really that fucking stupid they don't know not to cross the road when the man's red, or not to jump into the deep end of a swimming pool if the sign says no? What next? Are we gonna have Callum forgetting to wash his hands when he goes to the loo and getting explosive diarrhoea?"

Years of secondary school acting worked their magic. Melinda scuffed her feet, and mumbled:

"Hey... uh, I'm Callum. I do sod all for the band and never speak, so I'm literally just there, so, uh—"

"Callum writes the songs!" said Ashley, scrambling to her feet. "He *does* do a lot, he's just shy."

"The names Kenzie. I work out, lounge around on sunbeds, and spend more time in front of the mirror than a teenage girl." Melinda shook her hair just like he did. "Check out my hair, man. It's cool."

"Kenzie does that because he cares about himself. And his hair is *nice.*"

Melinda could see Kenzie singing his solo. She wished for that criminally-high blond hair to fall from his head, and his brown eyes to melt out of their sockets. "No," she said. "It's disgusting."

"Why are you so horrible about them?" Ashley asked. "They haven't done anything to you."

At long last, Melinda moved on to the third, and Ashley's favourite, member. Speaking in a posh drawl, she made sure to pronounce all of his words to the exact letter. "Oh dear, whatever is this monstrosity on the screen of our television?"

Melinda reached for the remote. Ashley dived, but Melinda was too quick for her!

"It looks like we will have to terminate this television show," Melinda continued. "It is most disgraceful."

Ashley stood up and started screaming:

"Shut up! Just leave them alone! Tom *doesn't* talk like that, Callum does do things for the band, and Kenzie is a *much* better singer than *you!*"

Melinda flinched. She tossed the remote to the floor. "Fine," she sat down, and opened her magazine. "Watch your stupid band."

Ashley went back to the TV, just as their mother Julie came bustling into the room.

"For Christ's sake. Can't you two just sit quietly for ten minutes?"

Covered in flour, Julie looked both of her noisy daughters over, her face as red as the hair in her top-knot, and ranted:

"Melinda, you're ridiculous. You're meant to be the oldest; you're eighteen! And as for you, Ashley," the overweight Mom shook her head, nostrils flaring resentment at having her home-run baking business interrupted. "That show possesses you. I have a good mind to stop you watching it."

Her lip quivering, Ashley looked to her sister for support.

Julie continued. "I know everyone else loves them, but that's precisely the problem! They're everywhere, in every shop I go. And Melinda, you're no better about it yourself, with your snide attitude and silly remarks! I heard you, in there. I think the whole street did! Now, sit here and be *quiet* until your dad's ready to take you to—"

The fire alarm! Jack barked hysterically, and Julie's expression transformed from furious to fearful:

"Oh god, the cakes!"

Gaining sudden speed, she left, leaving her daughters to stare each other out.

"Ash?"

Ashley ignored her. The alarm was switched off. Jack was told to shut up. And on the TV, the credits began to roll. June heat rippled around the room, and the magazine crackled under Melinda's fingers.

Ashley was crying.

Swallowing her pride, Melinda shuffled across the room. "Ash," she put her arm around her. "I'm sorry. I didn't mean those things I said. I was being an idiot. They're not *that* bad, I suppose. I was only winding you up. Ash, come on, I just…"

"I really like them."

"I know you do."

"I mean, really, really like them."

It was a pity that Melinda didn't look at Ashley properly, for if she had, she would have seen the smile break out on her cheeks. She jumped when she felt Ashley link her arms around her, and nestle into her neck, but the relief she felt was indescribable.

"But I like you better," Ashley said. "I'm sorry about what I said too. You're a *good* singer, nearly as good as Kenzie… nearly. I know *you* don't like them. I just don't get *why*. I'm sure you would if you gave them a chance. Tom's *so* fit. I love his curly, black hair. Most people think he's too pale but I like it. Its vampire-ish."

"Aw, bless ya."

"He's mine, though," Ashley warned her as they sat back on the sofa. "So don't try and steal him from me. Maybe you could have Kenzie?"

"I don't think so, Ash."

"Oh but come on, you'd make such a good couple!" Ashley insisted. "You could get married and write songs and have little blond babies and—"

"Ew, no! No, no, no, no, no—"

"Yes, yes, yes, yes, yes—"

Thankfully, the TV made an announcement that silenced Ashley:

"Would you like a chance to go watch, meet, and go on a private *backstage* tour with Three Beams?"

"What? Yes, absolutely one million percent *yes*!" Ashley screeched.

"What the heck... *no,* oh god. Ash, the TV doesn't talk back, you know, and you're not entering that, cause then I'll end up having to take you."

"But that means you can meet Kenzie and give him a massive sloppy kiss!"

Melinda lunged forward and covered her sister's mouth. "Ah, ah, ah, no, don't scream now, hush little child. *Shush,*" she cooed against Ashley's wriggles. "Hush now, you're dreaming, this isn't really happening, this—"

"Well, by entering our amazing contest." The TV drowned out Melinda's efforts. "And answering an easy, simple question."

Ashley broke free and ran to the TV.

"No, Ash!"

"Go online to Three Beams dot com, and pay our entrance fee. It could be *you* cheering them at next week's concert. It could be *you* meeting them, *you* being the special one, the envy of your friends, as the band take you behind the scenes!"

"No, no, we don't want to go behind the scenes," said Melinda as she caught up to her sister. "Come on Ash, come away now, school-time—"

"Hurry! The contest closes tomorrow," The TV announced, before the screen faded to the next show, which was something about bunnies in 'Bunnyland'.

Sitting back down with a bump, Melinda exhaled, and waited. From the kitchen, the baking tray scraped across the oven. The oven let out a roaring noise, followed by released heat, and voices:

"Oh, fuck!"

"Ignore her girls," their father called. "You know what Thursdays are like!"

Melinda prepared herself for the worst, and she was right to do so, for the worst was what she got.

"Oh Mel, can we, can we, can we—"

"No." Melinda shuddered. "Dear god, no."

"Please?"

"No, I said."

Undeterred, Ashley sat on her knees, and pleaded. "Pretty please?"

"No, I'm allergic to Three Beams. One interaction could kill me." Melinda gave a fake sneeze. "See?"

All it took was a stampede of 'pleases', and Melinda caved:

"Fine."

"I'll be extra, extra good. I'll do whatever you want for a week, no, a *month*. I won't tell anyone. I'll even let you hug Tom first! They're gonna take us backstage, they're gonna… Oh just please, please, please, please—"

"All right," Melinda hissed. "We'll enter."

"Oh, thank you! Thank you, Mel, I love you!"

As Ashley hugged her, hiding her distain was the most difficult thing Melinda had done that morning.

"And what are you smirking at, Miss Ashley?"

Ashley beamed from the backseat. "Nothing, Dad."

"Yeah, Dad, nothing," replied Melinda. "Ashley's gonna be quiet now."

"Mel loves Kenzie, Mel loves Kenzie!"

Melinda dug her in the ribs. "Shut up!"

Their father chuckled. "To be honest I think their songs are quite catchy, and he's quite dashing, if I do say so myself."

Melinda screwed up her nose, utterly repulsed. Shaking his head, Brad turned the radio up.

"Nothing can beat a good bit of rock! Here Mel, sing with me!"

"Oh no," Ashley squealed. "Dad, no!"

To Ashley's displeasure, Brad and Melinda started head-banging and telling the world how they wouldn't do what it told them.

Brad, having grown up a single child, would never understand sisters, he decided after he dropped Melinda at the college bus stop and Ashley off at school. One minute they were fighting, the next they were... best friends? As Brad walked to his dog groomer's, the sound of dogs barking echoed up and down the alley. Hairs lingered in the air along with the smell of shampoo and conditioner. The bins heaved with bags of dog fur, and later in the day, so did Brad's shoulder-length, wavy brown hair.

When his phone rang on his lunch break, he grinned. "Yes, Mel, what is it?"

"I'm on my break from college."

"Oh," Brad took a bite of his sandwich. "What you up to then on this fine day?"

"I'm at Poundland."

"And why are you at Poundland?"

"Because Dad," Melinda sighed. "Where else are we meant to get cheap stuff living in Stratford? D'you need anything?"

"I guess your mom could do with some more flour."

Melinda sounded crestfallen. "But she moans if we get it from Poundland, she says it's too cheap."

"And how's she gonna know? All we have to do is pour it into her old bag."

"Dad, you're a genius. Shall I get Ash some more sweets, or you some more Pepsi Max? I can't stand to be in college during my break. Dana's doing my head in with all her mates, and I can't just walk out of here with a bag of flour, it looks weird."

"Mel, just get whatever you like, it'll all go to good use."

"Oh my god, Dad, Dad, *listen!*"

He listened. And he heard it, his favourite song! Immediately he grinned, and started singing along to the rock ballad. "You'd best be head-banging, Mel!"

"I am, this bloke's giving me some right weird looks."

"Good, let him look! Mel, keep up at your Maths and Science," he said kindly. "You'll pass it. You'll get onto any course then, easy-peasy."

She paused. "Thanks, Dad, that means—Oh god, some bloke's just tried to rob stuff! The security are chasing him! Hang on, wait, I think… nah, they've caught him. I think he's drunk."

Brad laughed. "That's great, Mel. Look, I've gotta go. Have fun!"

He was *still* wondering what was going on between her and Ashley, and why Ashley was so hyped up, but it was a sister thing, and anyway, he had to go. He could see his boss glaring at him through the window of the staff room.

Brad rose his hands. "All right, I'm coming, sorry."

"These old moggies won't groom themselves, you know."

Biting back any retort, Brad went back into work and found his favourite pair of scissors: the lime green ones.

Chapter Two

The stage lights illuminate her; she can barely see, yet she can hear them. They cheer, louder than the drums playing behind her, and her voice as she thanks them. The lights dazzle her, and she blinks, smiling, as the crowd jump up and down. They thrust banners, wave lighters, but best of all, they shout her *name.*

"Everybody make some noise!" she shouts.

"Mel! Mel, Mel, Mel!"

"Mel!"

Melinda jumped.

Damn it, she wasn't at a concert; she was at the back of her house, stuck on the outskirts of Stratford-upon-Avon. At the top of the hill, her eyes shifted guiltily to the girl next to her. Arms folded, Dana was frowning, the blue in her eyes clouded over with irritation. The warm breeze blew her black hair from her shoulders and her forehead, which was startlingly white.

"Were you even listening to me?" she said.

"Uh…yeah?"

Dana glared. "Were you thinking about that stupid contest again?"

For once, Melinda was grateful of Dana and her need to jump to conclusions. Biting her lip, Melinda nodded, ridding herself of the memories of being banished to the back row in the school choir, and having to just 'nod her head to the beat'.

Dana sighed. "You do realise that thousands upon thousands of people enter those?"

Melinda looked away from the sunset and back at Dana. "Yeah, you're right."

In all of her six years of knowing Dana, Melinda had learnt that it was easier just to agree.

"So, Mel, what do you think I should do about—"

A joyous laugh came from the boy at the bottom of the hill. Melinda called:

"Jay, you're such an idiot!"

Scrambling up the steep, grassy hill behind her house was Jay. Seventeen going on seven, the boy was beaming as he tugged his shopping trolley along with him. Melinda had a hard job deciding which was more battered out of him and the trolley. The shaved, brown hair on his head exposed the bruises on his scalp, and the trolley matched his build in wiriness.

Jay gasped for breath. "Come on girls, give us a hand here, would ya?"

The girls watched, amused.

"You damn fool," Dana said. "One day, you're gonna break your neck."

Jay pushed himself up onto the embankment, blood trickling down his elbow as he pulled the trolley up to join them. "Aw come on, you've gotta try it!"

"No thanks!" Melinda said.

"Oh well, more for me."

The short boy lined the trolley up and hoisted himself up into it.

Dana scowled at him. "You look a right dick in that. Anyway Mel, Anna's being a right div, hanging onto Drew like she is."

"You're only saying that cause you fancy Drew. Are you scared Anna will take him away?" sneered Jay.

"Scared, me? I'll show you scared. Have fun!"

With one push of her sandal, Jay was sent soaring down the hill.

The air was filled with Jay's cries, the trolley's clattering, and Melinda rushing after him. Her feet skidded to a halt at the edge of the hill. She watched as Jay, laughing, whizzed across the desolate field, which was littered with small, yet dangerous bumps.

The trolley hit a rock, and tumbled onto the floor. What had Dana *done?* Was he hurt?

Jay stood, unharmed. "Wicked!"

A mix of relieved and furious, Melinda turned on Dana. "Dana, what the hell?"

Dana shrugged. "He irritates me."

"But there was no need to push him down a hill," Melinda said, feigning a grin.

"He can handle it." Absent-mindedly, Dana admired her manicure. "Anyway, as I was saying, what do you reckon I should do about Drew?"

Dana had made an excellent choice in choosing Performing Arts for her college course, since she was already so dramatic. Additionally, she was trying to get into modelling, which came as no surprise, because she had a perfect, heart-shaped face that had not a freckle or spot in sight.

Stifling a yawn, Melinda tried her best to seem interested in Dana's boy problems. "Oh, I dunno. Just keeping hinting, I guess."

"I've been doing that for the past three weeks! God, you're hopeless. No wonder you hate that band so much. It's totally messed up your brain—*Joking!* Nah, I'm being serious now. If you get to go, you know, on a backstage tour with *Kenzie Hudgson*, you may as well make the most of it. I'd give anything for him to take me backstage." Grinning, she dug Melinda in the ribs.

"Yeah, backstage." Jay interrupted as he re-joined them. "Hang on… backstage where? I don't get it."

"Oh, shut up, stupid!" Dana snapped.

"Ow! What was that for?"

"Cause you're an idiot."

"I'm not an idiot!"

"Oh *no*, you're just special."

"If Mel wins that contest, I'll tell her to tell Kenzie you kissed Dwayne Lester behind the bike sheds, then he'll put it on Facebook so that Drew will never wanna go out with ya."

As Dana made to hit Jay again, Melinda got in between them. "Oi you two, break it up!"

Devotion to her sister's happiness was the reason she was entering the contest, she told herself. Plus, it wasn't like she'd bought tickets. Smiling, Melinda shook her head as Jay flipped Dana off.

"Oi," she teased. "I said break it up."

"She started it!"

"Ashley," Melinda squirmed. "Ashley, will you get off!"

"Are you doing it?"

"Yes," hissed Melinda as her little sister clambered further into her lap. "Now get off will you? You're squashing me, and you're wrecking the bed-sheet tent."

"*Fort!* Now do it."

Roughly, Ashley made a grab for the laptop, but her older sister swung it out of her reach. "Ah, ah, not if you talk to me like that."

"Mel!"

"Oops, now it's over here… and now it's over there."

Eventually, after much struggling, Melinda placed the laptop back in front of her, which was the only source of light under the bedsheets.

"Ah, finally!" Ashley gazed at the members of Three Beams, standing together in the background of the website. It was as though they were begging her to come and join them! But Melinda was being infuriating:

"Have some *patience,* dear."

If Melinda didn't enter the contest *right now,* Ashley was going to lose it.

Melinda had filled out the form. All it had required was an email address, location, plus the ages and genders of the people receiving the tickets. Now, all she had to do was answer the question! Why was she being so difficult? All day, Ashley had been waiting and now, Melinda was trying to make her wait even longer? She had to enter, and she had to enter *now!*

"Oh *please,*" Ashley cracked. "It closes tomorrow, and it's already ten! I know we couldn't tell Mom—"

"Yeah, because the damn fee's nearly twenty pounds," interrupted Melinda, her fingers wiggling over the keyboard. "She'd have gone ballistic. You're lucky I still have money left over from my birthday. Right, let's have a look at this question then."

Ashley thought her heart would burst with relief, but she fell silent. She had to be good. She had to do as she was told if she wanted to see Three Beams for real.

Melinda read out the question:

"What colour beams does Kenzie Hudgson wear?"

What? That was all? Oh, that was easy! It was—

"Oh, come on," Melinda scoffed behind her. "Forget millions! *Billions* of people are gonna enter this rubbish, we don't stand a chance."

"Billions?"

"Aw Ash… fine, I'll do it, though I can practically *feel* them grabbing at my money through the screen! Now, what shall it be?" she mocked. "Yellow? Orange?"

"Red, red, *red!*"

"Nah, I reckon he's green... green with *envy*, at what a great singer I am."

Outside the quilt, time was ticking away, and Three Beams were vastly preparing for their concert *without* Ashley.

"Red," Ashley whimpered. "It's red."

"Fine then." Melinda sneered. "Yellow it is."

"No!"

Melinda took her fingers off the keyboard. "Say I'm the best singer ever."

In their empty concert room, Ashley could see herself weeping, because she'd missed them by minutes, and she could hear her worst enemy, Bryony Milner, giggling because she'd won instead.

"You're the best singer ever!"

"*And?*"

Ashley exhaled. "You're better than Kenzie."

"Good girl," Melinda praised. "And now, you get your prize."

Ashley sat bolt upright. She watched, agonised, as it all unfolded. Melinda ticked the answer as red. She clicked her tongue. She took a deep breath. And then, she pressed 'enter'.

Ashley gawped as the answer was flung into cyberspace, and a message appeared:

Good luck! Thank you for entering. Love from Callum.

"Yeah," Melinda grumbled. "And thank *you*," she prodded her sister's side, "for wasting my money." Just as Ashley's lips puckered indignantly, Melinda linked her arms around her waist, and grinned. "Oh, you know I love you really." She kissed the top of her head. "I just don't love *them.*"

"But I'm sure they'll love you when they meet you."

"Yeah, whatever."

Ashley could taste the excitement, and smell the exhilaration as Tom took her by the hand, and hurried her backstage.

Ashley wound her hands around Melinda's neck, and whispered into the darkness of her bed:

"*I* love you." Resting her head on her shoulder, Ashley smiled.

"You're the best sister ever, and we're gonna win."

"Oh come on girl," Melinda replied. "It's a one in a million chance."

Ashley's smile lit up the dark, brighter than the screen of the laptop. "But we're still gonna win. I know we are."

When Melinda opened her eyes, she was greeted by the cheery, colourful atmosphere of the shared bedroom. She saw the pink of Ashley's bed covers, and the array of posters featuring her favourite band above the headrest.

Melinda placed her hand on her forehead, still tired underneath her own white bed sheets, and empty cream walls. There was a big canvas featuring a set of rabbits on her left. Above her was the window. But her side of the room wasn't completely plain! She had her set of drawers, with her lamp, and a tower of techno-rock albums...

"Wake up!" Ashley shouted. "Mel, wake up, get up, we need to check your email! Mel!" Running over, the girl shook her, then she started bouncing on her bed! "Mel, get up now."

"Ashley, for the love of god, piss off!" Melinda snapped. Never was she a morning person, especially when it was six in the morning, and her alarm wasn't even due to go off until half past. "Shut it. You'll wake Mom and Dad."

Ashley took no notice; she shook her again. "Oh, come on, Melly, come on, please!"

"Don't call me Melly!"

Of course, the competition closed today, and Ashley wanted to know the results. Melinda swatted her away, and pulled the duvet over her face, grumbling as she did so. "Fine. Get my laptop. Anything for a quiet life."

Melinda moaned as she heard Ashley scrabbling under the bed, searching for the white laptop. As Melinda got out of bed and sat on the edge, her hair flopped over her face, a tangled mess. Half-open, her bleary eyes followed Ashley as she hopped back onto her bed with the found laptop.

Ashley sat cross-legged in front of her with a pleading expression. "Come on! We've gotta see if we've won."

Oh, it had to be a no.

After typing her password wrong three times due to the fact that she was so damn *tired,* Melinda logged onto her laptop, then her emails.

"Well? Did we win?" Ashley leaned. "Did we, did we, did we—"

"Wait a minute, it's loading!"

College the previous day had provided her with the opportunity to do some research, and never had she regretted entering a contest so much in her life. The concert was in the heart of London! It was a two-hour train journey away from their isolated country house, plus a half an hour walk. Somehow, Melinda knew they wouldn't make it home by, what their mother would call, a 'suitable time'.

What was the point? Even if they *did* win, they probably wouldn't be able to go. Plus, she didn't *want* to see Three Beams, and she *certainly* didn't want to be stuck backstage with them for a whole hour, having to pretend she actually *cared* about how many pets Callum had or when Tom's Nan's birthday was. So, she prayed, to her disbelief, that her money had been wasted.

"Oh, look! Mel, click on it, click on it!"

"I'll click on you in a minute, and press the delete button! Now hush."

On the screen, sneering at them through evil eyes was the email that said better luck next time.

Melinda gulped. "Oh…"

Shockingly, she wasn't relieved, or pleased, or happy. From outside their bedroom, Julie could be heard clumping around downstairs. While Brad sung to himself in his own room, Melinda broke through the cloud of despair that now hung over their bedroom.

"Ashley, I—"

Ashley scrambled off of the bed, and rushed out of the room.

Grabbing her mascara from her desk, Melinda flung it at a Three Beams poster. "Hyped-up pricks."

With a satisfying thud, the tube hit Tom square in the face.

Chapter Three

Bacon sizzled, egg browned, and a delicious, tantalising smell wafted through the kitchen as Brad flipped it over. Green eyes attentive, the dog groomer watched the bacon cook. Next to him, his wife was packing the cakes from the previous day:

"Thirteen for Mrs Green, thirty for the nursery, and one for Ashley's lunch…"

Brad interrupted:

"And two for me."

"No, *none* for you, you greedy git."

"One for Jack?"

"No," Julie snapped. "Brad, you're making me lose count. Now… after Ashley's lunch we've got the bakery, they want ten for the front of the shop, so that's one, two, three…"

Melinda nudged Ashley.

"Hey, Ash, you all right?"

"Hmm."

Ashley was prodding her scrambled egg, sad as it drowned in brown sauce. Melinda looked away. Her grey mood wasn't uplifted even when Brad came with her favourite breakfast.

"Here you are, breakfast for a queen."

Melinda feigned a smile back at him.

Jack hurried out from under the table, and trailed Brad as he went back to the pan.

"Oh, 'ello boy!"

Hopefully, the overly-hyper Jack Russell barked.

"All right." Brad grasped the remaining piece of bacon; licking his lips, Jack stood on his hind legs. "Catch!"

Jack's jaws munched the bacon eagerly.

To the beat of the radio music, Brad walked over to Julie, and peered over her shoulder as she stuck labels on the cake boxes. "Whatcha doing?"

"I'm labelling the boxes, what else does it look like I'm doing, unpacking them all? And the dog isn't meant to have bacon! It's unhealthy."

"Yeah well," Brad whispered, snaking his hand around her plump waist. "I'm sure he can take lessons from us and, you know, burn it off."

Melinda choked on her egg. "D-Dad! That's just... *ugh.* Ash, seriously, isn't that disgusting?"

As her mother smacked her father's hands away, she could feel a sickness brewing in her stomach, but it was nothing to do with her father's innuendo.

"Sorry," Melinda mimed.

Ashley smiled, and held up her finger, signalling Melinda to wait.

Melinda nodded back. Out of the corner of her eye, she glanced at Julie as she scolded Brad for stealing a cake. They were too busy to notice Ashley writing on her plate in the brown sauce. Ashley held up the plate, and it said 'it's okay'.

Without warning, Jack leapt onto Ashley's lap.

"Jack!"

Julie turned back. "What's he doing now? Hey, get him off that—"

Jack licked away the message on the plate.

Melinda and Ashley and Brad burst out laughing, however, Julie wasn't so pleased:

"Jack, get off that table right now!"

Unphased, Jack just wagged his tail.

Click. Flash.

"Okay boys, one more!"

Click. Flash.

"Perfect!"

Satisfied, the photographer of the photoshoot stepped back. "Well done, boys."

Kenzie pretended to rev the motorbike he was sitting on. As though it was the funniest thing in the world, Tom laughed, while Callum just looked bored.

"Hey," called Doug to the photographer. "Bring that here, lemme see."

The photographer hurried his prize to Doug, the band manager, who was stood on the balls of his feet.

"Thank god that's over," Tom grinned at Kenzie. "I can relax."

"And talk normally."

"Yeah, that too. I don't understand why they make me talk like a posh twit when filming."

Kenzie left the bike and sauntered around it to Tom, his long fingers gliding over the glossy, red colour of the beam that shot down the front like an arrow. He gave one look to ensure the photographer had actually gone, then smirked. "Oooh, come on, big smiles now boys, big, *big* smiles."

"I know! What is it with photographers and great big smiles? Still, it could've been worse," replied Tom. "Remember the last one?"

"Can I choose not to?" Kenzie said as in the back of his mind, disgusting images of the last photoshoot haunted him. He'd been surrounded by kittens, and one had pissed in his hair. "I mean, isn't the number one rule never to work with children or animals? Fair enough, there were no animals in this one but God, the *set up.*"

"Hey," Tom prodded the taller singer. "*You* got to sit on that awesome bike."

Kenzie curled his lips. "It's got bloody w*ings* on. You can't get much sadder than that." In discomfort, he rubbed at the skin-coloured make-up that covered his muscular arms.

Tom stared as it crumbled to the floor, and revealed the two tattoos underneath.

"Jeez, am I glad to get this stuff off. The last time I checked, tattoos didn't kill kids."

"You think you've got it bad? I hate having to talk like a posh person, it drives me mad."

Giving a brief glance at Callum, who was on his phone, Kenzie grumbled:

"Look at that sulky bastard, ignoring us."

"Oh, I know."

"He needs to think himself lucky. He'd be shit on the floor without us. Oi," snapped Kenzie. It was obvious Callum had sensed they were talking about him. "We're talking *about* you, not to you!"

Embarrassed, Callum turned his back on them.

"Just leave him Kenzie," Tom said. "He ain't worth it."

"Yeah, whatever. The sooner we finish this promotion stuff the better; at least with concerts we can do our own thing. I've got to find out who's won this silly contest."

"Remember that thirteen-year-old from last time?"

"Erm, hello? Of course I bloody remember." Walking away from the motorbike, Kenzie re-lived the scene. "The fat bitch sat on me, and wrote her number all over my arm, in permanent marker. *Permanent*, Tom!"

Tom sniggered. "Seconds to write, hours to get off."

"You're telling me?"

That night was horrendous. Scarred for life, Kenzie had never quite been the same afterward. While Tom performed bad impressions of wobbling jellies and thundering elephants, Kenzie hovered near Callum. The older band member was crouched down on the floor. Frowning in concentration, he twanged his wooden guitar.

Kenzie dragged his fingers over the strings. "Oops."

Callum tensed. "Dude."

Kenzie waited, eyebrows raised. "Yes?"

"Nothing."

As he predicted, Callum made no complaint. Instead, he just continued to play. In the background, Tom revved the bike, making childish engine noises.

"Whoa Tom," called Kenzie. "Careful, you don't know what you're doing—"

At the same time, Callum jumped to life. "Oh, Kenzie!" Scrambling to his feet, he pulled a folded piece of paper from his cringe-worthy yellow trousers. "You said you'd look at the new song I wrote."

"Did I?"

"Yeah. Here. I spent ages on it. I reckon it'll really help kids who are grieving the loss of a parent, or a friend—"

"No."

"No? But I think it's a really important subject."

"You know what isn't an important subject? You. No is no. We're not doing a sappy song about grieving."

Pitifully, Callum's big eyes blinked, and he ran his hand over his shaved head, in an attempt to hide the disappointment on his face when Kenzie crumpled his song and threw it on the floor.

"Ugh, I need to find out who's won this contest." While the crew chattered in the distance, Kenzie called for Tom.

"Yes, boss!"

"Grab your phone and pull up your emails," ordered Kenzie. "If I don't find out who this winner is soon, I'm gonna have a meltdown."

"I'm doing it right now, Ken-Kenzie. Sorry, forgot you don't like Ken…" Eagerly, Tom scrolled through his emails as Kenzie joined him near the motorbike. "I wanna find out too. I've gotta spend an entire hour with them as well, so I wanna at least know how old they are. One thing I get in trouble for is using 'inappropriate language'."

Kenzie rolled his eyes. "Yeah, cause the word crap is *so* traumatic for Mommy's little princess."

The lights were turned down. The cameras were zipped up in their boxes, and Tom searched for the email. Finally, he pointed to the screen in triumph. "Ah, here we are."

Kenzie peered over Tom's shoulder. Finally, he'd know whether he was risking once again having his thighs crushed.

"Oh, can I see?" called Callum.

Taking a deep breath in, Kenzie ignored Callum as his eyes scanned the names, ages and genders of the winners, and when he saw what was written, he grinned.

"There's paps outside." Hitching up his glasses, Doug always spoke so fast it was hard to keep up. "Want me to see them off?"

"Nah, it's cool, I'll talk to 'em."

Leaving his bemused band members behind, the twenty-five-year-old strolled out of the photo shoot, and walked down the corridor toward the exit. Outside, a crowd was waiting. In the eyes of fame, he could be anyone, and do anything.

Immediately, Kenzie was bombarded with reporters and photographers, microphones and cameras.

Click. Flash.

"Kenzie, Kenzie!"

"Yes, over here Kenzie!"

Click. Flash.

"So how does it feel, knowing you're the leader of one of the top boy bands?"

"To be honest," Kenzie said. "Pretty damn good. But I gotta thank my fans, of course."

"Kenzie, Kenzie!"

"Yeah, that's it, smile!"

Kenzie smiled, just how they wanted him to, because according to the form the winner had filled out, there would be two people coming on the backstage tour. One was seven years old, and the other was an eighteen-year-old girl.

A pencil case, two textbooks (one for Mathematics, one for Core Science) an empty lunchbox, a make-up bag, a bus pass and house keys…

Melinda frowned. "Nah, there's something missing…"

She carried on rummaging.

"Aw, shit."

There was nothing missing. She knew that, but she had to 'look busy' while waiting for class. God forbid anyone try to make small talk with her. She wasn't in the mood. Huffing, Melinda gave up after a bit, and zipped up her bag with a satisfying wrench.

"Hey, Jade?" someone said.

"Yeah?"

"Did you do that assignment?"

"Ah bugger! Did you?"

"Melinda," Dana approached her with a magazine. "I found this in class just now. I know you're still pissed about the contest but *oh my god*," she paused. "You *have* to see this. It's just—oh my god, just *look at him.*"

"Dana, I can't, Maths is gonna start in a sec and I need to ask my tutor if—"

Dana thrust the magazine cover in her face.

"Wait, is that—"

"Uh-huh."

As Dana joined her side to stare too, Melinda pondered whether she would ever be able to breathe again.

"Well," Dana said triumphantly. "What d'you think? I told you he was hot."

On the cover stood Kenzie Hudgson, lead singer of children's band Three Beams, and not just any Kenzie Hudgson. It was the one they didn't show on TV. In glossy, high-definition print, the man stood side-ways on, shirtless. Kenzie's pointed chin was resting on his hand, so every viewer could see the sculpted muscles that covered every inch of his arm. Under his shoulder sat a tattoo of a patterned skull, then a row of black triangles further down his arm. Out of the corner of his eye, he was looking into the camera, smiling teasingly.

Melinda gawped. She didn't think he looked like *that!*

"I didn't think he modelled in his spare time," Dana babbled. "I wonder if he'll do a catalogue…"

"I… I doubt it. I mean, this is just advertising how to get his body but, if he is modelling as well as being on TV, and recording songs for their more 'normal' albums, I doubt he'd have time for a catalogue."

Dana was still drooling over the photo. "I mean wow, I didn't know he had tattoos, did you? They must censor them for the show, although god knows why he's even in it. He'd be better off just sticking to the albums they do outside the show. Or he could do a film instead. I'd happily star alongside him! Bloody hell, if I could spend even one minute alone with him—"

"Dana!" Melinda pushed the magazine away. "I *really* don't need to see this right now, especially after how they screwed my sister around. If I wanted to get a body like Kenzie flippin' Hudgson, I'd stand in front of a mirror all day and be a pompous *dick.*"

Dana flinched. "Oh Mel, I'm sorry…"

"So you should be. I can't stand them," said Melinda.

Rolling the magazine up, Dana pouted. "I know you can't. I'm gutted you didn't win the contest for Ashley. I just got a bit… carried away. But there's no need to be rude."

The pale-blue floor became the most interesting thing in the world. "No, I'm sorry. Ignore me, I'm being an arse." Laughing to herself, Melinda shook her head. "I shouldn't have entered that contest anyway."

"Nah, it's cool babe." Dana tore the cover off the magazine. "But I think I'll keep this for… emergencies."

Melinda smiled. "Yeah, okay, 'emergencies'. Got it."

As if on cue, her maths tutor popped his wrinkled face out of the door, and beckoned the students in.

Melinda glanced at him, then she looked back to Dana, surprisingly grateful for the interruption of tiresome algebra. "Look, I gotta go. I'll see you after lesson."

Dana burst out into giggles as she pocketed the photo. "Yeah, I'll enjoy my lesson."

"Don't get too excited over that," Melinda scolded. "Your drama character doesn't care about boys!"

"Yeah, but they said nothing about *men*!" Dana winked. "See ya later hothead."

Melinda cheerfully waved the girl off, then, she stepped inside the classroom, and was absorbed in a land of numbers and boredom. Heading straight for the seat at the back next to Sophie, she raked her dull hair out of her face.

"Another lesson, ay?" she said. "Let's see who needs help first out of me and you."

Hopelessly, Sophie smiled at her.

"Arnold," called Jade sweetly. "I haven't done the assignment; can I have an extension?"

Secretly, Melinda didn't mind this class, because she could just zone out and picture playing with Jack in the garden.

Chapter Four

Sophie Mares was a quiet girl; she kept out of trouble. Looking down at her work, she frowned at the various mistakes on her paper. Melinda gazed at her long, blonde plait wishfully; it hung down her back like a climbing rope.

"Oh, come on, class," the tutor sighed. "Surely one of you is awake today?"

Fed up, Melinda resisted the urge to sigh as the tutor questioned the class. She could *feel* her life slowly slipping away, yet she longed for that C grade in Maths; it was such a dilemma!

"*No*, that's wrong," moaned the tutor. "Come on, one of you, any of you!"

"Do you even understand any of this?" Melinda asked the girl that wasn't quite her friend, but listened to her problems as if she were.

Sophie shook her head hopelessly.

"I can't believe it." In front of them, Jade Grant's thick brown hair, packed with blonde streaks, was shaking back and forth as she rambled to her best friend. "To think I was pleased I won. What a waste of my precious time!"

Sophie turned to Mel. "So, did you win that contest in the end?"

Melinda tapped her pen. "No. We got an email this morning that said 'better luck next time', as if I'm gonna allow there to *be* a next time."

"Oh. Never mind, those contests run pretty regularly, so maybe one day your sister—"

"*It's just really pissed me off,*" Jade's loud voice overshadowed Sophie's whisper. "To think, I've robbed some poor mite of their ultimate dream, cause guess what? Guess bloody what?"

"Mel—"

"Hang on, Sophie," Melinda hissed. "Shush a minute."

"What, Jade?" said Jade's friend.

"Turns out Carmen doesn't even *like* Three Beams anymore."

"Huh? No way!"

"Yes, way! Apparently, cause she's 'nearly eight' she's too old for them."

Melinda nearly bolted out of her seat. "Jade!"

Jade half-turned. "Yes?" She looked the girl up and down. "Can I help you?"

Suggestively, Melinda's fingers traced a circular pattern over her work. "I think I have an answer to your little problem."

The girl raised her eyebrows. "Oh, do you?"

"Uh-Huh. I sure do."

Jade's friend turned around. "Well go on then, we haven't got all day."

"Tracy, Tracy, please," Jade said. "I've got this."

"No, no, I'm serious," Melinda insisted. "Sophie, ain't I being serious—"

Jade huffed. "Go on then, but don't bore me. I need this grade."

Casually, Melinda wound her blonde streak around her finger. "Well, my sister loves Three Beams, and would love to go. We entered the contest actually, but we didn't win. So I was wondering—"

Sigh. "You want the tickets, don't you?"

Melinda lost her edge. Slowly, the thin hair fell from her finger.

Already, the beginning of a sneer was forming on Jade's tanned face. "Well, I'm not going to just give you them."

The laughter of Jade's friend pierced her, Melinda saw their tutor glare at them warningly, and she felt all hope begin to drain.

"Babe, I know you can't afford to pay me," said Jade… kindly? "So how about you come round mine tomorrow morning, and do me a job instead?"

Melinda blinked. "O-Oh my god… yes!"

"Girls, stop that noise!" barked their tutor.

"Right, sorry sir. Yes, Jade, I'll do it."

Jade approved. Holding up one finger, she turned around in her seat, and began to scribble on a stray piece of paper. Melinda didn't notice, for in front of her, she saw Ashley cheering, and herself surprisingly not minding, as she put earplugs in to block out the band's warbling. Best of all, she saw the previous highlights of Ashley's life banish to the shade as she finally gave Tom Landsby a hug… because of her.

"Here's my address," said Jade, quickly handing Melinda the paper. "You can get the 6Y bus by the college. It drops you pretty much right outside. Wear scruffy clothes, it's a big job. You sure you can cope with it?"

Next to her, Sophie stared, truly amazed.

Melinda nodded. "I'm sure I'll manage."

She stayed calm. She stayed quiet, all throughout the lesson, but the second the tutor dismissed them she grabbed Sophie and cheered:

"Oh my god, Soph, I can't believe it, I just… bye!"

She rushed out of the room. Down the corridor she went, half screeching, half skipping, intent on going to Poundland and buying all the chocolate she could get her hands on.

Jay saw her on his way to lesson. "Mel? Mel, what's—"

"Jay," she screamed. "Jay," she threw herself at him. "I'm getting the tickets! I'm getting them!"

"What? No way, how?"

"Oh, I'll explain later! I'm going to see a band I hate, but fuck it, I'm getting the tickets. I'm going… shit," she stepped back.

Jay stared at her, trying to work out why all of sudden, she'd gone from ecstatic to sounding like she was about to get the electric chair.

"I'm going to see a band I absolutely hate," Melinda realised.

Below Callum, the lights seemed like fireflies, with how they shone in the dark. Captivated, the back-up vocalist watched from the nightclub window as the city of Birmingham came to life. In each car, who was the person driving? What was their story? Callum's brown eyes skimmed the tops of the buildings, traced over the straight rulers of road, and slowly made their way toward the view, where beautiful, endless stretches of untainted countryside awaited.

Tom appeared behind him. "Hey."

"Hey."

Tom shoved his hands in his jean pockets. "So… what are you doing over here?"

"So, what are you doing talking to me all of a sudden? Oh wait, Kenzie's not here."

"Erm... the party's that way, dude," said Tom, guiltily.

Callum raised his eyebrows, then shrugged. "It's quieter over here."

Tom chewed his bottom lip. "But... you're always hanging back."

Why did he suddenly care? Going to the other side of the room, Callum looked through the glass screen. There were so many people Callum could see dancing, laughing, drinking—

Wait.

Past the leather sofas, exotic fish tanks, and bright colour schemes, the confident man clad in dark clothing was unmistakeable. He had his arms around a busty blonde's waist. She gasped as Kenzie tugged her closer and whispered in her ear. A teasing smile creeping across his face as his hand slid over her backside. In response, the girl laughed, nervously. Kenzie leant closer, and Callum didn't have to hear him in order to know what he was asking.

Biting her lip, the blonde shook her head, and tried to pull away.

"Ey up," Tom said. "There's some drama going on over there, ay?"

Kenzie repulsed Callum. Callum was going to look away, until Kenzie tugged the girl back.

After he asked her again, the blonde appeared to have a change of heart, for she looked up at him, and nodded. Dejected, Tom watched too as the band leader snaked his arm around her waist and guided her toward the lift. On his way there, he caught them watching, and waved goodbye at them.

Callum shuddered.

"That's Kenzie huh?" Tom commented. "Always pulling someone."

Kenzie had it all: model good looks, a muscular body, a great singing voice, and sky-high confidence. All Callum had was a guitar and a pen. "Yeah, he'll never change."

"Figures."

Just because Kenzie was no longer there, Tom had come crawling back to him as if he were a back-up plan, and it was driving Callum nuts.

"I'm buzzing for this concert actually," burbled Tom. "You've written some really good songs for this one, you know."

"Thanks."

As a curvaceous woman approached, Callum was not at all sorry to see Tom go. In fact, he was happy to see the woman ask Tom if he wanted to dance; he was *perfectly content* to see Tom vanish with her without even a backwards glance. Huffing, he sat down on the sofa in front of him, and reached into his pocket. He pulled out his pen, plus a written draft of his latest lyrics:

Whatever the weather, whatever the time, I will be there, to make you shine.

With gritted teeth, Callum scribbled all of it out.

Wrapped up in her pink bed covers, Ashley stretched her legs out below her. Carefully, she traced her freckly fingers down the paper, her fingers gliding over the dimples in Tom's cheeks, the roundness of Callum's face, the outline of Kenzie's muscles…

She'd drawn them perfectly. Even her art teacher had thought so. It was just a shame that ticket sellers didn't accept gold stars.

Resting her head on the pillow, Ashley hummed softly as Three Beam's lyrics soothed her. Come Sunday, there would be an omnibus of their weekday shows, plus a special clip at the end.

"Ash," Melinda whispered, sliding into the bed with her. "Why aren't you asleep? It's nearly twelve."

"Don't matter," Ashley bit back the tears. "I'm not tired."

"Not tired? You? But you spent ages helping Mom clean up again."

Melinda looked over her shoulder. "Ashley, that's brilliant! It looks just like them."

Ashley lay to face her. "I did it in Art today. Miss Jeans asked us to draw ether our favourite TV show, or our favourite band, so I did both. At playtime when everyone had gone, she said it was the best in the class."

Melinda returned her smile. "Well, I had a good day too."

"Why?"

Slowly, the girl sat up in the bed. "That's for me to know."

Ashley sat up too. "Mel, what have you done?"

"Oh, Jack was just really hyper today. Don't tell Mom, but those are my leggings in the bin. You know Ash, you should draw more often, you're really good. Not like me, I can't even draw a stick-figure."

Ashley looked at her imploringly. "Yeah, but you can sing."

She scoffed. "Oh come on, we both know *that's* not true."

"Sing me a Three Beams song."

Melinda's eyes widened. "You what mate?"

Ashley giggled. "Sing me a Three Beams song."

"Oh piss off!"

"Oh please, please! You can sing it in Rock mode if you want! Just please sing me one... It'll be like I'm at their concert."

Just like she predicted, Melinda buckled. "All right, fine." She clambered out of the bed. Their father's old black t-shirt trailed around her knees. "Throw me the microphone. I'll show Three Beams how it's *really* done."

As commanded, Ashley reached under the bed, and threw Melinda the fake microphone that had come with her latest pop magazine. Clumsily, Melinda missed the catch; Ashley pulled her phone from underneath her pillow, and just as Melinda opened her mouth, she set the camera to record.

"Are you filming?"

"Yeah, is that okay?"

"I swear, if you show it to anyone—"

"I won't!"

"Okay, fine. Hello boys and girls, men and women of the UK!" Melinda boomed. "Are you ready... To be utterly blown away?"

"Just get on with it!"

"All right, all right, *bossy.*"

With a teasing wink, Melinda stepped back, the black t-shirt gradually merging with the darkness of her side of the room. The phone shook in Ashley's hand as she stood it up. It was only when she thought she was going to *explode* that Melinda began to sing:

"In the darkness, the stars shine so brightly. And you smile at me so lightly."

How did Melinda do that? How did she just take a song, and make it completely, and utterly, hers? Ashley didn't know, and she didn't care; she just loved to hear her sister sing. She never understood why people thought she was awful.

Melinda shook her hips and twisted her body as she stood on her bed. "And in that moment, I know..." She stomped her feet, pointed, then shouted:

"That you are the one!"

"You are the one for me!" Ashley joined in.

"And under these stars,"

Leaping out of bed, Ashley abandoned her phone and charged over to Melinda. "I know that we'll be free!"

"Cause forever and always." Melinda hoisted her sister up onto the bed. "Day and night, our love will win the fight!"

The microphone became real. Thousands of adoring fans cheered Melinda on as she sang, not one of them moaning about the assistant vocalist she'd hired. In the middle of the crowd, their parents cheered, and at the back were Three Beams.

Their father burst into the room. "Girls, girls, girls!" He flicked on the lights. "For goodness' sake, it's twelve o'clock."

The pair were red with embarrassment.

Brad pushed his long hair back, and chucked. "What are you like, say? It's a good job your mother hasn't gone to bed yet."

The girls looked at each other. Melinda smiled. Ashley smiled. Then, they descended into laughter.

At first, Brad frowned. But afterward, he laughed too.

It took the trio a nearly a minute to regain themselves. When they did, Melinda hurried an apology, and got into bed. Meanwhile, Ashley rushed back to her own bed and turned her lamp off.

Brad shook his head in bemusement. "Right," he exhaled. "So, I originally came up here to ask you two something. Your mother baked too many cakes yesterday, and the weather's meant to be nice tomorrow. Fancy a picnic?"

"Oh yes!" Ashley bounced on her pink covers. "Yes, yes, yes Dad!"

Melinda shrugged. "Yeah, sure."

"All right, it's a date." Brad reached for the light. "*Goodnight,* girls." He winked at Melinda. "And keep singing, my little dreamer."

Melinda gagged. "Ugh, night Dad!"

Chapter Five

Water dripped from his chin as he looked in the bathroom mirror. Icy-cold, the remains of the water in Kenzie's hand slid down his throat.

There was a girl in his bed. Smile breaking out over his flushed cheeks, Kenzie plucked at his now-messy hair, and out of the corner of his eye, he saw the digital clock on top of the toilet blink three a.m.

Kenzie stepped back. The outline of his bare, broad shoulders reminded him of who, and what, he was, and who, and what, he had become. Along the way back to his bedroom, his fingers brushed the walls of the mansion, the home that had never been owned by anyone except him. As he reached his bedroom door, he peered through the crack in the doorway, and grinned at the sight that awaited him.

The gorgeous blonde was wrapped in his ruby-red bedsheets, the curls in her hair splayed across his pillow.

"Mommy?"

Suddenly, fear consumed Kenzie and froze him to the spot. In utter disbelief, he blinked. The blonde was gone, and her replacement wasn't a stranger. His eyes widened, and his world slowed to a crawl. No. Surely it wasn't...

"Mommy..."

The clock seemed to rewind. He was five years old. He was scared. He was alone. And in her bed, his mother slept, chest unmoving. Weak, the words slid from Kenzie's lips in a confused whisper:

"M-Mommy..."

His mother didn't answer.

As he neared the edge of the bed, he began to crumble. "Mommy, please wake up." It couldn't be true. It just—it couldn't... he was only little! "Mommy..." Shaking, Kenzie's hand covered his mother's shoulder.

His mother moaned. Turning to face him, her full lips parted as she murmured sleepily:

"Kenzie? Wha—" A yawn. A rumple of bed sheets. "What's up, babe?"

What was up? What was *up?* The sudden chill of Kenzie's blood, and the memories that stalked him in his fame was what was up!

Sitting up in the bed, the blonde was amused. "What are you doing, silly? Calling me Mommy... Come back to bed."

"Get out."

The blonde did a double take. "You what?"

"You heard me," Kenzie's voice rose to a shout. "I said get out!" The blonde jumped, and Kenzie pointed to the exit with a snarl. "Get the fuck out of my house. And don't you ever," he spat at her as she clambered out of the bed. "Ever come back."

While she struggled into her clothes, completely forgetting her heels in her frenzy, Kenzie crossed the room toward her.

"No! I-I'm sorry, I'm—"

"*Out!*"

His voice was so loud, so strong that it sent the girl running from the room, whimpering. Kenzie reached down, and plucked the girl's heels from the floor. With swallowing strides, he went through the bedroom door that moments ago, his five-year-old self had entered.

"Fuck you!" Kenzie tossed her heels down the stairs. "Fucking slut!"

He almost cackled with maddened laughter as they bounced from the wall, near missing her head.

"I'll ruin you if you tell anyone, you hear me?"

Slamming the wooden door shut, he leant his sweaty back on the polished wood.

"Shit," His legs gave out; he slid to the floor. "The fuck am I doing, man?" Tormented, he buried his face in his hands, and the entire time, screams of his five-year-old self reduced him to quaking.

"Mommy, wake up."

No.

"Mommy, wake up."

No!

Kenzie stood, let out a screech, and,ploughed his fist into the wall.

Melinda didn't know Jade was so... rich. The mansion, cream and gleaming, was *humungous*. It laughed at Melinda's own cluttered house, with its chipping paint and tatty curtains. Perched in a field of overgrown grass, separated from everything by a mile-wide wood, her little house suddenly seemed like a shack.

Melinda knocked again.

She'd done what Jade had said; she was wearing her oldest black leggings and one of her father's cast-out, long t-shirts. It was pale green, with picture of a cobra coiled in the middle. How fitting, for in that moment, the cobra seemed to be hissing at her.

She could turn back right now and get the bus home, but Ashley *wanted* those tickets.

Melinda heard Jade hurrying down the stairs.

"One second, babe, don't go running off! Mel," Jade swung open the front door, her hair freshly straightened. "Sorry about that, I've got someone upstairs see."

"Oh, no, it's fine."

Please don't let it be a group, please don't let it—

"Anyway, I'm so glad you could come. I thought you weren't going to. I really, really need you, see. It's vital." Jade smiled, the perfection of her teeth setting Melinda on edge. "I did say it was a big job."

Melinda's fingers clenched around her shirt. "And I said I could do it."

Jade wrinkled her nose. "All right then, I'll take you through. Just don't touch anything." She waited. "Are you coming or what?"

"Yeah, erm... do you want me to clean all of it?"

"All of what?"

"Erm, the house?"

"What, the *house?* God no, it's much too big, and the antiques much too precious. Nah, I wouldn't impose that on you, at least for the crappy prize you're getting. For Pete's sake, come in quick, before I change my mind."

With a certain seven-year-old's voice nagging her, Melinda stepped into the mansion without a backward glance.

Overtaking Melinda, Jade shuddered as the girl's ancient canvas shoes made contact with the white fur rug. "Careful of the rug, it's new. My parents won't be happy if they come back from their honeymoon and it's covered in filth."

"Oh no, sorry, I was meaning to put these shoes in the charity bag, but..."

Melinda couldn't stand Jade and Jade clearly couldn't stand her. But Ashley needed those tickets, and Melinda didn't have the guts to take them by force. Where would she even get a gun, for a start?

"Oh, like the paintings?" Jade said. "I chose them. My mom has no sense of artistic culture."

Melinda decided that the further she ventured down the corridor, the more the place baffled her. Painted pictures, gold-etched mirrors, ornaments and antiques worth more than her father's car... she and Jade moved into the big, big kitchen, and Melinda couldn't help but gape. The counters were *real* marble, and everything *shone*.

"Do you have a maid?"

Jade stopped. "Yeah. But she's on 'maternity leave'. The last time I checked, pregnancies were nine months, not eight and a half. She could have at least held the baby in until my parents got back. Then again, if she had of done, you wouldn't be getting those tickets today."

As she wondered if she knew how to get away with murder, Melinda noted the coloured panes in the door's window. "Baby Jesus in a manger... pretty."

"Uh-huh," Jade jiggled the door open. "I don't believe in it myself, but it makes a nice picture I suppose. So your sister's into music then? Ugh, stupid door..."

"Well, not really. It's just this one band."

"Yes, finally! God, I've got to get someone to fix that. Anyway... seriously, *Three Beams?*"

Melinda hurried after her. "She likes Tom, though I can't see why."

The garden was smaller than she thought it would be. It was disproportionate to the mansion.

Jade sniggered. "Him? He looks like my auntie's dog, all big-eyed and annoying. And don't even get me started on Kenzie! Everyone acts like he's some sort of Greek God, yet he looks like a bucket of sick dyed orange. And that other dude... Callum, is it? See, I don't even know his name! They're everywhere nowadays. I can't stand them."

Jade strolled down the pebbled pathway. Absent-mindedly, Melinda took in the shed at the back, and the hutch in front of it.

"Well, you're not alone," Melinda offered. "I can't stand them ether."

"The hyped-up bastards."

"Burn them all!"

"Meh, you're not so bad." At the end of the path, Jade veered to the right. Placing a hand on top of the hutch, she raised her eyebrows. "Yeah, I sort of gathered you didn't like them. I sit in front of you, you know. I hear how often you witter on to that Sophie about it."

Jade had said her name like she was rotting fruit in a compost heap. Falsely, Melinda simpered as Jade leant down and unlocked the hutch door, yet when she pulled out a beautiful black rabbit, her gasp was real:

"Oh!"

"Cute, isn't she? This is Maxine. She's an ex-show rabbit."

Maxine nestled in her arms. Cutely, her nose twitched. Oh, Melinda wanted a rabbit! She'd *always* wanted a rabbit!

"She won us fifteen medals and five gold trophies. I reckon it's the eyes."

Sure enough, Maxine's eyes were a wonderful shade of pure gold.

Earnestly, Melinda wrung her hands. "She's beautiful."

"She wants cleaning out. And that's where you come in."

"Wait, all you want me to do is clean her out?"

Melinda was almost blown over by the hilarity. Jade had dragged her out of bed at seven-thirty in the morning, just to clean out *one* rabbit? And the reward in return was two concert tickets *plus* backstage passes?

Smirking, Jade dumped Maxine back in her hutch. "Sort of." She beckoned Melinda forward. "Follow me."

Melinda hadn't seen the wood-carved door; it blended perfectly with the brick wall. Unlatching the bolt, Jade went inside. Drawn by both confusion and curiosity, Melinda went in after her.

"Oh my god, Jade!"

"Mel! For heaven's sake darling, you nearly gave me a heart attack."

In retort to her earlier mockery, the garden was a garden straight from her childhood dreams. On either side, trees with ripened apples overshadowed the dusty floor, while bushes, flowers, and shrubs bordered it. Baskets and pots contained excess flowers, flowers every colour Melinda knew. Butterflies fluttered freely; bees drank in the beauty. In the centre, hedges formed their own private square.

Melinda hesitated to believe she was really there. So absorbed in the smell of flowers, she almost lost Jade as she walked into the corridor the hedge provided.

"Hey, where're you going?"

"Just follow me, and you'll see."

Melinda followed the cocky fairy as it pirouetted down the wonderland, and came out into... into...

A stretch of wood-chippings; numerous fences, each forming a small box. Inside the fences, there was a hutch, plus a rabbit dashing back and forth.

There were fifteen rabbits, plus the one in the smaller garden.

Next to her now, Jade beamed, cruelty dripping from the smile as Melinda's mouth dropped open. "Everything you need is in the shed."

Tapping the girl on the shoulder, she whispered:

"Have fun."

With that, she slunk away, leaving Melinda fuming.

"Ashley," mumbled Melinda as she looked at the rabbits running around. "I'm gonna kill you for this."

Sometime later, the hot, sweaty, exhausted Melinda tied her final bin-bag to a close.

"There we are," she said, to the grey rabbit by her feet. "All clean."

She was about to leave, but the rabbit nuzzled her leg. "Oh, hello gorgeous!"

Kneeling down, she stroked it, proud when she realised that this was the last hutch; she'd done it. In precisely three hours and two minutes, she'd cleaned out every single rabbit hutch.

Honestly, she'd enjoyed herself. Upon arriving, her mind had been cluttered with worries: what if she didn't pass her exams? What if her mother's baking business failed? But while cleaning the rabbits out, they had vanished. It was like... the litter in the bin bag was actually her thoughts.

"Okay, Mel," she mumbled. "Don't get cheesy now."

How could she not be? The rabbits had been lovely to her; she'd even?" been able to stroke some of them. Truthfully, she was sad to have finished the task. But at least she was going to get the tickets! Finally, after all this time, she was going to be sitting in a hall watching Ashley cry tears of joy... over a band Melinda hated.

Grabbing the bin bag in one hand and her box of sawdust and straw in the other, she left the run, trying not to look at the offended rabbit.

She paused by the gate. She overlooked her handiwork. At college, she'd taken Maths and Science in order to bump up her D grades from school. Many of the other courses required Cs to get in, as did many jobs. It was also partly because she didn't know what she wanted to *do*. Yet now, as she dropped her stuff and saluted the hopping creatures, she knew:

She wanted to do a course in Animal Care.

The second Melinda arrived inside the mansion, she searched for Jade. She wanted the tickets, and she wanted them now.

"Jade?"

Melinda checked the kitchen... no Jade. She checked the living room... no Jade. She prowled the corridor, calling her name, but still no-

"Mel," Jade was running down the stairs, panting. She raked her hand through her suddenly messy hair. "You've finished already?"

"Oh, yeah, just about."

Melinda wondered what was going on. Immediately, her inner thoughts were answered when at the top of the stairs, a long-haired, shirtless man appeared.

"Finishing at the same time as us?" he jeered. "Nice one."

"Cody!" Jade shrieked.

Raising his hands, Cody chuckled as he went on his way.

Jade sighed. "Sorry about *him*. I guess you want your tickets now, huh?"

Melinda smiled sweetly. "That would be nice, yeah."

"Okay then, be right back."

Thankfully, the girl did return. And in her hands, she held... did Melinda dare hope? Yes, she did. The tickets! Oh, the *tickets!* They were peeking out from the seal of the envelope. A smile spread, mile-wide, on Melinda's cheeks. Jade stepped in front of her, and she came dangerously close to losing control.

"Wait, one minute."

It all happened so fast, it could have easily been mistaken for a fantasy: Jade hugged her.

Melinda's eyes widened.

"Thanks, babe." Quickly, the girl pulled away from her. "I had a quick look through the window before I came down. Judging by that, you did a great job. If ever you need anything," she handed Melinda the envelope, "let me know."

Trembling, Melinda took her prize. "Jade, I... thanks."

"You can pay me back by cleaning out the rabbits again. They're my mom's. I'm not into animals, aside from the one up there. It'll be quite often..." Her eyes clouded over. "My parents holiday a *lot.*"

Melinda gulped. "Tar, I'll bear that in mind. Rabbits are nice—"

"Jade!" Cody shouted from upstairs. "Hurry up, will you? I'm dying here, you left me hanging."

Jade groaned. "Sorry babe, gotta go. You can see yourself out, can't you?"

Bounding up the stairs, Jade went back into her bedroom.

Oddly, Melinda was sympathetic. Maybe being rich wasn't all it was cracked up to be. Maybe Jade wasn't really perfect, or privileged, or *happy*. Melinda folded the tickets into the envelope. She listened to Jade's bedroom door slam. She listened to the obviously fake giggle that sounded from Jade herself. Then, she left the girl to her feelings of bitterness and headed home.

Chapter Six

Mel,

Just a quick note to say thank you. The concert organisers wanted double-check last night who was doing the backstage tour, and how many tickets to provide. I put it in your name. I knew you'd come. You're welcome to clean out the rabbits anytime.

Jade xx

Melinda's smile was wider than the bus she was on. She wound the red ribbon of her backstage pass around her finger. Among the three beams that streaked down them, the letters VIP were etched with silver glitter. Melinda cast a look around at the quiet, miserable people that sat below her.

She studied the printed email that Jade had attached to her note, and realised the concert was perfect. Due to the young ages of most of the audience, it was on a Saturday night. It started at six, and ended at nine. Her parents always went out on Saturday nights and didn't come home until at least twelve. She'd beat them home easily!

Outside the window, the cars became less frequent; the road became dusty. Returning home was a gift today; Melinda watched a stranger, someone *without* a special VIP pass, leave the bus.

One day, it would be *her* giving out the VIP tickets. It would be *her* people were flocking to see.

Ugh, Three Beams... for three hours. Lyrics of poison, and tunes of venom; a private tour, and forced conversation. Stuck-up Kenzie, immature Tom, and sulky Callum... What fun.

Fun for her *sister!*

Melinda yanked the pass off, and shoved everything back in the envelope. The private tour was after the concert, and only lasted half an hour. The final train home *was* due at ten. They had more than enough time; they'd be fine. *She'd* be fine.

Melinda's stop came into view. Trying to stay positive, she pressed the stop button, and left behind the old ladies and screaming kids.

That evening, even her father, who was usually oblivious, sensed there was something different. "You're in a happy mood tonight."

"Good boy," Melinda rubbed Jack's head as she took the ball. "Now fetch, off you go! Dad, aren't I always in a happy mood?"

Brad ran his fingers through his hair. "Ah, you girls, you and Ash… you're growing up fast."

"Well, I am technically an adult, Dad. And Ashley's eight soon."

"I know, but it still feels like you're babies to me."

"Hmm," Melinda swung the lead back and forth. "We still doing that picnic thing tomorrow? Can we take Jack? He hasn't been to the lake for ages, and look, he's found that ball already. He knows all the best spots."

Her father chuckled. "Ah, for you Mel, anything."

Melinda grinned. Ashley was *not* finding out until tomorrow, simple as.

The car ride was stuffy, quiet, and *boring*. Ashley blew out a breath to cool down. Panting, Jack was sitting on Melinda's lap, head out of the window. Melinda was also feeling the heat; on the other side of Ashley, she panted almost as heavily as the dog.

"For god's sake Jack," she huffed. "Your breath stinks."

In front of the exhausted pair, their parents nodded their heads to the tune on the radio:

"Hey Jules, remember this song?"

"Course I do," she said. "We danced to it back in the day."

"Back in the day? I ain't that old yet, you know—"

"Oh, hush up and turn it up!"

Ashley's Dad did just that, but the radio announcer interrupted the end of the song.

"Ugh, why do they do that?" Julie sighed. "No one wants to hear them yap yap yapping—"

"Television stars Three Beams have hit roaring success," the radio announcer boomed.

Ashley sat up.

"Ever since branching out from their hit children's TV show, and releasing their own albums, fans from all over the globe have flocked to see them perform life. This week is a perfect example. Tickets for the London Three Beams concert have already sold out, and it's been less than…"

Realising suddenly, Julie turned the radio down. Lips quivering, Ashley bowed her head.

"Ashley," her father said knowingly. "You all right?"

"Oh Ashley!" snapped Julie." Stop moping about that silly concert. You know my views on it. You're not trekking all the way to London on a bloody train just to watch that band do what they do on TV, and that's—"

In the mirror, Ashley's tearful expression softened her frown.

"Fine. If you're good, I'll buy you the tour DVD."

Ashley simpered. "Thanks, Mom. Hear that, Mel? We can watch it on TV before school."

"Oooh, can't wait," said Melinda sarcastically.

"Oh, about Saturday," their father said. "Me and your mom *are* going out, but after what happened last time," Brad shuddered at the memory of pillow fights and an overly hyper Jack. "Aunt Flo will be coming to babysit."

Around the sad seven-year-old, arguments exploded. Melinda was *eighteen* years old, an *adult;* she didn't need a babysitter, especially old-fashioned, frumpy Aunt Flo! Brad was quietened as Julie retorted that if she couldn't behave like an adult, she wouldn't be treated like one. Jack barked, and Ashley moped.

Ugh, it was so *hot!* From their house to the park, it was only meant to be a ten-minute drive! This was the longest drive of her *life.*

Everyone perked up when Brad cheered:

"Here we are, girlies!"

With a pleased swing of the car, Brad parked in the only remaining space. Immediately, Jack dived out of the window, and hovered outside of the sizzling death-trap, yapping excitedly. Ashley readied herself for the taste of cupcakes, but Melinda beat her to it:

"Oh Mom, can we play fetch with Jack first?" Ashley was jolted out of her misery as she grabbed her hand. "Look, he's so excited! Look at him. He's going 'yap, yap, yap'. Oh please, can we?"

"Ugh, if you must."

Brad laughed. "Oh Mel, what are we gonna do with ya? Go on then, we need to set up anyway."

"Yes!" Melinda opened the car door. "Come on, Ash!"

"*Mel!*"

Melinda pulled her across the stretch of concrete, past crowds of fussing families, and underneath the wooden banner. Behind her, Jack followed, barking happily. They were running even faster than him; Ashley tried to slow down, but Melinda just pulled her into a faster run, and snapped at her to keep up. Puffing, Ashley did as she was asked, her frilly summer dress billowing around her knees.

"Mel, why are we—"

"Come on, slowcoach!"

The trio ran past the playground, past a rounders game, and over the football field.

What was going on? What was Melinda up to? It wasn't until they came to the weeping willow tree that Melinda stopped. Ashley jolted forward, unglamorously bumping into her. Jack went straight for the mound of dirt on the tree trunk, and meanly tore apart the buried set of nuts. Melinda leaned against the tree, panting.

"Mel! Seriously, you know Jack just chews the toy and doesn't give it back. Why did you—"

"Close your eyes."

"Why?" Ashley demanded, suspicious.

"No reason," With one foot, her sister pushed herself off the tree. "Just close 'em."

"But—"

Melinda's lip curled. *"Close them."*

"Okay!"

Melinda was right in front of her now. So close was she that Ashley could feel the warmth of her voice:

"I was going to give this to you in a week, on the exact night, but I couldn't wait any longer. Keep still. Don't move."

Melinda sounded serious. She never sounded serious, unless she was bringing with her a series of 'adventures'.

Ashley clenched her hands together. There was another rustle… another round of her blood thrumming in her ears. No more waiting, surely no more!

"All right," said Melinda. "You can open them."

Ashley hesitated. It could be something scary. It could be a *snake*! Trembling, Ashley opened her eyes, and saw a miracle.

Ashley stared. She stared, and stared, and stared. On the bottom of the ribbon sat a plastic rectangle, but not just any old rectangle. Red, orange, and yellow raced down the black background in three spectacular beams. Ashley's hand shook. Could it be? No, it couldn't be… they didn't win! Yet…

Engraved at the bottom was her name!

"Mel, I-I…"

"Nope, there's more," Melinda pressed a piece of paper into her free hand.

Stunned, Ashley gazed at the ticket; a tear of happiness slid down her freckled cheek.

On Saturday the 14th June, she was going to see Three Beams perform live. In addition, she was going to go on a private tour with the band themselves.

"Well, babe."

Ashley looked up to the sound of her sister's voice.

Tucking the envelope away, Melinda cocked her head to one side, and enjoyed the sight of her shell-shocked sister. "*What* do you say?"

Behind Ashley, her misery became buried in the hole Jack had dug, never to resurface again.

"Oh my god!" She jumped up and down, and screamed. "Oh my god, it's amazing, it's brilliant, I love it!"

As Melinda descended into happy laughter, Ashley threw her arms around her, and made her cringe as she bellowed into her ear:

"I love you! I love you so, so much." Pulling away, she clapped her hands. "I thought we didn't win; how did you get them? No, wait, I don't care, just… *ah*!"

Shoving the ticket into the casing of the pass, Ashley raced around the tree. She performed cartwheels, gambols, and screeched triumphantly as she capered around, while the world was flipped upside, right-side, downside.

"Yes, yes! Bryony's gonna be so *jealous!* I'm gonna hug Tom and he's gonna love me! I'm gonna marry him and live with him and have babies with him and—"

"And live happily ever after while I use the other two as punch-bags? Yes!"

Crowing, Melinda swept her up in her arms, and both of their patterned dresses flew in the wind as she swung them around. Jack raced after Ashley as she was swung in a circle. Laughing and crying at the same time, both sisters became lost in the glory of being VIPs. The only thing that interrupted them was the planning:

"Mel, Aunt Flo's coming Saturday!"

"I know! Don't worry, I'll take care of her, just don't tell Mom and Dad."

"I won't."

"Good!"

"Mel, stop a minute."

Melinda halted the merry-go-round.

"Thanks, I was getting dizzy, and I wanted to tell you something." Giggling, Ashley pressed her nose against her sister's. "You're the best sister ever."

"Oh. Thanks Ash, that means a lot."

Suddenly Ashley ran. "Race you to the picnic!"

"Aw, no way are you getting the strawberry cupcakes, or *you,* you greedy little mutt!" retorted Melinda, running after her with Jack in toe.

The picnic that followed was the best Ashley had ever had. The cupcakes were delicious. Jack was calm. Her parents chattered happily under the glow of the sun, while she and Melinda winked at each other, honouring their brand-new secret.

"For god's sake," Dana wacked Jay on the side of his head. "It couldn't happen, you absolute moron!"

Jay winced. "Oh, but it so could! I'm sure if you shot it high enough—"

"You know what I wanna shoot right now? *You!*"

She gave the boy a shove. Jay lunged back at her to ruffle her hair, yet she caught his arms mid-air.

"Hey," called Melinda uselessly. "Don't get—"

Dana pushed. Jay stood his ground, matching her strength, and Dana sneered:

"It isn't scientifically possible to shoot a guinea pig into the sky, and have it land on the damn moon. Although maybe if it was"—she grinned as she released Jay, and sent him into a stumble—"it may find the brain you obviously left up there."

"Oh, with yours, you mean?"

Dana simply smirked. "Oh, so you're admitting you left it?"

"No! Dana—"

Melinda, sensing an opportunity, stepped forward. "Guys, stop it." Each of her arms held one enemy back from the other. "Jay, why would you even want to launch a hamster to the moon? Aw, who cares! Break it up. Just *chill*, okay? Look at the lake," she gestured behind her. "It's lovely, so why don't we concentrate on that?"

Lily pads floated on top of the clear water. Bushes and plants sloped around its border, some venturing into the water's edge. Willow trees hung over the sides, providing shade from the heat of the Sunday afternoon. Swinging ropes hung from scattered apple trees. In the back-right corner of the lake, Dana's other crowd of friends splashed. One of the beauties of living near woodland, was that it provided hours of entertainment in the summer.

"Drew, come here!" shouted a girl.

"Oh, don't you dare splash me, Anna, I—"

"Oops!"

Despite Dana and Jay's outburst, Melinda was happy. Ashley had kept the tickets a secret.

"Oi, Mel, watch me."

Melinda tittered as the swim-trunk clad Jay saluted her, and dived into the water.

"He's so stupid," scoffed Dana.

"Oh, Dana," Melinda moaned. "You know he can't help it. Ashley's kept quiet, by the way."

"Really? I thought she'd have caved by now. Geez, you were lucky getting those tickets. Looks like I was wrong, ay?"

Dana was wearing a stylish blue bikini, and Melinda couldn't help but be envious. The girl's thighs were perfectly small. Hers, on the other hand, seemed bigger than ever hidden under the sarong she'd consciously wrapped around her one-piece.

"What you staring at?"

"Oh, nothing—"

"Still thinking about cleaning rabbits out, are ya?" jeered Dana.

"No," Melinda replied. "Just dreading that silly concert."

"Oh come on! It's Kenzie Hudgson," Dana said. "You might finally 'do it' with him."

"Gross, no!"

"You've gotta pop your cherry sooner or later."

"Dana!"

Dana's laugh trailed off; her jaw locked, and her petite hands balled into fists. Melinda followed her gaze. Instantly, she understood the problem. At the back of the lake, Anna was giggling… with Drew.

Rage evident, Dana grasped one of the ropes. "Wait here."

"Dana, what're you doing, don't—"

"Stand back!"

Giving up, she stepped away, just in time to avoid the fireball's angry bellow:

"Jay, *move!* Drew! Drew, watch this!"

Dana grasped the rope with her feet and swung herself into the water. She should have looked ridiculous, but she simply landed with a dainty splash.

"Shit," cried Melinda.

Immediately, Dana's head bobbed back up.

"Wow babe, *nice,*" Drew swam over to her.

"Oh my god, did you see her, Mel?" Jay clambered up the embankment. "Come on, it's cool in there."

"Nah, you're all right, I'll wait here."

Stretching her legs out, she pulled her sarong over her knees. She looked out. To Anna's dismay, Dana and Drew laughed together in the water.

"You sure you don't wanna come?" asked Jay again.

Melinda shook her head.

"'Kay then."

Sitting down next to her, Jay mirrored her position; Melinda took in the bruises on his body, the cuts on his arms, and shook her head playfully. "What are you like, ay?"

"Awesome. So, when's the concert?"

Melinda swallowed. "Saturday."

Only six days to go, until Three Beams would contaminate her body with their horrendous lyrics, and blacken her heart on a backstage tour.

Chapter Seven

The news studio had cameras of every make, and every model. The view from the big glass windows behind was phenomenal. Tom couldn't resist looking at the view, mainly because it was fascinating, but also because the interviewer, Rose Clarton, was so direct it was scary.

"Well"—leaning forward, Kenzie clasped his hands over his red jeans— "I gotta admit, coming back to where it all started has been a mind-blower for me, for all of us."

"Oh, I'm sure it has," replied Rose. "You must have all worked very hard."

Kenzie wrung his hands together; the bruises he wouldn't answer for had long since faded. "Maybe, but we owe our fans so much."

Tom could see the muscles in Kenzie's arms flexing as he spoke; his tattoos stood out even more in the bright light. With the back of his hand, Tom wiped the base of his neck. It was a news studio! Why wasn't the air conditioner on?

Next to him, Callum nodded in agreement with Kenzie. He didn't cope well with interviews. He never had.

"Yes, the fans are crazy for you guys," said Rose. "How about we cut to a video clip?"

Behind Rose, a video of fans crowded outside their last concert building played; through their excited screams, Rose Clarton of Watch News smiled at Tom, and he shuddered. A heavily made-up, straight-haired blonde, she was dressed in a tight, low-cut dress. Opposite them on a matching armchair, she sat, one leg crossed over the other.

"So, you're performing a big concert today in London. How does it feel, knowing just how much you've risen to fame these past three years?"

"You know, we haven't really thought about it," said Kenzie. "There hasn't been *time*. It's all been a bit of a blur. One moment we were all waiting in line for the auditions, all excited because we may be going on

TV. Then suddenly, we're plonked in front of cameras and are filming our own show."

"Y-Yeah," stuttered Tom. "And we've got this manager, telling us what to do and stuff."

Rose nodded. "And how did you rise to such fame, exactly?"

"After the first season of the show, we were given album deals, small venues to start with," Kenzie replied. "After a while, we got *big*. We had fans at our doors, fans at our windows, fans everywhere. One day, our manager just whisked us away to an exclusive headquarters in Birmingham, and boy where we stunned when we were faced with security gates and bodyguards!"

Rose chuckled.

Ugh, Tom had to say *something!* "Yeah, it was crazy."

Kenzie looked at him.

"A-And it still is," continued Tom. "We have a lot to do. Its constant. We're recording, rehearsing, sometimes both, and it gets so tiring and sometimes we wanna go to bed. But we love our fans!"

Rose was amused. "I'm sure you do."

Great. Now hundreds of people had seen Tom in a flustered, panicked state. Perhaps he didn't like interviews as much as he thought he had.

Rose continued to speak, with a glint behind her fake eyelashes. "This band has come such a long way since their individual auditions," She leaned in, her gaze directly on Kenzie. "Especially you, Kenzie."

"Me?"

"Yes, you. To end the show this morning, how about we take a look back at that life-changing day?"

While Callum fidgeted, and Kenzie stared, bewildered, Tom was defenceless as the video exposed Kenzie to all.

May 27th, 2016

Exhaustedly, the judges on the panel shuffle through the papers. The older man sighs. The woman frowns, and the other man, dressed smartly, grumbles:

"Hell no."

In unison, they mark a definite X next to the previous contestant's name.

"All right," says the woman, preening her dark, curly hair. *"Next!"*

The security guard ushers on the next contestant. He wrings his hands as he stands in the middle of the audition room, a lost child who's wandered away from the ball-pit and into a bar of adults.

"H-Hello."

All of the judges assess him. He's tall, but there's not an ounce of muscle on his stick-like arms. Blond hair is flattened across his forehead by sweat. He's wearing a plain white t-shirt, and light blue jeans; an unremarkable, forgettable outfit for an unremarkable, forgettable boy.

The older judge rests his chin on his hands. "Hello, and what's your name, son?"

"For god's sake," mutters the mixed-race woman. *"He's not five."*

The boy stutters:

"My names Ken... Ken Hudgson."

Kenzie gave a false laugh, which was clearly an attempt to push his humiliation away:

"Oh god, what did I look like, ay? Let's switch it off before—"

"And how old are you, Ken Hudgson?" chirps the female judge.

The boy runs one hand down the microphone beam, and then back up again. "Twenty-one."

"And why are you here? What makes you so different from all the others that have come through here?"

"Erm..."

A sigh comes from the smart judge. "Look, kid, we really don't have all day—"

"I've come to audition, for the show. And I-I just think I can do it, if you just give me a chance."

Silence.

The camera zooms in on the judge's reaction. Two are smirking, the third judge, a suit-clad man, clears his throat, and speaks gently:

"Why do you want this?"

The question takes the boy by surprise. "I wanna be famous. I wanna make something of myself, start again. Ever since I was kid, I've wanted to be on TV. Heck." *He rubs the back of his neck.* "I guess I'm not that much different from the others. But... I was always told I could sing."

"Well okay then," offers the smart judge. *"Off you go."*

"All right, here it goes."

He sings... really sings.

His voice is shaky, but graceful. It grabs the judge's attention and holds it.

Ken finishes singing, and smiles to reveal straight white teeth. "Well, how'd I do?"

The smart judge rights his expression, the traces of a smile lingering on his lips. "Very, very well, Ken."

"Good times, ay?" Smiling, Kenzie pushed away all signs that he cared, but Tom wasn't fooled.

Callum and Tom had their auditions played next, then Rose finally called an end to it all:

"Wow, what memories! From all of us here at Watch News, we wish you the best."

Callum mumbled sincere thanks, and Rose turned back to the camera and spoke to the hundreds of people watching:

"Right, everyone, this was Three Beams. TV stars, boy band, and global sensation."

The theme tune of the news played, and petered gently out.

Rose stood. Briskly, she thanked the band, and shook every member's hand. Kenzie avoided her eyes completely, but Tom glared at the vulture, his usually friendly blue eyes teeming hatred.

"Thank you," gushed Rose. "Thank you so much for coming. You've spiked our viewings by over half!"

Tom turned to Kenzie, but he'd already left.

"I don't care, Doug." Pacing between the rubbish skips, Kenzie hissed into the phone. "I specifically asked you to make sure that video didn't get out!"

Doug wasn't agreeing. "Yeah, and I said to you it would be excellent to look back on and—"

"Ugh, fine, be like that."

Kenzie hung up. Hiding his face, he leant against the wall.

From his position in the doorway, Tom blinked. Agonised, he battled with the sight of Kenzie hurting. He looked so unlike the person who Tom had grown up with for the past three years.

"Kenzie?"

"What do *you* want, Landsby?"

Taking slow, steady steps forward, Tom came to the middle of the gap between them. "I just wanted to see if you were okay."

"Well I am, all right?"

Tom backtracked, his hands in front him. "Well, obviously you're not. I'm sorry. I know this has pissed you off. It's annoyed me too. I didn't want mine and Callum's audition played ether, but I had no idea they were going to do it. Now everyone knows I originally auditioned with him! How embarrassing is that, ay?"

Kenzie's fists unravelled. "Pretty embarrassing, but not as bad as mine. The conniving bitch... they get more desperate by the damn day."

Tom nodded. "I know. Paps are always trying to leak things about me." Embarrassment of the time he was caught picking his nose outside Costa crept up on him. "Trust me, it drives me mad. But as for today, it's only an audition video. There was nothing bad on there. Why are you so annoyed about it anyway?"

"Because I didn't want the fans damn well seeing it!"

Instead of backing away from Kenzie's outburst, Tom simply allowed his next rant to mix with the odour of the rubbish.

"Do you know how stupid that video makes me look? How pathetic it makes me seem? I've worked hard to be where I am today. It took months, Tom. *Months!* Now what are the fans gonna think? They'll think I'm a right god-damn moron, that's what." He punched one of the skips. "Fuck!"

Tom waited until Kenzie had calmed down, then said:

"They'll think it's cute."

"*What?*" Kenzie lunged at Tom, grabbing his t shirt.

"I-I said," Tom repeated. "They'd think it was cute."

Even when he was angry, Kenzie was breath-taking.

"They'll love it," continued Tom. "Think about it, you already get most of the fanbase. I mean, do you ever go on the website? Oh wait, course you don't. Anyway, there's always posts about you. 'Oooh, isn't Kenzie hot, what does he look for in a girl?' And there's nothing fangirls love more than seeing a tender side to a guy. It makes them seem real."

"Remember that episode of the show when Doug made us sing that food song?" he continued, as Kenzie released his t-shirt. "Everyone knew pizza was unhealthy already, yet we still had to do an episode about healthy eating. Our ratings went down that day, so guess what Doug put as the omnibus clip to spark 'em back up again? Come on, you know this."

"Yours and Callum's audition video."

"Yep. Our special omnibus clip for that week was mine and Cal's audition video. Oh, that audition! I was so nervous I gave the judges puppy-dog eyes at the end. But guess what the fans thought?"

Kenzie grinned, and to Tom's joy, started to tease him:

"They thought you were oh-so *adorable*. Come here, Tom," Kenzie got him in a headlock. "Little puppy-dog Tommy!"

"Hey!"

Kenzie pulled him into a one-armed hug, then slapped his back roughly. "Thanks, mate. You're right. The fans'll wet themselves over it. Maybe I just need to chill, huh? Anyway, I'd best phone Doug back, I bet the dude's shaking in his boots. Ah look, I can feel the phone vibrating. He's panicking already. Anyway, see ya Landbsy, so long as Doug don't kill me."

If Kenzie hadn't winked at him then, Tom would have been okay.

"Okay, girls," said Julie. "Flo's coming soon. She's really looking forward to it. Now, she said she'd be here in about half an hour," Consciously, she checked her watch. "But if she isn't—"

"Mom, Flo's *always* here."

"Not always, Mel, she does have her own life."

From the floor, Melinda scoffed.

"Me and your dad will be out for a while," Julie glowered at her. "And I'm not trusting you on your own. Why should I worry, on our night out? Nineteen years marriage is something worth celebrating. We'll back by half twelve, so Mel, make sure Ashley's in bed."

Cross-legged on the Living room floor, Melinda saluted. "Yes, mother!"

Julie rolled her eyes.

Ashley giggled, not because Melinda was being silly, but because that night, she was going to see her favourite band perform live! And maybe… Tom would ask her to marry him.

"Brad, what time did you book the restaurant for?"

"The usual."

"And you sure you booked the right one?"

"No, Mom," Melinda interrupted. "He booked a two-seater in a back alley, where all the teenagers go to smoke weed and piss up the wall."

"Melinda, if you don't shut up…"

All of the drama, anticipation, and sleepless nights all came down to this event! Ashley was so excited she missed the rest of her sister and mother's exchange, plus her father interrupting them to say he'd wait outside.

The car horn blasted.

"All right, Brad! Ugh." Julie smoothed down her black dress, and fiddled with her ginger bun anxiously. "Time to go. Have a lovely time with Flo. Don't stay up too late, don't let Jack dash about, and *don't* give Aunt Flo a hard time!"

"*All right.*" Indignantly, Melinda sat up on her knees. "But if she nags me again about swilling things before using them, or putting antiseptic on the *tiniest* little cut, or making sure everything's—"

"Have fun, girls."

Carelessly, Julie waved them off as she left, her flowing dress swirling around her plump ankles. There was another beep of Brad's horn, a shout, a sigh, a click, and then… silence.

"I love winding her up," smirked Melinda.

"If only she knew what we were up to."

"Yes, if only."

Ashley and Melinda observed the car's lights shine through the glass, then pull away. After they had gone, Ashley bounced up and down, babbling about the concert.

"Ugh, stop," groaned Melinda. "Pass me the phone."

Finally, after all this time, she and Three Beams would be together! Ashley could hardly wait as Melinda dialled Aunt Flo's number.

"Oh, hello, Melinda," Flo answered, her overly posh greeting making both sisters cringe.

Melinda placed the phone to her ear, and then hacked and coughed so realistically even Ashley was stunned.

"H-Hello... Oh god, Flo, I'm sorry but... No, I'm fine." Cough. Splutter. "Well, not really. I'm ill. We both are... No, we don't need anything. Oh god, *please* don't come! I don't want you to catch it... No, we'll be okay...I'm sorry, I really am. Aw, I was looking forward to playing board games too!"

Melinda winked at her sister, causing the girl to grab the cushion, put it over her face, and burst out into hysterical giggles.

"Yes, you too. And yes, we will. Oh no—" Moan, gag. "I think I'm gonna hurl, *bye!*"

Melinda hung up. Ashley continued to gasp, until Melinda snatched away the cushion. "Race you to the top of the stairs!"

Yes, the sisters were really, *really* ill.

They raced out of the room and took to the stairs, alive with glee.

Chapter Eight

Three hours were left of precious, precious sanity, before Melinda had to hear Kenzie warbling, Tom acting ridiculous, and Callum mumbling.

Melinda put down the wand; her mascara had been finished a while ago. Her hair was in plaits, her foundation smooth. Sat in front of her bedroom mirror, she stared at Ashley.

Ashley was kneeling up on her bed, *kissing* her Three Beams posters!

"Ashley!" Smirking, Melinda reached behind her, and took the VIP passes. "Well, well, well, girl, looks like we can't go backstage after all."

"What?" whimpered Ashley. "Why?"

"Because," she uttered dramatically. "*It's* happened."

"What? What's happened?"

Melinda drummed her foot against the stool leg. "The turning. I knew it would happen eventually, that soon, you'd become…"

Melinda waited for the tension to build, before saying tauntingly:

"You'd become possessed! You'll turn into a zombie!"

"Mel!"

Melinda chortled. "There's only one way to help people like you, and that is to kill the zombie virus before it takes over, and that's with a full-on exorcism."

When Melinda tickled her, Ashley cracked up laughing. "Y-You don't do that with zombies, you cut their heads off! Stop!"

"Oh, babe!" Melinda stopped her attack. "You know I'm only joking, So Ash, be honest… do I look okay?"

The dress was her favourite, however, the size ten was a little tighter than she remembered. Fitted at the waist, yet petering into modest flows afterward, the dress was a mix of gold and black flower patterns, and looked great with black tights and black plimsoles. But Melinda still feared she looked ugly.

"Mel, you look lovely. But I thought you hated plaits?"

Melinda held up one finger, then unravelled her secret.

Ashley gasped. "Oh wow!"

Pretty waves cascaded past Melinda's shoulders, and came to rest above her chest. Ashley ran her hand down the freshly washed hair, and the blonde streak that was freshly bleached. Beaming, Melinda took one of the few clips she owned, which was a small, black butterfly.

"Oh, Mel," Ashley simpered. "You look so beautiful."

Securing the clip at the back of her head, she dared a glance at the mirror. "Aw, thank you, Ash, that's so sweet. You've scrubbed up well too; you're good at putting outfits together, kind of like Mom. Honestly? Tom will be on his knees. You look stunning."

She did. Ashley was wearing a white dress, cutely decorated with orange ribbons. She'd constructed herself a French braid, and tied an orange ribbon around the bobble. Wavy wisps framed her delicate face, and orange tights matched well with her white pumps, discarded from the long-ago, hated ballet lessons their mother had forced on them.

Her sister was a little beauty.

Melinda quelled her jealousy. "Here," she gathered the backstage passes, and placed each around their necks. "Keep this on you for the way there. We can let the whole train know we're VIPs."

After a few more minutes of bickering and fussing, they said goodbye to Jack.

Melinda scrutinised herself. Yes, her thighs were well hidden beneath the dress, and no, she would not die a gruesome death at the concert. Warmth graced the sisters as they stepped outside; overgrown grass weaved around their feet. Straight on, they left the expanse of greenery and the wood around it behind, and braved the dirt road for the long walk to the train station.

Ashley broke out into a Three Beams song. Melinda rolled her eyes.

In the tour bus, Three Beams were approaching the concert entrance. They were sat at the back, where there were four seats all facing each other. So far, they had been undetected by the obsessed 'Beamers' that had already crowded the venue, desperate for even a glimpse. Now, all the band had left to do was get to the back entrance and sneak inside.

"Kenzie," Tom moaned. "Pass me a Kit-Kat."

"Get it yourself, you lazy shit."

"Oh *please,* I'm starving."

"Yeah," Kenzie reached into the bag next to him. "Practically wasting away."

Doug turned from his seat in front of them. "You had a massive dinner, *plus* dessert. How can you be hungry already? You'll lose that fast metabolism if you don't watch out."

"Nah, man." Casually, Kenzie rested his feet in the Tom's lap. "This dude needs to beef up."

The band manager grinned. "Beef up? Him?"

"Yeah. I could teach him how."

Tom fidgeted.

"Have you ever tried protein shakes, Tom?" Kenzie asked.

"Huh?"

"Protein shakes, dummy," Kenzie repeated.

"O-Oh, erm, no, I haven't tried them. I don't like them."

Kenzie rolled his eyes. "So you haven't tried them, but you don't like them?"

Tom shrugged, while Callum typed hurriedly on his laptop, to no doubt his meagre fanbase. Kenzie smirked. He was the only person they really wanted to see.

"Guys," Callum said. "Look at this! The fans are so excited for the concert."

"Yes, Callum, thanks for pointing that out," said Kenzie sarcastically. "I never would have guessed from the way we're literally sneaking inside the ven—"

Crash!

"What the—"

Cheers bounced from every side of the tour bus; even the windows shuddered. Then, there was a psychotic bellow:

"Kenzie, I love you!"

More crashes, more voices. Callum's laptop clattered to the floor as he backed away from his window, for it was at Callum's window, that the Beamers swarmed, and a humongous, sinister girl leered.

"Oh *shit,"* Doug cried. "Driver, floor it. Get a move on, before they mob the damn bus."

"I can't just run them over!"

Kenzie shouted:

"Well do *something*!"

The driver slammed his hand on the horn.

Bang, bang. "Kenzie!" Rattle, rattle. "Kenzie, please marry me, *please!*" Oh no! It was the fat girl from the last year! The beast's dyed-red hair whipped over her eyes as she launched herself forward, splaying her palms on his window's glass. "We can have *babies*!"

Babies? Oh hell no, hell no! More teenage Beamers latched onto her side. Trying to pull her away, they screeched similar obscenities:

"Tom, take me home!"

"I love you all so fucking much!"

"Kenzie, if you don't follow me on Twitter I'll kill myself!"

Groaning, Kenzie and put his hands in front of himself, because Phones, iPods, and cameras were flashing. More Beamers surrounded the back of the bus. Kenzie craned his neck back, and saw them banging on the window behind him.

Tom, in a silly attempt to hide his fright, simpered and waved at the lunatics. Outside, a security guard yelled:

"Step away from the bus, *now!*"

The horn honked.

"Oh, fuck this," Doug cursed. "All security guards, out!"

The security guards inside the bus rushed outside. The Beamers stood their ground. Together, the Beamers coursed adoration for their favourite band, their cries morphing into endless noise as they pinned posters to the bus frame and their lips to the glass.

Callum whimpered. "Oh come on, I only posted that we were nearly there and about to stop at Costa."

"You did *what?*" shouted Kenzie. "Do you have no common sense?"

"Kenzie, Kenzie," Tom called. "Look outside, it's actually really funny-"

Kenzie looked. "Oh jeez, this *is* amazing!"

It was. Tom joined Kenzie's side, and they watched, grinning, as the fans became hysterical. Desperately, they were trying to get past the guards, who were herding them back. One fan punched a guard as he picked her up and carried her back to the barriers. The fat girl tried to run around the other side, but she too was seized.

Kenzie waved. Tom mirrored him, and Kenzie laughed. The guards from inside the building brought another barrier in, and penned the fans behind that.

"Callum," asked Tom. "What're you doing? You're missing out."

"I don't like watching the fans get upset, you know that."

Oh, touché! Kenzie aimed kisses specifically for the fat girl, teasing her.

"Go!" Doug snapped at the driver. "No, leave the guards, they'll be fine."

The bus pulled away, but that was not the end of it. Some of the sheep escaped from their barrier and c*hased* the bus. As Tom enjoyed the comedy sketch, Kenzie allowed his mind to wander. Adoring fans, an exhilarating concert, and a backstage tour that was going to be perfect? Yes... his life truly was great.

Melinda and Ashley approached the queue. Dumbly, they hovered on the pavement, not knowing what to do next. As if the entire Christmas holiday was taking place there, it was lit up with spinning lights. Glowing in the dusk, lamps lit up the red carpet in the entrance.

"Mel! Oh Mel, we're here! Come on, let's queue up—"

"No, Ash, wait!"

In the venue, Three Beams were waiting, lurking backstage. She didn't know London. She'd followed a group of girls out of the chip shop her and Ashley had just had chips in, because they had just happened to be wearing Three Beams shirts. Despite her predictions, she hadn't thought anything through properly.

"Mel, where are you going?"

Melinda's jaw tightened. "We need to wait in the queue."

Fans were chattering. Whispers flew from one to the next. Security guards stood either side of the queue, eyeing all tickets suspiciously. The line was impossibly long, yet the security guards didn't delay the procedure, and it was actually moving quite quickly.

"But we have VIP passes," Ashley piped up again. "Shouldn't they just let us through?"

"Oh! Quick, give yours here, we don't want the fans seeing them, they'll kill us."

"But how are we gonna—"

"Ash, just do as I say!"

Hastily, Melinda shoved both of their passes into her black handbag. "We'll just wait in the normal line and show the men the tickets; they have VIP on them too."

Ashley squealed with excitement. "Oh, whatever, I can't wait! This is going to be so, so amazing! They're going to take me backstage… Kenzie's gonna love you. Oh, just watch, he'll take one look at you and he'll say, in that deep voice of his: 'Mel, please, come away with me. Come to my mansion and be my baby girl.'"

There were small children with their mothers, teenage girls in groups, and girls and boys with their younger siblings. Three Beams had truly brainwashed everyone, but she was stronger.

"Right, Ash, do you remember the rules on the email?" asked Melinda.

"*Yes.*" Ashley rolled her eyes as they moved forward. "No hitting, insulting, or asking the band personal questions. Always wear your pass when backstage. Stay seated during the entire performance. Do whatever security says. And—" she paused. "Leave as and when the tour is over."

"Good girl, but just remember my rules too." Melinda ignored Ashley's second eyeroll. "Don't get throwing yourself at Tom. He's not a set of skittles in a bowling alley. Don't pester Callum. He's not a turtle, so he doesn't have a shell you need to bring him out of. And, don't you *dare* try setting me up with Kenzie. I *don't* like him. I think he's a twat."

"You're a twat," mumbled Ashley jokingly.

"Don't go asking them dumb stuff ether, like, 'What's it like to be famous?', because they get that all the time. And also—"

"Yes, yes, I get it!"

"Tickets, please?"

They were at the front of the queue! Fumbling with her bag, Melinda got her tickets out. Nauseatingly, the chips churned in her stomach. Thanks to the tracks she could hear playing from inside, it had randomly, but powerfully hit her that she was meeting a famous band. What would they think of her? And why did she even care?

"Mel, you have got the tickets, haven't you?"

"*No,* I threw them down the drain. Course I've got them, look."

Ashley bounced around, giggling, while Melinda thrust the tickets at the man. The man turned away and whispered to another guard behind the door.

"So, you're the lucky winners?" the man said kindly.

"Yes, we are, that's us, Ashley and Mel!" Ashley cheered.

The man chuckled; Melinda and her excited sister looked at him. He was broad, yet welcoming; his blue eyes were gentle, his smile genuine. He had stubble, and tousled blond hair that reached his shoulders. "Well why didn't you say? And why did you wait in that massive queue? Come with me. My name's Aston, and I'm gonna be looking after you both."

"Yay!"

"Ash, for god's sake, just—"

Ashley let go of her sister's hand, and rushed in.

"Ash, wait for me!"

"She's eager, isn't she?" Aston said.

"Not just eager, but bloody irritating." She placed a hand on her sister's shoulder; thankfully, she hadn't run off as far as the door. "Ash, stay with me, okay?"

Ashley was still. To the left of her was the stage. It was enormous. Rainbow lights hung down, waiting patiently to be switched on. Projected images glorified the band; a trampoline was located at the back. Various workers milled around, adjusting beams, tightening bolts and testing microphones. Melinda could taste the heat of the lights, the sweat of the fans. As she and her sister followed the guard, Melinda inwardly screamed at herself for insisting on getting the tickets.

"So, girls, where you from?" asked Aston.

"Stratford," said Ashley proudly.

"Oh, that's a long way. Did you catch the train?"

"Uh-huh. Mel wouldn't shut up about how much she wanted to meet Kenzie."

Melinda seethed. "Ash, I swear to god, I'm gonna brain you in a minute."

"Aw, you two remind me of my girls." Aston led the way up a set of dark red stairs. Various sets of them cut through the brighter red rows of soft chairs, after every sixth seat. The security guard led them on, to two seats on the third row brandishing a 'reserved' sign. Removing it, he seated them. "Here you are then, girlies, seats eleven and twelve. You can see the whole stage from here."

Ashley jumped into the seat more than eagerly, while Melinda sat on it as if it were going to bite her.

"So what happens after the concert?" Melinda asked Aston.

"I'll come and collect you, and take you to the band. Then, you're on your own."

"Oh."

"Yeah, it's not normally within our protocol for me to leave, but we're short-staffed, and the band insisted on it." Aston smiled. "But I will be back to show you out. Have fun, and make sure you put your backstage passes on."

"Thank you!" Ashley said.

Aston nodded at them, then left.

"I think I'd better put earplugs in," teased Melinda, in an attempt to calm herself. "I think I may need them if I've gotta listen to this crap for three hours—"

"No, you can't! It's *rude.*"

Melinda scowled.

At that moment, a girl with frizzy ginger hair flopped down in the seat next to Melinda.

"Hey! Mind if I sit here?"

Her eyes were mischievous. Melinda liked her already. "Course not."

"Thanks. That stupid damn queue," the girl mumbled, shoving her bag under the chair. "It took forever to get my sisters in. I swear those guards only check the tickets so they can stare at you, the perves. And then there was Shell and Darc, nearly pulling my bag off my shoulder. 'Oh Cassidy, hurry up and get us in, I wanna see 'em'. Yeah, cause they're gonna come dashing out." Puffing with the effort, Cassidy sipped on some water.

Melinda couldn't believe her luck. Another band hater! "So, you're not having a good time then?"

"Oh yeah, brilliant," replied Cassidy, pulling a face. "I've been forced here by my mom, as my sisters' 'adult guardian' 'cause she doesn't wanna come. There they are." She pointed at two smaller replicas of herself, who were giggling on the second row. "Those 'Beamers' next to them robbed my seat. So who dragged you here, babe?"

"I did," Ashley butted in.

Melinda smirked. "There's your answer."

"Well, at least I've got a sane person next to me," Cassidy replied.

Hmm… maybe this concert wouldn't be so bad after all.

Chapter Nine

Anxiety held Callum behind his fellow band members.

In front of the excited Tom, Kenzie poked his head through the backstage door; his whisper proved Callum's fears as true:

"Oh... my god, it's rammed out there."

Tom hurried towards the door, stood beside Kenzie, and peered out. "There are loads of them!" he exclaimed. He shook Kenzie's arm and pointed. "We're in business, Ken."

Doug grinned. "Hey." Giving Callum's shoulder a reassuring squeeze, his eyes radiated kindness behind their expensive lenses. "You'll be fine. You always panic like this before a show, but it always turns out okay."

Oh, but this time it *wouldn't!* Callum could sense something bad was going to happen, like the trampoline collapsing, or the lights catching fire. Yet at Doug, Callum smiled and shrugged.

All too soon, Kenzie turned back. "Come on guys, let's knock 'em dead."

Suddenly, he rushed outside. Tom followed. Cheers almost shook the place down, and screams nearly shattered the light bulbs.

Doug had to shove Callum out. "Go!"

Callum skirted around the trampoline, the one *he* would soon be jumping on, and came to a stop on Kenzie's right, in front of his microphone.

Cheers, shouts, cries... Don't look, don't look, don't look—

Callum looked up.

The arena was heaving! Fans occupied every seat. Banners floated in the sea of faces, but the *real* sight was on the front row. As the music began to play, Callum began to strum the guitar, and his eyes welled up with happy tears.

The banner had said 'I love you, Callum'.

Callum may not have had Kenzie's good looks, or Tom's adorability, yet he had fans who cared about him. Mentally, he took a photo of the moment, and watched them cheering for him, because he wasn't due to sing properly yet. His line wasn't until the end of the song.

"Took you long enough, didn't it?" Kenzie sneered, before belting out the theme tune lyrics.

Callum blew a kiss in the direction of the banner. The sound of Tom backing Kenzie was a bit pathetic, really.

Unknowingly, Callum's few fans had changed things for him. Yes, the screams did near deafen him, but when his time to sing came, he did so without hesitation.

Sheer, pounding volume... Dreadful, cheesy music... hot, sweaty air... Melinda was in hell. It was too *loud!* Which was worse, the band or the audience?

Cassidy placed her freckly hand over hers.

"Hey babe," she called over the music. "You okay?"

"Yeah, it's just my first time, if you get what I mean."

Ashley was bound to her seat. Eyes wide, mouth grinning manically, and knees hugged to her chest, she looked *insane*. Melinda shuddered. During the past two hours, Ashley *had* become a zombie. And soon, Melinda would too; she would be forced to bite down on flesh from the remains of the fans, who had died from a mysterious, yet fatal eardrum explosion.

Cassidy was sniggering.

Quickly, Melinda backtracked what she'd said. "My first time seeing them live, I mean."

"Hun, I knew what you meant!"

Melinda's 'first time' was something she hadn't had yet, and probably never would, because she didn't like any of the boys at college, plus, the idea of sex repulsed her at the moment.

Three Beams were hilariously awful. After a while, her and Cassidy had great fun taking the mick out of them, and 'dancing' in their seats. Never would Melinda forget the video of Kenzie's audition, now plastered all over the internet. The fans had loved it, and so had she, because he looked a complete fool.

Sometimes, Melinda felt bad for hating on a band so much, but when her sister and even her best friend was so obsessed with them, it couldn't be helped. The night before the concert, Melinda had discovered Three Beams fanfiction, where the band participated in orgies, or got shipwrecked and ended up killing each other. She made a mental note to send Cassidy some links to them.

Ashley sighed happily:

"Callum, you're so amazing."

He actually was. The boy was performing backflips on the trampoline, which he was clearly an expert at. Melinda stared, fascinated. With all due respect, he actually had a decent singing voice; briefly, Melinda wondered why he didn't sing more often. But then she looked at Kenzie, and the answer was revealed: she'd clocked him shooting a quick glare at Callum.

Melinda glanced down. An instrumental played over the speakers. Out of the corner of her eye, she could see Ashley bouncing on her backside, pointing, and saying 'Mel, Mel, look!'.

"Oh, fucking hell." Cassidy cursed under her breath.

"Mel!" Ashley was shaking her sister's arm, grinning. "Look, they're coming!"

Ashley was right. The band was heading up the stairs, toward them.

Cassidy had slid down in her seat. Melinda held back her whimpers. Oh, what was she going to *do?* She could barely cope now. How would she cope meeting them? She hugged her knees to her chest. The band came closer. Girls behind her, in front of her, and around her stuck their hands out enthusiastically.

Please, Melinda prayed, don't let the band come near her.

Kenzie and Tom were on the other side of the stairs, and were quickly making their way up, up, and... past them!

Melinda felt a surge of pure relief. Her chest deflated with a breath she didn't even know she'd been holding. They were gone; she was safe. Only Callum was lagging behind. He was one-arm hugging some idiotic teenagers on the front row with a banner.

Meanwhile, in front of Melinda, Cassidy's seat-hogging Beamers practically clambered over one another, snatching at Kenzie and Tom as they went past. Smartly, Kenzie and Tom avoided them.

Further down the stairs, Callum peered around for his band mates, looking lost when he realised they'd left him behind.

"Dude, come on!"

Startled, Melinda craned her neck back. It was Kenzie. There was no mistaking his voice as he grabbed Tom's wrist, and shouted at Callum to just 'run up the stairs to meet them' because 'they were running behind now'.

Melinda turned to her sister. "Don't worry babe, we'll see them later on—"

A set of screams followed a strangled cry.

Melinda looked to see a Beamer on Callum's shoulders. She kicked him in the base of his knee! Another two charged at his side, shoving him down. From then, the entire concert went into slow motion. The girls descended on top of Callum, squealing.

Some fans gasped, while others stood, beside themselves. Two security members pounded up the stairs, shouting at them on the way. Where were the other two? Why weren't they helping Callum? Melinda looked up to where Tom and Kenzie were. Tom was calling to Callum, worried... but Kenzie was laughing.

Ashley jumped out of her seat. "Callum!"

"No!" shouted Melinda, holding her sister back. "Stay there, he'll be fine."

"Oh god," Cassidy sniggered. "Best concert *ever*! Look, they're practically humping him!"

They were, and all Melinda felt was a burning, burning sympathy for the tiny boy. Thankfully, the security guards were fast. They grabbed a Beamer in each arm, barking orders.

Aston scaled the stairs. "Hey! Calm it, *now!*" He hurried to where, Melinda presumed, the other band members were standing. On the way, he coldly instructed the standing fans to sit. Smartly, they did.

Callum was on his back, his limbs splayed out.

Tension beat with the sound of the instrumental.

Callum scrambled to his feet. Running a hand over his head, he fearfully looked about him.

Melinda gawped. Lipstick covered his face. One knee of his yellow trousers was torn. His hands were cut. But other than that, he was unharmed. He blinked. He trembled. Fans called to him; others made to stand but were shouted at by security. The Beamers sobbed as they were 'escorted' down the stairs and to the exit.

Biting his bottom lip, Callum scurried down toward the stage.

"Oh, Callum," Ashley whispered, hugging her knees.

Wheezing with laughter, Cassidy hid the view with her hands. Eyes following the retreating figure as he ducked behind the trampoline, Melinda watched him vanish backstage. Tom, head down, passed their row with Aston. Only Kenzie didn't follow.

Looking away, Melinda folded her arms. "Damn prick. He did that deliberately."

"Did what?" Ashley asked.

"He made Callum hurry up so that those girls would grab him. The instrumental is still playing, so they weren't running behind at all. He's a prick."

"Aw, Mel, he'd never do that, it was an accident. Oh, Mel, look!" Ashley exclaimed, shaking her again. "Quick, stick your hand out."

Oh, anything to keep her happy! Without thinking, or looking, Melinda thrust her right hand behind her.

Shock juddered over her skin when she felt a hand slap against hers, and hold on. Eyes bulging, Melinda turned around, inwardly screaming for it not to be a Beamer. What she got was much, much worse:

It was Kenzie.

Melinda stilled, her entire body flushing. His hand did not leave hers; the grip remained, strong and determined. Behind his brown eyes, a glint sparkled as her eyes locked with his.

He winked. "Later babe."

Clicking his tongue, Kenzie continued down the stairs.

"I can't believe you," huffed Melinda. "I specifically told you *not* to set me up with Kenzie, and what did you go and do?"

Ashley gazed at the stage as the final song faded away.

"Shush Mel," she hissed. "Kenzie is talking."

"Well, Kenzie can go and choke on a bourbon."

The band stood in a line. Callum had been given a new pair of trousers, new make-up, and new confidence.

Kenzie took centre stage. "Before we go tonight, we just want to say thank you for a great three years. It's been so, so amazing. Truly, it has. And we couldn't have done it without the patience, the support, and the love from you guys."

The lights started to go out. Tom gave the crowd a thumbs-up.

"So from all of us here at Three Beams," Kenzie combed his hair back. "Thank you! Thank you so much!"

Applause erupted; fans cheered.

Ashley clapped, and wiped away a tear. The band joined hands, and took a final bow. The remaining lights dimmed. And then, darkness took over the stage, the crowd's noise died down, and people began to leave.

Various fans milled on the stairs. "Shall we wait by the stage?" they said, clapping. "They might come past us. We might get to meet them!"

Ashley smiled maliciously. It was *her* the band wanted, not them.

"Well, Melinda," Cassidy, who Ashley thought had been a pest, said. "I guess I'll see ya around, sister from another mister." She gave Melinda a quick hug. "If he bugs you again, just let me know, and I'll knee-drop him."

Melinda snickered back. Cheerfully, she said goodbye to the girl as she collected her two sisters, and departed with an infuriating wave:

"Ta-ta, darling."

Ashley glowered.

At the bottom of the stairs, Aston began happily climbing toward them, and the second Ashley saw him, she forgot her resentment for Cassidy. Throwing her arms around her sister, she bounced in her seat. "Oh Mel! You're the best sister in the whole wide world. We're gonna meet them!"

"Hey, enough sappy stuff." She rummaged through her handbag. "God, why did you bring this phone? You didn't even take any pictures. Anyway, with this around your neck"—Ashley nearly hugged Melinda again as she slipped the backstage pass over her—"I officially declare you royalty."

Ashley cheered so loudly, even her own ears felt the sting. Oh, she couldn't believe it! She, an ordinary girl, was going to meet Three Beams!

Aston called:

"Ready, girls?"

Melinda shrugged her pass on and sighed. "I guess—"

"Oh yes, *yes*!" With one jump, Ashley had left her seat, and was nearly running down the stairs. "Come on!"

To Melinda's protests, Ashley served past the Beamers making their way toward the stage. On her way down, she caught sight of Bryony, dumbly sitting in one of the further rows. She paused. She stuck her tongue out. Waving the pass, she drank in Bryony's shocked expression. After that, it was just her, and the stage. Behind it was where her new life lay: marriage, children, and love. So when Ashley felt the tug on her elbow, she was furious.

"No! The band—"

Melinda's glare turned her legs to jelly. "Ashley! Are you completely incapable of listening to a simple instruction? I said earlier to stay with me."

"I know." Consciously, Ashley mumbled as she peered around her. "Sorry."

"Girls." Calmly, Aston joined them at the bottom of the stairs. "No worries, okay? I'm escorting you to the band. No one's gonna nick your passes while I'm around."

Melinda seemed to realise her mistake. "Oh yeah. I'm sorry, Ash. I just don't want to you get lost. I need *someone* to endure the torture with."

"No, *you* just need to hurry up and marry Kenzie," Ashley retorted. "I want a blonde niece to play dress-up with."

The rest of the journey backstage was uneventful. Aston chatted. Melinda bunched and re-bunched her dress, biting her lip as they crossed the stage. As they skirted around the trampoline, her previous bravado seemed to have gone.

Ashley took no notice. They were on the same stage Three Beams had just stood on. Not even the start of Melinda's annoying nags could tear the exhilaration away.

"Now Ashley, remember; no bombarding, no screaming, and *definitely* no—"

As they entered the portal to Ashley's new life, Melinda's words drained away. Tom… the real Tom, was standing at the head of the hallway.

Cheekily, Tom smiled. "Ello, ello, ello!"

Ashley screamed. "Tom! Oh, *Tom*!" She ran. "Tom, Tom, Tom!" Shrieking, Ashley threw herself onto the boy, nearly toppling him over.

"Whoa." Tom chuckled. "Hey there!"

In love, Ashley clung to his waist. And despite his bewilderment, Tom clasped her back.

Tears dribbled down Ashley's cheeks. "My baby! *Mine.* I love you." Oh, he even *smelt* gorgeous. "I love you so, so much…"

Chapter Ten

Melinda lost her patience. "Oh, for goodness' sake!"

Protesting, Ashley whined her love to Tom as Melinda pulled her away. "*Mel,* what are you doing? He's—"

"I *told* you not to bombard him. Why can't you just listen?"

Callum awkwardly stared at his feet. Wearily, Aston hovered. Ashley gazed at the blue-eyed boy adoringly, and Melinda was about to apologise for being so harsh with her, then Kenzie stepped in front of her.

"All right, calm down," he said.

Anxiety rendered Melinda incapable of speaking. "I-I'm sorry. She's just a bit… um…"

Ashley glanced up at her questioningly. Melinda wilted, and the younger sibling gave her a look which said she would never let her live this one down. She, the careless Melinda, who'd made so many jokes about tying them up and shipping them to Antarctica, was suddenly scared of them.

"She's just excited." Melinda continued to apologise, as Ashley gave Kenzie and Callum big hugs too. "She really likes you all."

Casually, Tom placed his hands in his pockets. "It's okay. We're used to it."

"I bet you are."

Oh, what was she meant to *say?* They were all staring at her! Briefly, she thought back to the girls she'd seen pouncing on Callum. They'd have loved this opportunity. But why? Aston hurriedly said his goodbyes, and mentioned… something about getting the fans away from the stage? Melinda didn't know for certain; all she knew was that he had left, and she was suddenly grateful for Ashley's babbles:

"Oh, you were so good! How did you do that jumping Callum? And I love your hair Tom. Oh my god Kenzie, thanks so much for coming to us!"

Kenzie grinned. "What can I say? I love meeting you guys.".

Ashley looked at Callum, and simpered. "Are you okay now, Callum?"

"Huh?" Callum said momentarily confused. "Oh, that? Yeah, I'm—"

Kenzie slapped the boy on the back, winding him. "He's fine, aren't you, Cal? The fans were just wound-up. They come from all over the globe to see us. Travelling's stressful. We had someone come from Australia once."

Melinda couldn't help but be annoyed. Those fans had been *savage,* not 'wound up'.

"So…" Up and down, Kenzie's eyes roamed her body. "Did you enjoy the show?"

Melinda's breath hitched. Yes, Kenzie was very, very handsome, but the way he was looking at her was making her very uncomfortable.

Ashley parroted foolishly. "Yes, yes, yes, we absolutely loved it, didn't we, Mel?"

Swallowing, Mel nodded.

Tom flashed Ashley a smile. "So, where are you guys from?"

"Twenty-seven Larkridge Road, Stratford-upon Avon," replied Ashley, proud that she'd remembered it all…. wait, what?

"Ashley!" Melinda hissed. "They don't need to know our entire address, you fool. What if…"

Kenzie smirked. "We're a bunch of axe-wielding murderers? Don't worry hun, we're not."

Melinda looked away. At her, Callum smiled kindly, as if to say 'ignore him'. The other two band members nudged each other, and looked back at Ashley. Ashley hurried to join them, and jumped up and down, parroting endless rubbish about fame, lyrics, and her love for Tom. At this point, Melinda gave up. It was time to just give in, and let Ashley become a zombie.

"You girls are hilarious," said Tom. "What are your names?"

Of course, it was Ashley who replied. "I'm Ashley, and that's Melinda, she's my sister."

At Melinda, Kenzie stared. "Melinda, huh?"

Melinda gulped and nodded; she didn't dare mock him.

Litter fluttered in the wind. On a long road, cars drove past the building and past the two fans across the road from the concert.

"H-Hello. I'm Faye. I'm outside Three Beams' concert. It ended twenty minutes ago. There were more of us, but they went home... we're still here, though."

The recording camera was swivelled around, and the owner of the voice was revealed on the screen.

It was a girl. Lank, her brown hair was in pigtails; the glasses on her nose shielded her tears. "I just wanted to meet them. I waited. I didn't have to, but I waited on after the concert, b-by the stage." I wanted to see them, and I couldn't because... because—"

Cutting her off, her friend Kat took the phone from her:

"The damn security threw us out." Dressed in a Three Beams t-shirt, thick, orange make up was piled on her face.

Behind her, the lights of the venue went out. "We don't think it's fair. Three years. Three years, yeah, we've watched their show, and listened to their albums. We're twelve now. People think that we're, like, too old for them. But *we* don't care. *We* love them. We were here, right from the start, before they even released their albums. And where are we now, ay?"

Off-camera, Faye snivelled. "Standing outside their venue 'cause they didn't come out to us."

"Precisely!" The orange-faced girl was shouting now. "It wasn't like there were loads of us. There was only, like, ten. Surely it wouldn't have been too much trouble to meet us. But Kenzie, Tom, and Callum couldn't spare a moment. All they care about are those stupid contest winners. Well, what about us? We're the ones that truly care!"

Faye pleaded. "Kat, let me have the phone please, I wanna say—"

There was a huff, and then, Faye was back on the screen. "We entered the contest, but we lost. We had to buy tickets, and they're forty pounds each. We're not made of money. Some people aren't. It's not fair."

Off-camera, Kat began to cry. "We've been everywhere, right. Hereford, Wales, Manchester, everywhere. And what do we get? Nothing!"

Faye's finger hovered near the off button.

"No!" Kat said. "Don't turn it off. I just—I'm so fucking pissed. Some of these winners…"

Shaking her head, Faye was dangerously close to crumpling to the floor and bawling.

"They don't even care about the band," she said. "Like tonight, the one girl obviously did. She was wearing orange, Tom's colour. But then there was this other girl with her, who I think was her sister. I was behind them, and I could hear her taking the piss out of the band. She didn't care about them!" Faye burst into sobs. "She didn't care, she didn't—"

The camera was taken away from her.

Kat's tears were black with mascara. "Why do people like her get to meet the band? People like us, who, like, wait for them, and actually *buy* their albums instead of listening to them on Youtube are the real fans. But we get treated like dirt. Look at her."

She presented the camera with Faye, who was sobbing hysterically into her hands.

"Faye's crying. Faye never cries. But now it seems like it's all she ever does, and it's all because of *them*—Faye!"

Faye was running back across the road.

Kat hollered after her; the camera shook up and down as she ran. Nearly hitting her, a red car whizzed past. Kat screamed:

"Fucking *wanker!*"

When Kat got to her, Faye was sat, cross-legged, on the concrete floor outside the venue.

"Faye, don't do this again. It's pointless. Security will just move us on again. Come on, Faye. It's late. We need to be getting back—"

"No!" Faye howled. "No, I'm staying here. They might come out. They might—"

"Faye, don't be silly, of course they won't."

"Shut up!" howled Faye indignantly. "I don't care. I'm not leaving. I'm staying here."

"Fine then. I'm going home without you."

"Fine!"

A few awkward seconds passed. And then, from behind the camera, a sigh came. Kat's knees scraped against the floor, as she sat down with her friend, and turned the camera off.

"What are those for?" Ashley said excitedly.

"Oh." Tom bent to Ashley's level. "They're backstage cameras. We use them to record us sometimes before we come onstage. The fans can see it via the big projectors around the stage. It creates... dramatic effect."

Ashley practically swayed to the rhythm of Tom's speech. "Dramatic effect..."

"Nice." Kenzie took hold of Melinda's hair and wound some of the waves around his finger. "Very nice."

Melinda pulled away from him. Stupid Tom. Her sister hadn't spoken to her at all during the tour. Both her and Tom had their backs to her now. Ashley called Callum over, and Callum joined her opposite side. Ashley was, once again, trying to set her up with Kenzie. Melinda didn't even know where her sister had got the running gag that she loved Kenzie from, but she'd chosen the worst possible time to run with it.

"So," Callum said. "Did you say you guys were from the country?"

Kenzie was back. This time, he was playing with the edge of her dress. He was wrapping it around his hand, and slowly lifting it up.

"Don't!" Melinda hissed, snatching her dress back.

"Oh dear. What's up, babe? You look tense."

The trio in front had crowded underneath the cameras in the back-left corner, leaving her stranded in the centre, with Kenzie. They had to come back, they had to! Oh, where was the exit?

"Hey, come on." Kenzie etched closer to her. "Don't be all moody."

Melinda stifled a shout. Why couldn't he leave her alone? "I'm not. I'm just not..."

"Yes?" Kenzie teased her as she looked away from him. "You're not what? Come on, tell Kenzie everything."

Melinda hadn't finished her sentence, because she'd realised the person she was about to insult was famous. On TV, Three Beams had seemed like cardboard cut outs. The last thing she wanted was them making her name mud.

"I think we should go and join the others," Melinda mumbled.

Looking around, she saw the others on the other side of the room. Inching away from the lead singer, she made to follow them, but Kenzie pulled her back.

"No, leave them to it, they're having fun."

Oh god. Kenzie was standing millimetres away from her. She could feel the heat of his body and hear his breaths as they rose and fell. Tom, Callum, and Ashley's conservation trailed away as they rounded a corner.

Melinda went cold with fear when she felt Kenzie's hand on the small of her back. "Just me and you now, babe. Hey, what are you doing? Don't run away from me," he said, wounded. "You'll hurt my feelings."

Too close, too close, get away—

"So guys... Erm, guys? What's the best part of being famous?" Frightened, Melinda hurried in the direction of the others.

Kenzie's hands linked around her waist and pulled her back. "The fans... definitely the fans."

Melinda's heart almost *stopped.*

His mouth was right next her ear; she could *feel* it. The others hadn't heard her question. They hadn't even looked back. Kenzie could do... anything. Already, he was tracing his fingers over her body.

"You look good in that dress. But you'd look so, so much better with it off." Kenzie drew in a sharp breath as his hands glided over her breasts, slid down her waist, and came to rest at the top of her hated thighs.

When he chuckled at her reaction, Melinda grew angry. Growling slightly, she twisted away from him, and balled her hands into fists. He had way, way too much nerve. Just because he was handsome, and she couldn't care less about the band, he was trying to intimidate her. Melinda was having none of it.

Thankfully, Kenzie seemed to give up:

"Everyone," he called, flicking his hair. "Isn't it about time we took a look in the dressing room?"

Ashley clapped from far away. "Yes, oh yes, let's go Tom!"

The others came to meet them. Melinda was beyond relieved. Kenzie smirked at her. Hurriedly, Melinda looked away, blushing shamefully.

Kenzie led them toward the corridor to her right. Ashley and the remaining band members joined their side, talking breezily about their favourite breeds of dog.

Melinda snuck a peek at her watch. Fifteen minutes remained of the tour. After that, she could put the traumatising ordeal behind her. Maybe, just maybe, she'd be safe.

"By the way, I love your outfit," Tom complimented Ashley.

The younger girl blushed and grabbed his hand. Tom clasped hers back, a small smile producing dimples in his cheeks. Ashley asked him if he liked chocolate, and then, the pair floated in their own private bubble.

Melinda turned to Callum. "I read in a magazine somewhere that you had pets."

Callum looked surprised. "Oh, no. That was Tom; I don't have any. Why, do you?"

"Yeah. I've wanted a rabbit for ages, but we've got a Jack Russell called Jack."

Callum raised his eyebrows.

"Oh, Mom made us choose the name. I wanted to call him Boppers."

"Boppers… that's actually kinda sweet. Does he bop around a lot then?"

"Yeah, he's like, majorly hyper. We don't know one hundred percent why. We did try him on medication, cause my mom insisted, but it kept making him sick."

"Aw, bless him."

"Yeah. It took a *lot* of arguing with Mom before she saw sense."

Melinda had been wrong about the other band members. Tom was brilliant with Ashley; he really cared about her. Callum was humble, yet chatty once he allowed himself to speak.

"Those fans really did a number on you, didn't they?"

Callum smiled sweetly. "Yeah, but I'm fine. It comes with the job. They didn't mean it."

Melinda didn't quite agree.

"Ah, here we are!" Kenzie brought them to a stop.

The door was the finest wood. Polished to a sheen, it proudly bore a star on the front. Three beams of colour ran through the middle of it, telling Melinda this was definitely theirs. Kenzie's eyes caught Melinda's, and she couldn't look away quicker.

"Let's have a look, shall we?" Kenzie chirped.

Pinching at her dress, Melinda tugged it further down. No, she would not cry. As she blinked the tears back, Kenzie opened the door.

"Girls, this is where the fun begins."

Ashley charged in first. Kenzie went in second, followed by Tom and Callum, while Melinda stayed where she was. On the way down, she'd spotted an exit. Now was the perfect opportunity. Melinda dithered, until she heard the excited squeal of her sister.

Ashley needed her. She was with three boys who she didn't know, one of which was obviously perverted.

Taking a deep breath in, Melinda readied herself, and prayed the ground would swallow her up as she stepped inside.

Chapter Eleven

"Wow, so this is where you guys get ready and socialise and have fun!"

No, Kenzie thought to himself. It was where they all dealt drugs and got high.

Desperate, the younger girl had hung around Tom constantly. The stupid pest was gazing at him, utterly entranced. Callum hung back and lingered in front of his mirror. What the heck was he staring at?

Tom placed a hand on the girl's shoulder and answered her kindly. "Yeah, we've had some good times here, Ash."

Oh, so she had a name now? Below the chair, Kenzie's fingers scraped the leather material. He wanted her to leave; her voice was beyond irritating. As Tom joined her side, the little girl took in the three colossal mirrors on the right, each with matching black swivel chairs.

Kenzie had to be patient; he knew that. Yet when he glanced at the crimson red sofa opposite him, his thoughts of what would go down later almost caused him to foam.

Suddenly, Ashley seemed to spot Kenzie for the first time.

Oh no. Kenzie placed his foot over his other knee. Not on his lap again, not—

Giggling crazily, Ashley jumped onto the empty chair next to him, and began to spin herself around.

"Oh, not without me, you don't!" Tom called.

Tom charged over to Ashley, and spun her around on the chair. Wow… the look on her face reminded him of his own when his mother used to spin him on the roundabout.

The blond pinched the bridge of his nose. There was no time for that. Watching the girl spin, he willed for the orange pest to keep spinning until she vanished into thin air. Where on earth was—

"Tom, stop," protested Callum. "She'll be sick."

Tom sighed. "All right."

"Hey, Ash," Kenzie asked. "Where's your sister?"

"Oh, I don't know," the girl replied. "Mel? Mel!"

She was coming! She entered the room, clearly scared as hell. As the girl fiddled with her dress, an animalistic growl tore through Kenzie's head:

Mine.

"Mel," Ashley called to her sister. "You've gotta come and sit on one of these chairs, they're so cool."

Giving Kenzie a quick glance, Melinda shook her head.

Her sister pressed. "But you can look in the mirror, and pretend it's *you* getting ready to perform."

"*Ashley!*"

Everyone's eyes landed on Melinda. The girl glowered at her sister, and her eyes said it all: Shut up or else.

Ashley didn't quite get the hint. "My sister loves singing. She's really good! I've got a video I can show you."

"No!" Melinda pointed. "Ashley, don't you dare."

"Oh, you can sing?" said Kenzie.

"No," said Melinda. "Ashley's just being stupid. Ashley, forget it, please."

"Aw come on," said Tom. "Show us!"

That was all it took. Ashley's hand ducked inside her sister's handbag, and retrieved a black phone.

Snatching for it, Melinda blurted:

"Oi, give that back!"

"Nope, it's *my* phone!"

Melinda made a grab for her. "Ashley, I'm being serious—"
Dodging out of the way, Ashley leapt back onto her seat. "My sister wants to be a singer, just like you guys. You've gotta watch this, she's so good—"

"*No!*"

Melinda lunged. Kenzie leapt out of his seat at the opportunity: when she rushed past him, he grabbed her. "Hey, hold on a minute, babe." He tightened one arm over her collarbones, and the other over her waist. "I wanna see this video."

Melinda was furious. "Ash, don't, I swear to God. Kenzie, let go of me, please!"

It was too late. Ashley was already playing the video, and it was the most horrendous, ear-splitting singing Kenzie had ever heard.

"*No,* Ash," Melinda wailed. "Turn it *off!* Ash, stop it, they'll laugh, they'll… ah!" Clawing at the hands that held her, she seemed to have no clue who they belonged to. "No!"

Kenzie snickered. Melinda turned back to him, and hissed:

"Get the fuck off of me!"

"She's great, isn't she?" said Ashley.

Tom nodded fervently. "*Yeah,* she's not half-bad."

And Kenzie snarled under his breath, right into the thrashing girl's ear:

"Stop.*"*

The girl froze.

"Don't you *ever* talk to me like that again."

Kenzie slid his arm from her waist, to just under her breasts. She quivered. He squeezed one in his hand. From her forehead down, he saw her face drain, and felt her breathing come to a complete stop. Already, he could hear her screams; there were so many of them. Already, he could taste the saltiness of her tears.

The video began to fade out, and Melinda began to whisper her apologies over and over:

"I-I'm sorry, I'm sorry."

Kenzie slid his hand over her thigh. Sorry? Oh, he would make her very, very sorry indeed.

In the glass of beer, Brad could see his reflection. He bit back his yawn. He would not fall asleep, he would not fall asleep…

Julie laughed. "Oh Vicky, I can't believe you sometimes!"

Julie was clutching a wine glass, and cackling at Vicky, her friend that they'd bumped into after the restaurant.

Vicky tossed her sleek red bob. "Yep, I said to him 'if you're not gonna deliver, don't bother coming round in future'."

Brad turned away, cupped another yawn, then poked the beer with his finger, watching as his touch gave the beer rings.

Truthfully, Brad was never into pubs. The sheer thought of drinking pint after pint while exchanging small talk over pork scratching's made him shudder. Secretly, he longed for a flood, a small fire, or even a beer shortage at the bar. That way, everyone could just go *home*.

"He sounds like a keeper, Vicky!" Brad joked to her.

Just then, his phone vibrated, and Brad remembered he'd forgotten to turn the tones off. He'd broken his wife's number one rule of nights out: all phones stay off. Spinning away from her burning eyes, Brad tugged the phone out of his pocket.

Aunt Flo? What the *hell* did she want now? "Flo, I told you not to ring us while we're out, what the—"

"I'm sorry." The sound of Flo weeping on the other end of the phone shut Brad up instantly. "I know. I know I was meant to be looking after them, but they were insistent they were too ill for me to come!"

A rowdy set of drinkers cheered. Vicky grumbled, and Julie hissed at Brad to turn the phone off.

"Flo, get to the point. What's happened?"

The drinkers cheered again. Why couldn't they be *quiet*?

"I went round to drop some medication off," Flo wept. "But no one answered the door, so I let myself in, and-and…"

Flo paused.

Brad's fingers curled with impatience. He was growing angrier by the second, and was about to shout, when Flo unexpectedly wailed:

"They were gone! The house is empty Brad. They're not home."

Panic sent shockwaves throughout Brad's entire body. "Flo, stay at the house. We're coming home."

Just as he hung up, Vicky and Julie appeared behind him. Tartly, Vicky slurred:

"Ey up, what's going on here then?"

Brad caught a glimpse of Julie's gritted teeth.

"Julie, the kids are missing."

At that moment, Julie's face transformed from an angry pink to a stark white. "Shit. Come on."

Past the cheering drinkers, away from the crude Vicky, Brad tugged Julie while she rambled:

"You're driving. You haven't even drunk that beer. Jesus Christ… the kids are missing…"

The kids are missing.

"Julie," Vicky called. "Text me, let me know what's happening."

"Will do!"

Brad blew out a frustrated breath. Flinging open the pub door, he and Julie stepped out into the warm night, and together, they raced for the car park.

Melinda whimpered as Kenzie's touch slid away.

"I-I'm sorry. Look, I know it's bad. I was only messing around." Thankfully, Kenzie did not pursue her as she joined the others, flapping her hands madly in an attempt to stop herself crying. "Ash couldn't sleep and she wanted me to sing, so I did. Here, I'll delete it." She snatched the phone from the smiling audience.

Behind Melinda came a dance of fingers over her shoulder, and the heat of another body near hers.

"I thought you were really good," said Kenzie.

Callum's reply was muffled; "Yeah, you're all right."

Ashley gushed. "She's brilliant, isn't she?"

"Hmm, I agree." Kenzie insisted. "You know, it's unfair of you to keep it all for Ashley here." Melinda felt his fingers leave a ghostly trail, from her shoulders to her elbows. "How's about you give us a little song, ay?"

"Yeah," Tom agreed. "Go on Mel, it'll be fun."

Memories pounded in the back of her head, about a train, and beating her parents' home. Kenzie stepped away, sat on his chair, and wheeled the seat so he was behind Ashley. Ashley clapped her hands, Tom leant on the desk, and Callum sat cross-legged on Ashley's other side. They were all watching her. They were all waiting, and soon, Melinda was treated to various forms of encouragement.

No way; absolutely no way on this earth was she doing it. She *knew* she was a terrible singer; she knew Kenzie and the others were only winding her up.

"Aw, don't be all shy," Kenzie jeered. "Do it Mellbell. Give us a show."

Melinda was mystified as to why Dana liked him, and how he could make a stupid nickname sound so scary.

"Please, Mel." Hunched forward, Ashley pleaded. "Please, you'll be the best sister ever if you do."

Melinda snuck a glance at her watch. There was ten minutes left. If she sung, then Kenzie was more likely to stay away from her. And, if she dragged it out, it would then be time to pull Ashley from the room.

Kenzie looked her up and down, and winked, while Ashley continued to beg:

"Please! Callum writes songs! He could write you one, and then you could get a record deal!"

Melinda caved. "Fine, go on then."

Ashley cheered. "Yes! Tom, Tom, pass her something to sing with."

Tom tossed her a hairbrush. Melinda caught it and smoothed down her hair. She opened her mouth and sung one of their more tolerable songs with zero hesitation, because if they liked it, maybe she could get a record deal, and even if they didn't like it, it was a better alternative than having Kenzie touching her again.

Tom whooped, cheering her name.

"Give us a dance as well then," Kenzie commanded. "Come on!"

Oh, did she have to? Shyly, Melinda swung her hips from side to side, earning a wolf-whistle from Kenzie.

Ashley clapped her hands. "Go Mel!"

"Yes, that's it," Kenzie called, punching the air with his fist. "Show us how it's done!"

"Oh, I can't be without you, and I know you feel the same way too." Melinda continued to sing, wishing the ground would swallow her. "So dance with me baby, my baby girl, *dance...*"

"Dance?" Kenzie grabbed her hand. "Bring it on, Mel!"

Unaware, Tom whistled, and Ashley clapped her hands even faster, squealing.

Uneasily, Melinda feigned a laugh. "No, no, I think that's enough now—"

Kenzie yanked her into him. Her hands collapsed onto his shoulders. He hissed into her ear:

"I said *dance* with me, you stupid slag."

On her left, she caught a glimpse of the reflection in the mirror. She was starting to tremble; his hands were sliding lower down her back, and something hard was stabbing her in the stomach. He was too close, too close, too close! Oh, she needed to move, *now!* What the hell had she *done?*

Kenzie licked his lips tauntingly.

Melinda's legs almost gave out. The band were watching. How the hell could they not see the problem? Kenzie tightened his hold, and pushed his body further into hers.

Melinda started the song again. "It was only yesterday, when you said you didn't love me…"

She only managed a few more lines of the long; a few sways alongside Kenzie, and one occasion where he twirled her around, before she relented.

"Well"—she prised his hands away— "that was fun."

"It was, wasn't it?" Kenzie chuckled, and at long last moved back. Turning to the audience, he called to them. "What d'you think boys? She can both sing, *and* dance. Reckon she's record material?"

Tom chirped falsely. "Oh yeah, Ken, she's *totally* record material."

Clapping, Ashley jumped out of her seat, her squeal so high-pitched it was a knife to the tension in the air.

Melinda hid behind Kenzie, and adjusted the hands on her watch to 9.30.

It was time to *leave.* Melinda tapped her watch at Ashley.

Ashley reacted perfectly. "Aw," she whined. "It's time to go already?"

Melinda sighed. "Yeah. I'm sorry, Ash, but you know what I said."

Callum clumsily stood. Tom moaned about it being so soon. But Kenzie appeared annoyed, and that was the best reaction of all. Melinda bit down on her lip to stop the laugh escaping. She'd won. Never would she have to see Kenzie again, *ever*.

Ashley threw her arms around Tom's waist, and buried her head in his shirt. "I'm gonna miss you, all of you, so much."

Tom tugged her braid playfully, and hugged her back. "Aw, I can't believe it's gone so quick. We'll miss you too, kid."

Callum patted Ashley's back, and thanked the pair of them, and Melinda even managed to thank them back, because it was at long last time to escape!

What Melinda hadn't counted on was for Kenzie to bring her plans crashing down.

"Leaving so soon? But you can't go." He paused. "Without a band shirt. We've got loads of spare ones backstage."

Ashley craned her head back, a lone tear tricking down her cheek. "Really?"

"Yes, really. You can have it for free, both of you, for being such *good* fans. Callum, Tom?" Kenzie gestured with his thumb. "Take Ashley with you to get the shirts. She can pick one for Melinda here, too. We'll wait here. Maybe I can get Mellbell that record deal."

Tom saluted. "Coming right up, boss. In a bit, Mel."

No... surely they wouldn't—

Callum followed.

No! She couldn't be left alone with *Kenzie!*

"Wait," called Melinda desperately. "Maybe we should all go?"

Kenzie shook his head. "No, no, Mel, I need to get you to sign some papers, and didn't you say you were going in a bit?"

Melinda absolutely knew Kenzie was bullshitting her. Ashley didn't, though, and she kept telling her to wait with Kenzie as she scurried off with Tom and Callum.

Melinda was defenceless as Kenzie opened the door for his band mates.

Frowning, Callum walked out first. Melinda heard him mumble:

"Stop taking the piss, man."

Kenzie said nothing back. Tom and Ashley slipped through the gap under his arm and disappeared.

In a surge of panic, Melinda made for the door, yet Kenzie was quicker. He slammed it shut, and he locked it.

Melinda jumped back. "Erm, erm..."

Kenzie turned and leant against the wood. Gradually, his head rose up, up, up, and his smile... oh, his *smile*.

At that moment, Melinda truly feared for her life.

Chapter Twelve

Melinda broke the gag that fear had fastened over her mouth. "Erm, Kenzie..."

Smugly, Kenzie folded his arms.

Melinda swallowed. Alone in a dressing room with Kenzie Hudgson; it was every fangirl's dream, but his leering eyes were reducing her to a wreck.

"My train comes at ten. I really have to go—"

"You're not going anywhere."

"What?"

Kenzie just shrugged. "I said you're not going anywhere. Are you deaf or something?"

"B-But I..."

"Well, don't you have any questions to ask me?" He began walking toward her, his gaze trailing up and down her body.

Melinda let out a strangled squeak, and stepped back, back, back, her arms out in front of her, while Kenzie got closer, closer, closer—

"What's the best part of being famous?"

"You already asked me that."

Oh, *fuck!*

"W-Well, erm, uh... How did you get famous? W-What's your favourite song, on your albums I mean?" He wasn't answering. He wasn't even listening! "Performing! Do you like performing?"

Unknowingly, Melinda had shot her final arrow. Kenzie grabbed her waist, and pulled her against him. A tiny sound escaped her as Kenzie's hands slid from her waist to her hips. Kenzie chuckled, and dug his fingers in. He towered her; she hardly grazed his shoulder.

One of his hands danced down her back, and rested on her backside. "No more talking, beautiful."

Melinda didn't move.

As Kenzie leaned down, his lips brushed against her ear, and his taunting tongue licked from top to bottom. "To answer your question, yes, I do like performing. But I'm gonna have so much more fun performing with you."

Suddenly, Kenzie's lips were over hers. Melinda screamed. The tall blond thrust his tongue in her mouth, silencing her. She felt her handbag fall from her shoulder. In her struggle to get away, she stumbled, but managed to re-gain her balance.

Kenzie pushed her.

Melinda's vision was uprooted. Her head crashed against a cushion, and she landed on her back.

"Oops." Kenzie was clambering onto the sofa. "Come on now, babe. No need to go falling for me already."

Frantically, Melinda did a backstroke to the opposite end of the sofa, the safe place, but Kenzie was too quick. Grinning, he grabbed her ankles, and yanked.

"No!" Her dress rode up, exposing her thighs as Kenzie dragged her. "Kenzie, my train—"

"Can fucking wait."

Melinda's chest caved in as he crawled toward her. This was all a joke. He was only messing around, surely, he wouldn't—

In a flash, Kenzie was looming over her. "Do you really think I'm that fucking stupid?" He grabbed her watch, and undid the clasp. "I saw what you did with this. That's what mirrors are for."

Melinda whimpered as he tossed the watch behind the sofa. "Please, this isn't funny."

"Oh, but I'm not playing. Can't you see that? Or, do you want me to prove that to you?"

Paling, Melinda shook her head.

"Oh, you *do*. I can see it in your eyes!"

Swallowing the bile that rose in her throat, Melinda paled as Kenzie planted a kiss on her neck.

Kenzie chuckled. "See? You want this. You want me."

No! No, she didn't want this! Teasingly, his hands rubbed from her shoulders, down to her hips. Melinda quaked when she felt his tongue come in contact with the skin on her neck. Hot, slimy, and *burning,* the sensation sent qualms of disgust throughout her entire body. How had she gotten herself into this situation?

Melinda wanted to scratch, hit, scream, *anything,* but her arms were glued to her sides and her throat was stapled shut. Alternatively, she could only stutter:

"K-Kenzie, p-please..."

"Oh, the things I'm going to do to you," Kenzie hissed as he met her wide-eyed stare. "I'm going to make you *scream.*" Slowly, he rubbed his bulging crotch against hers.

"No! Get off me, get off me *right now.*" Of their own accord, Melinda's hands reached up, and shoved at Kenzie's chest. "Move!"

One after the other, Kenzie grabbed her wrists. "Ah, ah, ah, I wouldn't do that."

When Kenzie put his thighs down over her legs, Melinda felt her courage evaporate; suddenly cold, she was bolted to the sofa as Kenzie placed both of her wrists into one hand.

"Trust me beautiful, you're only making it worse."

"I-I'm sorry. I'm sorry, I didn't mean that. Please." She pleaded, in vain. "I just wanted to please my sister, she loves you guys. And I've gotta go now. They'll be back in a minute... please!"

"You can beg me all you want," Kenzie sneered. "But it'll mean nothing." She felt his free hand slide up her dress and circle her inner thigh. "Because guess what?"

Melinda tried to pull away, but she was glued to the sofa by both Kenzie's weight and her own fright. The lead singer bumped his nose against hers. Gulping, his prey began to whimper. This couldn't happen to her, surely it was just a nightmare, surely—

"I'm gonna fuck you till you can't walk straight."

Kenzie smirked, delved under her dress, and twanged the base of her underwear through her tights. Terror at last forced Melinda's scream out. It bounced from the walls of the room, and it made Kenzie angry.

Melinda heard the slap before she felt it. Red sizzled over her cheek, and her instincts finally told her: Stay still. Don't move.

"Don't you *dare* do that again," snarled Kenzie hatefully. "Or I'll break you like a twig. This is your fault, you know."

Her fault?

Kenzie regained his composure. "You shouldn't have smiled at me like that, or danced at me like that."

His hand slipped past her thigh. Bare skin to bare skin, his hand was spreading heat over her clammy stomach and making her feel sick, yet, she could do nothing. She could say nothing. She was frozen in the expanse of time, and could only stare as his hand ventured further.

"You're a decent-looking girl, and I'm a hormonal singer. What did you think was going to happen, hmm? You deserve this, you little cocktease. You're a frigid bitch. Look at you, crying your eyes out over a bit of sex. I bet you've never been fucked before, have you?"

Melinda hadn't even known that the tears were rolling down her cheeks, shaking her. "I-If you let me go, I won't tell anyone, I promise, I *swear.*"

"But I know you won't tell anyone. Because think about it... no one's ever going to believe you."

Melinda sobbed as Kenzie toyed with the wire of her bra.

"Kenzie, please."

Kenzie suckled her neck.

"P-Please! Kenzie, I'm sorry if I ever did anything to you. If I said anything that annoyed you, I didn't mean it, and I'm sorry if I led you on in any way—"

"God, don't you ever stop talking?"

"*No.*" Kenzie's hand had slipped under her bra. "Please just get off!"

Oh, his touch was hot and rough and horrible!

"Please! I'm sorry, I'm sorry, I don't want to, I don't—"

Suddenly, Kenzie retreated. Melinda gasped, relieved, but then, he yanked down her tights and underwear in one swift movement.

Melinda yelped. She was going to be *raped*, and she *couldn't* stop it!

"*Please!* D-Don't. I-I'll do a-anything else!"

"S-Sorry, n-no can do," he mocked her. "This'll have to be quick, babe."

Still holding her wrists, Kenzie sat up. The sound of him undoing his zipper was unmistakable. Spluttering on tears, shaking her head, Melinda tried one last time:

"No! Please..."

Knocking! Quiet, persistent knocking? It was coming from the door! Oh, at *last!*

"Mel? Mel, you've gotta see my new shirt," said a soft, excited voice.

Kenzie sighed, irritated. Turning back, he barked:

"One second!"

He glowered at Melinda. He released her, then commanded:

"Go."

That one word was enough. Melinda scrambled to her feet, pulling up her tights as she did so, while Kenzie sat back on the sofa.

She was lucky. To escape unharmed was a privilege; never could she speak of what had happened, for if she did, she knew Kenzie would come back for her.

As she bent to pick up her handbag, Melinda was at a risk of falling her legs were so shaky. Wiping her tears away, she sniffed and put her bag back on her shoulder. Only when she was certain she wouldn't howl did she turn the lock and open the door.

"Mel, look!" Ashley beamed. Wearing a Three Beams t-shirt, the excited little girl pointed her finger in the air, revealing a Haribo ring. "I got you a shirt, Mel! And Tom asked me to marry him! Oh, it's so wonderful, Bryony's gonna be so jealous. Did Kenzie do that for you too?"

Kenzie... *Kenzie!* Melinda turned. Kenzie was walking toward her, grinning. Oh no. No, not again! Nodding hurriedly at each band member, Melinda babbled:

"Thanks guys, you were all great. Thanks for the tour. Ash, come on, we need to go home *now.*"

"Oh yeah, the train—"

Ashley was cut off by Melinda yanking her out of the doorway. There was no time to see the band's startled reaction. They had to run, run far, far away from this *madhouse.*

Ashley's ballet pumps tapped the floor as she ran. The sound of their passes hitting their chests was excruciating. But, the noise was nowhere near a match for Ashley craning her neck back, and shrieking:

"I love you, Tom!"

For goodness' sake, they had to *get out.*

"Mel, where's your watch? Why is your face red? Why is your hair a mess? Have you been crying?" Gasp. Pant. "Can we stop running? I'm getting tired—"

"No, we'll miss the train."

"But Aston said he'd show us out."

"Forget him, there's no time! Come *on!*"

The pair clattered down the corridor, and turned the corner.

The dressing room faded away. However, Kenzie's words played in her head, an echo in a dark tunnel:

"No one's ever going to believe you..."

They found the doors to the stage.

"Ash, through here."

Taking the trampoline down, security guards were milling around on the stage, chatting. Stray litter and debris were scattered on the stage, and the seats. Compared to a short time ago, it seemed eerie.

"What's wrong, Mel?"

"Oh, erm... Ashley, nothing's wrong. I'm fine. We just need to hurry up."

She was trembling, all over. She hadn't noticed that her hair had come loose, and one side of her face was red. Past the seats, she pulled her sister, despite her desperate cranes back toward the stage. The band was behind there. Tom had asked Ashley to marry him, which had sent Ashley's excitement into overdrive. But now, as Melinda went on, she regretted ever getting those tickets.

"Mel," Ashley said quietly. "Are you okay?"

Melinda swallowed. "Yeah, I'm fine, I've already said. Stupid Aston. He was supposed to show us out."

"It's not Aston's fault! You were the one that was rushing. We should have asked the band, and said goodbye. Tom would have—"

"No," snapped Melinda. Yanking her backstage pass off, she shoved it in her bag. "You being so desperate for a shirt has already made us late."

Ashley missed the tear Melinda wiped away. "Sorry, Mel." She put Melinda's shirt into the big front pocket on her dress. "What did Kenzie say to you?"

"This is your fault, you know..."

"I don't want to talk about it."

"Why? Wasn't he signing you up to a record deal?"

"No, Ash, of course he bloody wasn't-I, I mean, yeah… yeah, he told me he thought I was good, but I need to practice my singing and dancing way, way more."

"You shouldn't have smiled at me like that, or danced at me like that…"

Ashley was crushed. "Oh, I'm sorry, Mel. Maybe next time, ay?"

Next time? As if there'd *ever* be a next time!

Melinda at long last found the exit. "Ash, I think this is it…"

"The exit? Oh, I can't believe it's over already," whinged Ashley.

"Yeah, well, tough. It is over now, and we need to go."

"Why couldn't we have spent longer with them? Tom *is* going to marry me one day, after all, so Aston should have let us stay longer. And you shouldn't have been so rude to them! They treated us so nicely… why couldn't the contest have been better? We should have gone on a proper outing all together rather than just half an hour with them."

Bubbling with fury, Melinda pulled them to an abrupt stop outside the exit. "Christ's sake, is *nothing* ever good enough for you? I scarified a *lot* for you. I paid for the train tickets, I brought you here, even though I can't stand this stupid band, and if you don't stop moaning and fucking me about, I'll go home and leave you in the street."

Ashley fell silent.

Melinda pulled her from her concert and out into the night.

Chapter Thirteen

Melinda stumbled over an ungainly heap.

"What the *hell?*" she yelled.

It was a girl. She was crying; she didn't even look up.

"Why are you sitting there for?" Melinda asked. "I nearly fell over y—"

They were stopped in their tracks by a plump, frightened blonde. "I'm sorry. I know it's late. I-I know you probably need to get home, but please, can you help me?"

"Erm…" Melinda hesitated.

"It's my friend. We wanted to meet the band, but it didn't work out. S-She's been sitting there ages, and I can't get her to move."

Melinda just shrugged. "And what do you want me to do about that?"

"I-I-She used up all the battery on my phone. I need to use yours, if you have one. Please, I have to get her home."

Melinda wavered.

Ashley watched her. Melinda been acting horribly since the concert, but now Ashley's hopes rose as Melinda begrudgingly reached into her bag. The blonde clasped her hands, grinning with relief because they were going to be helped; they wouldn't be left stranded in London.

"Why are you asking her for?" shouted the other girl. "You said *she* was a fake slag."

The blonde flushed scarlet. "Faye!"

"You said what, now?" snapped Melinda.

Panicked, the blonde shook her head frantically at Melinda, who was now red-faced and fuming. "I-I didn't say that! I was just angry cause—"

"Whatever. Get yourselves home."

"Oi!" Aston's booming voice made the blonde, Ashley, and Melinda jump as he stormed towards the awaiting Beamers. "I've told you girls before! Shows over. Go home."

"Come on, Ash, we're going." Melinda snapped.

"No."

"Fine then, bye." Her sister stalked off, leaving her.

"Mel, wait, you're going the wrong... Mel, *wait*!"

Desperate not be alone in the dark scary streets, Ashley followed. She ignored the blonde's cries, the other girl's sobs, and Aston's apologetic calls toward them about how he was sorry he didn't get chance to see them out, and that he'd got caught up in something.

Oh, it was getting so *dark*. Frightened, Ashley clutched her sister's waist.

"Don't touch me," Melinda yelped. "I-I'm not in the mood..."

Ashley wrapped her arms around herself. When? Why? It had happened so annoyingly fast. One moment Melinda was fine, then the next, she was all angry and mean. Kenzie had been humble, Callum chatty, and Tom brilliant. What could possibly be the problem?

Left to Aston's wrath, the blonde they'd left behind descended into angry bellows:

"Stupid bitch! You don't even like them!"

Melinda kept walking. Ashley limped behind her, not even daring to whine.

Callum rolled his eyes at the irritating sound of Kenzie clapping his hands, and roaring with laughter on the sofa. Tom rocked on the floor, wheezing. Still, the pair were in hysterics over the fact that Tom had failed to catch an M&M in his mouth, had fallen onto a spinning chair, and in the process, cracked Callum's mirror and snapped the shelf.

"Oh man," Kenzie gasped. "You absolute fucking idiot."

"Oh jeez, Doug's going to scream."

Callum ignored them, comforting himself with the knowledge that the concert was over, and he'd enjoyed it despite the... mishap. The crowd were great, the songs were performed perfectly; even the backstage fans had behaved.

Callum pondered. Did he really want this night to end?

Kenzie wiped water from his eyes, and Tom spluttered on sniggers.

Yes, he did. There was only so much immaturity, foolishness, and broken items Callum could take. Turning to Kenzie, he waited for the pair to finally calm down, then asked:

"What did you say to Melinda?"

Tom sat up. "Oh, Ken, you didn't give her a record deal, did you?"

Kenzie smirked. "No, are you mad? She was terrible. Of course, I did let her down gently. I told her the usual, you know: 'You have potential', 'You're very entertaining'. But deep down, I really wanted to tell her she sounded like a dying cat."

Clenching his fists, Callum remembered that she had never wanted to sing in the first place. It was her sister and the boys who'd pressured her. Briefly, Callum wondered who was the youngest: Ashley, or his fellow laughing band members. Normally, he'd keep quiet, but you know what? He didn't feel like it tonight:

"Well, from what I remember, it was you and Tom who goaded her into it. If you had no intention of signing her up, why bother?"

Kenzie, surprised at Callum's question, shrugged. "Funny."

"Well, you probably really hurt her feelings, and I don't think that's very funny at all."

"And who asked you?" scoffed Kenzie.

"No one, but I was there, and in my opinion, you shouldn't have told Aston we'd be fine without him. I didn't like the way you were dancing with her ether."

A switch seemed to flip in Kenzie's head. Callum, suddenly, was very scared when Kenzie jumped up from his seat, and grabbed him.

"Are you accusing me of what I think you're accusing me of?" Kenzie growled.

"Guys," said Tom. "Come on, break it up—"

"I ain't no perve, if that's what you're thinking!" Kenzie shouted.

"No." Swallowing roughly, Callum bit his lip, regretting opening his mouth. "I knew you were only messing about, sorry."

"Good. You're just jealous cause no girl would ever wanna dance with *you*."

Callum slumped back in his seat.

Tom sighed. "So, season four, ay?"

Callum kept his eyes down. "Yeah, it's crazy. I can't believe we start rehearsals Monday; it seems like only yesterday we posed for the photo—"

"I can't believe we only get one day off." Tom shook his head. "And that we have to spend it in the Brummy house."

Longingly, Callum pictured Doug bursting into the room, and giving Kenzie a brilliant punch on the nose.

Kenzie's fingers edged closer to the M&M bag. "Oh relax, Landsby. We get our break in a few weeks anyway, so we can all sod off to our loving families."

Ping! An M&M bounced from Tom's forehead.

Mischievously, Kenzie reached into the bag again. "What? I thought puppies liked fetch."

Ping!

"Right, that's it Hudgson!"

The second Tom's hand connected with the bag, Kenzie lifted it up, and dumped the entire contents of the bag onto Tom's head. The M&Ms mirrored hard bullets as they fell out of Tom's curls and onto the floor.

"Hey, boys—"

Doug halted by the door. He gave a slow, agonised sigh. Peering around, he took in the carnage. One, two seconds passed. And then, the frazzled, overly-tired man descended into fury:

"What the hell has happened in here?"

"Blame the M&Ms," replied Kenzie carelessly. "They'd always been Tom's downfall."

"For goodness' sake, look at all of you. How are we even gonna survive season four if you can't act your ages?"

Kenzie placed a hand on the man's shoulder. "Hey."

Of *course*, Kenzie going to use his manipulative charm and model looks to get himself out of this. He *always* did it.

"I'm sorry," Kenzie said gently. "It was my fault. I'll clean it, and pay for the damage. We just got a bit overexcited about the new season. It's gonna be huge, you know."

Like everyone else, Doug was a moron. At Kenzie, he smiled. "Fine, no worries then. Just clean this mess up, yeah?"

The stars stared down, cold and judging on the London streets. A lone fox hurried across the road. Puddles reeked with an odour, and the various old buildings sagged under the weight of the mould that clambered up their walls...

Ashley snivelled. "Mel, I don't think this is the right way—"

"Of course it is. Just stay close to me. We'll be fine. I'm sure it's just down this road."

Ashley protested that she'd said that three roads ago.

Melinda was scared. How could she have been so stupid as not to remember the way back? They'd blundered down road after road, turned back on themselves, and peered around. Yet, no matter how hard they tried, they could *not* find the way, even with Google Maps. Ashley was squeezing her hand, probably even more scared.

Melinda concentrated on putting one foot in front of the other, and moving forward. She *didn't* concentrate on the burning of her cheek, the feel of Kenzie's hand on her skin, and her own shrill scream as it rattled her mind.

A rat darted over Ashley's shoes, and her scream echoed.

Crack.

"Don't you dare *do that again."*

"Mel, I don't like it here!" Ashley cried, clinging to her sister's waist. "It's dark and wet and scary. Oh please, can we just go home?"

"We're fucking lost!" Melinda glared hatefully into Ashley's frightened face. "How can we go home, you moron?"

Ashley began to weep.

Immediately, Melinda pulled the girl into a hug. "Oh, Ash, I'm sorry, I didn't mean that, I just... come on, let's go."

No one would believe her; he was as famous as he was terrifying. Further down the anonymous pathway, Melinda chattered as she edged around the corner:

"Tell me about Tom, Ash. Tell me how he proposed to you." When Ashley didn't answer, Melinda bluffed frantically. "It's just around this corner, I'm sure it is."

There was an array of clubs, awaiting taxis, people scurrying back and forth, tight dresses shining, and happy laughter floating... but no train station.

Whimpering, Ashley gazed up at her sister. "You said it was here, and it isn't."

Just then, Ashley uttered the words Melinda couldn't bear to hear:

"We're never going to get home."

Melinda stopped a passing pair of party girls. "Excuse me,"

The girls jumped.

"Sorry, sorry! Please, we need help. Do you know where the train station is?"

A chorus of laughter sounded from a club.

The older girl looked at them pityingly. "Ah, Three Beams? Sorry, I noticed your shirt, little'n. My youngest loves them, especially Kenzie. Her room's covered in posters of him. She wanted to go to the concert, but we couldn't afford it this year. As for the station, you've completely missed it, girls."

Melinda's face drained.

"Oh Mom, you're terrible." The younger girl gave a kind smile. "To get to the station, just carry on down, then turn left. Bypass all the clubs and you'll get to Churchall Lane. Follow that. It's a long, winding road, but there's no creeps down it. After, you'll find a load of shops. Go past them, and you'll get the station, easy. Funnily enough, there's an alley just outside the venue that takes you right there."

Ashley giggled triumphantly; she'd been right. Melinda *had* gone the wrong way.

Thanking the women, Melinda ushered Ashley away, while Kenzie's words devoured her bit by bit.

"Look, Ash," Melinda called as the pair clattered up the stony staircase. "These are your stairs, and tonight's your night, because—"

"I'm gonna marry Tom!"

In the train station at last, the girls raced to the top of the stairs.

Ashley clenched her sister's hand, happy. That red side of her face wasn't red anymore, and she seemed normal again. Ashley was so relieved, that she didn't see the falseness of her sister's smile, or the Oscar-worthy laughter she gave, because her finger was warm with the ring that still remained.

It was time to say goodbye to the concert, yet it didn't matter. Soon, Tom would come for her. Soon, they'd be embraced in each other's arms, with Kenzie and Melinda smooching opposite them.

"There!" Melinda panted. Hoisting them onto the platform, she hurried to the edge of the tracks, pausing behind the yellow line to turn to Ashley. "We're here. See? I said we'd..."

Her voice trailed off.

Ashley 'blinked. Puzzled, she hovered in the archway, until she realised Melinda's gaze was directed behind her.

Ashley gulped. Slowly, she turned around, and looked at the indicator board.

"Fuck..." Melinda gasped.

It was ten forty-five p.m. They'd missed the train.

Ashley felt physically sick. Trembling, she looked to her sister. "Mel, what do we do now?"

"Fuck. Fuck, no. No..."

Ashley watched her sister slide to the floor, her hands over her face. Her bag fell down next to her.

"*No!*"

Smack. Smack. Madly, Melinda banged her head against the wall, showing no signs of stopping despite Ashley's cries.

"It's all my fault, it's all my fault." Hugging her knees to her chest, Melinda howled, and banged her head again. "I-I'm sorry. I'm sorry. It's all my fault..."

Poor, poor Mel. What was Ashley going to *do?*

There was only one thing she could do. Breaths ridged, she reached into Melinda's bag and retrieved her phone.

Nine missed calls, fifteen texts, all from Mom.

Ashley called the number, and as she dared a glance at her chuntering sister, she knew she'd made the right decision.

Immediately, her mother's voice boomed from the phone to her ear. "Ashley! Oh, thank God. Ash, where the hell are you?"

"L-London..."

"London?" Her bewildered mother echoed. "Is this a joke? Why the hell would you be in..." Silence; the penny had dropped. "Oh no." Ashley could sense she was shaking her head, seething. "No, don't even tell me—"

Ashley wailed:

"Mom, come and get us, *please!*"

Chapter Fourteen

What was he doing? Tom couldn't take a shower! He'd wake everyone up.

Thankfully, no one was there to mock the uncomfortable hardness between his legs. One moment he'd been asleep, and then the next... how had it even *happened*?

Tom had no idea what he'd been dreaming about, or what exactly had caused his not-so-little problem. All he knew was that he'd woke up boiling hot, and if he didn't get to something cold *right now*, he was going to pass out.

Hurriedly, Tom exited his bathroom, grabbed his robe off the bed, and snuck downstairs.

"Ken, come on. Ash was a laugh!"

"Yeah, fine, she was all right."

In the early hours of the morning, on the sofa of the Birmingham house, Tom swallowed roughly. Mentally, he screamed at the muggy air to cool down. He could see every inch of Kenzie's muscles as he raked a hand through that stunning blond hair. Quickly, Tom looked down, his face flushing.

"Aw man, I can't believe you proposed to her, Tom. With a bloody Haribo as well."

"She loved it though," Tom popped another ring on his finger. "I swear, her face lit up like—"

Kenzie's lips wrapped around Tom's finger.

Oh, his tongue. In mere seconds, the ring was gone from his finger. Gawping at his friend, Tom watched as Kenzie ate the ring, and he wondered:

Who had switched the air conditioning off again?

The flustered boy shuffled down the corridor, his slippers scuffing on the lightning bolt rug. The rug was his choice, and it seemed painfully childish as he stood in front of the fridge.

There was no need to look around; no one would be awake now. Callum had retired to bed hours ago, and Kenzie was such a heavy sleeper.

Tom gritted his teeth. Now was *not* the right time to be thinking about his friend's morning voice.

Tom opened the fridge.

Cool air! Oh, a lovely, wonderful breeze…

Now he was hungry. Hmm, what could he eat? Frozen vegetables? Nah. Vegetarian sausages? Nope, he'd have to cook those. The ice cream?

Yes! The *ice cream*. It would fill him up, *and* cool him down.

Damn it, was he really that desperate?

Yes, Tom decided; he *was* that desperate. He tugged the lid off. It hit the red-tiled floor with a loud clatter, but that didn't deter him. Mint chocolate chip, Kenzie's favourite! Tom devoured the ice cream with the biggest spoon he could find, and he held no regrets, because finally, the heat had gone, leaving him with a clear head.

Kenzie was right; mint chocolate chip really *was* the best flavour.

"Enjoying that, are we?"

Disaster occurred. The tub thumped to the floor, upside down. Ice cream splattered the red tiles, covered the freezer door, and speckled the walls in flecks of green.

"Shit! Kenzie." How could he not have noticed the lights were on? "What are you doing up?"

Kenzie was standing in front of the window, and Tom was hypnotised. His hair ruffled, he wasn't wearing a shirt, just grey tracksuit bottoms.

Kenzie shrugged. "Couldn't sleep, it's too hot."

"Yeah, it is."

Tom could barely focus. But he'd seen Kenzie shirtless tonnes of times before, so why was it so important now? Oh, the *mess*.

Tom knelt down.

"Oh, leave that," said Kenzie. "Callum can sort it. I guess I don't need to ask you why you're up."

"Well, erm." Flustered all over again, Tom stood. "I was hungry!"

"Of course you were. Then again, if you weren't meant to have midnight snacks, there wouldn't be a light in the fridge."

"Y-Yeah, you're right, it's dumb that people say not to snack at night, cause the calories... you know..."

Oh, what did they do again; how did it work?

Kenzie narrowed his eyes. "Can I help you?"

"Oh, it's just, erm... Your tattoos!"

Kenzie cocked his head to one side, amused. "My tattoos?"

"Yeah. I... I've always wanted to know... why you got them?"

Why couldn't he just fall through the tiles?

"Well"—Kenzie hoisted himself up onto the counter—"the pointed triangles I got 'cause I thought they looked cool." Kenzie traced the ink with his finger.

Oh, the ice-cream was everywhere... Callum had some serious cleaning up to do.

Kenzie's finger moved upwards, circling the other tattoo, which was the patterned skull. "And the skull I got to cover up something else."

"Something else? What was that?"

"Jeez, I don't remember. But I do know that *you* have a tattoo all over your *face*."

Tom frowned. What was Kenzie—oh. Of course, the ice cream was dripping down his cheeks. Quickly, Tom wiped it off.

Kenzie smirked at him. "Why don't you hop off to bed, Landsby? All that ice cream seems to have frozen your brain."

"Right, yeah. Goodnight, then."

With that, Tom scampered out of the kitchen and back to the safety of his bedroom.

Warm, the blanket was like a pair of comforting arms around her.

"This is your fault, you know."

Now that she was no longer walking the streets of London, or panicking, *it* had come to back to haunt her, but inside the blanket, she was safe. Melinda breathed, slowly. The dull thrum of the car... the silence, was nice.

Her father was driving. Her mother was sitting, stony faced, and Ashley was sleeping. Melinda hugged her knees.

She didn't want to go anywhere ever again.

"Mel?" Brad whispered. "You okay back there?"

"You shouldn't have smiled at me like that, or danced at me like that."

Melinda bit her lip, and trapped the pain before it could escape her lips.

All too soon, the car rolled to a stop.

Julie sighed. "Right, we're home. Now get out."

Slam! The car doors bore the brunt of Julie's anger.

Reluctantly, Melinda pulled the blanket from her head. Bleary-eyed and bushy-haired, she leaned over, and shook her sister awake.

Ashley grumbled. "Tom?"

"No, it's Mel. Come on, we're getting out."

Swatting as if Melinda was a pesky fly, her eyes remained closed. Normally, Melinda would have laughed, but not tonight.

"Ash, now, before Mom gets angrier."

Ashley awoke sharply. "Oh! I forgot to give you your Three Beams shirt Mel, it was in my pocket. Here."

Melinda gritted her teeth. "Keep it." She got out of the car.

Looking the sternest he'd ever looked, Brad walked to the other side of the car, his mouth a hard line as he opened Ashley's side, and helped the tired girl out.

Melinda grumbled:

"She can get herself out, she's not two."

Julie glared at her. "Get in the house."

Melinda didn't have to be told twice. With her spare key, she unlocked the house, and opened the creaky, wooden door. Jack raced over, barking with a wagging tail.

"Jack…"

Immediately, he jumped up to Melinda's knees. Melinda wanted to cuddle the yappy Jack Russell, and hold him tight. So, when Julie stalked in front of her, and Brad closed the door while holding her little sister, that's exactly what Melinda did.

Brad put Ashley down, and whispered at her to go upstairs. Rubbing her eyes, she did as she was asked.

The phone rang.

"Oh, that'll be Flo." Julie stormed toward the phone. "Yes Flo, we've got them... No, we don't need you to come back down. Yes, yes... Goodnight."

That was the end of the conversation; head bowed, Julie rested her hand on the kitchen doorway. Burying her head in Jack's scruff, Melinda waited in the hostility that was obviously directed at her.

"Right," Julie snarled. "It's three o clock in the fucking morning. I'm too tired to discuss this now. But I'll just let you know, I'm not blaming Ashley, she's seven. But you? You're eighteen years of age, Melinda. You should have known better to drag her all the way up to London, *behind our backs,* only to get her completely lost."

Melinda opened her mouth, but was quietened when Julie shook her head.

"No, don't you dare interrupt me. You're not gonna be looking after Ashley overnight anymore."

"What?" Melinda felt like she'd been punched. "Dad?"

"I'm sorry, Mel, but I'm with your mother on this one."

"But why? I don't understand..."

Julie slumped into the kitchen chair, and had buried her hands in her frazzled ginger bun. "Because we can't risk this happening again, obviously."

"But it won't!"

"Melinda, drop it, I'm tired!"

Brad skirted around his tired wife, and placed his hand on her shaking shoulder.

Melinda realised it was time for her to go to bed. There was no point arguing. Snivelling, Melinda left her parents to clean up the shards of her mess and began scale the stairs, Jack in her arms. Jack peered up at her, and licked her nose, his paw touching her shoulder.

"You can put that fucking dog down as well." Julie jeered from the kitchen.

Up the stairs and to her bedroom, Melinda left without him.

Upon entering, she didn't look to see if Ashley was asleep. Instead, she made for her own bed. Accidentally, she knocked over the tower of Ashley's Three Beams CDs. Although, she couldn't say she was sorry. She tore her dress off, the one she never wanted to see it again. Flinging it on the floor, her underwear that crawled with Kenzie's touch went with it. Instead, Melinda shrugged on her father's old black t-shirt, paranoid that somewhere, somehow, *he* was watching.

How had it even happened?

Hating Three Beams, laughing at their dumb TV show, and dancing with Cassidy on the red seat... It had all been so innocent. Baffled, Melinda retreated to the safety of her burrow.

"Don't worry Mel," came Ashley's reassuring voice. "Tonight's been the best night of my life."

No answer.

"I've put Tom's ring in one of those ring boxes."

Still no answer.

"I love you."

Melinda shut her eyes.

"Well, goodnight," Ashley called.

Yes, *goodnight*. Under her bed sheets, Melinda curled into a ball, and shut off completely.

When Ashley finally got out of bed, it was one in the afternoon.

She yawned. She stretched. And then, she jumped out of bed like a singer in a music video. Despite the night's ending, she felt reborn. Her parents would calm down, eventually. Cascading down her back, Ashley's hair swished as she rushed. The dress had taken pride of place at the front of her wardrobe; she was wearing it on her wedding day.

The Three Beams omnibus was to start in half an hour. But, due to her mother's anger, the possibility of her watching it was very, very slim... unless she got to the TV first.

Downstairs, the smell of cakes wafted toward her. Cherry! Oh, they smelt *nice*.

Picturing eating a cherry cake for breakfast, Ashley stood in front of the shower door.

The water was running.

Ashley frowned. Briefly, she had awoken at twelve, and saw Melinda leaving the room, carrying her shower things with her. Was Melinda *still* showering?

Nervously, Ashley knocked on the door. "Mel? Are you done?"

Downstairs, the oven was opened. The smell got stronger. Brad hummed in appreciation, and Julie hissed at him to shut up.

Ashley put her ear to the door. A frantic rubbing, a soft gasping, and a mournful... sob? What was Melinda *doing* in there? In her quest for an answer, Ashley was about to knock again, until Melinda replied, and the tremor in her voice made the younger sister even more anxious:

"O-One second..."

The water stopped. Ashley waited, while Melinda called to her, her voice getting higher and higher. Finally! Melinda was finished! Ashley could take a shower, settle in front of the TV with her mother's cakes, and see Tom's gorgeous smile.

Life couldn't be any better.

The door opened, and Melinda came out, her hair plastered to her head. Her face was pale. Her brown eyes looked at her, yet she didn't seem... there? Smile trembling, she clenched her dressing gown flaps in her hand, and her shower bag in the other. Ashley stared. The redness on Melinda's chest was clearer than day. It looked sore, and itchy.

Ashley sniggered uncertainly. "Why have you done that?"

"Done what?"

"Scrubbed like that," Ashley said, pointing. "It's bad for your skin, you know."

"I know, but I-I..."

"I call dibs on the TV!"

"What?"

Grasping her things, Ashley charged into the bathroom. Smugly, she jeered as she slammed the door:

"I call dibs on the TV!"

Chapter Fifteen

"Mel," Brad said softly, leaning on the living room doorframe. "Are you all right?"

Melinda didn't answer.

Shaking his head, Brad went back to the kitchen, while Melinda pulled the blanket further around herself.

Ashley stared at her. Melinda's eyes were looking, yet they were lifeless, like they were made of glass. Where was her real sister, the cheerful girl that always mocked her favourite band? Ever since she had come downstairs, she'd sat on the sofa tugging at her bottom lip with her fingers.

"Mel... Mel." Ashley prodded her sister's knee. "Mel, what's wrong?"

"Nothing, Ash, I'm just tired."

On the TV, the characters of the soap mourned the loss of their barmaid.

Melinda wiped a falling tear away, while Ashley's own eyes filled with a deep hurt. She didn't understand it. The concert had gone okay, and their parents hadn't been *too* mad at them. Looking back at the door, Ashley heard her mother and father mumble; they were discussing Melinda. Julie said to leave her to sulk.

Rummaging under the sofa, Ashley pulled out the chocolate bar that was meant to be for her mother's cake icing. "Hey Mel, wanna share?"

"Yeah, go on then."

She took her share from Ashley's hands, completely disinterested.

This was not a simple problem that chocolate could make better, Ashley realised. As Melinda took a bite, Ashley resolved to find out the truth:

"Come on, sis, tell me what's really up."

Melinda shook her head.

"Please, you can tell me, honest. I won't tell Mom if it's something really, really bad. I just wanna know, 'cause you're really upset, and we're sisters, and—"

"Nothing." Melinda shrugged, and swallowed the last of the chocolate bar with a toothy grin. "I'm fine, I'm just tired and worried about my college exams."

The Three Beams omnibus came on the TV, and Ashley tried one more time. "Mel—"

"Doesn't Jack need walking?"

"But you normally walk Jack."

"Please, Ash, just do it." Melinda stood up suddenly. "I need to go upstairs, I don't feel well."

Forget the omnibus; Ashley never missed an episode anyway. She went to the kitchen.

Julie was taking cakes from the oven, while Brad was on the phone to a client who couldn't understand that he didn't work weekends.

Julie turned to her, brandishing the tray. The cakes were pink this time. They hadn't been iced yet, but they looked nice. Julie rolled her eyes, and said something about ignoring Melinda because she was sulking? Whatever it was, Ashley didn't hear, because she was too busy wondering if it was her fault. Had she done something wrong?

In Melinda's bedroom, the metallic noise of techno-rock blasted against the walls. Magazines, college assignments, Jack... Melinda had tried to distract herself, but later in the day, *he* had come on the TV, and sent her running upstairs.

Melinda buried her face, and screamed into her pillow.

Why did she dance for him? Why didn't she scream louder, fight rougher, alert the others, or tell K—*him* in clearer terms that she did *not* want him? The music pounded, but even in her bedroom, she couldn't escape from Kenzie Hudgson, and that horrid, vile night.

"I'm gonna fuck you till you can't walk straight."

Muffled, Melinda's scream tore through the pillow again, and she shook violently.

"Melinda!" shouted Julie.

Oh, what did *she* want?

"Tea's ready, turn that crap off!"

Melinda looked up. She unravelled herself. That night was over. She was still alive, at least. Melinda switched her stereo off. Then, she went down the stairs, because she just wanted to have a normal family dinner like everyone else.

Throughout the day, nausea had been a rock in her stomach. At dinner, it had taken her almost an hour to finish her sandwich. Along the banister, her hand slid, drenched in sweat. Melinda readied herself.

From the dining table, her family watched her as she entered the kitchen. They smiled, while cottage pie steamed on the plates. Uneasily, Brad gestured:

"Nice of you to join us Mel, why don't you have a seat?"

Melinda's family began to eat, chatting casually. Bile travelled up Melinda's throat. She was going to be sick—No, she *wasn't*.

Melinda picked up her knife. She picked up her fork. Bite, chew, swallow. It was that simple, even toddlers could do it! But she just... couldn't. Prodding the potato, she mourned as it oozed gravy, and she made no attempt to eat it, because she just wasn't hungry.

Julie's stern voice was no help. "Melinda, eat."

Melinda shivered as Kenzie's hands ran down her body. Her fork trembling, she picked up a forkful of potato and shoved it in her mouth, thus silencing the voice that jeered in the back of her head. She bit, chewed, swallowed, and complimented her mother on the food.

"Well, I did try," Julie replied.

Great. Now all Melinda had to do was finish the meal.

Ashley reached for the tomato ketchup.

"Oh god," Brad joked. "Must you?"

"You know I have to have ketchup on cottage pie."

"Yeah, that's true. So, I know you don't want to talk about it, Julie. And I know *I* shouldn't be talking about it, but how was the concert, girls?"

"Oh, it was *amazing!*" Ashley gushed. "Tom even asked me to marry him! And Mel got on so, so well with Kenzie, didn't you, Mel?"

Melinda dropped her knife and fork, and charged out of the room as if lightning had zapped her from behind.

"Mel? Hey Mel, what's up?"

Underneath the stairs, there was a toilet that was rarely used. Melinda flung the door open. She only just made it in time; the smell of vomit stung her nostrils, and the taste burned in her throat.

Hair shielding her, Melinda slumped over the toilet, gasping. When Behind her, she sensed someone, a plump, frustrated someone, kneel beside her and pull her hair from her face.

"Oh, Mel, why didn't you tell me you were ill?"

Not looking up, Melinda shrugged.

Julie sighed. "Well, you'd best stay off from college tomorrow."

"No!" Melinda protested. "I'll be all right, I'll be—"

Much to the displeasure of Julie, Melinda vomited once again into the long-ago pristine toilet.

"My poor Mel," Brad said kindly. "Why don't you go on up to bed? I'll bring you some water in a bit."

Melinda didn't need her mother to help her up, but at the same time, it felt nice to be looked after. She went upstairs to sounds of Julie shouting at Jack not to dare put his head in the toilet; when she got to her bedroom, she buried herself in her bedsheets. Starting a texting conversation with Jay, she lost track of time inside her safety cocoon.

As light turned to dark, the bedsheets soaked up her tears, and Melinda gave up texting Jay. She bit her wrist, thus quietening the sounds she was making. The chicken noodle soup (her father had insisted on bringing it to her bedside later that evening) was battery acid in her stomach.

Oh, why couldn't she stop *crying?* It wasn't even helping! '

She needed someone to hold her, and say it would all be okay, that Kenzie was going to be arrested, and would never be free to hurt anyone else. But she couldn't have that, as she wasn't allowed to tell anyone, because when she thought about it, no one would ever believe her.

Reaching down into the space between her bed and the wall, Melinda pulled out Flossie.

Flossie was blind in one eye, due to a tragic accident with a stray cat. Her pale blue fur had almost faded to white. She had one floppy ear missing, frayed paws, and a patch of red material over where her twitching nose once was. But, as she hugged Flossie to her chest, Melinda felt slightly comforted, until she felt two little arms slide around her and pull her back to reality.

"Mel," whispered Ashley. "Please, Mel, don't be sad anymore. I had a great time at the concert, really I did."

Hang on... There *was* a way out. Melinda *could* have control. All she had to do was act like it never happened. Placing her hands over Ashley's, Melinda turned her body toward her, and was met with her hopeful gaze. Flossie was pushed out of the bed; Kenzie was pushed to the back of her mind.

Melinda smiled. Ashley smiled back. Melinda cuddled her close, and in response, Ashley rested her head in the crook of her neck.

"Oh, Ash, I'm a silly nana, aren't I?" Melinda cooed, ruffling Ashley's hair.

Squirming, Ashley giggled.

Melinda blew a raspberry on her forehead. "Hey, you could at least tell me I'm not!"

"But you are," Ashley retorted. "Oh, and leave the blankets off. You're boiling. I know you felt poorly, but why were you so upset?"

Damn it, Ashley was so close to just forgetting about it! Thankfully, Melinda had a lie ready to shut Ashley up and, ironically, it was the exact thing that had gotten her into the mess in the first place. Wiping her eyes, because she had to seem as though she actually cared, she murmured softly:

"Cause Kenzie couldn't get me a record deal."

"Oh." Clasping her hands, Ashley gasped with a new idea. "Wait, I can get you one! That video! I'll post it on YouTube like Justin Bieber did, and then—"

"No!" Her, being on YouTube singing *that* song for all to see? "No, Ash."

"How come? I thought you wanted to be famous?"

"I wanna finish college first. I've only got this year to finish, then I can get my Cs, move onto Animal Care, and get a job working with animals."

Melinda didn't remember telling Ashley about her newfound dream. Yet she must have done, for Ashley nodded eagerly.

"But then"—squeezing her sister tighter, Melinda lied once more—"*then,* I'll think about it."

Ashley sighed. Content, she snuggled into her sister, and Melinda snuggled back. She started telling Ashley about how she planned to rehearse *really* hard while looking after those animals. However, deep in the bottom of her heart, she knew that after what had happened the previous day, she would never sing again.

"I'm sorry, I'm sorry, I don't want to, I don't—"

Kenzie exhaled.

Hot damn, he was so *messed up*. When she'd sobbed and begged, Kenzie had almost combusted as he dawned over her, the superior he knew he was. And when she'd screamed... oh, when she'd *screamed*...

The man shuddered.

Of course, he'd never intended for things to go *that* far. Yet, on that sofa, he'd drunk the life from her glossy eyes.

Kenzie rolled the butterfly clip between his fingers.

"Mel? Mel, you've gotta see my new shirt."

Ashley! That ridiculous little peasant! When she'd knocked that door, he'd longed to knock her *down*. He'd ached to snap her, just like he'd just snapped that silly, tatty clip that probably cost no more than a pound.

Kenzie morphed the memories in his head. In this version, his fellow band members had not returned when they did. Ashley had not knocked that door, and Melinda...

"No, you're hurting me, no!"

Growling, Kenzie sat up, and tossed aside the clip. He stared into the darkness of his room. The uncooperative cow! She'd been lucky to escape when she did. In the dressing room, as the moments had gone on, Kenzie had planned much, much more for her.

Raking his hands through his hair, Kenzie clung onto the fantasy, but despite his best efforts, it slipped away.

Fantasies were just that: Fantasies. He knew that his made-up version of the backstage tour wasn't true; he understood that really, she'd gotten away.

Like a child who'd been given the trifle without the cherry on top, Kenzie wasn't satisfied. So why should he stop now?

Kenzie laid back in his bed. He'd made his decision, but for now, he was perfectly happy to bask in the memory.

"Please..."

He wasn't finished with Melinda Stevens, not by a long shot.

Chapter Sixteen

Julie slipped her thirtieth cupcake into the second plastic tub she'd used, muttering under her breath. "That stupid programme. I don't know *why* I'm still letting her watch it."

"Aw, come on, Jules, I'm sure she's learnt her lesson," said Brad.

The atmosphere was nagging Melinda to move, but she just kept lingering. Brad was also in the kitchen, packing his work bag at the table, and Jack was sleeping in his basket. Melinda fiddled with her college ID. The TV was blaring at her through the living room:

"Stay with me, let me in…"

Melinda leant back on the doorframe, and questioned awkwardly:

"Mom, d'you need any help?"

"No thanks, Melinda."

Melinda knew she was getting on everyone's nerves lingering in the doorway, but surely her mother couldn't pack all of those cakes herself? Forlornly, Melinda stared at her college ID, knowing she'd be bombarded by Dana and all her friends about the concert the moment she walked through the doors:

Oh, how was the concert, Mel? Was the tour any good? Did anything happen?

Brad picked up his bag. "Well done, kid. I know it's hard when you feel like crap."

Zoned out, Melinda didn't realise it was her dad's arms trying to hug her:

"No! Don't touch me."

Julie gasped. "Melinda!"

Brad startled. The hands that had been on her shoulders slowly retracted, instead choosing to rake through his long, brown waves. The TV sung from the living room; Ashley joined it in its chorus while, looking down, Brad hurriedly nodded. "Sorry, erm… don't forget breakfast."

"Brad," scolded Julie. "Don't let her talk to you like that, and Melinda, apologise to your father."

"No, it's his own fault. He should have known not to try and hug me when I'm not feeling well."

Brad fled from the room; Melinda watched him go, and wondered: Why was she acting so horrible?

Julie seemed to be wondering the same thing, except she was angry.

"No, Tom," Ashley exclaimed from the living room. "Don't do that, you'll hurt yourself!"

"Shouldn't you at least go and join him in the car?" Julie remarked.

"No, I'm walking today."

Julie turned away. "Suit yourself then. But this isn't over."

Reaching for another box, Julie continued packing her cakes. The front door was re-opened, and from the stairs, Brad's footsteps sounded. He'd forgotten his dog records again. Of course, Tom *did* hurt himself in the programme and, most likely, Julie would give her random baking away to friends at work, Ashley's classmates, or Brad's work colleagues.

On edge, Melinda reached for a banana from the fruit bowl. It was easy to understand how angry her mother was, but Melinda chose not to leave, because no matter what came of it, she could *not* face walking past that TV.

"For goodness sake, Melinda." Julie slammed another lid. "Go and do something. You've annoyed me enough this morning."

"But it's not time to go yet."

"Melinda, I swear to god—"

Barking, Jack suddenly jumped up and ran for the front door. The postman had come.

"I'll get it," said Melinda.

Ashley's protests got louder. Through the crack in the living room door, she was sat on the floor next to a bowl of cereal, gawping at the TV.

Onscreen, Tom lay on the floor. Various children were dark shadows above him. Callum's shouts echoed, while the overturned motorbike roared. Melinda's lips parted. Season three, episode nineteen, the finale… Life lesson: never put yourself in danger to please others. Tom had wanted to please the children of Funville by jumping the dumpsite on the motorbike, and Kenzie wouldn't let him. Tom had done it anyway, and it had ended terribly.

"Tom," said *that* voice. "Oh, Tom!"

Why? Why did she look? Hurrying to the letterbox, Melinda tugged the letter free. She was about to head back, when she noticed something. There was no address on the letter... it just had her name on, in block capitals.

Melinda frowned. She never got letters. She even looked out the window, but the person who'd posted it was clearly long gone.

"What is it?" called Julie.

"Nothing, Mom," Melinda replied. "Just another pizza leaflet."

Biting her lip, Melinda shoved the envelope into her college bag, and continued with her day.

"Excuse me," Tom mumbled, barging through the swarm of observers, producers, and directors. "Sorry, excuse me, sorry."

A woman huffed as he elbowed past her, and a man grumbled as he trod on his foot.

"Doug, Doug!"

If only he'd read the script the night before, instead of wasting time playing Mario Kart with Kenzie. And where was Doug? It was just crowd after crowd, suit-clad person after suit-clad person. To the side of him, the green-screen was near blocked by children and crew members, but none of them were Doug.

"Here, how about this?" someone said.

It was Callum. He was knelt on the floor. Strumming his guitar, he was blind to the hustle and bustle around him, and Doug's quiet voice as he knelt and replied.

Tom charged over, grabbed Doug's arm, and yanked him up as if he were a naughty schoolboy. "Doug, there you are, we need to talk—"

"Bloody hell, Tom! What is it? Can't you see I'm busy?" He placed a hand on his head. "It's all going wrong today. Kenzie isn't even here yet, and I specifically told him half eight on the dot; it's nearly nine now."

Tom beckoned the annoyed band manager backstage.

"Doug, I can't do this scene."

"Okay, what scene, and why?"

A director told Callum to put down his guitar. An electrician shouted to turn the lights down.

Without looking at Doug, Tom flicked to the offending page in the script. "This, here. I can't do this bit."

Doug peered over the shorter boy's shoulder and read the stage direction out:

"Kenzie puts his arms around Tom, and pulls him up from the floor, calling frantically. Tom wakes up, and the pair throw their arms around each other, relieved Tom is still alive."

Doug scoffed, and shook his head in disbelief. "And what's wrong with that?"

"It's... weird."

"Weird? How is it weird?"

"It just is," said Tom defensively.

"Oh for goodness sake, grow up. It's only acting, Tom. No one's gonna take any notice, especially Kenzie. Besides, you texted me okaying the script." Smirking, Doug patted Tom's cheek. "Next time, read the script before you approve it, okay?"

Humiliated, Tom followed Doug with his eyes as he went back to centre stage.

"Kenzie!" Doug called. "There you are. What the heck took you?"

While Kenzie explained the cons of traffic to Doug, Tom prayed for Kenzie not to come around the corner.

"Tom!"

Tom inwardly wept. Arms folded, Kenzie was clad in his usual attire of dark clothing. Strands of blond hair hung in his eyes, shining and golden.

"So Landsby, you've read the script then?"

Never had Tom wished so much for a fire to burn down the building.

"Excuse me," Melinda said to the cleaner.

"Sorry, sweet." The cleaner moved the trolley from her path. "I like your top!"

"Oh, thanks."

Pushing *his* touch away, Melinda continued down the corridor, wringing her hands as her footsteps echoed. Thankfully, there was no one here. Melinda was early. Brad had ended up leaving extremely late, which in turn made Ashley late. Because Melinda had walked to the bus stop, she'd been on time, unlike when she'd missed a certain train home.

The lack of people in the college pleased Melinda. In a longing to be invisible, she'd worn black leggings with a long, black, frilly shirt. Sophie was already at the classroom. From the opposite end of the corridor, Melinda could see her sitting outside the Maths room, her nose buried in her favourite manga.

Hands landed on Melinda shoulders. "Hey!"

Kenzie, Kenzie, *Kenzie!* Melinda screamed.

"Oh my god, Mel, your face!"

"For fucks sake Jay, get a life!"

Jay shrank back. "Sorry, I just wanted to tell you about, I mean..."

Melinda raised her eyebrows.

Fiddling with his battered hands, Jay looked down. "I just wanted to show you this draft of a new kart I was thinking of building. We learnt some good stuff in DT and I was thinking of applying it to the go-kart. And I was trying to cheer you up about the concert. I know you probably hated it."

"Yeah, of course I did."

"So what was the tour like? Did you give the band a good battering, like you said you would the other day?"

"I was joking about that, you idiot!"

"God, Mel, you're moody today."

"Oh just piss off, Jay!"

Before regret had chance to sink in, Dana appeared behind her, and added her own sharp tongue to the mix:

"You're so immature, Jay. Everyone knows you don't *really* have a go-kart, and that it's just some trolley you robbed from ASDA. Now get lost."

Obviously upset, Jay left.

Melinda couldn't apologise to him, not in front of Dana. Trailing her, her other five friends sniggered. Dana slid an arm around Melinda, and urged her toward the window. Briefly, Melinda caught a glimpse of Sophie gawping, which only made her feel worse.

"Anyway"—to Dana, Melinda avoided eye contact—"the concert... Tell me *everything.*"

"Oh, well, me and Ash just watched the show."

Dana smirked. "You don't say?"

"And there were all these lights and a trampoline and I met this girl who also hated the band and—"

"No, no, I don't care about *that*. I meant Kenzie. What happened with that stud muffin?"

"Nothing. And funnily enough, he's butt ugly."

Instinctively, Melinda began to perform a script she'd written herself. In this one, all had gone okay. She'd just watched a concert, had a tour, and gone home, on time.

"Seriously, Dana, he's like, really ugly. Don't get me wrong, on stage he looks nice, but when you see him up close, he has a tonne of spots and never brushes his teeth and never washes. I swear his breath smelt like your sister's socks. No, *worse*, and…"

Dana laughed. "Oh, *come on*, don't try and tell me that, especially after the look on your face when I showed you that mag cover. I know you wanted to jump him. I certainly would." Dana licked her lips. "As soon as we'd have got in that dressing room, that would have been it."

Melinda almost threw up there and then.

"Oh my god!"

Two of Dana's friends jumped into the conversation that was quickly going wrong.

"You met Three Beams didn't you? Dana told me."

Another other one of Dana's friends leapt on the bandwagon. Her tanned skin glowed against her short, plump figure, and her hair was so brightly purple it was startling. "Did you meet Kenzie? Was he buff?" Glancing at her friend, she squealed, and clapped her hands. "Oh, I bet he was."

Melinda ignored them. Yes, Kenzie was 'buff', but Melinda didn't know, because she *wasn't* there.

"Oi, tell us!"

Wait, which of Dana's friends had poked her arm? And which one blurted:

"Don't leave us hanging, that's proper rude you know."

"Come on, Mel," Dana nagged. "Spill!"

Melinda's chest tightened. Through her nose now, her breaths became shallower, and shallower. In the dressing room, Kenzie pulled down her tights. At college, the cleaner from earlier smiled warmly at her as she pushed her trolley past.

"Erm…" Melinda looked from one expecting face to the other. "He was good. Really hot and buff and stuff." Melinda had to leave, now, or else she'd miss the train home… "But I need the loo, so I'll be back in a sec."

"Hey," said Dana indignantly.

Her calls came a millisecond too late. Melinda had already taken off down the corridor.

"Wait for me!"

Melinda bustled on, wishing she could grow wings, and fly away. Australia was meant to be nice. It was always warm there; never did it rain like in England. And it was full of cool animals. What bliss! Wiping her eyes, Melinda barged into the toilets, which were blessedly empty. They smelt like disinfectant; they'd just been cleaned, unlike her.

Ignoring Dana's irritating babbles, she headed into the last cubicle on the left. Bolting the door shut, she sat on the toilet seat… and took deep breaths.

Dana huffed. "You could have waited, you know."

"Sorry."

There was a spraying sound. It was hairspray, peach scented. "Ugh, my hair's a mess."

Melinda clamped her hands over her mouth. She wouldn't cry, not here.

Dana snorted. "God, what's up with you today?"

"Nothing. Just period pain."

"Ah, I get it. I suppose my mates didn't help, either. Rach and Em… They're lovely, really, they are, but they can be a bit full on sometimes. Plus, Em's all moody cause not only did she get hair dye all over her favourite shirt, but her boyfriend dumped her again. I don't get why she's even shocked. I *told* her that Ted Parker's an arsehole…"

Dana's voice trailed off. None of what she'd said mattered anymore, because Melinda had spotted the envelope poking out from her bag. She may as well open it, she decided.

It was a message, typed in bold:

Just remember Mellbell: Thanks to your sister, I know where you live.

Dana called to her:

"So, back to Kenzie. Did you talk to him?"

Melinda didn't answer.

"Oh, so you're not gonna speak to me now either? Don't worry though, I know period pain can be a bitch. Anyway, see you later. But just remember, he's mine."

Melinda waited for the sound of Dana's shoes, then the door opening. Only when she was sure Dana was gone did she break down and cry.

Chapter Seventeen

"Tom, Tom! Speak to me, mate!"

As Kenzie began to lift him from the fake grass of Funville, Tom's breaths hitched.

"Please, come on." Kenzie began to shake him. "Come on, I'm sorry. Tom!"

The children of Funville whispered. The script said that soon, this moment would be over. It would be time to open his eyes. Tom clamped a hand over Kenzie's shoulder. He didn't want to leave. This was so warm, so nice, so passionate…

Wait, what?

Tom's eyes snapped open. Children were huddled in the background, gasping in their brightly coloured wigs. The crew and their director were fast running out of patience. However, they may as well have not existed; Kenzie was so *close!* The only issue was, he was wearing *way* too much clothing…

Growing impatient, Kenzie mouthed, out of sight of the director:

"Come on, say your line."

"Erm… I need a wee!"

A confused pause was followed by Kenzie and Tom bursting out laughing.

Doug face palmed. "Right, that's it!"

Holding his hand up, the director glared. "Take five. I'm out. Carly, get me a coffee."

To the cackling boys, Doug stomped forward. "You two, here, now."

Tom looked at Kenzie. Still grinning, the taller, confident blond looked back, hands in his pockets. Neither of them moved.

Doug advanced on them. "What on earth are you playing at? This is a simple scene. This is the *seventh* time you've screwed it up."

"Hey," said Kenzie defensively. "It wasn't me."

Doug didn't even look at him. "I know that, Kenzie. I'm talking about this one here." He gestured at Tom. "Why are you acting like such a child today? None of this 'I need a wee', or 'wait, this isn't McDonalds' crap is in the script, and you know it!"

"Soz Doug, I'm having a bad day."

"A bad day? We have a tight schedule here! Tots TV want this episode done by *next week.* But you just *have* to keep messing around like a complete imbecile—"

"Hey. Doug, chill out, man," said Kenzie calmly. "It's not his fault."

Eyebrows knitting together, Doug's lips curled; he was about to get even angrier with Tom, until Kenzie stepped into his sight.

"Look, we're all a bit stressed." Kenzie said. "Like you said, the schedules are tight. We've literally been thrown back into this, right after a concert."

Out of nowhere, Callum joined Tom's opposite side, and smiled timidly.

Kenzie continued. "It's just… riled us a bit, that's all. Please, just give us a chance, okay?"

Milling around, the crew poked at the bike, muttering amongst themselves.

"Kay, fine, whatever, I guess you're right," said Doug. "Just get yourself sorted Tom, okay?"

"Oh, fuck this," huffed Tom.

Doug did a doubletake. Furious, Tom walked away from the green screen, away from the shocked crowd, and away from that stupid, *stupid* man that was the sole cause… Huffing, he shoved open the door to the little garden where they kept abandoned pieces of the TV studio.

The red car, the first design for the band's method of transport, was one of the best places to sit when you just wanted to take a breather.

It wasn't his fault. The lights in the room were too bright; even Callum had moaned about it. Plus, the new episode was cringy as hell, so how was Tom expected to concentrate? Tom banged his fists on the car, and cursed at the cloudy sky above.

Creak…

Oh, why couldn't Doug just stop bugging him? A pair of feet emerged from the back door, and stopped.

Tom was about to snap at him, but then he saw it wasn't Doug.

Hanging in his eyes, Tom's curls were shielding his vision, but there was no mistaking it. Kenzie was in front of him, his hands by his sides, his red trainers gleaming.

"Hey, Tom."

"Hey. You all right?"

"I should be asking you that. Come on, Landsby." The car creaked as Kenzie sat on it too. "Don't take it personally, he's just stressed. You know what Doug's like."

Yes, Doug. The problem was just Doug, being snappy as usual. Tom grumbled:

"He's a twat. I hate him."

A rat squeaked from beneath the car.

"There's some fans outside," said Kenzie suggestively. "From what Callum said, there ain't that many. How's about we go see 'em, ay?"

Tom smiled in spite of his misery. "Okay." Looking up, he took Kenzie's hand, and allowed the blond to pull him from the car.

"Ha, see? You're not a complete imbecile after all."

"Maybe we'll see that red-headed elephant, also known as 'The girl of your dreams'." Tom winked, even though he was rubbish at winking.

Kenzie tittered, and went toward the back exit. Tom gathered himself. Then, he followed.

Melinda regretted sitting in the middle of the classroom. Anyone could snatch at her bag, yank the envelope free, and find out. Painfully, she dug her fingers into her temple. She stared at the Maths questions in front of her. Papers rustled, students sighed, and the tutor barked answers.

Question one was three quarters. Question two was an improper fraction; two and four fifths. And question three—

Kenzie Hudgson had been to her house! Melinda quaked. Kenzie Hudgson, the man who'd violated her at the concert of her worst nightmares, had walked past the window where her sister had been sitting! He'd been stood *outside her front door!*

Biting her lip harder, Melinda commanded herself to concentrate. What was the answer to question number four?

"Mel?"

Oh, she wasn't safe! Kenzie knew where she lived, and he was going to break into her bedroom and finish what he'd started!

"Mel?"

It was all fucking Ashley's fault! If the girl hadn't blabbed their address—

A sudden shake to her shoulder brought the classroom back.

"Hey, Mel!" Sophie was the picture of concern. "You good?"

Unusually, the girl had torn herself from her Maths problems to see if she was 'good'. Why couldn't everyone just leave her alone?

"It's just—" briefly, Sophie glanced back to the Maths tutor. At present, he was explaining one of the problems to Jade, who was looking completely baffled. "You've been so quiet today. Usually you can't stop ranting about random things."

Thank goodness Melinda had Science tomorrow, *without* Sophie. "Sophie, it's nothing. Can you just leave it? I don't wanna talk about it."

"But—"

"I said I don't want to talk about it!"

The Maths tutor sighed. "Is there a problem, Melinda?"

"No, sir. Sorry."

Wiping the whiteboard, the tutor mumbled something, then turned to face the class. "All right guys, class dismissed. See you Wednesday."

Students chattered, pulled out their phones, and headed for the door. Snippets of conservation drifted over to Melinda: What was everyone doing after class? Was anyone going to the café. They were having a half-price reduction. And had anyone checked Three Beams' Twitter accounts lately—

Melinda bolted from the classroom faster than humanly possible. Vaguely, she was aware of her bag smacking against Sophie, and other students protesting as she shoved past them. She didn't care. She was too angry, too worried, to god damn s*cared*.

Students lined the corridors. Did they know Kenzie? Melinda jumped as someone brushed past her. Was he hiding amongst the college students somewhere?

After a short run down the staircase, Melinda was free from the college. Outside, it was muggy. Flecks of rain sprinkled on her. There were few students outside; not many finished at half past two, so no one saw her lean on the bin, and catch her breath.

She couldn't go home, not by herself.

Reaching into her bag, Melinda tugged the envelope free. Fleetingly, her eyes scanned the message that practically glowed through it. Then, she tore it up and threw it in the bin.

Ashley had Art Club today. Apparently, parents and siblings were now allowed to attend.

The Birmingham House stretched out in front of Callum. With its clean white walls and floors, colourful sofas, various TVs and even a games room, it was every boy's dream, but Callum didn't like it. He'd much rather be outside. Outside, there was a peddled pathway, which seemed to slice through the perfectly cropped grass. Two apple trees loomed either side. Rain hung, mist-like, over the front garden. Huge, black iron gates sported two security guards.

Behind him, Tom laughed at the TV. "Aw man, that's brilliant."

The shower was still running. Kenzie was taking an age; there was no way there would be any hot water left.

Taking one last look at the stern guards, Callum exhaled through his teeth, and yanked the curtain shut. The Beamers were fans, not rabid animals. Well, most of them.

"Oh, what I'd give to do that to Doug." Tom laughed.

Callum shot a glare at the back of his head. He'd cheered up quickly, considering that filming had been a waste of time. They'd barely got anything done because of him and his 'best friend' mucking around. Callum sat in the blue armchair.

"Jesus Christ." Clapping, Tom pulled his legs onto the chair. "He's getting slaughtered!"

Callum reached for his laptop, which he kept under the chair.

"Hey, Cal, we should push Doug in there. Those piranhas would love him, and he deserves it after how he acted today."

"Yeah, well"—Callum typed in his password—"I've said before not to wind him up."

"But he doesn't have to be such an arse."

Eventually, Twitter loaded. Callum remembered a crowd that had waited by his house last Christmas, the presents he'd been sent on his twenty-third birthday, and the loyal group that had held up a banner for him at the concert. Tom's stupidness forgotten, Callum anticipated the joy his fans would bring him once the screen loaded.

It didn't.

Stuck in the chair, he sat, staring, at the screen in front.

There was a photo of Kenzie and Tom, taken when they'd gone to greet the fans earlier that day. Tom was looking down, smiling toothily. Fans could be seen taking photos in the background, yet that wasn't what was making Tom smile. The cause had his arm around Tom's shoulders, and was smirking into his ear while the boy flushed scarlet...

Callum refreshed the page. The photo, originally posted by a fan, had been edited. Around the pair was a gigantic pink heart, and at the base of it...

WE SHIP TOMZIE!

7,900 re-tweets, 201 comments...

Callum refreshed the page.

8,001 re-tweets, 243 comments...

Aw bless, they look so cute!

Ha, told you so!

OMG, Tomzie forever!

From Callum's pocket, a cheerful ringtone sounded. He knew it was Doug. What would he think? No, what would *Kenzie* think?

"Ignore it," said Tom dismissively. "That stupid git's rung me about it twenty times."

Panicking, Callum minimised the screen. Kenzie wasn't gay. It was obvious! But...

Callum stared at Tom. They locked eyes, and at that moment, Callum knew.

"Tom, come look at this," he said.

The boy flopped down on the arm of the chair. "Ey up," he ruffled Callum's shaved head. "What's going on here then, Callum-boy?"

From upstairs, the floorboards creaked.

"I think you need to see this."

The back-up singer reacted as though he'd been tossed into an ice-cold freezer; he froze, and he did *not* move. He seemed so scared, Callum wondered if he'd pass out on the spot. Beeps sounded. Callum had forgotten to turn the sound off. At both of them, the screen went wild, tossing up comment after comment, re-tweet after re-tweet.

Tom gulped. "Oh shit..."

Videos and photos leapt onscreen from concerts, the TV show, and the earlier filming session, every one of Kenzie and Tom, with the hashtag 'Tomzie'.

"N-No," Tom scrambled to a stand. "W-We're not, we were just... we were by the fans! And Kenzie was winding me up."

Callum continued to stare. When Tom noticed it, he cried out:

"We saw an old lady. She had black curly hair and Kenzie said I was her boytoy, and that it wasn't okay cause she was secretly my granny and that... Callum, *please!*" Red-faced, he raked his hands through his curls. Some came free in his hands. "You have to believe me—"

Urgently, Callum slipped the laptop back under the armchair. "Tom!"

"Stop looking at me like that! I'm not gay, you know I'm not."

Callum reached out. "Tom—"

"Oh god, what if Kenzie sees it, what if—"

"Tom!"

"Oh god, this is fucked, this isn't happening, it isn't—"

Kenzie put his hands-on Tom's shoulders.

Slowly, Tom turned around. "Oh, Kenzie, hi, how was your shower? We were just—"

Kenzie snarled, his words a cold, hard lash:

"*What* is going on?"

Chapter Eighteen

"Oh." Anxious, Tom wriggled away from Kenzie's grasp. "Nothing, Ken, everything's fine."

Looking the boy up and down, Kenzie came closer. "I'm going to ask you one more time," he said menacingly. "*What* is going on?"

Tom's shoes were sticking to him. "Honestly, Kenzie." He put his hands out. "It's nothing to worry about. Me and Callum were just—"

"What do you take me for?"

Tom squeaked; Kenzie had grabbed Tom by his purple shirt, and brought his face into his.

"Do you think I'm a dickhead?"

"Tom, just tell him," cried Callum from his chair. "He's gonna find out anyway—"

"Damn right I am!" Kenzie tossed Tom to the side as if he were simply a plant that stood in his way. "Give me that laptop, Callum, now. I can hear it going off from here."

Tom's curls fell in front of his eyes; the only thing he could do was watch as Kenzie stormed toward Callum and demanded his laptop.

"All right, just don't break it!"

Kenzie snatched it. "Whatever."

"Now Kenzie," said Callum. "Don't freak out, it's just the fans having a laugh."

Around the device, the squeeze of furious fingers made it creak. Twitter continued the rampage; the pictures, videos, and comments kept pouring in, faster, faster, and faster.

Kenzie's eyebrows came down. A ripple of hatred stirred in his eyes, and then…

Crash!

"Kenzie," howled Callum. "I told you not to break it!"

The whole left side of the laptop screen had come away. Sparks of electricity showered the white carpet. On the screen, Callum's Twitter began to flicker.

"Those little shits!" shouted Kenzie. His foot sent the laptop soaring once again.

The laptop hit the wall; Callum bent next to his laptop, and prodded it, sighing when he realised that it truly was useless now.

Kenzie turned back on himself. Foaming at the mouth, the man fled from the living room; all that could be heard was the ground-shaking thud, thud, thud of him scaling the stairs.

Tom stared at the door his best friend had fled from. "So," he chuckled awkwardly. "He's not gay then…"

"No." Knelt near his destroyed laptop, Callum raised his eyebrows. "But are you?"

Briefly, Tom heard himself promising Callum a new laptop. Mentally, he cursed as he called his best friend's name over and over, and longed for the stairs to cave in as he scaled them. Callum was stupid anyway, a fool who'd grew too big for his boots. Following the sounds of Kenzie swearing, Tom plotted a malicious revenge on him.

Soon, Tom found Kenzie raiding his closet, tossing out item after item. Shoes thumped off of the floor. Sprays and brushes rolled along the floorboards. A forgotten tennis racket bounced along the wood.

"Oh, Kenzie," Tom huffed. "It took me hours to organise all of that stuff."

"Fuck off."

"Kenzie, come on, I—"

"Aha!" Kenzie gave a triumphant gasp.

The pair locked eyes, but only for a moment, for Kenzie turned his back on him, his jawline hard. In his hands, he held Tom's video camera from his days at college. Tom made to reach out, but Kenzie had already switched the camera on, and when he growled into it, Tom *felt* the sound.

"Now listen, you little fuckers—"

"No, Kenzie!" Tom pushed the camera down. "You can't say that!"

"Why the hell not? I'm not fucking gay Tom, and neither are you."

Carefully, Tom eased the camera from Kenzie's hands. "I know that. But we can't speak to the fans that way! They'll be so upset. We could lose thousands of them, and that would be catastrophic. What's the point of ruining what we've spent years working hard for?"

Kenzie sighed.

"This happens to a lot of bands, Kenzie, a lot, but mainly the really famous ones. If anything, it just means we're up there, with the best of the best. All we've gotta do is tell them the truth... nicely."

That last sentence extinguished Kenzie's fire completely. "Yeah, I guess you're right."

"Plus, this means that the girls really *are* crazy for us." Tom winked.

"Dude, don't do that."

"Why?"

Kenzie jabbed him in the stomach. "Cause, you can't do it right! You just squint like some blind bat."

Standing by his side, Kenzie took the camera from his hands, and held it up, high. "Here, stand by me."

Again, Kenzie switched the camera on, but his time, he was smiling. His eyes were twinkling playfully, his perfectly-white teeth glowing, and his hair all messed up in that oh-so wonderful way...

"Hey guys," Kenzie said, tossing his hair. "Kenzie here, and this is my best mate, Tom. Note that I said *mate*. We've just been on Twitter, and saw all the... stuff. And we just wanna say that we're not gay. We're just *mates*. I'm sure you've all got that one friend, the one you can tell anything to, the one you'd trust with your life but not your phone."

"Well, that's me and Ken."

"We rehearse together, we perform together, we even live together sometimes. So we get where you guys are coming from, really, we do. But we're not kissing backstage, or cuddling in the tour bus, or smooching in bed together, and we never will be. Still, we'll be more careful of what impression we give in future, won't we, Tom?"

Tom jolted; Kenzie had dug him in the ribs. "Yeah, we will."

"I'd also like to take this opportunity to remind you all that, if Tom and I had girlfriends, this could have ended very, very badly for us. So please be mindful when posting on social media, because spreading fake news can really impact people's lives. I'd have hated to see Tom get hurt. He's my best mate."

"Yeah." Pushing his curls back, Tom blew out a grieving breath, and put all his focus into holding himself together. "Kenzie's awesome. Without him, I don't know where I'd be."

Kenzie slapped the back of his head playfully. "Oi, enough with the sappy stuff. Now, time to say bye-byes."

They both waved goodbye, before ending the video.

Kenzie switched the camera off. "Nice one, dude. I'd best go and post this then."

"Not using my laptop, you won't."

"Aw, poor Callum. Ah, screw him, he can buy a new one."

Without closing the door, Kenzie left. Tom closed it for him. He leant on the wood, and waited. The creaking of the stairs, and the mean laughter at Callum told him Kenzie was truly gone. With no idea *why* they were there, Tom allowed his feelings to break free. Pulling his skinny knees in, Tom sat back against the door, and replayed Kenzie's words over and over:

"We're not kissing backstage, or cuddling in the tour bus, or smooching in bed together, and we never will be."

Around the dinner table, Ashley watched her family's eyes land on the painting. Jack had been captured perfectly, and so was the moment her teacher had handed her the prize in Art Club. For the entire day, she'd been the centre of attention. She'd had countless people grab her, and ask about the band:

Was Kenzie's hair naturally that colour? Did Tom really have three brothers? Did Callum really travel the world in his spare time?

"Well done, Ash, nice one." Brad nodded.

As Brad enjoyed his meal, Julie took her seat. "Yes," she laughed, looking at Ashley's prize. "Another bag charm to add to the millions that are already dangling off your school bag."

Ashley sliced a fish finger. "Sixteen, actually."

"I wish I could draw like you Ash," babbled Melinda. "But we all know what my drawings are like, don't we, Dad?"

Julie scoffed. "Anyway, I have some great news. Guess what girls?"

Ashley sat, on edge. What was going on? And why was Melinda not eating?

The breadcrumbs were dryer than usual, Ashley noted as she swallowed a fish finger. The TV blared with current chart music, and Ashley waited, impatience nearly making her toss her knife to the floor.

Finally, her mother put everyone out of their misery:

"This may be your last cooked dinner for a while, because my baking business is taking off."

Melinda's empty knife and fork clattered to the table. "Wow Mom, that's great."

Julie did a comical squeal. "Yes! I've had a huge order today. My friend wants a great big set made, all for her son's birthday party. And Karen wants a wedding cake, *and* the head of Ashley's school wants a set for the school fete on Friday. I'm gonna be in the kitchen for days practising, but it'll be worth it."

Cakes, wonderful cakes, baked constantly in the kitchen for her to eat! With the new excitement, Ashley was able to ignore the fact that Brad was mouthing at Melinda to eat, and still, Melinda wasn't. Because, all she could envision was cakes, cakes, cakes covering every surface—

The doorbell rang.

Leaping up in her seat, the yelp Melinda did startled everyone. They stared, baffled. Jack could be heard scrabbling down the corridor, yapping madly.

The doorbell rang again.

Gripping her sister's elbow, Ashley questioned her. "Mel, what's wrong?"

The snooty voice of Aunt Flo jeered from the unopen door:

"Hello? I know you're there."

Jack was scratching the door. Melinda, realising it was Aunt Flo, rolled her eyes.

"Everyone," called Flo. "Please stop ignoring me, and let me in."

Chair scraping along the floor, Julie rose to answer the door, not hesitating to barge past Melinda's chair on her way out. "For goodness sake, Mel, you made everyone jump. Ugh, I've *told* her not to come round during dinner."

Bustling from the room, Julie was quickly pursued by the bemused Brad, leaving Ashley and Melinda alone.

Ashley was going to ask: Why the scream? What was the problem? However, Melinda shushed her the second she opened her mouth.

The older sister listened to the chatter going on outside. She looked to the door. She looked back at the table. After that, she snatched a tissue from the middle of the table, splayed it on her lap with one hand, and swiped her white fish and several potatoes into it with the other.

Ashley did a doubletake. "Mel!"

Melinda's hard eyes and deadly reply was enough to silence even the loudest Jack Russell:

"What? I've *told* Mom I wanna go vegan."

In the darkness, a gentle, quiet thrum of limo against road sounded. Kenzie fiddled with the chain on his jeans. Callum hadn't come. Apparently, he'd arranged a video chat night with his 'fans'. Kenzie exhaled. If he'd had his way, the ones responsible for 'Tomzie' would have been burnt alive in a vat of acid.

Next to him, Tom slept. Tired out from a night of clubbing, the boy murmured:

"No, don't put mayo on my pizza, it doesn't go right..."

In the back seat of the black limo, Kenzie felt confident, smug, and powerful. Now he had fame, security guarded his life as if it were a sacred jewel. Money never ran out, and everyone adored him no matter what fucked up *shit* he did. As he leant back in his seat, he felt so tall, so strong... well, until the memories got to him.

As he turned his phone on, it blasted him with a blue light, and that was what took him back.

Suddenly he was helpless, because he was only five years old, and there were so many, so many of *them*.

"*Daddy, where are you? Daddy! Daddy!*"

Wildly, Kenzie looked around. His palms began to sweat. Scary people with white torches were coming after him, and he hadn't found Mommy, because she wasn't there. Instead, there was just a torch, several torches, coming closer and closer and whispering amongst each other:

"*Is that the boy?*"

The horn practically *roared*. There was a shout. The limo swerved to avoid the oncoming car.

Unexpectedly, the shake brought Kenzie back to civilisation. He was twenty-five, not five, and a famous singer. He was in a limo, on his way home, and Tom was next to him.

Kenzie's back became ridged in the leather seat as his phone demanded a passcode. Slowly, the forbidden memories subsided back *down*, where they belonged.

"Stupid damn fans…"

They'd screwed everything up. And as Kenzie typed in his passcode (25082000, the day that *bitch* had left him) and signed into Facebook, he ground his teeth. He searched for Melinda Stevens in the search box.

Melinda's Facebook account hadn't been used for months, but he recognised the girl's photo instantly; he'd know that nervous smile anywhere, and that pest of a sister that smiled with her. After all, it was the same sister who'd knocked on the dressing room door and ruined his whole night.

The brilliant blue light of Kenzie's phone settled in every curve of his grin.

This was great. It was so, so *great*. Never had he expected to find what he found. Had the silly cow never heard of profile privacy?

The limo slowed. Kenzie sat up, and nudged Tom awake.

Despite being ridiculously drunk, Tom quickly caught on to what Kenzie saw. They'd arrived at the Birmingham House; outside, the security guards were talking to the car driver, ensuring he was who he said he was.

"Oh," Tom groaned, his head lolling. "Where's that-that girl, the one I was dancing with?"

"She went home, Tom." With no fear, Kenzie saved Melinda's mobile number into his phone. "You vomited all over her dress."

Ashley jolted up in bed.

"Ash, *ssshh.*"

"Mel, what—"

Placing a finger on her lips, Melinda shushed her again. In her hand was a plastic bag that bulged with promises. She shut the door, quietly, tiptoed over, and bent to Ashley's level. "Guess what I've brought?"

Excited, Ashley sat up. "What, what?"

Melinda placed the bag onto Ashley's bed, and hopped on so she was sitting next to her. "I've brought…" Rustle, rustle. "A midnight feast!"

Ashley gasped. Thrilled, she took in the various treats Melinda delved through: chocolate, biscuits, sweets, crisps, a jar of peanut butter, and even the cake icing on its own!

"Oh Mel, its lovely." Immediately, Ashley yanked the cake icing tube free, and unscrewed the nozzle. "How'd you get it without Mom and Dad seeing? What about Jack, didn't he bark? Mmm, *pink* icing! Oh, and why did you freak out when the doorbell rang—"

"Oh, it was piss-easy," Melinda replied. Snatching for a tube of gingerbread biscuits, she tore into them. "Jack's practically deaf when he's asleep, and Mom and Dad went to bed hours ago. Now eat up, I skipped dinner for this."

Oh, Ashley certainly would.

Melinda put the biscuits down, and leant forward. "It became dangerous for a bit."

The icing tube sagged in Ashley's hands.

"There I was, in the kitchen, alone, picking out food, thinking all was perfect. But then, suddenly…"

Melinda ate a biscuit.

"What? Mel, what happened?"

"The TV came on, out of nowhere," Melinda whispered. "And on it, were Three Beams. And you know what they did?"

Ashley leant in, crushing the bag as she did so. Melinda shut her eyes. Ashley swore she saw tears inside them, however, she was unable to think for long, because what Melinda said enraged her:

"Their stupid songs almost rotted my eardrums."

While Melinda burst out laughing, Ashley squirted the remainder of the icing all over her face, and together, they laughed their worries away.

Chapter Nineteen

Melinda's thoughts were bellowing at her, louder than her own scream on that horrid, horrid night. Thanks to her sister blurting her address out when she met the band, Kenzie could get to her whenever he wanted. The realisation was what had stopped her eating dinner the previous evening. It was only at night that her hunger had returned.

Jay's road was quiet, yet it wasn't safe. Nothing was.

Dana babbled, her footsteps matching Melinda's, and their shadows entwining in the afternoon sunshine.

"So anyway, Anna walked off in a massive huff..."

Melinda pushed her hair from her eyes. Oh, it wasn't Ashley's fault, she was only a kid! Did he know where Jay lived too? Was he going to sneak in with her, and slash them all to ribbons?

"And then Drew said to me that he didn't really like her anyway, that her family was just friends with his, and that her auntie was dieting with his auntie..."

What was that?

It was a long, winding concrete lane. It was houses with open garages, gardens with trimmed hedges. But—rustle, rustle. Clank, clank! Melinda jumped. He was behind her, or worse, behind Jay, who she could see in the garage to her right, engrossed in his latest trolley.

Run Jay, he'll hurt you if you dare scream but no one will ever believe you anyway—

"Oi!"

Melinda almost dropped the plastic bag she held.

"You're not even listening to me, are you?" Rolling her eyes, Dana confronted the plainer girl. "I said, do you reckon I'm in with a chance?"

"Yeah," Melinda looked away. "I think he likes you, I can tell."

Jay had his back to them. Knelt in front of an upturned shopping trolley, he hummed cheerily as his wrench abused the wheel, the bruises on his arms making him look like a Dalmatian.

Dana smiled. "Of course he'll accept your apology, Mel, you know how dim he is. Not that I get *why* you're saying it—"

"Jay!" Melinda called.

Another clank, and Jay's wrench met the floor.

Reaching the garage, Melinda ducked under the half-open door. "You're home. I have something to give you."

For once, she was thankful of her Tuesday extended lunch break. She'd been a bad friend, but now Jay was going to accept her apology and it would all be fine.

"Here." Holding the boy the bag, she mentally promised that she'd be a better person. She'd do well in college, and stop singing for good.

Frowning, Jay continued his 'work' of twisting the wheel's bolts aimlessly.

Melinda took a step back. "Oh, Jay. Look. I…"

Jay ignored her.

The splattered paints on the wall lost colour. Dana was watching, half in, and half out of the gap.

Melinda's bag felt limp in her hand. "I'm sorry, I didn't mean to snap yesterday. I was just angry cause—"

"Wait!" Pointing, Jay stood. "What's in the bag?"

"Well, it's just a few—"

Melinda had no time to finish her sentence. Jay snatched it.

"Oh my god, this is *off the chain*."

Jay's stupidity was hilarious, always hilarious. He pulled the small box of acrylic paints free, and tossed the bag to the floor. He ripped off the cardboard packaging, and grabbed the blue. Putting the others on the floor, he marvelled at them. Already, he was opening the blue. He was even sniffing it! It was going to get everywhere!

"Oh Mel, you're amazing; look at all the stripes I can paint on this now!"

When the shorter boy hugged her, still holding the blue, Melinda managed to smile.

Dana appeared at Jay's side. "All right then, stupid, let us have a look—"

"No, Dana! It's for painting the go-kart when it's done. I wanna paint the wood panels I'm going to put on. I don't want your mucky smelly fingers making it all messy."

"Aw, is the big baby protecting his paints?"

Melinda shook her head. Raising her hands, she at long last just let the pair go at it like cat and dog. It was normal; it happened every day, and today was no exception. She sat at the back corner of Jay's cluttered, paint-splattered garage, and watched the drama unfold.

The wicked witch was winning. She had the paint. Laughing, the witch dipped her fingers in, and flicked the paint at her worst enemy—but oh, oh! He was fighting back! Wrestling with her hands, he shouted about trolleys and the importance of their neatness.

The witch cackled. "Dick!"

The pair swung to the left. They swung to the right. The paint swung with them, back and forth, back and forth—

Melinda dived to the floor as a jet of paint leapt toward her.

Splat!

Letting the culprit have the paint, Dana said tauntingly:

"Well done, fuckwit."

Melinda sat up. Behind her, the paint, looking very much like an exploded firework, trickled down the wall.

Inevitably, Melinda burst into laughter. She laughed and laughed. Laughing too, Dana slumped by the trolley, slapping the metal wires. Jay sat near Dana, sniggering.

When Melinda's pocketed phone buzzed, she wasn't anxious to read the message onscreen:

Hello, Mel.

She didn't know the number, but she put the message down to one of Ashley's friends. She had so many; after a while, they'd jumbled together. Once her giggles had stopped, Melinda didn't think twice about texting back. With a brief 'who's this?' and a smiley emoticon, she put the phone down, and watched her friends.

Buzz.

Melinda sighed. Why couldn't they leave her alone? She was having fun—

The same person who had their hand up your dress. The same person who made you scream backstage.

Dana wiped her eyes. Jay bashed the handle, and Melinda almost descended into the floorboards.

Yeah, that's right. It's ME, Mellbell.

Thwack! Melinda hit her head on the wall, hard. Dana and Jay had both stopped laughing, and they were now bickering right in front of her, yet at that moment, it was like they'd been yanked away.

No… just… *how?* How did he have her number? Oh, she didn't care! She just wanted him *gone.* Melinda texted him back:

Leave me alone.

Maybe it wasn't even the real Kenzie. Maybe it was just a prank, or a dark, horrible dream that she would surely wake up from soon…

Or what? Is your little sister gonna beat me up? Nah, she can watch us fuck instead, if you're into that.

Dana scoffed. "You can't put your sister's hamster on there, pillock; it'll get squashed for a start."

"Oh, come on," Jay whined. "I could wrap it in tin foil."

Melinda dragged her hand down her cheek. Digging her fingers into her phone, she began to type another message, begging him to please leave her alone, but she erased it. Instead, she sat back, and watched the texts come through line by line:

You wanted it, just as much as I did.

You're a cheeky little minx. But you made me feel so fucking good.

I want you underneath me, right now, sobbing as I kiss your neck and fuck you hard.

Where was he? Was he out filming? Was he at his mansion on Twitter, cleaning up the 'Tomzie' incident Melinda had heard all about at college? Or, was he right outside the garage?

Just bear in mind whose fault it was, Mel. You're my little slut, and little sluts always speak to their masters nicely, understand?

"Hey Mel, who're you texting?" called Dana.

Melinda gripped the phone. "Oh, no one."

Words could not describe how godlike Kenzie Hudgson felt as he sat, on the stool behind the green screen, admiring the messages he'd sent to Melinda. His lips twisted into a sneer. The stupid girl, the stupid, innocent girl that had lay on the sofa, sobbing her poor little heart out.

Kenzie tittered. Leave her alone? Oh, no way. With the touch of a button, he had her, trussed up in terror as if she were dolphin caught in fishing net. As he tucked his feet behind the bar of the stool, he began to tap away, listening to the calls of the crew, the chatter of the children, and Doug going on about something boring.

"Hey, Kenzie!"

Kenzie squinted. Yes, he really was seeing what he thought he was seeing: the band manager was actually *happy* for once. Kenzie didn't care as to why, but this was odd behaviour, especially as Doug had been in a foul mood since the Tomzie incident, even though it was all calming down. As the band manager came over, all cocky smiles, jazzy hands and waving clipboard, Kenzie nodded at him.

"You're in a good mood."

Pushing up his glasses, Doug came to a stand in front of him. "Yeah, 'cause I've got *good* news. Well go on, ask me why."

Good news? The last time Doug had said that, Kenzie had been up to his eyeballs in kittens. Swivelling to fully face him, Kenzie pocketed his phone, leaving the next text unsent.

"Okay, why?"

"We're in demand."

"Seriously? How? When?"

"Well, it turns out Tomzie was actually a godsend. All day, Ken." Doug grabbed his upper arms. Ugh, how dare Doug touch him? How dare *anyone* touch him? "All day, my phone's been blowing up. Magazines, radio stations; they're not fussed about Tomzie. They're fussed about *us*. Word's spread, and now..."

Moving away, Doug raked his hand through his hair, and shook his head. "Geez, I don't believe this. I've booked a photoshoot and interview with Wow Mag on Monday, hopefully that will satisfy them."

"Damn, nice one, Doug."

Doug pondered. "Oh, but I don't think it's gonna be enough. We're getting *huge,* huger by the day!"

A cry from far away made Doug turn. That cheering, happy wail... Kenzie knew it anywhere. And as the curly haired boy, the only person Kenzie would ever call a friend, jittered on the corner as if he'd drunk five litres of fizzy pop, Kenzie realised he'd heard the entire conservation.

"Yes!" Tom bellowed. "Yes, yes, *fuck*, yes!"

Doug was sent spinning, as Tom whirled him around.

"Kenzie!" Tom threw his arms around him. "Come here, you big doofus."

Kenzie laughed. "See? It was worth it. it was all bloody worth it."

"I *love* photoshoots! It's so much fun to wind the photographers up! I swear we get more famous every year… it's so great!"

Folding his arms, Doug smiled as he watched two best friends live large.

"Yeah, its ace, ain't it?" Kenzie agreed.

It sure was. Wow Mag's studio was located just half an hour away from Melinda's tatty house.

"Whoa, what's all the fuss?"

Callum's puzzled expression was a silencer to the joy, but just for a moment. Tom burst out into more infectious cheers, hurried over to Callum, and swept the shocked boy into a bear-hug.

Kenzie finally sent his text:

Get ready Mellbell, cause I'm gonna fuck your life up.

"No, it's mine!"

The large boy reached for his football. His three shorter friends echoed, their whines merging together:

"I'm gonna get my dad on you."

"But Miss, we were only playing."

Around the dinner lady's feet, they were equivalent to goats jumping for a bucket of food. The dinner lady held the football higher, and the goats chorused. The dinner lady wasn't giving in without a fight, because the boys had been naughty. They'd kicked the ball at the staff room window *three* times.

Other children played. Some had toys, and some didn't. Some gossiped in small groups, and some wondered alone.

Ashley was crouched behind a dustbin.

"Why can't you just get it after school?" said Hamrit.

"Because, they'll be no more left after school, because everyone's moms will have got to them," Lucia hissed.

A pair of girls whooshed past them, giggling. A lone boy earned the applause of many others as he won the weekly hula-hoop contest. Ashley watched the dinner lady.

The playground was a long, concrete rectangle. The classrooms boarded the perimeter, with only the one middle door left open at lunchtimes. The gate was at the top of the playground. It was broad, and *locked. But,* there was a way, through classroom 3b.

The reception-turned-classroom continued past the gate, and stopped on the car park. If Ashley could climb out of the window, she could flee the school, and be to the corner shop and back within fifteen minutes. It was brilliant! But her partners in crime (the worried remains of what was originally a group of nine) were being contrary. And, that stupid dinner lady *still* wouldn't move. Briefly, Ashley heard Lucia grumbling:

"Oh, come on, she's gotta move in a minute."

Ashley gave her five seconds. "I've got a better idea."

Rising to a stand, she confronted her partners, which were the lanky, nervous Hamrit with a plait longer than some of the boy's bodies, and the stocky latino Lucia. Hamrit was hesitant, shifting from foot to foot. Lucia was looking to her for answers.

"One of us needs to distract her," Ashley said.

"I'll do it."

Lucia did a double take.

Ashley could wholly believe it! Timid Hamrit, taking a stand?

Hamrit held up her finger. "Wait here."

Her tiny shoes pounded on the concrete. Her tiny arms swung by her sides. Lucia stood behind Ashley, and uttered something about how Hamrit ran like a horse. She dodged around the crowds, jumped up, and smacked the football out of dinner lady's hands.

It soured across the playground. The boys charged after it, with the dinner lady pummelling after them. Hamrit darted into the toilets. Ashley was another member down, but, turning to Lucia, she sounded a battle cry:

"Now!"

With that, Ashley and Lucia clattered along the concrete. They swerved past groups, barged through playground games, and scattered through children's abandoned toys. In milliseconds, they reached their target, and were transported to musky red corridors and bright coats hanging on pegs.

As Ashley called for Lucia, Lucia called for her. The pair clutched each other, scared.

"This way!" Ashley pointed, sending their wild eyes to the right.

Down the corridor, to classroom 3b, Ashley led the way. Meanwhile, Lucia was ducking under the class windows, looking like a wannabe spy.

Annoyed, Ashley snapped at her:

"Stop!" Pant, pant. "You're making it look obvious."

"Sorry!"

They turned the corner. They were getting away with it! They were going to pull off a plan so daring, so devious, that their names would be forever in glory. Ashley ran ahead, and Lucia lagged behind, but they were soon reunited again in the classroom.

It was overpopulated by play-dough models of... animals?

Ashley made for the window. Once Lucia had caught up, she lunged for it, yanking it open so forcefully it bashed against the wall. Without waiting, without looking back, Ashley hoisted herself up onto the table. Play-dough sagged under her weight. It stuck in her shoes. It stained her socks. And she froze, because suddenly—

"Who's in here?"

A teacher!

Lucia slapped Ashley's legs urgently. "Quick, *go*, he's coming!"

Ashley looked down. It was a steep drop. Oh, she couldn't do it—

"Ashley, *move!*"

Leaving Lucia in the stench of playdough, Ashley dived out of the window, thankfully landing safely.

She'd done it; the concert DVD was hers. Bursting into triumphant cheers, she powered through the carpark, Tom's lyrics singing her a soft, congratulating melody.

She was halfway to the shop before the laughing Lucia caught up with her.

Chapter Twenty

"Dad, Dad!"

She wasn't going to tell. She wasn't going to tell...

"Mel?"

She nearly ran into her father. He'd been lumbering out of the kitchen and had halted when he'd spotted her.

"Oh, Dad, I just wanted to say I'm really, really sorry about yesterday." Oh god, Kenzie knew her number, Kenzie knew everything—" I was just in a really bad mood, and I'm sorry. Just... sorry."

From the living room, Three Beams sung:

"If only you knew, my heart beats for you..."

Tears blurred Melinda's sight of Jack chewing on his bone in his basket.

"Aw, Mel," sighed Brad. "You've already apologised for that, and I'd forgotten all about it. Why the sudden apology again?"

"Because, you're my dad and I love you."

"Okay, what do you want?"

What did she *want*? The calmness, the normality of just a few short days ago, when Three Beams were poison, and Kenzie just a joke!

"Nothing Dad, I'm just going outside. It's too hot."

Melinda ignored Jack's protests when she accidentally trod on his bed.

The grass weaved around her feet. Melinda seemed out of place in the summer day as she scrambled up the hill. She had to let her scream out, else it would bolt her to a sofa and tear her from the inside. Melinda whimpered when she reached the top. The trees rustled, the birds chirped, and Melinda sobbed. On her knees, hands splayed in front of her, she clawed the grass as the tears rolled down her face and she shivered uncontrollably.

Why *her*? She'd only wanted to go to a concert, just like everyone else! In the midst of her tears, Melinda wondered why girls found Kenzie so attractive; he was horrible! Also, she wondered why she had danced for him, why she hadn't screamed, and why she'd just let him do it. She didn't understand... *why her?*

"Just please, leave me alone," she begged to no one. "Just leave me alone, please."

Or what?

Melinda shook her head. To Kenzie's question, she had no answer. She just heard that instinct, to keep quiet. For a while, she simply sat, calming herself.

Her apologies to her friends and family had been accepted. Her phone was no longer buzzing with messages. Kenzie was just an evil character in a story book. It was fine. *She* was fine.

A tap on her shoulder made her jump.

"Melly! Guess what?"

Melinda stood to see her sister jumping up and down, clapping her free hand on a DVD.

"Mel, Mel, oh my god, look! *Look*. Oh, come on, look, I thought I was gonna burst waiting for you to come home."

Heat gushed into Melinda's cheeks the second Ashley thrust that vile DVD in her face.

"Mel, it's the concert DVD! We've gotta watch it later so we can see ourselves in the crowd—"

"Just *fuck off!*"

Before Melinda could register what she was doing, she'd snatched the DVD from Ashley's hand, leant back, and tossed the object down the hill.

"Don't you get it, Ashley?" she shouted. "I don't give a shit about that stupid band, you annoying little brat!"

Ashley wilted like a sunflower that had lost its sun.

"Ash, I'm so, so sorry, I..."

It was too late. Ashley was racing down the hill, away from her...

"No, Ash, please. Wait!" Melinda could only watch, pleading, as Ashley re-discovered the DVD, which had landed in a bed of weeds. "I—"

With one slam of the back door, Ashley was gone, and Melinda sunk to the grass, shocked at her own behaviour. Weak, she hugged her knees, and waited… but Ashley did not return.

"Great… fucking great!" Melinda cursed. "Well done, Mel."

She retrieved her phone, switched it on, and was greeted by another text from *him:*

Get ready Mellbell, cause I'm gonna fuck your life up.

Filming the next episode was hell for Tom. 'The sounds of the children laughing were like pinpricks.

Kenzie called them to attention, then came closer to Tom.

"Yeah, guys," he said. "I'm still Tom's friend. I know he made a mistake. But, he's my best friend and he… he means a lot to me."

Were the children applauding Kenzie, or Tom's heart as it performed somersaults in the confines of the fictional village? As per the script, to the tune of Callum's guitar, Tom leant forward, and gave Kenzie a hug.

Kenzie clasped him back, and it was in Funville that Tom lost grip on reality, until…

"Right," the director boomed. "And that's a wrap!"

The music was switched off. Lights were toned down; Tom was freed from the arms of his best friend. Applause sounded from the crew, the children darted away for cake and biscuits, and Callum fiddled with his guitar. All around him, conservation began, leaving Tom to mentally insult himself.

Kenzie found Doug, and groaned:

"Doug, what have I said? No more sappy stuff! I can't take it."

Tom showed the crowd his back. He plucked at his own orange costume. He scuffed his foot. The beam, running downwards, easily mirrored the spiral he was on as the Twitter video's words lashed him once again.

"You absolute twat, grow up," he grumbled to himself.

Why had he allowed a script to transform him into such a helpless fool?

Tom told himself no more. He was done, completely, and utterly, *done*. He would make sure that this feeling could never hurt him again. Tom glared at the back of the green screen, then to the camera on the left. Currently, the image on-screen was a blue sky, endless hills and cottages, and a rainbow… it was sickening.

"Hey, Landsby! Filming's over," Kenzie said. "You coming with me bowling?"

Tom didn't hesitate. "Yeah, hang on a second, I'm on my way."

He practically sprinted over the grass, right back toward the man that grinned at him with that wonderful smile—

Tom tripped on a fake bush, and fell.

He got up to the sound of everyone's laughter. The cameraman sneered:

"Still rolling…"

Kenzie slapped him on the shoulder. "You dumb fool, trust you. Glad you found your feet, now come on before it shuts."

"Right, let's have a look at this DVD then."

"But what about Mom?"

Brad put his finger to his lips. Prying the DVD from under the sofa, he grinned a mischievous grin.

"She'll be fine," Brad said. "She's in the kitchen anyway. As long as you're very, very quiet, she won't find out."

From the kitchen, Julie whispered to herself:

"Beautiful."

Brad popped the DVD in.

Ashley grinned. "Yes! I hope I can see myself."

Exquisite smells of practice cakes caught in her nostrils. Yet, sadness filled her stomach where hunger should have been. Was she really an 'annoying little brat'?

Brad sat down beside her. He smiled, folded his arms, and sat back. "Well, here we go."

"Yep, here we go."

"Damn," her father mumbled as the concert began. "Looks like I did miss a lot, ay? Wait, not that I'm condoning what you and Melinda did! It was was very, very naughty."

Ashley let Melinda, and her father's voice trail away. Tom appeared onstage! Kenzie began to sing. Callum strummed his guitar, and then Tom sung. He clocked the camera. He waved. Ashley shot forward in her seat. She was back there. In that room, she was watching the concert as Cassidy and Melinda danced around in the seat like morons—

Ashley grimaced. She decided to pretend that Melinda hadn't been there. Neither had all those others, that the camera was swooping over. It had been just her, and the band. Kenzie had made her laugh. Callum had told her stories, and at the end, Tom had whisked her away straight after his proposal. On a white horse with three beams down its face, they had galloped into the sunset...

"Ash, Ash, *look!*"

Ashley squealed with excitement.

"Ash!" Urgently, Brad grasped her shoulders. "Ash, careful, your mom!"

"Oh, I forgot. Sorry. But look, that's me and Mel."

Chaining herself back to the sofa, Ashley watched the DVD. On edge, her father watched with her. Julie, from the kitchen, hummed.

Brad ruffled Ashley's hair, placed his hands behind his head, and continued enjoying the concert.

Hmm... maybe next time, Ashley would take her father to the concert.

Out of the corner of her eye, Ashley saw that the door was cracked open. She saw the pale fingers curl around the edge, and she knew who it was.

Melinda stilled.

Ashley was no longer watching the TV, but she knew by Brad's sniggers what her sister was seeing. She'd spotted herself. Performing a set of hand-jives with Cassidy, and cackling with laughter, she'd finally seen what a fool she was. Ashley was angry; she'd worked damn hard to get that DVD. She didn't *want* her sister there. She didn't want her spoiling *her* special night with her father.

Brad laughed. Kenzie sung. Tom backed him, while Callum did his somersaults, and far in the present, Ashley glared at her sister.

Melinda's eyes glossed over. Then, she slunk away.

What was she going to *do?*

Melinda had tried everything, but Ashley wasn't speaking to her. Kenzie knew her number; he could be outside the room right now.

Melinda bit Flossie's soft, velvet ear, hard. Facing the wall, she stared at her phone, and her tears became her only solace. Flossie embedded herself between her stomach and her arm, but was no help.

On her phone, numbers couldn't be blocked, not fully. The messages just went into a separate inbox, which Melinda knew she'd just keep checking.

I'm gonna fuck your life up.

Furiously, Melinda began to type the truth she couldn't bear to face, Flossie cheering her on all the way.

You already have.

The sound of the door creaking open pulled the rebel from her rampage; wisely, she abandoned the text.

Melinda panicked at the footsteps, although she knew it was Ashley.

"Ashley?" Melinda called, her phone getting in the way of her hand as she sat up. "Ash?"

Ashley ignored her.

Melinda heard Ashley's bed sheets being pulled back, and the girl getting in without as much as a backward whisper.

Buzz.

Melinda started. No, it wasn't Kenzie, she told herself. It was Jay, updating her on his new go-kart, or it was Dana, bragging about how Drew had taken *her* to Pizza Hut instead of Anna. Either way, it wasn't Kenzie, absolutely no—

Don't you get cheeky, else I'll put you over my knee and spank you till your ass is red-raw. But I know you'd like that really, cause you're sick. Maybe after you're done cumming all over my lap I'll flip you over and ram my cock in your mouth.

Melinda almost vomited on the white sheets. Without meaning to, she'd sent her earlier text.

Buzz. **You've gone quiet.**

Buzz. **Oh, I know why! You're too busy fingering yourself thinking of me, dirty slut.**

Buzz. **By the way, you're taking much too long to reply to my messages. Don't get ignoring me, Mel, cause if you do, I'll come over to your house, and we can pick up where we left off in the dressing room.**

Chapter Twenty-One

"Strike!"

Sounds of laughter, enjoyment, and bowling pins being scattered drifted from the hall, and filled the men's bathroom.

Tom exhaled. His breaths made plumes on the grass; he drew a smile in the mirror. But then he wiped the mirror clean, and returned to picking apart his face. His eyes were still big, and blue. And as for his hair, it was still curly, looking ever the more like the mop Kenzie never used to mop their house floors.

Everything was still in perfect order, so why did he feel so *different*? In the bowling alley, Kenzie yelled that he'd won. How was he so good at everything?

The door swung open from the opposite side.

"Shit!" Tom startled, and jumped back.

A flustered woman entered. "Oh god, sorry, wrong bathroom!"

"Oh, no worries."

The woman gasped. "Wait! You're Tom! Tom Landsby! I've been looking for you everywhere, my daughter—oh, please, can I have your autograph?"

"Yeah," he said, taking the notepad and attached pen from her hand. "How could I say no? You look lovely tonight, by the way."

The uniformed staff member practically melted on the spot. Quickly, Tom scribbled down his star signature, dotting the tail of the 'y' with a heart.

"Oh!" The woman gasped. "Thank you! Thank you so much! I'd best get back, bye!"

Had she even needed the toilet?

"Tom!" someone called when he came out of the toilet.

Roy, clutching a bowling ball, beckoned him over with his head, his quiff of dyed-pink hair magically *not* taking flight. "Come on, dude," he whined. "You're missing all the fun. We've started the next game, it's your go."

Tom took the ball. Trying not to look disappointed, he nodded back at Roy, who was one of the three extra people tonight who'd apparently gone to school with Kenzie, and knew him a lot better than he did.

"Well hurry up!" said Roy.

"Wait, where's Kenzie?" Tom asked.

"Dunno, he walked off somewhere. Why, you scared to be without him?"

Roy and his friends, standing, grinning in unison, looked like skittles. How wonderful it would be to bowl the ball right at them? As Tom took his stance at the edge of alley, his fingers itched.

Along came a sharp wolf-whistle...

Roy laughed. "Ey-up Kenzie, check you out, ay?"

Kenzie?

A pair of tanned fingers flipped Roy off, from the sofa to the left of them, which Tom had completely missed spotting.

A girl had Kenzie's hands locked on her body. Kenzie was kissing her.

From the back of the bowling alley, the game stations echoed: 'You lose'.

While Roy's other friends nudged each other and Tom watched, Kenzie swept another girl into those delicious eyes. His hand stroked down her weave, then pulled her in deeper. Giggling, she slipped her arms around his neck, and allowed his tongue into her mouth.

"Come on, Tom," Roy moaned. "Hurry up before he gets back and whoops my ass again."

Tom shrugged him off. Humiliation hissed in his ear, and so did frustration, endless, endless frustration. Leaning down, the back-up singer pursed his lips, swung the ball back, and sent it sailing. Straight, it continued, down the long, narrow alley, until it reached the centre of the skittles.

Clatter. Clunk. *Strike*.

Every witter of Dana's voice made Melinda wince; following Dana upstairs to her bedroom, she shuddered. Last night, she'd gotten no sleep. Every waking moment, tossing and turning, was spent staring at her phone, waiting for the messages to stop.

They hadn't. He'd kept her up all night.

"So," babbled Dana. "Your parents don't know you shouted at her then?"

"Nah. I stayed in bed this morning till college and avoided her."

Dana stopped by her bedroom door. "Don't blame you. So you really called her an annoying brat?"

"Yeah, I did. I've tried apologising."

Perhaps venting would make her feel better. Perhaps Dana would understand, as she had a younger sister too, who was currently at after-school Math Club.

"I've literally said sorry over and over. I got her a chocolate bar. I made her bed for her. I've tried everything, but she won't speak to me. And look what she left on my bed this morning."

Reaching into her pocket, Melinda pulled out the crumpled drawing of herself burning in a witches' pot.

Dana burst out laughing. "Oh Mel, bless her, she's got you just right."

"Dana," Melinda hissed. "You're meant to be on my side. Best friends stick together, remember, you're supposed to..."

Above Dana's bed, on an A3 poster, Kenzie Hudgson's lips seemed to move:

"Oh, the things I'm going to do to you."

"Yeah, yeah, I know I'm meant to be rooting for you, but still," Dana said. "You called her a little brat while she was all excited about the DVD she'd gotten. She snuck out of school to get it for god's sake, she's a badass!"

Plonking herself onto her bed, which was cluttered with one of her morning rushes, Dana caught Melinda's wide eyes.

"Oh come on, why are you even surprised?" she said.

"Cause Dana, I told you what a dick he was. He didn't even speak to my sister on that stupid tour."

Dana mimicked her. "I told you what a dick he was. He smells, he's ugly, I don't like him, meh."

Melinda inhaled, and told herself: calm down, just calm—

"Oh, come on, babe." Pathetically, Dana began to sing: "I know you want him, you know he wants ya—"

"No way." Melinda sat down, her back to the menace on the wall.

Tutting, Dana tugged her laptop next to her. "All right, fine, I'm sorry. Here, take some pics with me, will you?"

"Oh, okay."

"Awesome." Dana tossed her hair, and pulled the laptop onto her knees. "I'm dying for some new Insta pictures. I hardly see you nowadays. You're always with that weirdo Jay."

As Dana held the laptop steady, Melinda smiled her signature smile, showing her teeth because according to Aunt Flo, she had lovely teeth. The entire time, Kenzie's eyes bored into her back, and with a click, the camera captured them: two best friends, one locked in oblivion, one locked in a never-ending nightmare.

"Oh wow," Dana approved. "You look great, babe."

Just then, Melinda's phone buzzed.

Oh no... she'd thought he'd finished! With dread, Melinda silently enticed her phone from her pocket.

"Want me to send you it?"

"No," snapped Melinda. "You shouldn't even be on Instagram. You should be doing your assignment. This is your second extension."

Tap, tap, tap.. away Melinda went, texting Kenzie back:

Aren't you tired? You were up all night.

His reply back was instant:

Nah, I have insomnia anyway. And you were up with me! Well done, Hun. Ffs I'm so BORED. What are you doing with yourself, hmm?

"Do you think this lipstick looks okay on me?"

Bored? Kenzie was harassing her because he was *bored?*

"Yeah, Dana." Melinda typed away.

"You're not even looking!"

Melinda flinched. Sneakily, she pressed send, and the text saying she was with a friend vanished just like she wished Dana would.

"Hey," said Dana. "You're so moody lately. Are you okay?"

Buzz.

Melinda tensed. "*Yes,* I'm fine."

"You can tell me, you know. What's up?"

"Are you deaf? I said I'm fine, I'm just tired."

I'm waiting for Tom to get back from the pisser so we can carry on filming for the show. What's your friends' name?

Dana shoved her. "Oi, why're you talking to me like that for?"

Quickly, Melinda texted back a random name. "Cause you're annoying me."

"What's so interesting about that stupid phone, ay? You got a boyfriend?"

"No."

Buzz.

"Here, let me see!"

No, it's not. It's Dana.

The text (or Dana's grabbing hand, she wasn't sure which one) made Melinda jump back.

"No! Don't touch my phone!"

Luckily, her phone remained in her hand, but it buzzed again, and Melinda cowered. Oh, she couldn't look she couldn't look—

"Mel!" Dana shouted. "What the hell? You nearly knocked my laptop!"

If you're gonna lie to me, at least make it convincing. She follows me on Insta. Check her profile.

Before Melinda could register what she was doing, her phone was in her pocket, and she'd scurried back to where Dana was sitting. Baffled, Dana cried out as Melinda pried the laptop from her hands.

"Oi," Dana hissed. "Give that back right now, you little cow!"

Oh, how *dare* she! How dare Dana follow that manipulative maniac? Despite Dana's protests, Melinda scoured her Instagram, and spotted a photo Dana had posted just seconds ago.

Hands lingering on Melinda's shoulders, Dana's nails dug in as she realised she'd been caught out. Melinda didn't notice the pain. She was in the photo; it was the one they'd just taken. Dana had posted it right under her nose, and Kenzie was tagged in the caption, which read:

'Hey gorgeous, look who I'm with! Remember her?'

Kenzie hadn't replied yet. But Melinda did, right into Dana's stunned face. "Dana! What the *fuck?*"

"Oh my god Mel, it's only a photo," she scoffed.

Slamming the laptop in front of Dana's lap, Melinda readied herself for attack. She was going to rip her hair from the roots, tear her false nails from her fingers—

"Only a *photo*?"

"*Yes,*" Dana retorted. "A photo, of *us*. Why are you freaking out about it? It's not like he can see you naked or anything."

Melinda stood up so abruptly she almost lost her footing. "I don't care! How could you do that, Dana? I've told you and told you that I don't like him. I didn't like him before, I didn't like him on the tour, and I *certainly* don't like him now!"

"What the hell is your problem?" Dana shouted back, rising to meet her rage-for-rage. "All day you've been a miserable shit, and now you're telling me that I'm not allowed to post stuff on my own Insta account?"

Melinda had crossed Dana, which was the sin she'd always feared of doing. But as Dana prepared to burn her alive with her catty tongue, Melinda realised she was too annoyed to care.

"It's not you posting pictures of us that's the problem, and you know it, so stop acting dumb!" she shouted.

"No, *you* stop acting like it's your business who I tag in shit and who I talk to, because it isn't."

"It is when you involve me!"

"You're being such a baby about this it's unreal."

Melinda scoffed. She paced the room, one to help calm her anger, and to try and think what to say next.

Dana continued. "I took that picture because I was happy to be with you! We never hang out just us two. You always have to bring that weirdo Jay with you."

"Oh, speaking of Jay, I don't like the way you treat him. There's a difference being joking around and being a bully, you know. Now, back to this photo. My reason for being so angry is cause you fucking tagged Kenzie in it, you idiot, and said 'Ooh remember this girl?' And I've told you and told you, I just want to forget I ever went to that stupid concert but *no,* you don't seem to understand that, do you, you thick, airheaded Barbie-wannabe?"

Suddenly looking upset, Dana opened her mouth to interrupt, but Melinda cut her off, too angry to even stop for breath. Looking directly into her eyes, she sneered:

"Look at the state of you, fawning after some pompous prick. Did you know you're trying to contact someone who's a complete wanker, and will kill you inside if you allow him? Then again, you probably wouldn't care, because as long as you've got your lips round somebody's cock you're not bothered."

Wait…what?

Melinda covered her mouth, as if she could stop the words from coming out.

Dana backed away from her. "Mel… M-Mel, how could you?"

Thank goodness Dana's parents weren't home, because her sudden weeping was enough to burst down the walls.

Why couldn't Melinda just apologise? As Dana cried, she scrabbled for the remorse that would not come. Kenzie leered at her from the bedroom wall, and laughed. She could see him, hear him, *feel* him next to her…

"You can delete that picture, *and* all the ones of us two," Melinda said. "Because I'm done with your bullshit, Dana."

A door slammed in Melinda's mind. Dana was gone from her life now; she knew that. But then again, maybe it was a good thing. Blinking, she stood straight, and stared, stonily, at the door. She'd revealed too much to her about what was going on, in a way. Losing their friendship was a daunting sacrifice, yet she had to make it. Because if she didn't…

Dana snivelled pitifully. "Y-You never tell me anything, you never l-listen to me, you never— "

Melinda patronised her. "Oh dear, should I go?"

"Yes!" Bashing her fists on the bed sheets, Dana pointed to the door. "Get out, you little sket! Don't ever fucking talk to me again. *Get out.*"

"Fuck you."

Melinda left without looking back.

Chapter Twenty-Two

Callum's pride and joy was scattered all around the living room. On the carpet, in a circle of mockery, the other two band members sat around him, reading out his newest songs:

"Are you kidding me?" Kenzie said, one eyebrow raised. "You're casting me aside, pushing me out. Although I don't know why, I have no doubt? The fuck is this shit, man?"

"I-It's for episode ten—"

"No, it's for the bin, that's what it is."

"Look, I can re-word it," Callum protested. "If you just give it back to me, I can make it so it's a bit less—"

Kenzie crumpled the paper and tossed it. Although he bit his cheeks, Callum couldn't cover his hurt as Kenzie picked up the next song, and readied himself for the ultimate blow.

"Here," Kenzie ordered, slapping the next song on Tom's chest. "Read this one for me."

Tom began reading the words from the song:

"Day and night, when I lie awake, I wonder if my feelings will ever win the fight…"

Me and Dana aren't friends anymore. We had an argument today.

"Sorry Cal, but this one's a no-no," said Tom. "Do you not see how similar it is to Our Love?"

Melinda was getting better and better at replying to his texts. Kenzie quickly texted her back with an 'Aw, why?'. Then, he grabbed the song from Tom's hands.

"It's more than similar," he scoffed. "It's pretty much the exact same thing. Do us a favour, Callum." Kenzie bunched up the paper. "If you're gonna write songs, at least put some damn effort in."

Thwack! The paper bounced off Callum's head, and Kenzie was straight back to his phone, not pausing to take in Tom's laughter as he read Melinda's reply:

I don't know. But I needed it, really. Our friendship… wasn't the best.

Huffing, Callum grumbled a humiliated 'fuck this' on his way out of the living room, yet Kenzie wasn't sorry, and Tom didn't stop laughing.

"Oh man," the back-up singer wheezed. "D-Did you hear that? Oh." Puffing out his cheeks, he imitated the grumble so accurately, even Kenzie snickered. "Fuck this, man."

"Oh, I'm such a sap," Kenzie added. As he texted Melinda back to say 'Oh, poor baby, he knew how she felt, so why didn't she spread her juicy thighs for him and he'd make it all better?', He sent Tom into further sniggers:

"Read my songs Kenzie, 'cause I can't do fuck-all without your approval."

"Who you texting, anyway?" Tom glanced over Kenzie's shoulder.

Closing the chat quickly, Kenzie pulled up Twitter instead, in the nick of time. Kenzie should have been worried, but as Tom gawped at the photo of Dana Kingsley instead, Kenzie was just amused as hell about the near calamity.

"So, what d'you think? She sent me this selfie earlier today. What d'you reckon, Landsby? Shall I message her back, or not?"

"Yeah, sure," Tom replied. "S-She's pretty hot."

"All right, looks like she gets a message back then."

"I-I'm glad all that Tomzie shit's gone though, it was so dumb."

Raking a hand through his hair, Tom earned a raised eyebrow from Kenzie. Upstairs, Callum could be heard thumping around as Kenzie felt his phone vibrate. It was Melinda. Kenzie resolved to keep the stupid cow up all night again. He smirked at Tom, and began to mock the rubbish that had previously made his skin crawl:

"As if we could be doing all that though. Oh, Tom, come keep my cock warm for me, it's getting cold."

Tom blushed fire, fire red, although Kenzie was so busy texting he didn't notice:

Ready to stay awake again tonight?

Ugh, he could practically hear her stupid whingy voice as he read her reply.

Sorry Kenzie, I can't. I need my sleep. I've gotta get up early tomorrow.

Who did she think she was?

Oh but Mellbell, I know you wanna stay up all night with me. Come on… please? If you don't, I'll have to come over and wake you up.

Knocking Jay's door frantically, Melinda prayed he'd answer. She had some news for him.

"Mel," Jay opened the door. "You didn't say you were coming? I thought you were with Dana today?"

"I was, but we're not friends anymore. I told her to get lost."

Melinda *adored* the look of complete horror on Jay's face. She'd crossed Dana. Oh god, oh *no,* whatever was going to happen to her now, Jay's expression said. Truthfully, Melinda actually was slightly worried, but in comparison to knowing she, again, was going to have to stay up all night, it was nothing.

"I can't believe it, Mel. What happened?"

"She posted a picture of me and her, then tagged Kenzie. And when I told her to delete Kenzie's tag, she just flew off the handle, Jay. You should've seen her! I knew she could be a nasty piece of work, but wow, even I was shocked when she screamed at me. In all fairness I'd had enough of her a while ago, but this was the icing on the cake. I told her to fuck off and to never speak to me again."

"Wow…"

"I never liked the way she treated you, either. Don't hang out with her, Jay," Melinda pleaded maliciously, loving how he was just drinking in her lies. "She pushed you down a hill, remember, and she hits you all the time and calls you names. She's horrible."

"Oh no, I only hung out with her cause you did! I'll never talk to her again, Mel, I promise! Wanna come in? My go-kart's looking ace!"

On the way through Jay's kitchen, Melinda spotted a full litre of Bacardi sat on the counter.

"Oh," she said. "Who's is that? You don't drink."

"It's my mom's. She's had a bad day at work, so she bought that to calm down, but I told her to go for a nap instead. She's meant to be cutting down. I hate the taste of it, it's like gasoline! I hate the taste of all alcohol."

Melinda wasn't a massive fan herself, although she did like the odd bottle of fruit cider with her father. She got drunk once at Christmas, but absolutely *despised* the next day's hangover, so she didn't bother drinking heavily again. But there was something tempting about the Bacardi bottle. It seemed to glow at her as the sun came through the window. She was so riled up... surely one drink wouldn't hurt?

"Can I have some?" she asked Jay.

"Oh! Erm, yeah, help yourself! I was gonna tip it down the sink anyway."

"Oh my god Jay, what a *waste!* Come on, let's go out and get some coke and find somewhere to chill."

"Are you sure, Mel? You don't normally drink, and if you do, you tend to just get a couple cans of—"

"It'll be fine! Quick Jay, before your mom wakes up. I've just texted my mom, and said I'm out and I'll be back later."

She just *had* to forget about Kenzie. Please, just once! She was only going to have one, or two drinks, just to settle her nerves. She just couldn't take having to keep secrets, and lie to everyone around her. She'd lost track of how many people she'd upset; for once, she just wanted to enjoy herself.

It passed in a blur, the next couple of hours. Melinda had lost count of how many drinks she'd had after eight. All she knew was that the canal suddenly seemed a bit blurry, she was unsteady on her feet, and best of all, she was the most relaxed she'd been since she'd first gotten those concert tickets. In fact, she was having fun!

"I love drunk Mel!" Jay shouted with joy, as Melinda pushed him along the canal.

They'd found an abandoned trolley in the canal, and Melinda had pulled it out, filth, algae, and all. Bored of being in the park, and conscious it was starting to get dark, the pair had now decided to head for the street; the underground bit of Tesco car park was the best place for go-kart racing.

Unfortunately, their fun didn't last long. They were soon thrown out of Tesco car park after Melinda zoomed down a hilly bit in the trolley, and almost caused an oncoming car to crash. Briefly, Melinda had remembered Jay pulling her away when the worker had threatened to call the police; the trolley got left behind.

"I could have handled them, you know," Melinda slurred.

"Erm, I think you should stop drinking now, Mel. You've already had three quarters of this bottle, we have no coke left, it's dark and you're being really loud."

So what? So what if she'd been singing 'fuck you, I won't do what you tell me' at the top of her voice at ten p.m.? So what if she'd torn down a couple of Three Beams posters, or scribbled 'Kenzie Hudgson is a cunt' on a wall? She was having *fun*, and Jay was ruining it!

"Jay," she moaned. "Jay, Jay, Jay… lighten up, will you! Oh look, a billboard! Come *on,* Kenzie's on it. Let's rip it down!"

Melinda ran, so drunk her legs were like jelly. All she could see was the blurry, blurry billboard, and his smug face on it.

"No, Mel! It's too high up. You'll fall! You can't, you'll be arrested. *Mel!*"

Jay was right. It *was* too high up.

"Fuck this," screeched Melinda. "Come on. Put your music back on."

"Mel, please. We need to start heading back. You've gotta get home! Your family have been trying to ring ya, and you've just been ignoring them."

"But—"

"Mel, *please.* Look at you. You're *drunk.*"

Once again, Jay was right. Melinda could hardly walk at all now. Her fury had drained; a feeling of helplessness replaced it. Drunk, swaying, and vulnerable, Melinda allowed Jay to lead her in the direction of home, on the condition he'd put her favourite song back on. She sang along to it all the way. This night was *not* going to end.

"Mel, shush, we're going past Dana's."

"I don't care about Dana." Melinda took the bottle from Jay. "She can stay up all night just like I have to!"

Jay had the *nerve* to try and snatch the remaining Bacardi away from her. "No, you *can't* drink it from the bottle. Give it here! No, don't—"

The Bacardi *burned* her throat. However, it soon went from burning, to going all down her t-shirt, because Jay had taken it from her… and he was *pouring it on the floor.*

"Jay!"

"That's enough, Mel!" he bellowed. "Look at the state of you! I knew this was a bad idea!"

Sad… Melinda was suddenly so, so *sad*. She started crying. She couldn't stop. Jay hugged her, apologising, promising to take her home safe, and she couldn't stop crying, because…

"I'm sorry Jay. I'm sorry, I'm sorry, I'm really sorry!"

She just wanted someone to love her, and hold her, and…

"It's okay," Jay whispered soothingly. "It's fine, I've thrown the bottle in the wheely bin over there, and we're gonna go home now, yeah? People are turning their lights on though, and looking out the window, so we need to go now, okay? I'm gonna walk with you. Lean on me if you have to."

Leaning into him, Melinda sobbed for the rest of the walk home. Twice, she fell over. How did Jay find the strength to pull her back up? He was so tiny…

Jay knocked on the door of her house. Melinda stopped crying. The door opened, and there was her mother:

"And what time d'you call this? We've been worried sick!"

Her voice was echoing in Melinda's head; lost in the darkness was Jay's reply of:

"We lost track of time, Miss Stevens. I really am sorry. She's not well."

"No, she's been drinking. I can fucking smell her from here. I can't believe it. Brad, come here, *now*. Where's Ashley? I don't want her seeing her sister like this."

Head down, Melinda was groaning softly. Her father came out; Melinda couldn't see his expression. She couldn't see *anyone's* expressions. She could just hear their voices, echoing and echoing.

"Right, you, inside!" Julie snapped at her. "Brad, take her upstairs to bed. Ashley, you stay in the living room, and *you,* boy, get the hell off my doorstep."

Slam! Poor Jay was left outside on his own…

When she got there, Melinda pretty much fell into her bed. She heard her father plonk a bottle of water on her chest of draws. The oblivion of sleep washed over her, and she didn't wake up again until three a.m.

Ashley reached for the glass of water on her bedside table, her half-open eyes scanning the bedroom, and only just catching Melinda sitting up in bed being blinded by her phone's light—

Ashley choked on the water. Yes, that was Melinda, her mean, horrible sister, on her phone at three in the morning, frowning at the screen and tugging her bottom lip.

"Mel?"

Melinda jumped. "Oh, Ash!"

The DVD case that had gotten covered in grass stains no longer mattered. Gulping, Ashley whispered:

"Are you okay?"

Her sister's phone buzzed.

"Yeah," Melinda replied shakily, wiping her cheek.

"Are you crying?"

"No!"

"Were you really drunk earlier? I heard Mom shouting."

Melinda nodded. "I don't know why I did it, Ash. It was only meant to be a laugh with Jay, but now my head's *banging.*"

"But you don't drink."

"That's what I thought."

Her phone buzzed again.

"What are you doing on your phone, Mel? Are you revising?"

Ashley had noticed the open Science textbook over Melinda's blanket-covered legs. She knew her sister was struggling with her work. The lessons had gotten more difficult, or the assignments more complex. Whatever the problem, Melinda was pulling an all-nighter in pure desperation. But everyone needed their sleep... surely Melinda was tired?

Ashley glanced at her. Then, she smiled warmly. "You'll pass, Mel. You're smart."

"Thanks."

"Oh, I'm sorry, by the way."

"Why are you saying sorry for?"

"Cause I've been all moody with you. I've forgiven you for throwing my DVD now. I'm sorry it took me so long."

Nothing was wrong, Ashley told herself. Melinda wasn't hurting as she looked back at Ashley, returned the smile, said her thanks, and then went back to her phone, her fingers shaking as she pressed the buttons. Ashley traced her finger over the nearest Three Beams poster. Admiration filled her as Tom grinned back at her, loving the attention she gave to his curls.

Taking another drink from her glass of water, Ashley buried herself back under the bed sheets.

Another buzz. Another snivel, and a younger sister telling herself that everything was *fine*.

Chapter Twenty-Three

Melinda was no stranger to foreboding as she walked, fearfully, down the college corridor. She'd left class early; the tutor had believed her forged note. It was so quiet at the college, that if *he* was hiding there, she would surely hear him, and he would hear her.

Blowing a deep breath out, Melinda told herself: stay sane, and carry-on walking. It was fine. She'd managed to save the day last night, by texting him as soon as she'd woken up. He'd been angry, but she managed to talk him out of coming round. But she was so tired now, *and* hungover.

What had she been thinking last night?

Melinda forced herself to put it behind her. Jay was still talking to her. He was such a good friend, he'd told her he was going to pretend it never happened. He even laughed about it. Melinda tried to switch off by remembering her plan for the day, which was to make it up to Ashley, and avoid Dana if possible.

So far, part one of her plan was going well, although breakfast had been awkward. Her parents had given her an earful, which was the last thing she'd needed after being kept awake all night by a terrifying pop star.

Clack, clack. A set of giggles…

Dana was coming down corridor with Em and Rach in tow, engrossed in the video she was showing them.

"Oh god, Dana," shrieked Em. "Look at her! What a wreck."

Melinda turned back on herself, and hurried away. She had a stomach-ache, even though she had her loosest, comfiest pink rose-print leggings on. Into the haunting familiarity of the toilets, she made for the nearest cubicle, shut the door, hung her bag on the peg, and sat down on the toilet lid. She told herself:

There was no Kenzie. She'd never gone to the concert; he'd never gotten her number.

The door opened.

Along with the giggles, heels (Dana's favourite blue ones) stalked along the tiles, and paused outside Melinda's door. Clamping her hands over her mouth, Melinda hoisted her feet up onto the seat. Never did Dana actually *use* the college toilets. She'd surely be gone in a bit...

"Honestly Rach," Dana scoffed. "I don't know why I even bothered hanging around with her, or that creep Jay."

Rach snickered. "She's such a tag-along. She never actually does, or says, anything."

"Try having a conversation with her," Dana replied. "It's like talking to a brick wall."

"Is she a lesbian? She like... never talks to boys."

"I don't know. Sometimes, I wonder. She was always staring at my body when we were at the lake, and she hasn't shagged anyone, either."

Melinda trembled; she was going to cry.

"Why does she wear such oversized shirts?" added Em. "She looks like a charity case."

"Because she thinks her thighs are fat," Dana sneered.

What? Dana had promised never, ever to tell anyone that!

"And to be honest," she continued. "They are, really. No, no seriously! I've lost track of the amount of times she's asked me how to get a thigh gap. It's ridiculous, everyone knows thigh gaps are all about bone structure."

"And not constantly scoffing cake every five seconds," added Em.

Making a noise of disgust, Dana rummaged in her handbag. "Ugh, if I see her today I'm slapping her, the little bitch. Come on girls, lets watch this video again, it's brilliant!"

Through the tears that were now seeping down Melinda's face, she realised: the video was of her. It was when she was drunk, outside Dana's house. Dana had saw her, and she'd filmed it, most likely through her bedroom window.

"I know you're in there, you little alcy!" snarled Dana, banging the toilet door. "Now listen. Me, Rach, and Em are the only ones who have seen this video, and that's how it's gonna stay. But, if you do, or say, even the *slightest* thing to piss me off at all, then I *will* make this video go viral, understand?"

"Yeah…"

"Good. Now come on girls, let's get to lesson."

Melinda didn't realise her torture was over for quite some time. However, when she did, Dana and her friends had long since left the toilets. For a few minutes, she simply sobbed freely, feeling empty, until she remembered her plans with Ashley. Standing up, Melinda collected her bag and left the cubicle, her head held high.

"Oh, shut up Bryony, you're just jealous cause Tom wants to marry me and not you."

"That's rubbish," hissed Bryony. "Tom would never marry you, or your sister."

The clock said it was one minute until lunch. All throughout the dreaded weekly mental maths test, Bryony had been poking Ashley with her ruler, whispering snide remarks, *breathing…* anything to drive her nuts, and it was working. Even though she couldn't see her, Ashley knew she was smirking as she made her next dig:

"He probably doesn't even remember your name."

"I've told you a thousand times, stupid, I've met them. And he proposed to me with a ring and everything, so I'm pretty sure he'd remember—"

Slam!

Mrs Green made every child jump. Her hand still on the desk, she rose from her seat at the front of the classroom. "Bryony, stop bothering Ashley and get on with the test. And if I hear one more word about that wretched Three Beams, I'll keep the entire class back for lunch."

Ashley surveyed her posse of friends, and grinned. Now she had to make a tough decision about who to sit with at lunch.

"Right," Mrs Green said. "Now that our little… *issue* has been resolved, I hope you all have a good lunch. Leave your papers here and I'll collect them on my way out."

Bryony and her two friends were the first out, humming Three Beams songs.

Ashley snickered at them. They weren't even humming in tune.

Ashley's gang of nine were about to squeal over Tom's hair, sigh over Kenzie's eyes, and recite Callum's songs, but sadly, Mrs Green's voice pulled Ashley from that opportunity:

"Ashley, you wait there. There's someone here for you."

Ashley's heart began to thud. Oh no. Was it the headteacher? Did they know about—Ashley exchanged worried glances with Lucia and Hamrit—the DVD? Her friends each told her in their own words that they would meet her after, to tell them what had happened, and good luck.

"Go on, girls," Mrs Green said. "Out."

Uncertain, Ashley stared at Mrs Green, while the last of her friends, Lucia, bit her lip and left.

Oddly, Mrs Green was kind. "Don't look so worried, child. She's outside the classroom right now."

She?

Ashley walked out of the room. It was Melinda and Jack!

"Hey, Ash," she said timidly. "I've got—"

Jack threw himself toward Ashley, up on his hind legs as he panted and barked. Kneeling down to the Jack Russell Terrier, the girl rubbed his ears as he pulled on the lead.

"Mel, what are you doing here?"

"I'm taking you out for a picnic," Melinda replied.

No school dinners? No listening to the dinner ladies whine? As Jack licked her hands, Ashley agreed more than eagerly.

"Wait," Melinda said as she ate the strawberry cupcake. "She told *Bryony* to be quiet instead?"

"Yeah," bragged Ashley. "She got the blame even though I was the one that shouted at her."

In the park, the breeze blew the picnic blanket up and down. A squirrel scurried past them. Jack was chasing it. In the centre of the park's field, Ashley sat in front of Melinda, nibbling on the last of a tuna salad sandwich, while Melinda glanced up. The sky was so blue… not a single cloud obscured her world as she sat, happily, with her sister.

"You're a bad, bad girl, Ashley. Still, so am I. I really am sorry, you know, about the DVD, I'm not just saying it 'cause you did—"

"Mel, I've said its fine."

Jack darted along the blanket, sending the plates flying.

"Jack! You little shit!"

Who was Kenzie again?

Of course, Melinda hadn't *really* forgotten. Yet, it was so lovely at the park. After scrambling to their feet, the sisters chased after Jack, laughing and calling. Ignoring their orders, Jack soared past the duck pond, and ducked and weaved as the squirrel led him on the adventure of his life.

Ashley shouted:

"Jack!"

The night of the concert was left, stranded, all alone in the past. Swans cawed above her. Majestic and beautiful, they were flying...

Fuck Kenzie.

With Jack in her arms, Ashley came out of the wood, smiling, with twigs in her hair.

"Oh, you little rascal, you," Melinda cooed at him. "Thought you could go pestering a harmless squirrel, did you?"

She didn't know when, she didn't know how, and she didn't know why, but as Jack wagged his tail and licked her nose, Melinda knew she was *done*. Kenzie had taken far, far too much from her.

"Crap," Ashley said. "I think we left our bags."

Melinda didn't actually care; however, she took Ashley back to the picnic spot anyway, just in case someone in the deserted park really *had* stolen their bags. They hadn't. The picnic blanket was half-folded, the plates scattered thanks to Jack. But, their bags were safe, aside from the pecking of a few pigeons.

Melinda clapped her hands. "Be gone, little scavengers!"

Firmly, Ashley clasped Jack to the lead. "Is it time to go?"

Melinda drooped. "Yeah. Here babe, gimme a hand with this stuff, will you? And before you ask, no, Mom won't notice the cupcakes. They were her first batch. She'd shoved them in a box in the fridge. According to her, she'd gotten them all wrong, even though I *told* her Summer Fete kids don't care if their cake is a *tiny* bit lopsided."

"Her brain's lopsided."

"I've probably inherited it. Maybe that's why I'm such a meanie sometimes."

Within minutes, the picnic was packed away. Melinda bit her bottom lip. She'd better check her phone, just in case her mother *had* cottoned on. Getting her phone out, she knew with a heavy heart what was waiting for her, and she was right. On her phone was a message from an unknown number. She'd refused to save it as his.

While Ashley fussed Jack, Melinda fought off the fear that invaded her sanctum. She was still plagued with dread, however, her reaction this time was different. Instead of opening the text, she left it unread. Instead of sending her mind to war, she allowed it to rest, because she deleted the entire chat.

"Drat!" Tom hissed.

Standing up, he shook his curls free of the red paint, and called out:

"I'm going to get you for that one, Kenzie!"

In the game of Paint Wars, there were only a few rules: keep to the classroom provided, stay in view of the cameras, and absolutely no swearing. Other than that, Three Beams were allowed to roam free with the paint guns. Pumped by lack of sleep, the boys were taking full advantage.

Kenzie jeered:

"Well come on then, I'm waiting!"

Callum smirked. Crouched behind the teacher's desk, he was happy, because for once, the script had gone his way. Tom and Kenzie were forbidden to shoot him. At the end of the battle, when both had gone down, Callum was to jump out, and blast them all silly. It was just up to those two *idiots* who went down first.

Tom was acting very, very oddly. Usually, the sheer *thought* of injuring his beloved, treasured master reduced the back-up singer to whimpers. Yet now, the boy was more than eager to do so. Behind the goggles they had been forced to wear, Callum watched the two boys fight.

Tom popped his head out from the desk he was hiding behind.

Callum winced. No, no, *bad* move! Tom crawled toward Kenzie's overturned shelter.

Kenzie pointed his gun at Tom, and unleashed a squirt of paint.

"Oh, bother!" Tom squeaked.

"Got ya!"

Callum could sense Tom was thinking 'the mess, oh, the mess!' as he stood. His hair was dripping red, and worst of all, he'd dropped his gun.

Suddenly Kenzie's desk was sent crashing to the floor by his huge red trainer. Victory smouldered behind a set of goggles, and a gun with red paint was thrust at Tom. Tom cowered. Kenzie smirked, facing him head-on, while Tom stepped back, his free hand out, his voice frightened:

"No, Kenzie, no…"

The only thing Tom was treated to was a laugh:

"You've got five seconds to run."

The crew grinned. Doug clasped his hands, and Tom was sent running.

He slid under un-flipped desks. He ducked behind over-turned tables. He begged Kenzie not to shoot, but it was pointless. Kenzie shot anyway, and he shot *everywhere.* The crew held in their laughter as the red splattered onto the floor. Kenzie was missing Tom deliberately. He was winding him up. He even *gambolled* on the way!

Tom slammed himself to the floor, avoiding another jet of paint. He rolled onto his back. He found his gun, and pointed it up.

Callum dared himself to hope. They were on Tom's side of the classroom; there was nowhere else for the boy to go. So, as Kenzie advanced, he had to resort to fight, or flight.

Tom squirted Kenzie directly in the face.

Damn. Callum bit back his snicker.

The music was brought to a higher, more intense note. The crew were calling an end to the battle.

Kenzie, wiping his face, was lifting his gun back up. Tom tried his gun. It was jammed! On his back, legs flailing, he scurried back, back, back toward Callum's desk, while Callum forced himself not to shoot.

Tom's head slammed against the desk. He looked up. Kenzie looked down. Tom gulped. And then, Kenzie raised his eyebrow, and sneered:

"Game over, Tom."

He fired blast after blast of red paint until Tom was plastered head to toe.

Doug hopped excitedly. Tom swivelled away, his back dripping with paint as he presented it to the audience and his red, red face to Callum.

As per the script, Kenzie turned around to meet Callum..
Callum said his line:
"Fighting never solves anything, Kenzie."
Sadly, as Callum covered Kenzie in yellow paint, he wasn't even the slightest bit joyful to hear the crew switch the cameras off, and clap *him* for a change. In fact, there were no good feelings at all, because out of sight of Kenzie and the crew, Tom was crying.

Colourless cheeks, ridiculous curls, and a body so skinny he could fall through every crack in the ground? Tom was disgusted with himself. Grumbling, he picked the last flecks of paint from his hair, and fondly imagined himself being crushed under the tour bus.

He hated being so skinny, he hated being so weak, but most of all, he hated having feelings.

When he caught a glimpse of Kenzie in the dressing room mirror behind him, his misery only increased.

"Hey, Landsby."

"Hey."

In the reflection, Tom saw Kenzie look up from his stupid phone that had, oddly, been silent all day.

"Sorry," said Kenzie. "Didn't mean to get it in your eyes."

Tom picked at his hair. "It's okay."

It *was* okay. Tom had gotten 'got the point.

Kenzie had brought a girl back to the Birmingham House last night, and they did *not* 'fuck quietly' like Kenzie had promised they would.

Kenzie mumbled:

"Fucking bitch."

Don't look at him. Don't even say anything.

"What bitch?" Tom blurted. "Who's a bitch?"

"Oh, the one from last night," Kenzie replied. "You've missed a bit of paint by the way, right there. Ugh, remind me never to screw *her* again."

Tom turned around so quickly he almost crashed into the strong body behind him. "Huh?"

"Well, she had no clue what she was doing. She just lay there, man. It was like fucking a wooden board. I got her to leave straight after, but—"

Straight after? At the moment where Tom had shoved the pillow over his head and screamed? Grinning, Tom completed his best friend's sentence for him:

"And now she won't stop texting you? Aw, Ken. Try and be nice."

"I'm trying, but it's so hard. Anyway, I'm out of here. The traffic gets terrible at seven."

Tom relaxed. Relieved, he said a brief goodbye to his lead singer as he scurried from the room, glaring at his phone. Disregarding his far away cursing, Tom glowered at his reflection. It was official:

He hated himself.

Chapter Twenty-Four

Every table in the cafe was packed with laughing students and chattering tutors. Melinda bit the inside of her cheeks, hard, and looked for Jay in the crowd.

A body brushed against hers!

The gangly boy in front of her flinched at Melinda's shriek.

"Aw man, sorry! It was an accident mate."

"It's fine, don't worry."

Embarrassed, Melinda searched for the sniggers she knew were about her, and what she was faced with was Dana.

Dana was sitting at the table directly in front of where she was standing, surrounded by her clones, and practically in Drew's lap. She spotted Melinda staring, and glared a glare that cut right through her bones. She hissed something in Drew's ear, then to the rest of them, and suddenly, they were all laughing at her.

Melinda clutched her bag.

"This is your fault, you know."

Out of the café, down the corridor, Melinda hurried, not knowing, not caring about where she was going. Wait, what was she *doing*? What if someone saw her, running down the corridor like there was a fire? Gasping, she placed her hands on her forehead, breathed, and told herself to calm down.

Yes, ignoring Kenzie was scary, but she *could* do it.

To distract herself, she looked in a classroom window.

Twenty-odd students were watching another present a PowerPoint… about breeds of rabbit.

Melinda clasped her hands as she looked in. The course was Animal Care!

"Mel!"

"Oh, hi Jade!"

Jade frowned, her fingers drumming on her assignment. "What are you doing hanging around here? We've got, like, a three-hour break, and you don't even do Animal Care."

"Can I clean the rabbits out again tomorrow, Jade? I-I mean, if you're free, that is."

"Oh yeah, *that* was what I needed to ask you! My parents are out again tomorrow, so I kind of need you to. I'll pay you this time, though. Come round at nine, and by the way, that scrawny lad you hang out with is by the engineering cars."

"Oh, thank you," Melinda smiled.

It wasn't difficult to find Jay. God knows why she tried the cafeteria first, because he nearly always spent his lunchtime in his Foundation Engineering class, ogling the latest car the class had been working on. But, on this occasion, things were slightly different.

In the stench of the garage, Melinda hid her giggles. Jay was crouched behind the car, anxiously peering around the corner. It had taken a while for her to spot it, but Jay was hiding from Sophie.

The blonde was chatting to his tutor, and taking an enrolment booklet from her. Melinda could only see the back of Jay, yet she could tell by his never-ending gaze…

Melinda crept over, knelt down behind him, and cooed, teasingly, in his ear:

"What's up?"

"Ah!" Jay's fingers slipped off of the open hood of the car. On his bottom, he landed with a huff, his foot sending a spanner clattering. "Mel! You scared me."

"I'm not surprised. You looked quite… entranced."

"Entranced? With what? And what does entrance mean?"

"Changing the subject, are we?"

"No. Well… Mel, seriously, who's that?"

"That," Melinda said smugly, as she nodded toward the sweet, quiet blonde, "Is Sophie."

Sophie held the booklet, and smiled timidly at the tutor.

"Oh." Jay squeezed the hood. *"That's* Sophie, the girl you sit with in Maths? Is she enrolling in this course?"

"No, her brother is. He missed the open day, so she's getting a booklet for him." Melinda narrowed her eyes, picking him apart, because for once, she had the upper hand. "You like her, don't you?"

"No," said Jay defensively.

Standing up, Melinda called:

"Sophie!"

Jay dived behind the car.

Looking away from the tutor (who was now rifling through the tool cabinet), Sophie smiled when she saw Melinda, and came over.

"Hey Mel," Sophie said, slotting the booklet into her handbag. "What are you— "

Bang, clatter.

Jay groaned. To avoid her seeing him crouching, he'd stood up so quickly he'd banged his head on the car.

"Oh, you poor thing!" gushed Sophie. "That must have hurt. Come here, let me see."

They were the same height. Jay was wringing his hands, peering up as Sophie tenderly brushed her fingers over his shorn head. Screwing up his face, he ducked away from Sophie's hands, and puffed out his chest as if he were a pigeon. "Hey, I'm fine, I do this all the time."

"What, hurt yourself?"

"Oh, yeah. It comes with the job."

Sophie gazed at him.

Jay continued, his cheeks losing their redness. "I race Go-Karts, but I fix cars too. Want me to show you what I did today?"

Sophie blinked. "Oh. Yeah, sure!"

To Melinda's glee, the pair were soon absorbed in the wonderment of the car. She was a genius! Oh, she had to text her father the news; he was always asking after Jay! Pulling out her phone, she was immediately greeted to the messages that awaited her, and all she did was roll her eyes in annoyance.

Below the ten plus messages from *him,* was her mother:

I need you down here ASAP. Vicky's dropped out on me. I'm being bombarded by children with absolutely no manners.

"Oh, Mom, please!" Ashley begged. "We'll be extra, extra good, we promise!"

On the other side of her mother, Melinda united with her hopeful sister. "Oh, come on, please, please, Ashley really needs some new school shoes."

"How many times do I have to say it?" Placing a hand on her hip, Julie glared at both of her daughters. "You're not going shopping! Not after what happened with that stupid concert. Oh, come on, you haven't forgotten already, have you?"

In the midst of the Summer Fate, where children ran loose and the cakes never stopped selling, Melinda shuddered. Julie passed a cake to the child who'd just paid. More children queued up, gasping and clambering. Julie snapped:

"Come on girls, give me a hand here!"

Melinda jumped to life. "Okay, okay, I'm coming! Mom, *please* can we go shopping? I'm broke anyway, so we won't buy anything pointless, honest."

"Yeah, no more Three Beams posters, I promise, it's just that my school shoes are really, really rubbing me, look." Ashley tugged on her mother... while she had a plate of cakes in her hand. "Look at this massive red mark I've got right here—"

"Ashley!"

Springing into action, Melinda caught the plate in the nick of time.

Julie huffed. "All right, fine! You can go, if that keeps my cakes safe. I guess you're sorry enough now Melinda, and I did say you weren't to be alone at *night* times. But, not until next week, you hear me?"

"Yes!" Ashley cried. "Yes, thank you, thank you, thank you!"

"All right, all right," protested Julie. "Calm down now. Get on with selling these before I change my mind."

Immediately, the sisters went back to work. Around them, the fate continued. Children played on the Hook a Duck stall next door. They crowded around the Tombola, and pulled their parents across the playground.

"Oh my god, is that Mr Langston?" asked Melinda.

"Who?" said Ashley.

Melinda told her that he was the lifeguard who had taught the forced swimming lessons in year four, and now there he was, stood in the docks. Children pelted him with wet sponges. Over by the girl's toilets, the fair-haired, young lifeguard spluttered as water dribbled down his chin.

As Lucia asked Julie for a strawberry cupcake, Melinda thrust her hand into the coin jar.

"Mel!" Ashley exclaimed.

Melinda pocketed the change. "Oh, she won't notice. Just popping to the toilet, Mom."

In unison with Julie telling her to hurry up (without even looking at her, as Lucia wanted her cupcake *now*), Melinda charged over to the toilets, more excited than Jack when he saw a cat in the garden.

Ashley watched her sister pay the Maths teacher for the sponges, collect the bucket eagerly, and wait for her turn. When Melinda eventually reached the front, she screeched with laughter as she pelted the lifeguard so brutally, Ashley winced. Melinda was cruel sometimes, and cold with no mercy, but Ashley wouldn't have her sister any other way.

"Mommy," the little boy said as Mommy cuddled him close. "Why was that bad man here?"

He'd had a clipboard. He'd worn a suit. He'd frowned a lot, and was very, very mean...

Boxes fell. Cutlery clattered. Yowls echoed as the cats got twisted and bent out of shape; the apartment was rotting. The foundations were slathered in mould. It stank; the smell was so pungent even the cats screamed.

Mommy sighed. On her lap, the little boy nestled into her neck as another cat darted across the back of the urine-stained sofa.

"It doesn't matter, darling."

"But Mommy—"

"You're very lucky. Remember that."

"But that man didn't say I was. He said I was in danger. What does that mean?"

Two tom cats brawled on the once-blue carpet (It was Daddy's job to clean it; he'd given up long ago).

"It doesn't matter. He's just a grumpy-kins." Mommy stroked Ken's hair. "He thinks I'm an unfit Mommy."

Yowl. Screech. Oh, it smelt, it smelt so much—"But you are fit! You exercise all the time."

On the treadmill that hadn't worked for months, she could go all day, locked in that room... alone.

Mommy laughed. Clutching the four-year-old closer, her joy was enough for them both. Meanwhile, Daddy called from the kitchen about the meat stew. Oh, meat stew, Ken's favourite! The cats stopped fighting. Slinking away, the loser hid under a stray box, while the winner sat, proud, on an upturned stool that had gotten broken long ago.

Peering up at his Mommy, Ken smiled as she gazed down at him, then hugged him close.

"Oh, my Ken-doll, don't ever leave me."

'Ken' never left. Ken was always there for her. Ken wasn't the one that cried himself to sleep when the lights went dark and the cats stopped yowling.

"No! You listen to me, I did everything I could—"

Suddenly, the room fell into a hole; the memory changed.

Thump, thump, thump! The corridor juddered as the boy ran. He was panting, gasping, falling all over as terror grabbed at him.

He's not 'the boy'. He has a name! He's Ken! The bad men were *downstairs, but now they're coming up! They're shouting, and his Daddy, his lovely, kind Daddy is screaming for them not to take him.*

"Mommy!"

The boy was sweating. A light shone on the wall. It was blue. It was scary. No, get away!

The boy changed direction so fast, he didn't hear Daddy bellowing at him from the bottom of the stairs:

"Ken, wait, don't go in there—"

"Come back, we're not going to hurt you!" said another bad man.

"Mommy!"

The boy cried for her as he opened the door, and stumbled into her bedroom.

The smell sent him staggering back, clutching his stomach. It always smelt... but not like this. *The sheets, smothered in cat poop, seemed to slither around his neck and strangle him.*

The cats were guarding a mound on the bed, sniffing and pawing, meowing and scratching.

Despite their efforts, the mound wasn't moving.

Gulping, the boy put his hand out, and inched forward, hardly daring to breathe. Behind him, thumps slowed to steps, and shouts to whispers, whereas Ken's voice changed to screams of horror.

Kenzie escaped the bundles of cat faeces as they smothered his body, and fled from the strangulation of that vile, vile stench.

Sitting up in bed, he wiped his hands down over his face. The Birmingham house... it was back. His room was spotless; there were no disgusting, filthy moggies, and best of all, no shit in his bed.

"Damn it," Kenzie snarled. *"Fucking hell."*

Rage made his fists curl; Kenzie felt as if he would *explode*. He was twenty-five, not five. He was better, stronger, so much more damn superior than that stupid bitch and her 'lucky cats'... all one hundred and fifty-nine of them.

Kenzie pulled on some random clothes and stormed for the door. Yanking it open, his glare was so deadly, that a worried Tom cat was reduced to a quivering wreck.

"Hey man, a-are you okay?" Tom said. "I heard—"

Kenzie shoved him. "Go back to bed, Landsby."

"Ken, wait!"

Within minutes, the blond was in his blue BMW with the blacked-out windows. Driving toward the gate, he honked the horn, immediately attracting the attention of the guards. Did those morons have nothing better to do at two in the morning? From the centre of the gate, one put his hand out.

Kenzie opened the window, nodded, and smiled. "Hey, just me."

Looking bemused, the guard activated the gate. Slowly, it opened. And with one more creak, one more rev of the engine, Kenzie was free.

Kenzie exhaled as the rage began to fade. He knew exactly where he was going, and he tore down the desolate road to get there. Gradually, the overhanging trees lessened. Tarmac became dirt. The moon shone, and the stars were free to glisten. There were no potholes in the road, no houses blocking the view, and best of all, no people.

On and on, on and on, the car zoomed down the road at speeds of eighty, ninety miles an hour.

A ginger cat padded out into the road. Kenzie didn't even stop; he ran the nuisance right over, and as his car scaled the hill, he vowed that any damage to his car would be fixed in the morning, as the last thing he wanted were the fans seeing blood and guts all over his wheels.

Kenzie sighed. Relaxing completely, he slowed the car to a drift, then a stop. On the edge of the hill, he overlooked the fields below. He leaned back, and rested on the leather seats, which were *real* leather, and not the fake ugly kind that Melinda's shoes were on that night.

Teeth flashing in his smile, Kenzie basked in glory for just a moment longer. Then, he reached into his pocket to text the silly cow and scare her silly.

Wait.

He didn't have his phone. He'd been in such a hurry to leave that he'd forgotten it, and Melinda had been ignoring him anyway.

Kenzie thumped the wheel. His fingers curled around his hair. Who the hell did she think she was? Oh, he'd show her. He'd *show* her.

Kenzie would give her one more warning, one more order to respond, and if she didn't…

Kenzie really, honestly, hoped that she didn't.

Chapter Twenty-Five

"For goodness' sake, Callum," Tom protested. "I've already said—"

"Well I don't believe you," replied Callum, as they faced off in the Birmingham House's kitchen. "I know what I saw in rehearsal. I'm not stupid."

"I know you're not. But right now, you're acting it."

"No, *you're* the one acting it."

"I wasn't crying, I swear to God I wasn't, Doug just used shitty paint. No, seriously, Callum! I'm getting really annoyed now. It's bloody eight in the morning, I haven't even had breakfast yet. It's not the right time to argue."

"It's never the right time. I tried after filming, and last night, but you always say that same shit. I've told you, over and over again, that you can always come to me if there's a problem."

Someone was coming down the stairs.

"Callum—"

"We auditioned together, or do you not even remember that?"

At the door, Tom widened his eyes in an attempt to get Callum to turn around, and witness Kenzie bounding down, the chains on his black jeans jangling.

Callum went on:

"Jesus Christ, you don't, do you? You don't remember that I was your only friend at school, the only one who up with your sorry ass before Kenzie came strolling into our dressing room all like—"

Kenzie gave a throaty cough. "Is there a problem?"

Tom didn't hesitate to hang Callum head-first over a vat of acid. "Yeah, there is, Kenzie." Skirting around Callum, he stood on Kenzie's right. "Sort this dick out. He reckons I was blubbing at rehearsals yesterday."

"Blubbing?" Kenzie said curiously. "You? Oh, deary me." Speaking slowly, patronisingly, he came closer and closer to Callum. "Looks like someone's got their wires crossed. Is it really Tom that you reckon cries at rehearsal, or is it you? Is it you that wets your pull-ups, because the cameras give you 'bad dreams'?"

Ouch.

"L-Look, Kenzie." Callum suttered. "I was o-only asking. I was just worried cause—"

"Yeah, sure."

The kitchen counter wasn't far away. Soon enough, Callum met a dead end.

"And I'm sure those judges were tripping on crack when they allowed *you* to join the band," Kenzie sneered. "You may think you're all big, with your jazzy guitar and your self-written songs, but you're not. Now, are you gonna leave my Tom alone?"

"I said," he growled, slamming his hands down on either side of the counter. "Are you gonna leave Tom alone?"

"Yes!" Callum cried. "Yes, I'll leave Tom alone."

"Good, because if you don't, you'll have to think of a pretty interesting cover story, when you go to rehearsal with two black eyes and a broken nose."

Suddenly, Tom felt guilty. He'd turned his friends against each other like they were pitbulls in a fighting ring.

Releasing Callum, Kenzie looked at Tom. Tom snickered awkwardly, and Callum fled, not daring to look at either of them.

"Well, what do you say, Landsby?" said Kenzie.

"Nice. Thanks man, he was really on my case about it."

Kenzie smiled bashfully. "Eh, I've been an arse. Sorry about last night, I woke up all hot cause of this stupid weather, and I just needed to get out. You know what I mean?"

"Of course. It gets… claustrophobic being here all the time."

Chuckling, Kenzie put his arm around him.

"That's my boy. Listen, I've got some family stuff to sort, so I'll be out all weekend, but text me if that twat bugs you, all right? I'm gonna be bored stiff anyway. My mom's house is dryer than Callum's dick."

"Oh dear. See ya then. Have fun!"

"I'll try."

Tom had never felt such an urge to latch onto him, and beg to be taken along.

Melinda rolled onto her back. The grass of the park, the smaller one that was easier to get to, and the pond behind her made the breeze cool. Jack rolled around on her left, snuffling. In Melinda's hands, she held the phone up higher, and laughed again. Apparently, Jay had deactivated his Instagram account. He'd found it too confusing. Sending a private message was just too difficult for him. Therefore, he'd turned to Facebook instead.

Quickly, Melinda tapped out a reply, then checked to see who her newest text message was from.

Kenzie, again.

Melinda sighed. Oh, why couldn't he just leave her alone? On his back, Jack looked curiously at his owner.

"What d'you reckon Jack? Should I delete him, hmm?"

Jack grew boisterous. Sitting up, he whined enthusiastically.

"Should I delete him, boy, ay?"

Yapping, the Jack Russell batted the phone with his paw.

"I'll take that as a yes then."

Melinda deleted the chat, not stopping to read any of his angry messages.

Of course, fear hissed in the back of her mind: What if he hurt Dana, or worse, Ashley? But Melinda couldn't bear to think about it anymore. She rolled onto her back, shut her eyes, and just *breathed*.

Briefly, she heard Jack stand up, and trot down toward the pond.

"Don't go too far, Jack."

She'd adored cleaning the rabbits out. Jade had even paid her fifty pounds! She hadn't heard from Dana. And best of all, family life was finally going smoothly again. She was even able to give Jack his daily walk without Brad asking if everything was okay!

Splash!

Melinda crossed one leg over the other, and hummed.

Quack! Yelp.

"Jack!" Oh, what had he done now? "Jack. Jack, where are you?"

In the centre of the pond, the tiny dog whined. Splashing, yelping, going under, he struggled, tangled up in the pond reeds.

Melinda stayed still. As she glanced over, the murky green seemed to rise, and devour her.

"Oh Jack, I told you not to go too far! Why can't you just-you poor thing!" She knelt down, and reached for a long, thick stick that lay buried in the long grass surrounding the pond. "Hang on!"

She grabbed the rock in front. The water lapped her fingers; she whimpered. Dragging her knees forward, she leaned further, further, further. Straining, cringing as the water touched her clothes, she thrust the stick outward.

It just about made it.

"Yes!

Rejoicing, Melinda tugged the edge of the pond reed. Luckily, it was just one tangled lump. Jack was easily pulled over toward her as he thrashed in the middle. As he came closer, Melinda shrank back, relief hitting her as the water left her body. Eventually, she was able to lift Jack out of the pond, and toss the stick aside.

"Oh Jack, I'm sorry..."

Whining slightly, he looked up... and wagged his tail.

Sweeping Jack up in her arms, algae-slathered, smelly dog became Melinda's baby. She kissed him, soothed him, and told him over and over how sorry she was for being such a coward. She walked away from the pond, collecting her phone on the way.

Jack struggled in her arms all of a sudden, not liking being held one bit.

"Oh, you're a bad, bad boy! All right, fine, have it your way. But no treats tonight."

Blowing a raspberry on his ear, Melinda put Jack down, and confined him to the blue lead that had been bunched up in her pocket. When Jack looked up with those pleading eyes and that adorable pout, she couldn't resist running with him. Clucking him onwards, she allowed him to lead the way as they charged out of the park's big iron gates, her laughing, and him yapping madly.

They were almost home when Melinda noticed it.

"Jack, stop a sec."

A BMW? *Here?* It was a dark, elegant blue. Facing her, the windscreen was completely blacked out. There was a wing on the back, and—

Thrum.

Jack jumped up again, barking and barking, while Melinda grumbled:

"Down, Jack, down—"

The music started.

Within a second, Melinda went from mumbling with annoyance, to shaking with fright.

"So dance with me baby, my baby girl..." said the music.

It was *that* song! The one she'd sung in the dressing room. The car inched forward, crawling slowly, menacingly, just like *he* had done when he'd followed her across the sofa. No, surely it wasn't... surely he hadn't found her?

Jack was barking hysterically. The music was blaring, and the car was still coming toward her, the engine revving and revving.

Melinda veered to the right.

There was a squeal of breaks. The car was turning around. As Melinda ran down the pathway, her blood threatened to spill from a wound that would soon appear. The car was following them. Jack simply thought it was a game; he was enjoying himself as he ran alongside her!

"Jack, come on, *run!*"

Bump!

The car mounted the curb, in the exact place Jack had been just milliseconds ago.

Panting, Melinda quickly bent down, and scooped Jack up in her arms. Charging down another path, dry sobs racked her body. Why was there no one around? Not that it mattered. Kenzie was driving in a way that looked like he was casually going to the shop, whereas she looked a nutcase running for no reason.

Into the distance, she could see the wood that bordered her house, and the grass that grew wildly.

Melinda was left with no choice. Across the grass, she cut away from the car. The car screeched. The music stopped, and the horn was silenced. Spluttering, Melinda looked back. Leaves crunched under her feet. Jack whimpered in her arms.

Kenzie wound down the car window, smiled, waved at her, and then drove away.

Melinda put Jack down (still holding the lead just in case) and rested her hands on her knees. The wood didn't last forever. Already, she could see the long grass, and the slanted roof of her cottage... soon, she would have to go home, with no clue as to whether he had gone.

"Fuck," Melinda sat on the floor. She hugged her knees to her chest. "Shit, Jack..."

Jack came to a sit in front of her legs, head cocked to one side.

As Jack pawed her knee, Melinda began to weep. "I'm sorry!"

What if he'd parked the car somewhere? What if he was stalking through the wood with a ten-inch knife?

"I'm so, so sorry." Cuddling Jack close, she whispered in his ear, and sobbed into his odorous fur. "I'm such a stupid cow."

Melinda wasn't sure how long she sat there. But by the time she'd finally calmed down enough to go into her house, her father was baffled.

"Mel," he said, speed-walking along the corridor. "There you are. What took you so long?"

Julie came out of the kitchen, hands plastered in flour from her practise at her friend's wedding cake. "Melinda Stevens, that dog stinks! What the heck where you doing with him?"

"Oh, Jack jumped into the duck pond. I had to bribe him out with treats."

"Trust you! Oh, damn, the cakes." Julie left, flour dripping from her hands.

"Ignore her, she's just flapping about icing or something." Brad pulled an envelope from his jacket. "This came for you today. I reckon it's another joke from Jay, because there's no address on it, but..."

To Melinda, Brad's voice trailed off.

"Oh, right! Erm, thanks Dad. Sorry about Jack being smelly, I'll wash him later!"

Melinda snatched the envelope, raced upstairs, and locked herself in the bathroom.

She'd thought she was free. She'd thought that at long last, he'd give up and leave her alone. Yet, as she peeled back the seal on the envelope, the letter that accompanied it proved otherwise. And out of a folded piece of paper, a dozen photos tumbled.

Melinda fell to her knees.

Photos of *herself* littered the white tiles. In one, she was just coming out of Jade's house. How the *hell* had she not noticed the car? In another, she was in her own *back garden*, giggling as she painted Ashley's nails. He'd been in the wood, leering at her!

The girl dragged herself over to the toilet. She leaned in, and retched, but nothing came out. Her eyes swivelled to the right, and she spotted the piece of paper.

I don't like being ignored, Mellbell. Stop being a stroppy bitch and shoot me a pretty little text, yeah? Else you will regret it.

It was as though the roof was torn from the house, and her eyes were met with his. In her mind, he'd grown to the height of a true, true monster… Melinda scrambled back.

She couldn't text him! She couldn't, because… she'd deleted the chat, therefore deleting his number!

Melinda breathed in deeply—wait. Why wasn't she able to breathe? The car, the photos, the letter… texts, endless texts, and his smile flooded her brain. Melinda coughed. On the tiles, her legs were splayed out in front of her as she wrapped her hands around her throat. She gasped. But she couldn't *breathe*.

"Mel?"

A voice! Who was that?

"Mel…"

Wait, it was Ashley!

Melinda could see *black spots* in her vision—"Ash!"

"Mel!" Ashley called. "Are you okay? Let me in." Knock, knock. Rattle, rattle. "Open the door!"

Melinda froze. If Ashley saw the photos—"I'm fine," she wheezed. "Go back downstairs!"

"No, you're not! Stay there, I'm getting Dad."

"No, Ash, wait!"

All too soon, Ashley was hurrying back upstairs, and she had their father with her.

Like a thief collecting scattered money from a bank heist gone horribly wrong, Melinda scoured the floor, which was a distraction enough to allow her to get some of her breath back. She continued until she'd seized every photo, and Brad was banging urgently on the door:

"Mel, what's going on? Mel! Open this door, now. Mel, I mean it."

Melinda slid over to the toilet.

"If you don't open this door right now I'm breaking it down."

Hyperventilating, Melinda ripped, and ripped, and ripped.

"I'm gonna give you three seconds."

She dumped the evidence into the toilet.

"One."

Eyes streaming, she flushed it.

"Two."

Legs shaking, she stood.

"Three!"

At the last possible moment, she had the door open. Ashley was sobbing. Their father was staring at her, both furious and frightened.

Melinda laughed, and told them she was fine. She'd been choking on some chocolate that she'd snuck into her bedroom, and the letter had just been a prank from Jay.

Chapter Twenty-Six

Ashley slotted the last of her packing into her small, pink holdall.

"Yes," her exasperated sister sighed. "I'm still doing okay at college." Rolling her eyes at Ashley, she mimed an opening and closing action with her other hand. "Yeah, Ashley still likes Three Beams... no, we haven't been to another concert."

Melinda been telling the truth about choking in the bathroom, hadn't she? She seemed okay now. She was pacing back and forth, trying to get Aunt Flo off the phone.

Ashley zipped up her suitcase. She was spending the Sunday night at Hamrit's.

"Oh, yes, Flo," Melinda met Ashley's stare. "Ashley would *love* to speak to you."

Oh no!

Frantically, Ashley waved her hands back and forth and shook her head.

"Ashley, darling!" Aunt Flo near-screamed down the phone Melinda passed to her. "I've heard you're at Hamrit's tonight! Make sure you take some spare underwear, just in case."

"Flo," Ashley moaned, fighting to ignore Melinda's laughter. "I'm seven, I don't wet the bed anymore."

"Oh but darling, these things can always come back you know."

Melinda had gone downstairs. Maybe, if Ashley hurried, she could give her a thump.

"Oh no, sorry, Flo," she said regretfully. "I've gotta go now, Mom and Dad are going straight to that hen do after dropping me, so they need to hurry up."

"Oh, Ashley, hang on, do you wanna go and—"

"Bye, see you later!"

Ashley hadn't been lying. Her parents *were* going out, and they *were* dropping her off along the way, they just weren't in that much of a hurry to leave.

Ashley had to get her revenge on Melinda. Clumsily heading downstairs with her holdall, she followed the sound of her sister's voice. She pulled open the front door.

"Oh, come on, Mom," Melinda whined. "Surely you can give it a miss? You said yourself you don't wanna go."

Julie's eyes fluttered closed. "Mel…"

"Please," begged Melinda. "Stay here."

"Mel, get off me."

"Mom, come on, you don't even wanna—"

Julie sent Melinda sprawling back against the car door. "For god's sake!"

The car had started. Brad was clenching the steering wheel, his face hard.

Julie ranted:

"You're eighteen years old, Melinda. You've stayed on your own plenty of times before. What the heck is the matter with you tonight?"

Julie's green gown billowed in the breeze. "Well?"

Melinda shrugged, which annoyed their mother even further:

"Ugh, you're such a pest," she said.

Usually, Melinda loved having the house to herself...

To Julie's sigh, Melinda stepped to the right, her head still down, and allowed Julie access to the passenger side of the car. Shaking her head, Julie didn't even look at Melinda as she got in the car and slammed the door, but Ashley did. Oh, her sister wasn't a pest!

With a loud sniff and her hand over her eyes, Melinda ducked around Ashley, faster than Kenzie could flick his hair.

"Mel!"

Her father honked the horn. Rolling her eyes, her mother wound down the window.

"Come on, Ash, we're going!" she said.

Taking a deep breath, Ashley tore herself from the grass, carried her holdall to the car, and got inside. Over Julie's muttering about how many wedding cakes to practice tomorrow, Brad spoke casually, his eye contact firmly on the house.

"It was nice of Hamjit to invite you round, wasn't it?" he said.

Hamrit! Her name was *Hamrit!* Stroppily, Ashley shoved her holdall to the opposite end of the car seat.

The blue BMW was parked on the corner of the dirt road. Trees surrounded the left side. Opposite the remainder of the dirt was an expanse of yellowing grass. Not a soul walked by, but of course, the animals made a racket in the woods instead.

Little Kenzie didn't like this place. The five-year-old was cowering, calling for his mother.

Kenzie fidgeted. Eyes to his phone, he shoved the image back under the layers of his fame. He leant his head back, and took a deep, long breath.

He looked back at his phone again. 21.24, and still no text. Moving in the seat, he sat up straight, raked his hand through his un-styled hair.

Briefly, he wondered how Melinda slept in such a noisy place. He scrolled down his Twitter page, casually replying to all the girls on his Twitter. Well, only the pretty ones.

Damn it! The almost missed the car going past him.

It was 'the family's' car. Drifting past his, the pathetic little girl, the obese lard, and the goofy man in it conversed. Kenzie was thankful for his blacked-out windows, and his headlights being off. He could see them laughing, completely unaware of what he was up to?

Oh, what would they say if they knew? What would they *do?*

The car faded into the distance.

Hmm, what would Kenzie do? It depended on if Melinda was awake or asleep.

Finally, after all the waiting, Kenzie could make his move. He hadn't known it would go this well; he'd thought he'd have to push his plan aside, and wait for a more open opportunity. It was purely by chance he'd happened to be sitting near her house after spending the day at the gym and clubs. But chance was a fine thing.

Snickering to himself, Kenzie firmly forced the car to a start.

Melinda would be screaming with nightmares for weeks.

As it crawled toward the house, the thrum of the BMW blended perfectly with the wood's chatter.

Melinda was beside herself. She had to lock every door, and shut every window. She couldn't allow the lights on, so she flicked them off. She couldn't allow the curtains open. In fact, she couldn't allow any sounds, at all, so the TV went off and the radio was unplugged.

If he was here, her life would leave her in the blink of an eye, and if she couldn't text him, she had to protect herself by keeping guard.

Only when Melinda had deemed the living room safe, did she jump onto the sofa, and lay down. She pulled the cushions around her. She grabbed a magazine, and her torch, from under the sofa. She tightened her hold on the pages.

Animal Life, Issue 54.... she'd already read it, but she had to do *something*. Rushing down the page, her eyes barely took in the information as she pointed the torch down. As the minutes passed, and the grandfather clock ticked, Melinda waited, poised for any signs of life.

Scratch...

He was here! How did he get in? Oh, he was going to kill her!

The living room door was edging open. The shadow was huge, lumbering, and scary; on the wall in front of her, it came closer, getting bigger and bigger as Kenzie panted, and his tail wagged back and forth...

Wait...

Slowly, Melinda slid her knees back down. Jack was standing at the end of the sofa, his tongue lolling, his shadow lit up by the light she'd left on in the kitchen.

"Jack, what the *hell* are you doing?"

Jack whined. Nervously, he glanced back, but his tail still wagged, and this infuriated Melinda *so* much.

"Don't you look at me like that, you stupid mutt. Get out."

She grabbed a cushion.

"I said *out*. Get the fuck out!"

She threw the cushion at the door. Jack yelped. Turning on his heels, he retreated back to the kitchen, his whimpers echoing.

Melinda ducked into the corridor, turned off the kitchen lights, and slammed the living room door shut. Back to her watch station, the girl returned, even more on edge than she'd been before. Retrieving her torch and magazine, she lay back down, and resolved to get through every magazine in the cabinet before the night was over.

What if he broke in? What if he snuck in through the kitchen window? Yes, it was closed, but the lock had been broken for ages, which meant it was always slightly ajar. All you had to do was give it a little push…

"Get ready, Mellbell, cause I'm gonna fuck your life up."

Melinda was unsure what time it was, but through the noise of the woods, the paddings of an agitated Jack, and the occasional car that cruised down the road, Melinda's eyelids began to droop. Soon, she fell fast asleep, accompanied only by the tears on her cheeks.

Click. Thud. Bickering… lovely, lovely bickering!

Melinda stirred. She pulled the magazine from her face. She was safe! She could hear her mother, complaining about how bland the food was. She could hear her father, telling her lighten up. It was typical, so wonderfully, wonderfully typical!

Brad opened the living room door, and peered inside. "Hello Mel," he said cheerily. "How was your evening?"

Melinda shrugged. "It was good. I watched some horror films."

"Nice. Bloody hell, I didn't think we'd get back at four in the morning! Sorry about that."

"It's fine, Dad, it happens. Aw man, that film was ace! There was loads of blood and guts and stuff, it was great. But how was your night?"

"Jack?" Julie called.

Oh, *Jack.*

Her father pushed his long hair aside, loosened the tie on his uncomfortable suit, and chuckled. "One sec, darling, I'd best go see what's bothering your mother. Julie, what's up? Julie? Julie…"

How could Melinda have been so cruel? The poor, poor dog… he hadn't done anything wrong. It was just *her* that was the problem.

"Melinda!" snapped Julie. "Get your dopey little arse in here, now."

Jack was probably whimpering in his bed. He may have even wet it, like he did on Bonfire Night. Melinda slunk out of the living room and down the corridor. Whatever her mother had lined up for her, she deserved every inch. Hesitantly, she came right into the kitchen, and was met with the furious face of her mother, however, it was her father that spoke, his voice behind her grave and angry:

"What have we told you?"

"Huh?"

"Look around, you stupid child," Julie said. "Look around, and tell me what's missing."

Melinda looked. What did her mother mean? Everything was in place. The toaster was still on the table from that morning. Next to it, Brad's files were still speckled in toast crumbs. By the back door, Jack's bed was still a mess of blankets, toys, and dog treats. And inside, Jack was… Jack was…

At that moment, Melinda's entire body went cold.

"Jack!" Bewildered, she looked back at her father. "Where's Jack?"

"Exactly, *Melinda.* We've told you time and time again, to keep this window shut," he replied.

The window that Julie stood in front of, the huge window that spanned nearly the entire kitchen, was wide open.

"But I closed it!" Confused, Melinda turned to her father, her mother, her father. "I closed it, I know I did. I shut everything just after you went out. I closed it, honestly, I did."

"Bullshit!" Julie's shout engulfed the room. "What else could have possibly happened?"

"You know first-hand what he's like," Brad added. "You know he's hyperactive, that no medication can settle him. That the second an opportunity comes, he's dashing outside like a shot."

"You're a liar, Mel," Julie shouted. "And it's pissing it down out there! Every where's waterlogged. I swear to god, if anything's happened to him, you aren't going near another animal in your life!"

"B-But Mom, I-I closed it, I…"

"You fucking *liar!"*

Julie grabbed her and shook her by the scruff of her neck, as if she were a rabbit that had been caught eating the cabbages. In the background, her father huffed, and said he was going to make a start in the village, while in the foreground, Julie brought her face directly into hers.

"Get outside"—Julie shook her—"and go and look for him!"

The millisecond her mother released her, Melinda charged out of the back door and into the rain.

Jack was out, all by himself. He was running in busy roads, or falling down deadly ditches, or being chased by farmers who brandished shotguns—

"Jack!" Melinda called. "*Jack!*"

Chapter Twenty-Seven

Where was Jack? Oh, she was sorry; she was so, so sorry...
Melinda, soaked to the bone, stopped in the centre of the grassy verge. She looked about her, wildly.

Jack wasn't here. He wasn't *anywhere!*

A clap of thunder sounded. The rain only seemed to get heavier, and Melinda more frantic.

"Jack, please." Melinda charged toward the pond Dana used to play in. "Where are you? Oh, Jack, I'm sorry, just please..."

When she was confronted by quacking ducks and no dog, she erupted into sobs so loud, the whole wood shook.

"F-Fucking hell."

Oh, where was he? How had he gotten out? And was he even still alive?

"Jack!"

Melinda bypassed the trees, and charged away from the pond; she didn't look back until she reached her house.

"Jack... I'm sorry." She said'. "I'm a rubbish owner."

Melinda allowed her tears to drip freely, not knowing, not caring if anyone saw them. When a homeless man huffed and barged past her, she didn't even flinch.

Jack... Never would she see his bounding run, or the tumble of his body as he rolled in the grass. Never would she hold him again, or sneak him to bed with her like she used to when he was a puppy.

Melinda snivelled. She didn't want to go home, but home was the only thing that hadn't been taken from her.

Outside the house, her parents were hugging, wrapped up in loss.

"How are we gonna tell Ashley?" Julie said.

"No... come on Jules, we'll find him."

Melinda paused. Easily, she could flee unnoticed. She wouldn't have to see her mother, snuffling into her father's shoulder, and he, with his back to her, soothing the shivering woman.

Julie wept. "I can't believe she's been so stupid."

Brad hummed. "*Shush*, it's okay. Jules, I promise we'll find him…"

Quickening, Melinda veered past her parents. Eventually, she came to the back of the house. Dripping, her hand met the metal handle. She took a deep breath in, and opened the door to a house without the familiar yapping of a Jack Russell Terrier.

A whine from the tiles bathed her in dazzling, dazzling relief.

Cupping her mouth with her hands, Melinda eyes widened, but with happiness this time. She couldn't help but squeal, and throw herself down to the floor.

"Oh, Jack!"

Jack yelped when she tried to pick him up.

"Huh? Jack, what's wrong?"

Jack's back leg was broken.

Melinda was soaked through, and her parents were opening the front door, however, Melinda paid no heed, as neither of the events was a comparison to the poor dog dragging his leg as he tried to come to her.

Julie banged the door shut. Brad walked in front. As Julie wiped her eyes, Brad sighed, but suddenly, he stilled in the doorway, surprise wiping his frown clean as Julie bumped into him.

"What on earth… Jack?" gasped Julie.

"Jack, oh, thank Lord, *Jack*. Melinda, you found him! Julie, Julie, look, he's okay!"

Melinda scrambled to her feet. "No, he's not. His leg! Look at his leg. It's broken!"

Brad paled. "Oh shit, Mel, you're right. Julie, Julie, Jack's—"

"I know Brad, I can see," said Julie slowly, firmly. "Go and get the pet carrier. He needs a vet, as soon as."

"I'll come too!" Melinda cried.

"No, you can stay here. You've done enough!"

Jack whimpered, helpless, on the floor. Melinda's bottom lip trembled. Rain pattered on the window. Brad went to fetch the carrier, and Julie glowered at her.

Buzz.

Immediately, Melinda dived for her phone, taking it from the front pocket of her shirt.

She opened the text.

Jack the Jack Russell? Couldn't you have thought of a more creative name for him, Mellbell? Anyway, he's a very, very lucky dog. Ignore me again, and I'll send him back in multiple pieces next time.

Julie hissed:

"I was talking to you. Look at me when I'm talking to you, you insolent girl!"

"Mom, just sod off, will you! I told you it was an accident, me leaving the window open. Don't you think I felt bad enough when I found him under the window in a bush, crying his damn eyes out?"

"You just told me you closed the window."

"Oh my *god*, does it matter? *Look* at Jack! As if, you were crying about him! You've hated him since day one, you rotten cow!"

Silence.

Melinda's mind counted down the moments until her mother would blow:

Three...

Two...

Unsurprisingly, the volcano blew ahead of time.

"God," Tom marvelled, pushing his hair back. "These comments should really be monitored."

His laptop's light illuminated the freckles on his nose, and the surprise on his face as he waded through unfamiliar ground. Browsing the Three Beams fan site wasn't something he usually did, but he'd been bored. Tugging his blankets further around his crossed legs, he promptly exited the page dedicated to discussions about him.

What thousands of girls wanted to do to him was *not* what he needed to hear right now.

Kenzie was still gone. He'd texted Tom, letting him know he was staying another night at his hotel, and would meet him at WowMag studios in the morning, but... why hadn't he come back, like he'd originally said he would?

Tom clicked onto the Kenzie Hudgson page.

Immediately, he wondered why he'd even bothered.

As usual, the stupid page was busier than rush hour. Tom couldn't help but mimic the stupid girls:

"Oh, look at him." He tossed his hair, and pouted his lips. "He's so gorgeous! Be mine Kenzie. Be my baby forever darling, kiss, kiss, ex oh… twats."

He was about to exit the website, but, there was one particular post that caught his eye. It was a question that drove his curiosity enough to make an account:

Yes, there *were* boys on the board…

Tom decided on a screen name. After adding a few more basic details, he glanced at his bedroom door, before taking a deep breath, and plunging in.

With one click, Bouncing puppy signed in.

Should he post in the ongoing public discussion? No way. Chin on his hand, Tom pulled up a private chat.

Bouncing_puppy: Hey! Just saw your thread. No, you're not the only boy who's a fan of Kenzie. I am too.

Within seconds, Tom got a reply back.

TakenSoDon'tBother: Oh, thank heavens! I thought I was riding solo! It's full of girls on here, man.

Tom bit his bottom lip. Now what did he say? Mentally, he debated his options, yet ended up going with:

Bouncing_puppy: Tell me about it, they're all so desperate.

Tom drummed his laptop. Once again, the unknown boy replied within seconds:

TakenSoDon'tBother: Yeah, but how could you not be? His smile's to die for, and his abs are just perf! ;)

Tom grinned. Leaning on the bed board, Tom slid his legs out so they were under the covers, and pulled the laptop closer.

Bouncing_puppy: I know. I wish I had abs like that, but I can't be bothered working out. Anyway, does your girlfriend like him too?

TakenSoDon'tBother: Girlfriend? Nah mate, I'm gay.

Tom gasped. Heart pounding, he was about to press escape, and deactivate the account, but he sent another message instead:

Bouncing_puppy: Me too.

Tom closed the chat, buzzing in one way, scared in another. Calming himself with deep long breaths, Tom buried himself under the sheets, and not once did dreams full of heat and lust plague him.

I bet you've missed me, haven't you, Mellbell?

No, of course she hadn't 'missed him'.

How could you do that to Jack? He's just an innocent dog.

No Mel, he's a lucky dog. And if you bring it up again, his luck WILL run out, mark my words.

Melinda shook her head in pure, fuming rage. How dare he hurt her dog?

Melinda had had enough. Cursing, she shoved her phone into her college bag. Although, it wasn't like she needed the damn thing anymore.

She glanced out the window. Many people *died* doing what she was about to do, but the car near her house, those words manipulating her ex-best friend... those hands around *her* dog, taking him through the window, snapping his poor leg, and putting him back like nothing had happened, convinced her she was doing the right thing.

Jack had been so lucky; he hadn't had to have his leg amputated. A metal rod and bandage had been enough. He was still at the vets now, sleeping off the sedatives. Nonetheless, Melinda couldn't let anything like this happen again: Putting her family in danger was a fate worse than death.

Placing her hands on the windowsill, Melinda felt sick as she caught a glimpse of the tangled grass, and the looming wood.

"Prick."

With that mumble, she took out the letter she'd written the night before, and slotted it under her pillow. 'She'd tossed and turned the previous night, worry prying her eyelids open. After convincing him that Jay had peered over her shoulder, and she'd had to delete the texts, therefore losing his number, she'd been a mess.

Melinda zipped up her bag. She blinked back the tears, because it was time to go.

"I hope you're pleased with yourself, Mel."

Turning to face her mother in her bedroom doorway, Melinda felt the sadness hit her once more, because she *didn't* want to go, not really.

"Mom, I—"

"Shut up." Pointing at her daughter with a flour-smothered finger, Julie looked frightening. "I've got today only to get these cakes right; they're going off for the wedding tomorrow afternoon. I don't need your smart mouth right now. Ashley's worried sick about Jack. It's took me hours to calm her down. And don't think for a second you're going shopping with her, cause you're not."

Melinda shrugged. "Big deal."

"Melinda!"

Julie stomped over to her. "Did you not hear what I just said? I don't need your smart mouth."

Melinda knew without looking at her mother that she was trying to hold her temper. It was pitiful.

Glowering at her packed bag, Melinda shrugged again. "You never hear what I say."

Julie said nothing.

Melinda smirked. Did she dare count the seconds again?

"What the bloody hell is the matter with you? Oi!" her mother grabbed her wrist. "Look at me while I'm speaking to you, and drop the damn attitude, cause I've had enough."

"Aw," retorted Melinda. "How *sad*."

"What have you turned into?"

Her mother's spittle had landed on her nose, and it was vile. Twisting her wrist away, Melinda spoke through gritted teeth:

"Trust me. You don't wanna know."

Her mother shook her head. "God, you're pushing it. You're really, *really* pushing it now, Mel! Your behaviour lately has been a disgrace! You drag your sister off to see some demented band, you mope around like some saddo expecting everyone to feel sorry for you, you act like a spiteful baby when you're left alone for more than a few hours, you come home pissed out your head, and now… Fuck! I've just had enough! What more do you want me say?"

Melinda was unable to resist infuriating her mother even further. So, she gave no answer. Let her mother suffer. Let her feel the stress, the agony, the *fear* Melinda had felt as she lost control over her life. Taking her college ID off her bedpost, she slung it around her neck.

"I have a college to get to," she said.

Marching right over to Melinda, Julie grabbed her wrist again, and spun her insolent daughter around to face her.

"Right, you little... I'm gonna smack you in a minute."

"Oh, come back for more have you?" Sneering, Melinda broke free. "Well go for it then. You wanna hit me? Just fucking do it. I'm not scared of you. No one's scared of you. You're just a waste of—"

Melinda gasped as her mother's hand connected with her cheek.

"Who the hell do you think you are?" Julie bellowed.

Crack. "*Don't you* dare *do that again.*"

"Do you want me to throw you out Melinda? Well, *do you?*"

"Just leave me alone!" Melinda wailed. "J-Just... I have to get to college, or I'll be late!"

Melinda turned on her heels, and charged out of her bedroom, her tears blinding her vision so much she failed to see her mother cry too.

Chapter Twenty-Eight

"So"—the interviewer admired the band in front of her—"between the three of you, who do you think's the loudest?"

Callum's eyes met his shoes, then a black carpet, a sweltering room, and a sense of being locked in with no escape.

"Tom," Kenzie said, pointing to the curly-haired boy on his right. "I swear, whenever we arrive on set, the whole of the crew knows we're there. And he's always first in line to the snack bar, the greedy menace."

The interviewer giggled with Kenzie. Tom jokingly slapped Kenzie's shoulder, and Kenzie ruffled his curls. Down Callum's back, a bead of sweat ran. Behind him was a cardboard pin-up of the band. Well, the band and *him*. Callum made sure he didn't look, and was so busy doing so, he jumped when the interviewer asked the next question:

"Who gets the most girls?"

What a stupid question! Tom gestured to Kenzie, who raised his eyebrows at the camera, because it was always him... *always*.

"And who's the craziest? Who starts all the drama? Who has the manager on their case twenty-four seven?"

"Me," replied Tom. "Me without a doubt."

"You're telling us?" Kenzie retorted. "Don't even get me started on the time we went to the theme park on Halloween night. You frightened all the children away from Storm force Ten because you couldn't wait your turn!"

While the interviewer giggled once more, Kenzie smiled sickeningly at the camera.

Callum said nothing. He knew Kenzie would just moan later. He knew he'd slag off the interviewer for being overweight, rubbish the WowMag set, or complain about how the camera hadn't 'captured his muscles correctly'. Oh, how he longed to rub the blond's handsome, smug face in mud; *then* he wouldn't be so perfect. *Then* he wouldn't get all the girls, and the fans!

"Who's the father of the group?" said the interviewer. "I mean, who looks after the band?"

The other two looked at Callum.

Gradually, the woman smiled, and gradually, Callum shrunk in his seat.

She wanted *him* to speak. During the interview, he hadn't answered a single question. He'd been quiet, reserved... But that was *him*.

"Who keeps everyone together when times get hard?"

In the end, Callum was given no choice. "Kenzie. Most definitely Kenzie."

Kenzie smiled, and seeing his kind smile made Callum angry, because he knew what Kenzie was really thinking; he knew he thought he was a wimp who he could push around with as little as a drop in his tone of voice. Although, he *was* right. Callum shifted with the uncomfortable memory of Kenzie's face snarling in his.

Callum spent the rest of the interview in stony silence. He knew Doug would kill him, but when at long last, the interviewer asked her final question, he nearly burst into tears of joy.

"So," she sighed happily, staring at Kenzie. "You plan to keep this band going a long time, then?"

Eagerly, Tom nodded. Callum nodded too. Meanwhile, Kenzie, as usual, was the one to take the attention of the camera.

"Of course, don't forget guys, season four premiers tomorrow. Tune in." Smiling at the camera, he winked. "For me."

Everywhere, millions of girls sighed dreamily. A closing line was burbled from the interviewer, followed by cheesy waves from Three Beams. The camera was turned off, and Callum wanted nothing more than to get out of the studio faster than the abilities of human speed.

"Tar, babe." Kenzie kissed the woman on the cheek.

The interviewer shrieked. Giggling, blushing bright, bright red, she was oblivious to Kenzie's mocking smirk, or Tom's bitten lips as he attempted to hide his laughter.

Oh, Callum had seen *enough*.

Outside was a cream sitting room, with white polished floors, and a tall, tall ceiling. Underneath the chandelier, the back-up vocalist ran his hands over his head. He paced. Just because he hadn't spoken, didn't mean he was any less of a band member!

Kenzie and Tom strolled past, sniggering.

"Oh, get in that lift, boy!" Kenzie chortled, shoving his best friend inside. "God, why is it always the fat ones that have the most confidence?"

As the doors closed in the lift, Callum could see Kenzie mouthing spiteful remarks at him.

"Sorry, love," questioned the ticket man, his double-chin quivering. "What did you say?"

Melinda replied, her voice hoarse:

"One ticket to Coventry, please."

"Single or return?"

"Single, please. I'm not coming back."

Carelessly, the man took her money, then swivelled back on his chair to get the ticket to her fears—*freedom.* Standing proud, Melinda attempted to smile, to be brave, because her family would be safe. Yes, Kenzie would probably follow her, but she'd never have to wait in apprehension for him to hurt Ashley next, nor be forced to lie awake at night, staring at the posters.

The ticket man swivelled back to her, her ticket in one hand, and donut in the other.

Melinda should have been happy on the platform. She could finally tell *him* she was moving out, and starting a new life.

In the distance, a train rumbled. An announcement sounded: the train to Coventry was due in five minutes.

The last time she was in this station, she was with Ashley, and they were heading to a concert, happiness in one of their hearts, dread in the other…

It was a pity she'd never know her college grades; she'd been so focused on her assignments in an attempt not to think of him, that she'd handed them all in early, and blew through her exams without a single break.

Sighing, Melinda flopped down on the bench. She held back the fear that made her shiver despite the June warmth. She'd be completely on her own. She had no plans. She was just going to crash in a B and B until she made some. It was a stupid, stupid decision, but what choice did she have? Putting her bag beside her, she pulled out her phone.

Another message from Kenzie:

So, what are you doing with yourself, hmm? Fingering yourself under your college desk? Tut tut, you'd better message me back so I don't come down there and relieve you of your 'frustration'.

Another train returned from some unknown place. A group of people got off, and went... *home*.

Melinda texted Kenzie back:

I haven't gone to college today.

And why ever, you naughty girl?

My mom's had a massive go at me this morning. Melinda responded. **So I cba to**

Whoosh!

Melinda nearly dropped her phone. On the opposite platform, the train vanished into the distance. Oh, she was a stupid, stupid idiot, confiding in the enemy! Huffing, she erased her message, and told him she was ill. She'd tell him about her departure while on the train; she couldn't be bothered to faff about with it now.

When her train at long last rolled toward her, Melinda stood with no hesitation. At least she'd left a letter under her pillow. The last thing she wanted was a search party after her.

"Wait, lovie, the doors aren't even open yet!" A middle-aged woman barged past. "Oi, I said *wait!*"

The woman called again to her little girl as the train doors opened. Panting, she gasped a hurried apology to Melinda:

"Sorry, darling!"

Melinda simpered back. "It's okay."

Getting on the train, the little girl clapped her hands. "Mommy! A train! We're going on a train, into a *big* tunnel!

Her mother was nowhere near as excited, but she smiled all the same. "God, what're you like, Ashley?"

Melinda's lips parted.

Someone else made it to the train in the nick of time, and as the train began to pull away, Melinda waited...and she watched it go. But she wasn't sad, or scared, or angry. She didn't cry, or scream, or grieve. Instead, she took her phone out of her bag with a reborn smile, and left a cheery voicemail on Ashley's phone:

"Hey, babe, I'll be at Art Club tonight! See you there!"

Stratford's most glamorous pub was standing room only. Older men sat in corners, while the younger generation favoured the bar. Cheers from a game of pool filled the room. For a Monday night, the atmosphere in the pub was roaring.

"Ugh, are you taking the *mic?*"

Watching Tom getting angry at the fruit machines was hilarious.

The mop of curly hair cursed as he lost yet another game. "Damn thing, I swear it's rigged."

"You know," Kenzie teased as his phone sounded out promise. "It might help if you pressed the right buttons, dumbass."

"I am pressing the right buttons! It just won't fucking work."

"Yeah, whatever. Damn, am I glad for a drink."

The day's interview had been painful. The questions were excruciatingly cheesy, and the interviewer? Kenzie felt sick just thinking of her. Yet now, as he read Melinda's latest text, he was exhilarated. At home, she was lying awake.

Don't let that mouth of yours start snoring, replied Kenzie. **I want it round my cock later.**

"Oi, you, you lanky twat!"

She texted him back straight away:

I know you do. Don't worry, I'm awake.

"Hey, I'm talking to you, Hudgson! Get off your phone before I smash it up your head!"

Kenzie looked up sharply.

Around the bar, the crowd of other famous singers, writers, and stars were staring… at him. Tom was protesting various 'no's', and was touching Kenzie's arm, trying to pull him away. The football played without the sound of the crowd, but another shouted insult from the same person drowned that out too:

"Oh, so now you're looking?"

In front of Kenzie, on a stool, was a fat, bald, wrinkly man.

"Kenzie," Tom wavered. "Seriously, don't—"

Angrily, Kenzie shrugged his friend off.

"Oh god, Ken, no, just hang on a minute—"

Kenzie passed the crowd, and stood over the man. "Yes? What's the problem?"

The man's sweaty body swayed as he slurred:

"You don't remember her, do you? You don't remember my Nat."

"Nat?" said Kenzie, amused. "No. Who the heck's Nat, a fly?"

"Bastard! You do. Wipe that smirk off your ugly mug and *think.*"

"Why don't *you* calm the hell down and explain?"

"You chucked her out of your house after you slept with her," the father nearly fell from his stool as he shook his fist. "You nearly cut her face when you threw her shoes. She begged me not to confront you, but fuck it."

Uh-oh.

"Huh?" Tom said, from somewhere in the background. "What's he on about, Ken?"

Kenzie blinked. "Now hang on mate," he said to the man. "Let's not do anything rash."

"Do anything rash? I'll knock your fucking head off, you waste of sperm. If I knew your father, I'd have told him to drown you at birth."

The slurring voice trailed away, in Kenzie's head, the fat, bald man was morphing into someone else...

"Kenzie!" Who was hissing at him, and frantically tugging on his arm? "Please, let's just go."

No, they couldn't! They couldn't leave, because the walls of the pub were melting, and the floor was cracking. The fat man had suddenly turned into Kenzie's father shaking his fist, and ranting:

"You think you're something great, don't you? Well let me tell you, you're nothing! You'll be famous for two, three years, then everyone will forget your talentless ass ever existed."

Somehow, Kenzie managed to stay calm, until the man said the words that made him snap:

"I bet your mother would be so damn proud of you, prick."

For a moment, there was stillness. After that, came the noise:

Tom was yelping. The crowd were cheering. There was a sickening squashing sound as a powerful fist connected with the fat man's nose. Kenzie briefly heard his own screams, and saw his own fists swinging as he lost control and *did not stop.* And suddenly, he couldn't see anything, because suddenly, his whole world was black...

"Dad?"

The fourteen-year-old's father simply cracked up at the TV. He didn't even spare his son a glance. One of his veiny hands was slapping his thigh, and the rapidly balding man roared with laughter so intense, his beer-gut shook.

His son hated it. He hated the wobbly, disgusting thing that extended night after night. He hated the bleary eyes, the slurry voice, and the crabby attitude that always came the following morning. And most of all, he detested the fact that it never used to be this way.

Awkward on his feet, Ken looked down at the letter his father had thrown on the floor, then at his blood-speckled trainers.

"Go and do something, boy." His father regained himself. "Don't just stand there like a wet rag. Go out and get a job. God, look at you. You'll never make your mother proud."

The boy shuffled away.

At school, he'd won the fight; he'd been expelled.

"Kenzie," Tom pleaded. "Kenzie, please, talk to me! This isn't you."

Oh god, his *head*.

Kenzie groaned. Clenching and unclenching, his fingers *throbbed*. He was sitting on the pub's doorstep with his head in his hands. Why couldn't he stop shaking? People were gathered outside. There was an ambulance parked to his right; from the slits between his fingers, he could see the sirens flashing across the concrete.

What had happened?

"Kenzie, please, come on."

"Fucking hell, Tom!"

Cursing, Kenzie looked up, and was met with his best friend, who was crouched in front of him, his eyes wide as he stared at the pub's back door.

"Y-You really hurt him Kenzie, he's—"

A stretcher clanked, and a fat, aging, *injured* man was wielded into the ambulance.

Kenzie exhaled. "Jesus Christ…"

"Kenzie!" Tom said. "What happened?"

Scattered clusters of people mumbled. The ambulance rolled away, and as Kenzie raked his hands over his head, he mumbled:

"I don't remember…"

Oh, he never did. Just like with Nat, he hadn't remembered her fleeing downstairs, him throwing the shoes, or how the hole in the wall had gotten there—

"Wait, what?"

To Tom's voice, Kenzie swallowed as he looked up. He was no longer a lead singer of a famous boy band, or even a grown-up. Instead, he was a little boy being interrogated by a police officer, one who had caught him doing something very, very bad. As Tom's hands balled together and his tone grew serious, Kenzie struggled to regain that precious sense of stability.

"Kenzie, what do you mean you don't remember?"

"Oh for fucks sake, Tom!" Kenzie stood up. "Just leave it."

He lurched to the side, because he was *still* dizzy.

"Kenzie!"

Clutching his forehead, he kept his head way down. "I'm pissed out my face! Everything's a fucking blur, now shift."

Tom squeaked as Kenzie barged past him. He had to get out of there, before the police turned up.

The crowd mumbled. The ambulance vanished down the street. Tom called out, but he didn't give chase, and Kenzie was relieved, because as he stormed off in the direction of his hotel, he knew:

He'd fucked up, big time.

Chapter Twenty-Nine

Ashley shot out of her room, not even stopping to shut the door.

Kenzie... bar brawl... offering the man compensation... zero charges. She still had the newspaper. The incident had happened last night. She had to show Melinda!

"Whoa, little one!"

Her father's outstretched hand stopped her. He'd been leaving the bathroom. Now, he blocked the stairs with his large frame and jolly laugh.

"Sorry, Dad, I—*Dad!*"

Thankfully, her father gave her the newspaper back. "Flippin' heck, go show Mel that scandal!"

Surprised, he was. Never expecting that, he was. Ashley ran downstairs.

"Mel!"

Downstairs was a hushed conversation. Downstairs was somewhere Ashley shouldn't have been yet; she'd been early getting ready for school. However, she paid no heed to the tension lingering in the corridor, or Jack's startled whimper as he hovered by the living room, unsure of what to do now his leg was in a plaster.

"Look, Mel, I'm not discussing this anymore."

Ashley startled. She'd gotten the kitchen door open, but only by a tiny, tiny crack. Inside the kitchen, in the space between the table and the counter, were Melinda and her mother, and that tone had *not* sounded good. Worse still, her mother was holding Melinda back with her hands, and Melinda was *begging*:

"Mom, please, I said I was sorry."

"I know, Mel."

"But, Mom, how could you do that to me? I—"

"Ugh, just stop. You know I didn't mean to hit you."

What?

"But I can't—Mel!"

Melinda was still trying to hug their mother, something she'd never done, and their mother was rejecting her!

"I've said I can't discuss this now," she said. "I need to finish these cakes, then be at hers for this afternoon so I can bring her here and show—"

Melinda snivelled so horribly, Ashley felt her heart crack.

Julie shoved her. "Oh for God's sake, just get your breakfast and piss off, can't you see I'm busy?"

Melinda turned back, nearly smacking into the fridge in an attempt to hide the tears coursing down her face. Ashley was about to rush to comfort her, but Julie reached for the door! Ashley practically *dived* for the living room, nearly bowling poor Jack over. Confused, the tiny dog scatted behind her. Closing the door, Ashley leaned her head on it.

Stomp, stomp.

"The silly cow," Julie grumbled.

Ashley clamped her hand over her mouth; why couldn't she be *quiet?* Her mother—

"Brad?"

Ashley breathed a sigh of relief; her mother had gone upstairs. Licking Ashley's hand, Jack began to wag his tail, glad for the company, and Ashley bent to stroke him with her free hand, because finally, she could confront Melinda.

She lingered.

Did she really want to? Looking at Jack, she squeezed the newspaper in her hand. Pushing her light brown waves behind her ears, Ashley opened the door, stepped out into the corridor, and headed for the kitchen.

Jack beat her to it. So tense was Ashley that she squealed, and gave the game away. The Jack Russell slid through the gap in the kitchen door, thus pushing it all the way open.

Sniffing, Melinda dragged her hand across her face, then smiled toothily, and *that* was what had made Ashley shudder.

"Hey, Ash, you're early. I haven't even poured your cereal yet."

Melinda was closing the fridge door, her voice high-pitched, and her smile beyond creepy…

Ashley blinked rapidly, unexpectedly remembering the newspaper.

"Mel, look at this, but don't you *dare* laugh."

Melinda took the newspaper, her still-shiny eyes bolting down the page. When she let out a gasp, Ashley suddenly wished she *had* laughed.

Librarians patrolled the shelves, on edge for possible noise. Students read, or typed away on computers. Clicks echoed, but the quiet stood out; it was what Melinda wanted. Around her, shelves of books boxed her off from the world, and the computer she was using transported her to the past.

It was a time when she was oblivious, and had no cares about *him*. Plus, she couldn't go to back to her lesson; she'd asked her tutor if she could sit in the college library, because she couldn't stand to be around her class.

They were all so happy. It made her sick.

Browsing her old Facebook photos via a proxy site was strange. How had it all become so… messed up? Her mother didn't apologise, Kenzie wouldn't stop texting her, and all she could see on her old profile was her and Dana, her and Dana, and…

A friend request.

Melinda drummed her fingers on the mouse. "Leave it. Leave it, Mel…"

Click.

"Cassie Burnall?"

Melinda recognised her straight away. The concert had been about to start. She'd been sitting in the seat, winding Ashley up, dreading the music, when along came ginger hair, a cheeky grin, and a shared hatred.

Cassidy had a horse! In her profile picture, she was proudly clutching the lead rope of a bay stallion, the third-place ribbon on his shoulder billowing in the wind.

Melinda grew even more excited when she looked on her chat bar. Cassidy was online! Immediately, Melinda started up a chat:

Hey there, sister from another mister! I've missed you.

She replied straight away:

Melinda! So good to see you! We'll have to go for a coffee sometime.

Had she read the latest scandal involving Kenzie, the one that secretly, had filled Melinda with worry? He'd been in a Stratford pub. Maybe he was still hanging around somewhere. Melinda didn't have to wait long until Cassidy mentioned it:

I'm still pissing myself laughing at Kenzie's face in the paper, you know. Hope everything went okay back there, at the concert.

Sighing through her teeth, Melinda ignored that part of the reply. *It was her secret, and was too complex for anyone else to understand,* she thought as she typed her answer:

The prick deserved to be shamed in the papers, and lose all that money. I hope the press never let him live it down. He was a right arse when I met him.

Cassidy's next reply could have brought the shelves tumbling down, and their books flapping onto the floor:

Same. I took my sisters to meet the band once, and it didn't go well, put it like that.

Melinda bolted forward. **Oh god, are you okay?**

Yeah, why wouldn't I be babe?

Cause like, he's so creepy, and weird.

Clack, clack, clack! Melinda was typing so loudly, a librarian scowled at her via a gap in the bookshelves.

Actually, yeah, Mel. He did creep me out a bit, to be fair.

You must have been really scared. No, Melinda had to be careful… she had to coax the truth out of her. **Cause I've heard it's happened to other girls too. They've got too close, or he hasn't liked them, or he's got them to sing and dance for him, then he's shut the door and pounced.**

Cassidy was baffled. **What? What do you mean? What's happened to other girls? Why are you being so weird?**

Melinda near pulled her own hair out. What did she *mean?* What did the girl *think* she meant?

Please don't play dumb Cass; you're not alone, I swear.

MELINDA, WHAT DO YOU MEAN?

I mean, he forced himself on you, right?

All of a sudden, the previously tranquil silence of the library transformed into a torture. Melinda bit her nails. She waited, and waited. It took her an age to finally get a reply from Cassidy:

What the FUCK? No, of course he didn't! We only went to get

autographs, and my sisters got us chucked out cause they tried to jump on Callum. Mel, I hope you're not hinting at what I think you're hinting at… please, because I don't think he'd ever do anything like that.**

Melinda's stomach lurched. There was only one way to get out of this one:

Of course not! I was only messing, about all of it. Sorry, I hate him, and I have a sick sense of humour. The two together never end well.

Melinda knew she'd messed up even before Cassidy went ballistic:

What the HELL? That's NOT funny Mel! Seriously! You don't have a sick sense of humour, at all! You're just SICK. Goodbye.

The chat seemed to freeze, and then:

You can no longer reply to this conversation.

Cassidy had blocked her.

"Kenzie… Kenzie, just please, come *on*."

Behind the green screen, away from the prying eyes, Tom paced. He embedded his hand in his mop of curls, and begged into his phone:

"Stop being a div. Pick up."

Tom hadn't heard from Kenzie since the previous night; he'd ditched rehearsal, with no warning. Tom continued to pace, as his phone rang and *rang*.

"Kenzie, come on, I need you."

Oh, he did, so, so much. Yet, he had no other option, but to relive the crunching of the fist that was surely bruised now, and the unravelling of a mind that was well and truly—

Tom heard hurried footsteps; Kenzie's voicemail sounded:

"Sorry, I'm busy. Drop me a message if it's important."

"Tom, have you heard from him?"

His band manager's face was tense.

"No, Doug, sorry. I've tried."

"Well, try again!" he said. "Oh for god's sake, I could kill him! The press is all over this. I still can't get them to piss off from outside."

It was as if they were on cue. The press were tapping on the opposite side of every closed curtain, and pressing their cameras onto every window.

"We need him here!" Doug ranted. "There are barely any scenes with just you and Callum, 'cause it just doesn't work. God, if I could see him now…"

"Hey man," Tom placed his hand on Doug's shoulder. "Try not to stress. He'll call me back. He always does."

Doug took another breath. "Oh, he'd better, else…"

Tom raised his eyebrows. "You'll kill him?"

Callum's guitar notes drifted toward them. The lights brightened, slowly getting hotter. Smells of sweat and hairspray were more overpowering than ever.

"Ah, fine then," said Doug, shaking his head. "I'll leave it to you, Tom. See you in a bit."

For everyone else, it was business as usual. Doug dismissed himself at his usual rapid pace, and Tom restarted his pacing. He put his phone back to his ear, and called Kenzie again.

"Please," he whispered. "This time, come *on*…"

Ugh, it was so *hot*. Melinda was fanning herself as she walked home, her sandals sticking to her.

Cassidy…

Concrete was quickly becoming dirt; the particles were burrowing in between her toes, making her itch horrendously.

How could she have been so stupid? Her secret had almost been blown to microscopic shards, all because she'd wanted a friend!

But she was right. Maybe, she wasn't the only one.

No! What was she thinking? She had to *stop!* If Kenzie found out…

Melinda moaned quietly. She had a headache. She was on her way home; she was going to go to sleep. In fact, she was nearly there, for she could spot that hidden wood even in the dark. Despite her mother's mood, she couldn't wait to get back.

"Screw you, Kenzie."

On the drive now, Melinda quickened her pace. A thrum sounded behind her. Thankfully, it was just her family's car. Her sister was waving, and her father smiling back at her. Melinda waved back, relieved she wouldn't have to be home alone.

The car doors opened. Melinda's waving hand stilled mid-air. Brad must have driven past them on the way home, and offered them a lift!

Stepping back, Melinda watched as her mother and her mother's friend got out of the car.

Mother and daughter locked eyes. Did her mother know she'd nearly ran away? Clutching her friend, Julie grinned, while Melinda looked down.

"Well," Brad chuckled. "This is a coincidence. Wanna do the honours?" He tossed Melinda his house key.

For once, Melinda didn't miss the catch.

Julie bragged behind him:

"Wait till you see these Karen, you're gonna love them."

"You forgot your house key again, Mel," Ashley chirped. "It's a good job we were here."

Melinda laughed. It *was*! She'd have been sleeping in the long grass otherwise! Lifting the key up, Melinda headed toward the house, the tide of family, and one excited family friend, following her.

The instant the call finally went through, Tom crowed:

"Kenzie, about bloody time! Where the hell have you been? Doug's screwing!"

"Sorry mate," Kenzie replied. "I'm on my way. I've been... busy."

"Busy?" Tom echoed. "Busy doing what?"

Kenzie continued to drive.

"Kenzie?"

A bead of sweat dripped off Tom's nose. There was a snipping sound; Callum's guitar strings had broken. The crew were calling louder, but Doug's voice overpowered all; he was coming close.

In time with the press' taps on the windows, Kenzie replied:

"Oh, nothing for you to worry about."

And then he hung up.

Chapter Thirty

Melinda knew there was something wrong the second she stepped into the house. She could hear an odd dripping noise, and Jack whimpering. She could see that the kitchen door was ajar, and the lights were on. An aroma of cakes didn't seem like the aroma anymore; the jam clotted in her nostrils, and the cream turned her guts inside out.

"I can't believe you spent so long on them," babbled Karen. "I owe you so much!"

Along the corridor, Melinda's shoes were sticking to her. How were her family not noticing—no, no, she was imagining it. Everything was *fine*…

"*Dad,*" said Ashley. "Come on, even my teacher thinks Bryony's mean."

Why couldn't Melinda merge into Julie's babbling about the cakes, or Brad's hearty chuckles? More importantly, why were her instincts yelling at her to *move back?* She 'was at the door, and her families' footsteps were pushing her onwards.

Karen bolted forward. "Ah, I can't wait any longer!"

Melinda made for the handle, but it was too late. Karen barged past her.

Stumbling into the kitchen was like stumbling into a land of utter devastation.

In front of Melinda, Karen stood, her hands splayed, shaking. Was it winter? Melinda actually *felt* the colour drain from her face, because the sight in front of her—

Julie screamed. She staggered back, gasped, and screamed again. "What's *happened?* My cakes…"

The previously pristine kitchen was completely trashed. Earlier that day, Julie had finished her cakes. On every surface the exquisite range had stood, proud and beautiful. Yet now, they were beaten to a bloody, weeping pulp. Traumatised, Julie's eyes trailed the damage. Jam was smeared on the walls. Cream slathered the floor. The sink was overflowing. Water etched around Melinda, and Karen's feet, an inch thick.

Speckled by cake remains as he sat up in his basket, Jack howled loud enough for the room to crumble.

Brad leapt into action. Instantly he was by Julie's side, comforting her, while Ashley simply erupted into floods of tears. Karen stayed still; Melinda didn't make an effort to comfort her.

"Melinda," Julie wailed. "Melinda... what's *happened*?"

Beside herself, Ashley hid behind her parents. On the back door, squirted in icing, was the words: 'Fuck you, Mom'.

Melinda shoved everyone aside, and took to the stairs. She had to get out, she had to get out, she had to—

Panicked, Melinda barged into her bedroom, and stopped.

In the centre of her bed was a single, red rose.

Melinda ground her teeth. Within seconds, she had that mocking rose in her hand, and was ripping it to mere *petals*. When there were no more petals left, her mind flashed back:

Kenzie's body brushed against hers. He yanked her tights down, he leered at her through evil eyes, and she screamed out for help.

Her phone buzzed.

You could at least text me first for once, or save me some cake.

Bolting from her room, Melinda pounded down the stairs, not once aware of Karen attempting to tidy the kitchen, or her parents, then Ashley calling her as she opened the front door, and plunged outside.

She didn't feel the heat in the air, the grass around her ankles, or the graze on her knee when she fell halfway up the hill. All that occurred, all that spoke to her through her wave of madness, was that she had had *enough*. He'd taken Dana. He'd taken Jack. He'd taken *everything*. Although, it took Melinda another stumble to realize she'd have to protect him once more, because if anyone found out...

"I've had enough!"

From one of the trees, a set of pigeons took to the sky, frightened.

"You hear that Kenzie? I've had enough! Just leave... me... a*lone*!"

The crack of his slap, the kissing of his lips, the whispers and the texts and the pranks and the pain... they combined to form a girl who was breaking down, on the grassy hill that overlooked the wood.

"See?" Callum said, holding the guitar with pride. "Now you."

Sighing, Tom ran his finger along the strings, and flinched when a racket rang out.

The children winced. The crew mumbled. The cameras glistened, and Kenzie still wasn't back.

"No, no." Callum adjusted the strap. "Like *this*."

Oh, Tom didn't *care* about how it was meant to sound! Anxiously, he looked back. The window was still packed with press; the orbs of their cameras were glowing through the curtains. Tom's eyes met Doug, pacing at the front of the set. He saw the children huddled in the corner, whispering, wondering the exact same thing as him.

"Tom!" Doug bustled over, angry. "Have you heard from—"

"No, I haven't."

Doug huffed, and left.

Callum went over to the group of children, grinning as they clambered excitedly around him. The stupid boy! How could he not understand?

Doug was grumbling to the director, as if that would actually help. "I'm gonna throttle him when I get hold of him… no, seriously, he'll be in a body bag at this rate—"

Rabid, happy screaming sounded from outside.

Tom followed Doug to the window.

Outside the window stood a towering, tanned blond, completely cool as the reporters mobbed him. They thrust microphones in his face. They clicked their cameras, illuminating him with bursts of light. Meanwhile, the lead singer simply talked to them, his head nodding, and his teeth glinting in the sunlight, his power so strong even Tom could see it from where he stood…

"Out of the way, boy!"

Doug barged ahead, throwing Tom back. Furiously, he banged on the window, hollering at Kenzie to *get inside*. The crew anxiously rounded up the children, who were clapping and jumping, saying:

"Was he back? What had he done?"

"Oh, nothing for you to worry about."

Tom ducked out of the door and veered to the left.

"Kenzie!"

Hands in his pockets, the lead singer peered smugly down at Tom. His blond hair was gelled the way Tom liked best, which into strands where some fell over his forehead.

"Yes, you know me," Kenzie replied.

"How'd you get in so fast?"

"Never underestimate the power of Security."

Tom snickered. Of course, Security had dashed out last-minute, and hurled Kenzie away. Tom grinned a true grin, and when Kenzie laughed bashfully, he melted in the centre of the set's corridor.

"Aw, Tom, sorry about last night. I guess the drink just got to me, so to hell with it! No more alcohol. It took me all night to sort the mess out; that bloke weren't easily persuaded."

"Kenzie! You little scumbag—"

Kenzie saluted. "All right, Doug?"

Tom spluttered with laughter.

To Doug, Kenzie sauntered over, without a care in the world.

"Right, come with me," Doug snarled. "*Now.*"

As Doug pulled Kenzie away by his wrist, Kenzie turned back, stuck his tongue out at Tom, and Tom copied his best friend, because he was honestly, truthfully, at ease.

What had happened? Why had Melinda dashed outside? Why was the kitchen wrecked? Embarrassed, Karen had left. Julie was weeping, silently. Brad was cradling her in the doorway, his eyes shut, his head resting on her shoulder, in their own private bubble of adult situations.

With clenched fists, Ashley snivelled. She was just so confused.

A cake tower collapsed in the kitchen.

"I might as well p-pack up the fucking business," her mother said. "Someone obviously d-doesn't want me to be successful. I know it was Melinda."

"Don't be so silly." Kissing her forehead, her father wiped her mother's dampened cheeks. "I know she's been trouble lately, but still, that writing could have been someone covering their tracks."

As Julie mumbled that trouble wasn't the word, the front door opened.

While another cake collapsed, a cake that had been a waste of their mother's precious efforts, Ashley watched her sister; her stare was something that made Ashley stop crying.

"Ashley," Melinda said. "Go upstairs."

Jabbing her finger in her fae, Julie was having none of it. "Don't you tell Ashley to go upstairs! Who the hell do you think you are? You're gonna answer to all of us."

"Mom." God, Melinda didn't even sound scared! "It's for the best. I need to tell you something."

Julie's arm fell, slowly.

"Ashley," Brad said. "Go upstairs."

With a startled gasp, Ashley ducked around her mother and sister and headed for the stairs. Temptation was too much; she slowed completely down when she reached the top, and sat down. She peered over the banister, gaining a birds-eye view of the scene.

"Fine," Julie snapped. "Go on then."

Brad folded his arms. "Come on, Mel, we won't wait forever."

Neither would Ashley, she decided as she knuckled her now dry eyes.

'Melinda sniffed, and said it:

"It was me."

"*What?*" Julie snarled.

"I said," Melinda replied emotionlessly. "It was me. I smashed up the cakes."

Brad pinched the bridge of his nose, and Julie simply... simply...

Ashley buckled. Right as the woman blew, she buried her face in her hands. Only just did she catch the woman lunge forward, and grab Melinda's wrist.

"What the *fuck?* Why the hell would you do that, Mel? Do you not know how fucking long I spent making them? You fucking *bitch!*"

"Mom, I—"

"I can't believe you!" Julie continued. "Did you plan this? Did you sneak out of college? Oh, you little—"

"Julie, come on, be rational."

"Brad, piss off!" Julie retorted. "Jack, get the hell back in your basket, you mangy mutt. And *you,*"

Ashley snuck a glance, and regretted it.

Julie had Melinda in her grasp. She was shaking her. "I want you out of here, do you hear me?"

What? No. *No!* Ashley wept, her fists rammed in her mouth to hide the racket. Surely her family wasn't being torn apart in front of her?

Melinda cowered. "What…"

Waving his hands up and down, Brad came to Julie's aid. "Now calm down, we can sort this out, we can—"

Melinda squealed as her mother yanked on her wrist, then shouted at her father:

"Shut up! You have no idea Brad, *no idea* how much she's wound me up. Look what she's done to the kitchen! Do you know how long it'll take to clean this mess up? And how much I slaved over those cakes? I could have made some real money showcasing my cakes at that wedding, but *this* little bitch… why'd you do it Melinda, why?"

Ashley was only able to look for another split second, yet she easily saw Melinda twist out of her mother's grip and completely fall apart.

"I'm sorry!" wept Melinda. "But after the way you've treated me lately, and how you hit me, you deserved it. I just needed you, and you weren't there!"

Julie roared:

"That's *it*! Get out of my sight!"

Desperate, Brad tried to stop her. "Julie, no, don't—"

Jack howled. Ashley wailed, but it was no use:

Thump!

Ashley looked up from her hands. Melinda was in a heap on the stairs, her knees and hands on the carpet.

Their eyes joined, and they were united in terror – Julie advanced on Melinda, pointing hatefully. "Get up there," shouted Julie. "And don't let me see again for the rest of today, you stupid, stupid cow!"

Melinda scrambled to her feet. Ashley jumped up too, ready to chase after her as she scaled the stairs two at a time and made for her bedroom.

"You're so fucking immature," Julie ranted. "You don't understand the trouble you're causing, how much you're hurting everyone… Ashley, don't you dare go after her."

It was too late anyway; Melinda had locked the bathroom door.

"Get down here, love," her mother said mournfully. "I don't want you near her."

Brad came up behind her. "Hey," he rubbed her shoulders. "Shush, hey, come on…"

Into his arms, Julie mother wept. Ashley sniffed, climbed slowly down the stairs, and slinked into the living room, utterly distraught.

"She's going, Brad. I mean it, I want her out of here…"

Chapter Thirty-One

The creaking of the first stair was equivalent to a gunshot. Melinda clenched the banana in her hand. She didn't want to see her mother, but she'd had to come down eventually; she was hungry for a start! Brad had brought her supper up on a tray last night, but she'd left it untouched.

"Stay with me, let me in…"

Ugh! Never, ever would been able to escape those damn lyrics. Season four was showing. Ashley squealed out:

"Because together, we will win."

No, Melinda could *never* win. Why couldn't he just stop? She hadn't even done anything wrong this time! The fruit shaking in her hand, Melinda fought the tears, and continued up the stairs. Creak… she had to text him, and keep on doing it. Creak…it had taken hours for her parents to clean the kitchen. Creak… she'd had no option but to pretend it was her fault, and accept her fate just like she'd done when he'd kissed her neck—

"Oi."

Oh god! He had her by the wrist, and he was going to kill her—

"I'm not gonna repeat myself when I say this," Julie hissed, her cheeks flushed. "So, listen up."

She pulled Melinda so that she was standing in the middle of the staircase, ensuring she was down to her level in every way possible.

Melinda was just annoyed with her. She'd listened all night to the arguments her parents had had, and now, she was tired.

"Fine." She tugged her wrist free. "But make it quick, cause I'm running late for college."

Her mother inhaled sharply. "I'm gonna pretend you didn't just say that, because I just want you to know, that you're beyond fucked up. One more strike, and you're out."

The stairs gave way; Melinda near fell through the metaphorical gap.

Jack dithered in the kitchen; his claws could be heard, scatting along the tiles. Brad softly spoke to the dog, delighting when Jack began to yap back at him.

Melinda simply looked down, and nodded meekly. "Okay."

She turned around, and continued on her way not listening to hear her mother's response. She listened to her sister giggle at TV instead, and wondered:

How could she giggle, when life was completely falling apart?

When Melinda reached her bedroom, she tossed the banana onto her pillow. Was it karma that was sending her this hell? Had she really done something *that* awful? Taking her phone from on top of her drawers, she received no answer, just her reflection in the bedside mirror. Contrasting against the dark circles under her eyes, her blonde streak 'hung like a rope, a rope she could easily strangle herself with. She sent Kenzie a text:

Don't worry, I covered for you. Mom's probably gonna kick me out, not that I care. Hope you're having a good day. Try not to mess up your lines!

There were four orange walls, a glass window, and three boys singing into microphones, while the crew watched them.

Kenzie cringed as he sang. Something was ordering him to get out of the room. Callum was oblivious; he strummed his guitar. Behind the window, nodding sternly, their band manager looked as though he were about to tantrum, while the various DJs (Of which, Kenzie had forgotten their names) muddled with the buttons of the sound booth.

Kenzie raked his hand through the inside of his jean pockets. How long had they *been* in here?

"Take my hand," he sang. "Take me down to the water side."

Oh, how Kenzie *hated* singing children's songs.

"And together, we can stand and watch the tide…"

Kenzie continued with the song, singing the lead as always, with Tom backing him, as always. God, they were all so stupid! They had no clue of Kenzie's phone buzzing in his pocket, or the messed-up *shit* Kenzie was plotting.

Callum yelling suddenly cut Kenzie's thoughts off:

"Whoa, whoa." Placing his hands over his ears, he shook his head. "Jesus Christ!"

Tom stopped singing. Kenzie stopped singing. Doug tapped the window, angry... someone had messed up.

It was Tom. Rolling his eyes as he took off his own headpiece, Doug swung open the tiny door and stormed into the room, actual *steam* flowing from his ears!

Kenzie clocked Callum muttering:

"Serves him right."

The smaller boy was given a smack around the back of his head for his arrogance.

Callum gaped at Kenzie. Kenzie glared back.

"What the hell are you doing?" Doug's face dove right into Tom's. "You're supposed to be singing back-up, not screaming like a demented banshee."

"I'm sorry," protested Tom. "I was just getting really into it!"

Kenzie knuckled his laughter, and let the argument turn into a mime-show; he reached for his phone. Everything had gone perfectly, and was back to normal, because the press had submitted to his bullshit apologies, along with the bald fat man. Yes, it had taken a lot of persuasion, but the man had accepted his bribe, and looked hilarious with a black eye and a split lip.

"I swear, Doug, I'll do better in a sec!"

Doug turned his back on Tom, making for the door. "You say that every bloody time."

"But I really, really mean it! I'll go to bed earlier... no more Mario Kart for a *month*, I swear. I was only trying to welcome Kenzie back to the Brummy house."

"I don't give a crap about your personal life, Tom!"

Kenzie tittered as he answered Melinda's text:

Well, hello Mellbell! We're singing right now actually, recording our songs for the next episode! Tom's just fucked up. Soz about your mom... you could always come live with me, and ride my cock all night.

After sending the message, he gave the arguing pair an expression of false sympathy, because oh, he *hated* seeing poor, frazzled Doug upset. "All right, Doug, calm down," he said, carelessly smiling as he got in-between them. "Here, *I'll* sort him."

In surrender, Doug raised his hands. "All right, Ken, I trust you. Just please sort him out, cause I'm near breaking point."

Tom flushed, humiliated. Scoffing, Callum looked miffed, yet lost his pathetic attitude when both Kenzie and Doug narrowed their eyes at him. Back to strumming his guitar, he kept well clear of further confrontation, as Kenzie led Tom out of the room:

"The stupid twit!" Tom cursed.

"So, I don't have to ask you what's up then?" asked Kenzie.

"Hell no." Tom scowled. "I'm just sick of him, Ken! He's been down my throat all day. I've barely done anything, and it's so hard anyway not to laugh when he goes off on one, cause I couldn't help but notice that his face goes all tight. Like, what if one day it all cracks?"

What if one day, Kenzie became the biggest celebrity, and had his name engraved on a golden plaque?

"I know its vacation tomorrow," Tom continued. "But still..."

"Exactly," Kenzie said. "So just chill."

"I suppose I could."

Vacation... *that's* what Kenzie had been so het up about in the sound booth! "Just put up with Doug for now. He always gets like this, remember?"

"Yeah, I guess you're right."

"I'm *always* right, Landsby."

Tom broke out into a smile, then gave the man a one-armed hug. "Aw, sorry mate, he just pisses me off sometimes, that's all."

"One more strike, and you're out."

The breeze ruffled her black shirt, then crawled over her spine like *his* fingers. The sun was blazing; not even the grass was cool.

Jay was bragging:

"Yep, took me forever to do it, but here it is!"

Sophie was admiring Jay's newest 'go-kart', while Melinda was sitting, cross legged, plucking at her leggings, trapped in a black cloud that was coming closer and closer.

"Wow, its brilliant Jay!" Melinda said falsely.

Ashley had called to her many times in the night, yet she'd ignored her, because she was just so, so scared of breaking down...

"I'm glad you like it, guys! It took all my blood, sweat, and tears, but here is the Jay Racer Five Thousand!" Jay crowed.

On the trolley-turned-kart, the handlebars were painted blue, and the metal polished to a shine. Around the metal of the kart, Jay had stuck on wooden flames. He had painted the flames red! They matched a red scarf, tied to the back…

No, Melinda wouldn't cry… she *wouldn't*. The kart was fantastic. The three of them had chosen to spend their lunch break in a field, on the hill that overlooked their college. They were going to test the kart, and it would be worth it.

Sophie glanced at Jay, nervous. "But how are we gonna test it? Isn't it dangerous?"

"Nah, it'll be fine. Hey, Mel," Jay called out casually. "What do you think?"

Sharply, Melinda looked up. What did she think? What did she *think?* Oh, she *thought* she'd be okay going to a concert, but a certain band member—

"Well," the girl replied hurriedly. "M-Maybe Soph's right. It looks dangerous, especially with all those stones on the hill. We've gotta go back in ten minutes anyway—"

"And what do we have here?"

Melinda jumped up, and began to move back, because a crowd of hyenas were stalking her in the savannah, their grins leering…

Dana was the picture of glee. In the centre of the crowd of Drew, Em, and Rach, Dana, perfectly dressed, folded her arms. White teeth stood out in her smile; her black hair caught the sunlight perfectly. Jay and Sophie were standing together, trapped on the side-lines, because Melinda was the only target in Dana's sneer:

"And what the fuck are you saddos doing?"

"Nothing," said Sophie timidly.

Jay stuck out his chest. "We're testing our new kart, so buzz off."

"Hey, who do you think you are, scruff-ball?" Drew snapped at Jay.

"I think I'm Jay, and you don't scare me, you arsehole."

Drew headed for Jay, and Dana cheered him on:

"Go on, Drew, smack him!"

Clatter!

Drew had shoved Jay into the trolley. Melinda quivered. Earlier that day, she'd butted shoulders with Dana in the corridor by accident… she remembered the hiss Dana had given her. Now, she was paying the price, with Jay's self-esteem. Rubbing his arm, he was trying so, so hard not to look at Drew, but it was impossible, for Drew was taunting him, teasing him:

"What? What are you gonna do, stick-insect, huh?"

"Drew, come on." Jay laughed nervously, raising his hands. "I need to test it, the go-kart I mean. And you guys are messing that up. Someone's gotta get in."

Drew looked the trolley up and down. "Oh yeah? And who's gonna test that heap of shit?"

"And who's gonna be a lying little bitch?" Dana added.

Melinda was met with fiery blue eyes, and a set of gnashing teeth.

"Whose gonna fuck me over?" Dana poked her; the handlebars of the trolley dug into Melinda's back as she stumbled.

Em whispered that Dana was getting angry now. But... so was Melinda.

"Whose gonna climb into that shitty trolley," continued Dana. "And send themselves souring to their *death?*"

Melinda was met with the frightened faces of Jay, and Sophie next to him, holding his hand protectively. Slowly, Melinda trailed her eyes away, then down the hill. It was a straight-downwards slope, plastered in stones; falling on them would be oh-so painful...

"Hello, are you deaf?" said Dana. "I said, who's gonna—"

"I am."

The breeze seemed to come to a halt on the hill. Melinda glared right back at her ex-best friend, but then came a chorus of shouts:

"No, Mel!"

"Don't, you'll hurt yourself!"

"Fuck off!" Melinda growled back.

Em and Rach egged her on. Stepping back, Dana blinked, shocked. Yelling, Jay made for Melinda, but Em held him back, and Rach grabbed Sophie's arms in a vice, telling her to hold still and let the madness happen.

All of this passed Melinda by:

"Push me!" She leapt into the trolley. "Someone push me!"

She ignored Jay's startled cries, and Sophie's begging as Em and Rach hauled them back by their arms. Her mother thought she was fucked up? Melinda would show her just how fucked up she was.

"Dana," Jay screamed. "Don't—"

"Bitch!"

One push was all it took. Suddenly, Melinda was careering down; the release she'd craved was rushing to meet her. Slamming her eyes shut, Melinda clung to the trolley's sides, ground her teeth, and anticipated.

"Jesus Christ," Drew howled, clapping madly. "She's fucking mental!"

Mental or not, Melinda bumped down the hill. Adrenalin, adrenalin, bump, bump, bump, and… crash!

Melinda was flying through the air. It was complete numbness before she landed. But when she did, oh, when she did, pain powered through her veins, and leapt into her throat, yet she didn't scream. She just lay there, staring at the sky.

The trolley skidded toward the people that were gathering, pointing, whispering…

There was nothing but an eerie calm. Limbs splayed out, Melinda held her teeth together, juddered, and became one with the agony that flowed like a river.

There was chaos on the hill. Dana's crew doubled back, however, their shouting was merely a dull, listless buzzing, much like Em and Rach were making a few minutes earlier... The sky was spinning – Melinda felt sick, dizzy. Was that Jay she could hear, dashing to meet her? Were those other sounds people coming over to her, and Sophie worrying?

Melinda had no clue. She had no damn *clue,* because… she was smiling.

She felt high. She felt amazing. She felt… free.

Chapter Thirty-Two

Unfortunately, the beautiful numbness didn't last long.

Jay was like a parrot, squawking her name frantically as he descended the hill. Melinda groaned. It was as if she were back in bed, not wanting to get up and face the day. She wanted to lie there, on her bed of nails, for just a few more minutes.

"Mel!"

Jay waved in her face. "Mel, hello, Mel! Can you hear me, are you okay? Mel, please, speak to me!"

Melinda just snapped at him:

"For god's sake, I'm all right." Grimacing, she sat up and held her forehead. "It was fine." She spat blood, from the tongue she didn't know she'd bitten. "It was *fun.*"

"Oh god, Mel! I'm so sorry. You shouldn't have gone down. I shouldn't have let you go down…"

Melinda managed to hold herself together, until there was a terrified cry from the top of the hill.

Sophie was calling down to her. Melinda squinted, but couldn't hear her.

Jay slipped his arm around her, but she shrugged him away:

"Go away," she shouted. "I said I was fine!"

She noticed the suspicious whispers of the crowd by the college, and at last heard Sophie's words about getting a nurse, aka an overly-concerned woman with a frowning face and endless questions.

"Mel, stay with me," Jay said. "Sophie's just gonna get the nurse and bring her back here."

"Sophie," Melinda snapped. "Don't you dare!"

Sophie pushed through the crowd and vanished.

"Sophie!"

Jay put his scrawny body in front of Melinda's. And to make matters worse, there were points from the crowd, hushed whispers, and startled giggles, all directed at her.

"Mel, will you just *wait?*"

"No, we can't just fucking stand here!"

"But—"

"Look at them lot, they're all staring at me! T-They'll think I'm weird... they'll wanna lock me up!"

Jay gulped. "Yeah, we can't have them staring. It's making you worse. I'll take you inside, to C Block perhaps?"

"Ri-Right, C block..."

Sophie was getting the nurse; it didn't matter what Melinda did now, or where she went. Her legs were still shaky; her back was still stiff. Yet she kept walking. Jay was behind her, squawking once more about how sorry he was. Melinda ignored him, kept her head down, and exhaled as the sun burned her back.

Bodies milled around her, brushed her shoulders, *touched* her:

"Aw babe, are you all right?"

"Hey, come here, god knows what that fall has done to you!"

"She's fine," Jay blurted. "I'm taking her to the nurse, and—"

"Are you sure you don't want help?" Another kind voice interrupted.

"What were you twats doing anyway," sneered an arrogant boy. "Messing around with trolleys?"

"Just mind your own damn business!" snapped Melinda. "Move!" She slapped at the unknown hands on her arm. "Get off, all of you!"

A sob rising in her throat, Melinda allowed Jay to do the talking, and herself to be led away. She let Jay usher her through the back entrance, down the quiet corridor, then down the stairs. Her strides became ghostly footprints, and she let her tears pour out of her.

She knew what her fate would be. As they reached C block, and chose a seat on the floor outside the empty Computer Lab, she was ready to accept it.

Melinda slid down the wall, until she met the cold blue floor. "I'm sorry. I'm so, so sorry Jay. It's all my fault. I'm sorry!"

Jay just sat next to her, his arm around her shoulders. "No, it's not, Mel. Dana pushed you, remember?"

Seconds ticked by, seconds where no one else came down the corridor, and it was engulfed in silence. Melinda needed someone, anyone, yet when Jay said:

"Mel, what's wrong?"

She jumped to defence:

"Nothing, just piss off."

"No one's ever going to believe you…"

"Oh, Mel, please," Jay begged. "Come on, this isn't you."

God, she looked pathetic, crying on the college floor! Gulping back another sob, Melinda glanced at Jay.

"You're best friend. I'm worried," he said.

"Well you're just choosing to worry. I've told you, I'm fine."

Jay sighed. "You're not. I know, because you don't wear make-up anymore. You're always distant. You don't do your hair." He was checking them off on his fingers, one by one. "You have bags under your eyes, you're moody all the time, you got completely drunk a while back, and *now*, you've insisted on doing something that you knew would hurt you. You're just not *yourself,* Mel. Something's gotta be going on."

Melinda looked away. "I'm just stressed."

"About what? You're ahead with assignments. Your Dad's the town's favourite dog groomer. Everyone loves your mom's cakes. Ashley loves school again, and is getting good grades. So you've got nothing to be stressed *about,* unless there's something you're not telling me."

Oh god she was going to smack him, she was going to smack him, she was going to—

"Even that Three Beams concert went all right."

"No, it fucking didn't!" Standing up, Melinda glared at him. "It didn't, you damn moron!"

Jay's mouth was an O of fright. Melinda was delighted, and shot the bomb into the hole she'd already dug for herself:

"It went *shit,* 'cause he won't leave me alone!"

Melinda readied herself, for the fury of the high heels she could hear from a classroom a few doors along.

"Just remember Mellbell… thanks to your sister, I know where you live."

The heels got louder. Jay stared harder. And in her mind, Kenzie was storming toward her, his teeth gritted, a knife in his hand.

"Excuse me," said a cross tutor. "I'm trying to teach a class here—"

Melinda ran.

"Oh, sorry, Miss," Jay gasped. "She's just upset."

Melinda had resorted to flight; all she could think was:

"I'll break you like a twig."

She turned right, bolted up some random stairs, and ran *away* from Jay's startled cries. At the top of the steep staircase was a fire exit. She bashed it open. Hot air, sunlight, greenery... in front of her, the concrete roof stretched out, and in the distance, the hill loomed. The trolley was still there, discarded on its side.

"Mel," Jay was panting as he joined her side, his hands on his knees. "Wait..."

Melinda didn't answer. In an attempt to achieve complete stillness, she kept her fists clenched, her eyes forward. She didn't blink. She didn't breathe. She just watched the trolley's wheel as it spun, and the magpie that was pecking at the bars. Determined, she stood tall, proud; she could *not* mess up again.

Step, step...

Jay appeared on her right, looking out ahead, his hands in his pockets.

"Fuck off," Melinda snapped. "You won't believe me."

"About what?"

"And he'll get worse."

"Who? Who, Melinda? Who'll get worse?"

Melinda curled her toes. "Kenzie."

Melinda's 'fingers spread out, as if she was searching for something that wasn't there. Blinking rapidly, she dared not look at Jay. She simply listened to his voice as it grew raspy:

"Kenzie? You mean, Kenzie from T-Three Beams?"

Melinda nodded.

Jay came to her side. "You can tell me, you know. I'm always here for you! Alway!. You're my friend, and I can't stand to see you like this! Just please, tell me everything, all of it. I'll believe you, I swear."

"Shut up! Just leave me alone!" Aggressively, Melinda pushed him away from her. "Fuck off, just fuck off! You won't believe me... you won't!"

Hang on, Jay said to her. He had only wanted to help, he said.

Rubbish! Absolute *rubbish*. With an enraged scream, Melinda kicked the fire exit door once, twice.

"Melinda!" Jay grabbed her arms. "What have I just said?"

Melinda clenched her fists.

"I said I'll believe you," repeated Jay. "I believe everything you say, 'cause you never lie!"

"*No.* You'd believe me cause you're stupid, so stupid you failed a foundation course and had to do it again!"

Jay released her. His eyes, echoing hurt, signalled that he finally understood that she'd' changed. And now, he was going to leave her, like Dana, her mother, and everyone else. Melinda couldn't bear it.

From the back of Melinda's throat, a sob rose. She threw her arms around Jay, and wept onto his shoulder:

"Jay, I'm sorry. I'm sorry I said that. I didn't mean it! You're smart. Look at all the stuff you've built. I'm sorry I'm so horrible, and I'm sorry I didn't tell you, but I'm scared of him!"

"Mel, it's all right. It's all right, I just wanna—"

"No," Melinda grizzled. "It's not, I-it'll never be all right, because h-he'll kill me if I say anything."

"But I won't tell anyone…"

"Okay, okay," Melinda gasped. "It started on the tour. He k-kept kissing me in the d-dressing room, and he," she choked. "He wouldn't get off. I tried to get a-away but he hit me, and then tried to-he tried to…"

Jay was rubbing her back, soothing her. It felt so *nice*.

"He's so famous," she continued. "He can have whoever he wants. But he keeps texting *me*. And he took Jack, and broke his leg. He trashed my house and…and…"

Melinda trailed off.

"Oh god, Mel." Jay clung to her far, far too tightly. "I'm so sorry—"

"Oh, sod it!"

This time, Jay let her squirm free from the embrace.

Melinda hated being so cold, so heartless. She hated Kenzie, herself, and the thought she'd kept bottled up since day one, the thought she was now screaming at the bewildered Jay:

"You know what? I don't care if he kills me, I've had enough. I wanna die, Jay. I wanna fucking die!"

At the rear of the college, a lone student scuttled from one door to the next, his hands in his pockets. A flock of geese flew overhead. A small boy stood with a new weight on his shoulders, and a snivelling girl stood with her back to him, no emotion left in her.

It took another gust of wind, another flock of geese, before the scene changed.

Jay crept forward. He put his hand on Melinda's shoulder. Timidly, she turned to face him, her lips bitten, and tears dripping down her swollen face.

Jay smiled. "I don't know what to say, but I will say this: Kenzie's a bastard."

"Promise you won't tell anyone."

Jay hesitated.

"*Promise.*"

"But Mel"—Jay locked eyes with her—"you do know he tried to rape you, right? And that what he's doing now is stalking, and that both are punishable by law?"

"Yes, of course I know that."

"Well in that case, you could show all the messages he's sending you to the police! It's evidence."

"No, Jay, it's not as simple as that. Just please, promise me you'll keep quiet about it."

Jay was mortified. "But I can't just let you suffer!"

"I'll sort it myself, Jay! God, I just needed to *vent,* and now I can't even do that?"

Exasperated, Jay put his hands on his head. "I've gotta go," he replied.

Melinda had zoned out. She didn't know he'd gone until the fire-exit door closed. *Shit!* She tried to follow him, but after going down the first flight of stairs, she lost him completely. Instead, she was met with Sophie and the nurse:

"Oh, Mel!" Sophie beckoned the nurse over. "We've been looking for you everywhere. Are you okay? I'm sorry I took so long. The nurse was busy."

As if to prove her point, the nurse clutched her chest when she arrived, winded by the effort of rushing to a disturbed teenager who actually didn't need her; she scoffed when Melinda replied:

"Erm, yeah, I'm fine."

'She had to find Jay!

Sadly, Melinda had no luck. She couldn't find Jay for the rest of the day; he didn't answer the door when she knocked for him, or her calls when she got home.

She spent the rest of the night awake, terrified of what would happen next.

Chapter Thirty-Three

"Damn it."

Callum tried again. "Nope, still flat..."

The lyrics *still* weren't right... why? He'd been practising on his guitar all night!

Despite his glares, the brand-new laptop that sat on the coffee table didn't combust. Callum was thankful he was alone in the staffroom. Kenzie *still* hadn't bought him a new laptop, and he'd had to buy his own, which was so complicated to use, he'd have better luck puzzling out code languages.

"Tom, man, what the heck are you doing?" called Kenzie from the corridor.

Tom was bouncing on a space hopper, and Kenzie was laughing. Both looked like children from the set. All Tom needed was a wig, and all Kenzie needed was a hammer to knock his height down a few meters.

The staffroom smelt of coffee, along with sweaty feet and mouldy pizza. Ignoring it, Callum started a new recording on the laptop. It was essential he recorded a new song *before* he showed the lyrics to the others. He'd learnt that the hard way.

"Take me back in time, to where every sentence didn't have to rhyme. To where I was just me." Callum sung. "And you were just you, and we didn't have to worry, about where we're going to. I'm sick of pretending, sick of lying... So why don't I just stop." There was a crash; Tom had fallen. "Stop constantly trying?"

"Aw Tom," wheezed Kenzie. "Doug's gonna go mental... again."

"Just hide it, and say one of the kids did it." Tom protested. "Doug won't know!"

There it was again, a giggling sound!

Bewildered, Callum looked at the laptop. Frowning, he rapidly crossed off the electronic sound booth app, minimised his extra tabs, and the girl that watched him near fell off the edge of her bed.

She had brown plaits. She wore glasses, and had a very, very worried expression.

"Oh no, I'm sorry," she said. "I know, I should have disconnected, but…"

Callum couldn't be angry with her. All fault belonged with the boys that were stupidly trying to hide a burst space hopper. They'd used Callum's laptop that lunchtime to video chat fans, as apparently, his video camera was better.

"I-I'm Faye," said the girl. "Tom and Kenzie were doing video chats, and I was in the queue. I didn't get clicked though, until Tom gave the laptop to you. I knew I was part of a joke, but," she sniffed, "I was so happy to finally get connected…"

"It's all right."

Kenzie and Tom's running feet signalled their departure.

"I get what you mean. Look, I've got another few minutes of break left, so how about you chat to me instead? Those two have gone now."

Faye smiled. "I know. I managed to stay quiet, until that hopper deflated. It sounded like a fart!"

"They've hid it in a right stupid place. Even from where I'm sitting, I can see it. So, what do you do in your spare time?"

"I mainly follow you guys. My friends make fun of me sometimes. They think I'm too old for your show, but I try and ignore them if I can."

Callum scuffed his foot across the floor. "That's the best way to be. You've just gotta ignore hostility. The people that give it are usually jealous, or, they have issues going on in their lives, that they like to take out on others. And sometimes, it's just cause they're bad people."

"Thanks. I'm glad I got connected to you now. You're really nice. You should talk more on interviews and stuff. One second…"

The singer's eyes were too blurry from pride to notice the girl mute the microphone, but he saw her jump up and down on her bed. She saw her cheer, laugh, then nearly bang her head on the ceiling. Someone had finally given her the time of day, and she loved it.

"Back now," Faye panted as she turned her microphone back on. "Sorry," she smoothed her hair. "I've really annoyed my mom. Can you hear her shouting?"

"Yep!"

"She told me to stop being a fan of you guys after what happened at the concert," continued the girl. "Did you ever get round to seeing that video my friend Kat posted on YouTube?"

Callum stiffened. "Yes, I did. It was sad."

"For a while," Faye hesitated. "I was considering not being a Beamer anymore."

"Why? I-I mean… what made you change your mind?"

The watch on Callum's wrist signalled the end of his lunch break, but he still sat there, his eyes locked on the girl, until she answered:

"You."

As Faye's mother's voice boomed through the bedroom, and Faye's face transformed to one of panic, Callum barely managed to grasp her final words:

"Sorry, gotta go! Thank you so, so much. I love you. You should sing on your own, you know! You've got a much better voice than Kenzie. Actually, I reckon he's jealous of you. Anyway, bye for now!"

When Callum's laptop screen went blank, for once in a long, long time, he was happy.

Kenzie was leaning on the dressing room drawers, his hands splayed out on the shiny wood. Chewing his lip, Tom watched as the leading blond became absorbed in the Three Beams Facebook page. Kenzie hummed. He scrolled down the page.
In the dressing room mirror, Tom flushed redder than the cover on the back of the laptop, and wondered:

Where were the electric fans, the ice-cold drinks?

"Yeah." Feet tapping, Kenize clicked on the mouse. "I'm gonna have a great vacation, thanks…"

"Hey, Kenzie." Tom waved. "Hey, hello?"

"Yeah, babe, you're pretty fine too…"

Gulping, Tom retracted his hand. "What are you doing exactly? Isn't our break…"

He trailed off the second he spotted it. The screen… the fan page, the *fans*… Post after post was appearing on their Facebook timeline.

"Kenzie…" Tom said, his throat dry.

"This bitch is all over me," Kenzie snickered at the chat he had open.

"Look."

Tom's fingers raked his pockets. "Yes, that's very nice, but..."

A minute passed, of Kenzie being distracted by Dana Kingsley. Outside the dressing room, someone was spraying hairspray.

"Kenzie, close that a sec."

"Why?"

"Cause something's up with the fans."

Kenzie scoffed. "Ugh, who cares?"

"They're going a bit... mad."

Rolling his eyes, Kenzie finally closed the chat.

At last, Tom could see every post. One after the other, they were stacking, pushing the one he was reading further down the board.

Kenzie's smirk was wiped away. An unspoken wave of fear was passed between the boys. Tom saw that the post the fans were going crazy over had been screenshotted, and re-posted everywhere.

"What the *fuck,*" gasped Kenzie.

"*Arrrr,* you're not meant to be on Facebook."

Ashley blinked, slowly. She had to stay calm. One more snap at Bryony, and she'd get a detention.

"I'm gonna tell Miss," Bryony jeered.

Ashley's hand clenched around the mouse.

"Miss, Miss, Ashley's on Facebook!"

"Oh, shut up, Bryony!" Ashley said.

Bryony was already strolling across the ICT room, toward the teacher that sat at the front.

Ashley slammed her elbows on the table, dragged her hands down her face, and *seethed*. She hated ICT. She hated the boring presentations, the endless Word documents, and the teacher that couldn't be bothered to actually *teach*.

Melinda... why wouldn't she tell her anything? Click. Three Beams grinned at her on their Facebook timeline, yet Ashley couldn't smile back, not even at Tom. She scrolled. Melinda had smashed the kitchen, but why? As a lump came to Ashley's throat, the words onscreen were washed out; the chatter of her classmates faded along with the lyrics in her head.

Bryony returned, prattling on:

"Miss said to get off Facebook or she'll block your internet."

Ashley gave her worst enemy not even a murmur.

Young, hopeless Miss Crieg clapped her hands. "Right, get into groups of three. I want a PowerPoint on solids, liquids, and gases, and we will present these at the end of the lesson."

"Oh my god…" Bryony wheezed. "Move!"

Suddenly, Ashley was shoved out the way! Bumping into Hamrit next to her, she let out a squeak as Bryony snatched at the mouse, then zoomed in on the screen.

"No way, absolutely no way!" crowed Bryony.

A ripple of excitement bounced around the room; everyone looked. Ashley felt her temper at long last boil over, and she was going to hit Bryony, until the girl began to panic:

"Oh my god, oh my god, *guys,* look."

At the wave of her hand, Bryony's friends charged from their side of the room to hers.

A swarm of students appeared around Ashley's computer. More and more of the class got up, and raced over to see the commotion. Even Miss Crieg came, flapping around the girls like a demented chicken:

"Girls, calm down, get away from that screen, now."

Two of the girls were *crying.*

"Oh but Miss," wept Jenna, the bigger, rougher friend of Bryony. "He'd never do that, I know he wouldn't."

Miss Crieg screeched when she caught a glimpse of the screen. "Oh for goodness' sake, you girls and that *stupid* band."

As the hysteria continued, and more girls sobbed and turned away, Hamrit whispered something, but Ashley was too busy staring ahead.

There was a space by the computer, where a now-hysterical Bryony had been pulled away…

Ashley hurtled out of her chair. "Get off my computer!"

Miss Crieg tried to tell her to sit down or else, but she didn't listen. She was back at her screen now, savouring her split-second glance at the monitor.

"Miss, what does that word mean?" A stray voice questioned. "That word beginning with R?"

"What the hell do you think it means, dumbo?" shrieked Bryony. "It's when someone forces else someone to have—"

"Bryony, I'm warning you," Miss Crieg snarled. "If you don't be quiet, you're going straight to the head, and you girls, *move back!*"

Ashley staggered, because someone had shoved her away. Yet... she never *felt* her body right itself. She just knew that tears were running down her cheeks.

The headmaster popped his head around the door. The class began running in all directions back to their seats, but Ashley just stood there, in the middle of the classroom, her hands limp.

Back in the dressing room, Tom was staring at the print-screen, re-reading every word of what Jay Stanser was saying:

Dear... the band manager?

Sorry for sending this. It's really horrible, so that's why I've sent it on private messaging. Is this the band manager? I hope so. But if it's Kenzie I don't mind, cause it's about him.

I have a friend. I'm not gonna say her name, because she doesn't want me to tell anyone. She won a contest, and went on a backstage tour a few weeks ago. She's saying Kenzie (or you) tried to rape her. Is this true? She says he's/you're stalking her too, and sending her messages. She wouldn't lie. She's my best friend.

I want either Kenzie (or you, if you're Kenzie) to leave her alone, else I'm calling the police.

Chapter Thirty-Four

Fuck. Kenzie could feel adrenalin pooling around his feet, oozing all over the keyboard, and making the floor so slippery he was barely able to stand.

"Ken..."

He cowered like... like a five-year-old. Who kept calling his damn name? He couldn't tell, because there were so many noises: cats scratching, a woman yelling, then hiding in her bedroom while she rammed those pills down her throat. Oh, where was his dad, where was—

"Kenzie, come on, stop ignoring me, I'm only trying to help."

Doug's running footsteps sounded in the background.

Tom rattled Kenzie as if he were a coin jar. "Come on, Kenzie, I know you didn't do it."

Kenzie opened his eyes. He was back in the real world. His fame, his life was collapsing like a sandcastle on the beach, all because his stupid Mellbell couldn't keep her damn mouth shut.

Kenzie glanced at Tom. "Jesus Christ, I knew we shouldn't have done that contest again." The shouts outside were getting louder. "I knew it was too risky, after what happened last time..."

Doug, hands either side of the doorway, called, worried:

"Kenzie, are you all right?"

Tom faced him, his hand firmly on Kenzie's back. "Not really, Doug."

Kenzie watched himself in the mirror, ensuring he mastered his performance:

"Oh god, Doug. 'I didn't do it, I swear I—"

"Hey, come on, don't be daft." Doug walked over, trying to smile. "Most of the Beamers are defending you. They know you didn't touch her, and so do I."

Wow... *Everyone* knew he wouldn't dare do such a horrible thing... Kenzie felt his confidence return, and he nearly smirked... nearly.

"But guys, we were alone with them. O-Oh god, I was alone with her, I-the band shirt..." Years of dancing in pathetic music videos proved at last useful. Kenzie fell, gracefully, to the floor. "I was alone with her... the little girl only wanted a shirt, so Callum and Tom went with me. And it was just me and her, that Melinda girl. How could I have been so stupid? I know I should have let Aston come with us on the tour, but I told him to go. I could see how busy it was and he kept telling me how well-behaved they were. I'm sorry, Doug, and Tom, I'm sorry, I just... *fuck*!"

It took a lot of determination to release the false sob, but it was worth it. Immediately, Tom was heartbroken, and both him and Doug knelt beside him.

"No, Ken." Tom rubbed his back. "Don't blame yourself—"

"Ah, screw 'em! It's the fans who've got a problem, not you." Doug reassured him. "I knew I should have put a stop to those fucking contests! They cause nothing but aggro."

Kenzie continued to release those ugly, ugly sounds. Kenzie didn't need to look up to know they'd fell for it. '

Uselessly, Tom rambled:

"God, those girls seemed so nice! If it was them, that older one I mean, then I'm shocked. I mean, it was obvious she weren't really into us but geez, there's just no need for that. Some people just need some help. Put a stop to those contests, Doug. It's just not worth it."

"Yes." Doug agreed. "I'm going to right now, and I'm getting a camera, so don't go anywhere. We're all gonna write a statement for the page, then we're making a video message. Written posts won't do jack, really. Videos are the only way. They make an impact. We learnt that from Tomzie."

While Doug left, and Tom comforted his sobbing best friend, Kenzie nearly grinned.

Melinda Stevens had *no idea* what she'd done to herself.

In the college corridor, Melinda's footsteps squeaked on the freshly polished floor.

"Is that her?" someone said.

Keeping her gaze straight, Melinda clenched her fists.

"Aw, I hope she's okay," commented someone else.

Students were lined along the walls of the corridor. She was in the centre. They were staring, then texting on their phones. It was near-impossible to keep ignoring it. Away went the paranoia that everyone might be talking about her, because it was obvious now... they *were*.

"The stupid cow," hissed a girl. "Everyone knows she's lying."

Melinda gulped.

"Slag!"

An empty bottle hit the back of her head, to which Melinda yelped. "W-Who threw that?"

A sharp-faced girl lingering behind near the lockers was the one to speak up:

"It was me. Got a problem, you dumb shit?"

"Leave her alone," someone else said.

"It might have actually happened, you know," a random voice added.

Melinda realised that this was Dana's class, and as for Jay, she hadn't been able to find him yet, despite skipping her own classes. There weren't even any tutors around! Most had gone for lunch.

Melinda had a horrible idea of what they were all talking about, but she didn't want to face it. Oh, *everyone* was staring at her! What was going on?

Out of nowhere, a pair of heels clacked down the corridor.

"Oh, this is gonna to be good," the bottle-thrower said, rubbing her hands together.

The girl's small huddle of friends moved out of the way. Through their centre, storming toward Melinda with her two girlfriends, her heels clacking, and her arms crossed, was Dana.

"You sick little bitch!" Dana yelled.

A million cameras were pulled out. Melinda turned to run, but Dana grabbed the back of Melinda's unbrushed hair. There was a snarl, an audience's chorus, and then, suddenly, Melinda was facing Dana.

"Don't you dare run away from me, Mel!"

"Dana, what the hell? That hurt!"

Dana shouted at her, spittle flying from her pursed lips:

"To think, I was gonna apologise to you earlier."

The crowds were taking photos, and recording. Em and Rach were hurrying to Dana's side, faces alive with evil excitement. Dana was pushing Melinda's shoulder, trying to get an answer.

"Oi, are you listening? You're not, are you?" Dana rose her voice. "You don't know what you've done!"

Melinda shrieked back:

"Because no one will tell me!"

"You know what you did. Don't try and deny it!"

"Yeah." Em—Or was it Rach?—added. "It's all over Facebook."

Melinda tasted her tears before she felt them. "B-But... I never said anything. I didn't! I don't know what's happened, honest!"

"Oh, fuck off! You're going round telling everyone Kenzie Hudgson tried to rape you, that's what's happened!"

No... no! This couldn't be happening! Kenzie... he was going to *kill* her!

"But I was lying. Dana," Melinda gasped. "I was lying, okay? It never happened! I was just messing about, I..."

Melinda howled. Her hair was practically yanked from the roots! The crowd were cheering 'fight, fight, fight!'. They were chortling, and throwing paper at her, and Dana was screaming directly into her ear:

"How *dare* you! I've told you! 've fucking *told* you my cousin was raped. Do you find that funny, huh? Do you?"

"No!" Yank. Screech. "Dana, Dana, please just listen—"

"As if Kenzie Hudgson would ever fancy you! You're disgusting. And don't you *dare* try and make excuses! If anything, it was probably you begging for it off him."

Fuck this! Melinda launched her nails into Dana's face, and scratched as hard as she could. *That* would ruin her beauty, Melinda thought as they grappled with each other's hair. They practically spun each other around, slapping and grabbing.

Somehow, they toppled onto the floor.

"Fight, fight, fight!"

Melinda had landed on top of Dana. She had the upper hand! It was *her* turn to do some damage this time, and it felt fucking great. Ripping Dana's hair from her scalp, she laughed when Dana cried out in pain; she adored the adrenalin that rushed through her as her hand connected with Dana's face over and over.

Of course, Melinda had never fought anyone before, so she wasn't the hardest hitter. And, what she hadn't counted on was Em grabbing hold of her and pulling her right off her victim.

"You've done it now, you really have," Em hissed. "After college, you're getting jumped."

Students clapped, and gasped to each other, thrilled. And poor Melinda, poor, devastated Melinda, just sobbed, trying to redeem herself, although she knew everything was just *over*.

"I-I know it was wrong, and that I shouldn't have done it, but I wanted a record deal, and he-he wouldn't get me one, even though he'd said he would!"

Dana clambered up from the floor.

Melinda had to *scream* over the crowd shouting for another fight:

"I'm sorry! I was angry. I wanted to get back at him. He treated me and my sister like shit. He wouldn't even talk to us, but then he started promising me all this stuff…"

She was shouting to no one. The story Kenzie had told her to tell, just in case anything ever came out, was wasted. The hawks had lost interest their feast, because Jay appeared, with a tutor.

He stuttered:

"Mel, I-I posted it privately. I sent it on messenger, I swear, I—"

"You bastard! You fucking bastard, *come here*!"

While everyone else watched, grinning, egging her on, she practically flew across the corridor to the boy. Her hands itched to tear him down, until a voice boomed 'Oi!', and her Maths tutor grabbed her and held her back.

"That is *enough*, Melinda. What the heck is going on?" he demanded. "And turn those cameras and phones off, everyone, immediately! Shows over."

At that moment, everyone discovered they had pressing engagements elsewhere. Dana, Em, Rach, and the others all departed.

Jay, who once seemed so loyal, stared mournfully back at her.

"I think I screwed up again," he sniffed. "I'm sorry."

Of *course*! Jay had always struggled with private messaging. It was the reason he left Instagram for Facebook. But that wasn't good enough!

"Mel." The tutor got between them. "What's happened?"

Melinda ducked. She ran around the tutor, down the corridor, and away from the fleeing students; ignoring their resentful snarls, and their frightening threats, she burst out of a door, and ran away from the college.

Callum exhaled. His space had been invaded; *everyone* was in the staff room now. Banished to the armchair, he was forced to simply watch the scene in front.

Down at the laptop in Kenzie's lap, Tom was grinning. Doug was sighing in relief. Yet most infuriating of all, Kenzie was sitting in the middle of them, chuckling.

"Wow," he said.

Wow, it was *so* damn hilarious that the band had been thrown into jeopardy again. Callum seethed to himself.

"It worked," Kenzie marvelled. "It really worked."

It had. Doug was clever. On Facebook, the comments were *pouring*. Callum was playing the now-viral video on Tom's laptop. It was on mute, although, he could still hear it; he'd never forget it, that cocky voice:

"I swear to you guys, I'd never do that. I couldn't even hurt a cat, let alone a girl. We were only alone for two minutes." Kenzie had raked his hand through his hair then in the video, taking a breather. "She asked for a record deal, but of course there was no way…"

A saddened man apologised to his fans; oh, he'd done no wrong…

Harder, harder, Callum's hands clenched around those laptop sides.

Tom ruffled Kenzie's hair. "See? I told you they had faith in us! Just don't be alone with a fan again, please."

"Yeah, for the sake of my sanity, don't." Doug smiled along with Tom.

"I wanted a record deal, and he-he wouldn't get me one, even though he'd said he would."

It was *odd* how Kenzie and Melinda both had the exact same story, word for word. In fact, it sounded almost… rehearsed.

Kenzie sighed happily. "Don't worry, Doug, I certainly won't. Ah well, they're a good bunch really."

There were so many comments from them, such as:

I knew you didn't do it Ken, stay strong!

Reluctantly, Doug agreed. "Yeah, we'll have to thank them later."

A record deal? All that over a bloody record deal? That girl's so

pathetic, and ugly! Ignore her.

"Damn, she's getting it in the neck!" Tom whistled. "Those fans are warriors. I reckon they need to take a break. Should we send them Kit-Kats?"

Kenzie groaned. "Again with the dad jokes? Shut up!"

Chin up, Ken, we all love you!

Callum dumped the laptop on the floor, and stormed from the room without a backward glance.

The car against road was the only sound. It had been some time since Ashley's father had sighed, and turned the radio off.

Ashley knuckled her eyes. Food shopping, jokes, CDs on the car ride home... Brad had gone to every length to cheer her up. In the driver's seat, he'd been watching her in the rear-view mirror. Ashley wriggled down in her seat, trapped in the middle of the back row by an army of plastic bags.

"Ah, Ash, what are we like, ay?"

Ashley didn't answer.

They passed green trees. Stones began to crunch. Neither needed to say that they were approaching home, but Brad announced it anyway:

"Well, back to the happy house."

"Yeah," Julie grimaced. "With bloody police outside it! Look."

The *police?* Ashley gasped. Were they going to take her sister away? Just when she'd thought the day couldn't possibly get any worse! At school, it was like she'd caught a virus. The entire class had edged away from her; only Hamrit had remained, kind and supportive. But when the Facebook videos had emerged, even she had wavered.

Even mean Mr Martin had taken pity! He'd sent her to the staff room, a sought-after privilege in the school; Ashley could still feel her tongue burning, the tea the year one teachers had kept giving her, to comfort her.

Melinda had hurt Kenzie. She'd damaged his life forever. But why?

The engine was switched off.

Brad's voice was shaking. "Okay, Ash, we're home now. No jokes, okay? Your mother's very upset, and Mel's probably upstairs. We had a phone call from the college, but she was already home. I'm not sure she knows the police are here, so you need to go and get her, okay? Don't worry, you don't need to speak to the police; we'll do that. Just carry on in."

Ashley climbed over the bags, and got out of the car. Stepping onto the drive, she looked at the police, her eyes filling with tears. They looked cold, and unsympathetic. She muttered about getting the shopping in.

"Ash, please…" Brad said. "We can bring the shopping in later. Just go and tell Melinda we want to speak to her."

Ashley protested:

"W-Why can't you do it?"

"Because I need to keep your mother calm."

Ashley nodded forlornly, then slowly make her way toward her house.

Chapter Thirty-Five

Breathing shallowly, Melinda just lay there. Clawing her hand down her bed sheets, she embraced the feel of her tears sliding down her face.

"You stupid, stupid idiot," she cursed to herself.

She pulled the Flossie to her, nestled into her faded ears, and inhaled the scent of babyhood. She didn't want to feel, to think; below her, voices mumbled, and quiet footsteps were edging their way up.

Why had she told Jay?

More like, why had she destroyed her own life? Thousands hated her, and Kenzie was probably sharpening his blade.

Her cavern of bedsheets was dark, and comforting; she exhaled, breathing onto the rabbit that watched her with glass eyes.

"Mel…"

It was a squeaky voice, one that had previously meant so much to her…

Melinda grimaced. Releasing the rabbit, her hand delved under her pillow; crackle, crackle. The letter was still there. Her plans to run away were still sealed in that beautiful envelope. The Beamers would rejoice, and Jack would easily find someone else to walk him.

Ashley came closer. "Melinda, D-Dad wants you. The police are here. They wanna speak to you downstairs."

"Oh, for fucks sake."

Shoving Flossie back down the side of the bed, Melinda sat up. Ratty and tangled, her hair flopped over her face, hiding the dark circles, and the pale cheeks.

"M-Mel, you need to go now."

"All right, all right," she huffed. "I'm going."

"Why did you do it, Mel?"

Melinda waited by the door, gritted her teeth, and gave Ashley that glance back that she was so damn desperate for. Leaning her hand on the doorway, Melinda simply smirked at her and went downstairs.

Why did she do it? Oh, Melinda didn't know; after all, she was just fucked-up, wasn't she?

Her mother was sitting on the armchair as she turned into the living room, while her father was standing in the centre of the room next to two policemen, his arms folded.

"We've had a phone call from the college," he began.

"They don't want you back," continued Julie hatefully. "For your own damn safety."

Melinda stared at the floor. "So... I'm out of college? I've just gotta stay here, on my own?"

"No," Julie replied. "We don't want you skulking around here, making a nuisance of yourself."

"But what about my classes, and my attendance?"

For a moment, her parents remained silent, obviously stunned. But then Julie spoke up, much to the annoyed 'shush' of Brad.

"The college know you've submitted everything, you silly cow. They've said you can have compassionate leave. Not that there was anything compassionate about what *you* did."

"I can't believe you're thinking of college at a time like this! Look at us, Mel, for god's sake!" her father raised his voice. "You lied about being *assaulted,* how could you possibly..."

Trailing off, Brad trapped his hands in his hair, and turned to face the window.

"Sorry, sir," said one of the policemen. "Can we take over from here? I promise, we'll be two minutes. We just need to hear it from her, without the pressure of loads of students round her."

Slowly, Julie stood, and slowly, she said:

"Fine. Me and Brad will wait in the hallway."

Melinda was left alone with the policemen. They were both old. They could have been twins, for all Melinda cared.

"We're ever so sorry to bother you this evening, Melinda. But we understand you made an allegation against Three Beams singer Kenzie Hudgson. Don't worry, you're not in trouble. Kenzie doesn't want to go down that road. This is just an informal chat, really, so that we can tick some boxes and close the case, okay? Then we'll be on our way. So please, tell me, in your own words. What happened?"

Melinda knew she should have felt a glimmer of hope upon being alone with the police, however, she knew his kind, caring eyes and his gentle words were all a bunch of bollocks. They wouldn't help her anyway, and they'd already decided she was a guilty liar!

"It was literally as I said in the video that was posted of me," she said.

The policeman looked as though he was holding back a sigh. "No, Melinda, we need you to tell us in full, for our records. I know this is difficult, but once you've told us, that's it. It'll be over."

"Okay, fine, that makes sense, I suppose. I sang for all of them as a joke. Kenzie said he'd get me a record deal. Ashley, Tom and Callum went to get a shirt. Then, Kenzie told me I had no chance, blah blah blah, and Ashley just wouldn't stop talking about him. I just wanted *everyone* to stop talking about him like he's some sort of God, because he's not."

"You sound very resentful still, Melinda. Are you sure you're telling us the truth? Because if something did happen, we can help you with that. Please, don't be afraid to say."

"No. I-I mean yes, I'm telling you the truth. There was no assault. He isn't stalking me, and he hasn't done, or said, anything to me since the concert."

The policemen looked at each other. Melinda read their thoughts instantly: hey thought she was wasting their time. And she was probably right, because they left shortly after that.

"I've lost track now of the amount of times I've asked you this, but what the *fuck* is wrong with you?"

Melinda trembled.

"Do you get a kick out of it?" Julie was shouting. "Do you like seeing your sister cry, and me asking what the heck's the matter with you? Do you feel good when we go out of our way to ask you if you're all right?"

Melinda said nothing.

"Melinda, god help you you'd better fucking answer me," her mother threatened. "Do you have *any idea* of the impact you've made on that poor boy?"

While Brad added his part, Melinda swallowed bile.

"When you make an accusation like that,"

Her father had taken Julie's hand. In an attempt to stay calm, she was opening and closing her eyes, and her mouth. She looked like a fish. Did Melinda dare laugh?

"It doesn't matter how many times he says he didn't do it," continued Brad. "That accusation will always stick with him. I don't know why I'm telling you this. You're eighteen years old. You're an adult! How could you have been so ridiculous?"

Julie's eyes snapped open. "How could you *lie,* Mel, about something like that?"

"I didn't."

"What?"

"What?" Melinda replied to her mother, looking up.

"Right, I've had enough. You," Her mother shoved her down onto the sofa. "Are gonna tell me—"

"Tell *us.*" Brad flopped into the armchair.

Julie rolled her eyes. "Tell *us* what happened at that stupid concert. And no more lies this time, do you hear me?"

"But I've just told two policemen, and a load of people at college. I'm sick of repeating myself."

"Well it's not just about what *you* want, Melinda!"

"We need to hear this for our own peace of mind," added Brad.

"Okay, fine, whatever. W-We all went into the dressing room. Ash wanted me to sing. So I did, and…"

"Then what?" her father said coldly.

Her mother leaned in. "*Then what,* Mel?"

Melinda pursed her lips. Seeing Julie for what she was, which was an overweight, red-faced woman who'd never loved her anyway, allowed her to rant with no fear:

"The band all started going on about how great I was, then Ash and Callum and Tom fucked off to get a band shirt, then Kenzie basically told me I was crap. He made fun of me. He said I'd sounded like someone who'd swallowed a mouse. *Revenge* Mom, have you never heard of it? He deserved it! And with Ashley going on and fucking on about Three Beams, and how she was gonna marry Tom bloody Landsby, I just got annoyed, and since no one was listening to *my* side of the story, I thought hey, fuck it, let's *lie*! Everyone believes the poor, innocent fan, right?"

Brad stared at her, his jaw slack. Julie shut her eyes. There were more of her 'calming breaths'; she was fumbling with her apron, spinning out the time with her hands. Upstairs, Ashley was playing Three Beams.

"Oh, you wanted revenge? So, you thought you'd just mess up some poor boy's life, did you, because you were annoyed?"

Julie's voice was so quiet it was barely audible above Kenzie promising he'd always be there, all of the time. While Brad whimpered into his hands, Julie continued in a high-pitched voice Melinda had never heard before:

"Well, do you want to know what I'm annoyed about? You *really* want to know?"

Melinda watched, waiting for it.

Suddenly, her mother turned back, grabbed the bottom of the coffee table, and flipped it over.

Melinda screamed.

"I'm annoyed because you're sick, Mel!" Screeching, Julie grabbed Melinda's shoulders. "You need fucking help, a therapist, *something*."

Melinda stilled in the deadly, deadly waters, because all she could remember was the dressing room sofa, and all she could see was… was…

"Julie, Julie!" Brad shouted.

Calling desperately, he was trying to calm her, but it was futile. Julie was shouting manically. To the curses, Melinda hid her face, because his hands were on her body, and his grin in her soul.

"Julie, stop, come away. *Stop!*" Brad pulled Julie away from Melinda by her forearms.

Julie, her hands by her sides, was in disbelief: "What the heck are you doing? Why are you protecting her?"

"Because—"

The phone rang.

Julie stormed over to it, snatched it to her ear, and bellowed:

"*What?*"

Brad pointed at the ceiling, and mouthed 'go upstairs', while Julie hurriedly apologised to Aunt Flo. Melinda didn't wait. She got up off the sofa and made for her bedroom.

Stomp. She was glad she hadn't told the truth. Stomp. What had it ever done for her? Stomp. The world had sided with *him, then* turned its back on *her* as if she were the devil, and the comparison suited her, because she was already in Hell.

"You want this... you want me."

Melinda grumbled. "Screw you."

The bedroom she stormed into wasn't hers anymore. It was a stinking mess of Three Beams worship.

Ashley was sat in the centre of the space between their beds, the place that had now become a no man's land. Humming, she was cross-legged, her tongue poking out in concentration. The musical beat was the credit song on the Three Beams TV show, the final song that had played at their concert before the stage had gone dark.

"Ash."

Ashley hummed louder, drawing another picture, one where she was holding hands with Tom. Meanwhile, Melinda stepped to meet her enemy.

"Ash, that picture's rubbish. And what the *fuck* are you looking at?" she asked a poster of Kenzie.

Her copy of the dreaded t-shirt was draped over Ashley's bedpost. The CDs were next to the player that rested on the floor. Meanwhile, on the walls, Callum simpered. Tom grinned, and Kenzie? He was mocking her.

How dare he? How dare he defile her, taunt her, and then prance around as if her life wasn't being *fucking ruined?*

"Mel," yelped Ashley. "What are you doing?"

Before she knew it, Melinda was on Ashley's bed. "I said what are you looking at, huh? Fucking cunt!"

Her claws reached out, scrunched up his face in the centre of the centre of the t-shirt, tore a hole in the middle, and threw it to the bed. At last, he was gone!

Wait, no he wasn't! He was still all over the walls, all over her body, all over *her.*

Ashley inched forward, and whispered, scared:

"Mel?"

Melinda lunged to the left, the right, and grabbed every poster. Some she ripped carelessly, others in half, some just to shreds for the sheer fun of it.

Ashley was frenzied. Capering up and down, she tried to climb onto the bed, but Melinda didn't hear her. She was having too much of a good time. Bits of Kenzie were falling on the floor, the bed, Melinda's *feet.* Oh how wonderful he looked down there—

"Stop it, Mel, stop, *please!*"

Melinda pushed her off the bed. She *had* to get that poster of Kenzie by himself. It was just difficult, because it was stapled to the ceiling!

"Oh, so you think you're funny, do you?" she hissed to the lead singer who sat, smiling, on the red stool.

Ashley sobbed. "Melinda..."

"Come here!"

Oh, she didn't even *recognise* her own voice now. It was so fantastically terrifically *insane*. Jumping, she seized Kenzie, then yanked his face and torso from the ceiling. And after that, she kept going, kept darting from wall to wall until every poster, every face of a god-damn *snake*, had gone. When it had, she shook from head to toe, panting with exertion.

"No!" Ashley cried. "They're all ruined!"

From her bed, Melinda hopped down. "Good."

"Y-You've ruined them... Mel, how could you?" Ashley wailed as she ran for the bed, and gathered the paper like a farmer gathering loose straws in a barn. "I hate you, Mel. I hate you!"

Melinda caught site of the autographed t-shirt still hanging on the bedpost.

Ashley shook. "No, not that one! Please, don't!"

Please don't? No? That was what she'd damn-well pleaded to him. A few seconds was all it took for her to grab the t-shirt.

"Fuck you," she said.

Her parents were running up the stairs; she could hear them.

"You can't hurt me anymore." She unravelled the shirt. "I won't let you."

"No!"

Ashley came rushing forward to stop her. Melinda's palm connected with her chest; she shoved, hard.

Yelp, thump...

"Time to say bye-byes, Kenzie." Melinda grasped the shirt with both hands, fully prepared to rip it—

The door burst open.

Melinda's parents' faces were pure, pure horror. The shirt fell from her hands. Following her parents' gaze, she finally saw what she'd done:

Ashley was on the floor. She was on her back, her legs straight out in front of her, cradling the rear of her head, wincing. Her eyes were half-closed, and when she took her hand from her head, Brad cursed. The CD player was underneath Ashley's head, and on her hand...

Ashley shrieked.

Brad shot forward, knelt down on the floor, and cradled her in his arms. "Oh god, Ashley!"

Melinda watched, speechless, as Ashley sobbed over the smear of blood on her finger.

"D-Dad," she said. "I'm dying! Look, I'm bleeding! Mel, she—"

"No!" Melinda whimpered. "Ashley! Ash, I'm sorry, I-*Dad!*"

"Why can't you just *go,* Mel?" Ashley howled. "You're making everyone sad!"

Brad said not a word, but the way he'd protectively hugged Ashley to him said it all. Melinda let out a screech, her nails dragging down her neck. Her sister, the floor, *blood*... Melinda was not fit for the world, no, not at all.

She screeched again.

"Brad," Julie said firmly. "Get Ashley out of here."

Ashley's legs clamped around her father's waist. He rushed her from the room, his head bowed. Melinda moved back. In time with Julie coming fully into the bedroom, an alarm bell rang in her head, and signalled:

Game over.

"That's it. You"—Julie pointed—" are gonna book yourself some plans, 'cause I want you out of this house. I know I've said it before, but now, I well and truly mean it. You're done, finished."

Downstairs, Ashley was trying to protest her sister's innocence suddenly, yet Brad was talking over her, telling her that her sister was bad, bad, bad—

"Okay," Melinda murmured.

"Okay?" Her mother echoed. "Is that all you can say, just 'okay'?"

"Yeah, okay."

"Fine then, if you wanna fuck your life up, fine, fuck your life up. But you are *not* fucking Ashley's up too. By the looks of it, it's just a graze, but it could have been really serious."

Lamely, Melinda nodded. "I'm sorry, it won't happen again…"

"But how do I know I can trust you? How do I know you won't lash out again? Exactly, I don't. I don't know my own daughter anymore and that, oh, *that,* scares me Mel, and I don't like it. So that's it, you're out."

"But where do I—"

Julie simply flounced from the room, leaving Melinda to nothing but the lead singer of Three Beams, who grinned at her from the shirt on the carpet.

Chapter Thirty-Six

The Birmingham House was so packed with activity, so shaky with thumping music and flashing lights, that it may as well have been alive.

Kenzie strolled through the room, smiling when people noticed him and moved out of the way.

They'd invited everyone from Tots TV. The music was so loud Kenzie couldn't speak, the disco lights so dazzlingly bright it hurt, yet he was happy. A girl stroked his shoulder, and he winked at her as she sashayed away.

It was finally the band's summer holiday.

"Kenzie!" Roy high-fived him.

How long, Kenzie wondered, before some fool tumbled down the stairs, and broke their neck in a drunken stupor?

The lead singer weaved through the dancing bodies, searching for Tom. He didn't fancy going after the girl. Yes, he did need a good fuck, but he was holding out for Melinda. Nothing was more fun than keeping her dangling as if she were a fish on the end of a line.

After what had happened that day, nothing was off-limits as far as she was concerned.

Callum's efforts, which was the coffee table risen by some old tyres, was hardly a stage, yet Tom was holding the microphone as if it were. Ugh, it was high-time Callum was sacked! Hiding upstairs, he was as much good as the lead superhero from other kids show called Heroes Unite, who was vomiting in the back corner.

Tom tapped the microphone. He cleared his throat, and tried to no avail to get the crowd's attention.

Cupping his mouth, Kenzie shouted:

"Oi, everyone shut the fuck up!"

It took every ounce of his lung strength, but the crowd quieted, and turned to face the stage.

"Now, Tom, what you doing singing without me?"

The microphone *squealed*. Kenzie face-palmed; the crowd let out a series of moans over the music.

"S-Sorry, guys!" Tom turned down the boom box. "I just wanted to say something."

A voice sneered:

"Well hurry up pretty boy, I'm dying for a fag."

"Um, it's just quick…" Tom shifted.

Kenzie rolled his hands around each other, and mouthed encouragement.

Gulping, Tom gripped the microphone. "I just wanna say thanks to you all, for sticking by us as long as you have. You couldn't have given better support. It's been a mad few weeks. There's been stress, arguments, blow-ups on Facebook… but it's our holidays now. It's time to relax and forget about it, and I just wanna say you're all always welcome here, whether it be a party or not."

Wait, had it suddenly gone cold in the room? Kenzie felt a shiver.

A smile broke out on Tom's face; his eyes glittered in the now-yellow light. "You've all been wonderful, so don't hesitate to keep in touch. I know the break can be boring sometimes, but we're happy to come out and play."

Kenzie clenched the chains on his jeans. How could little Ken just go and play? He wanted his Mommy, his Mommy that was just so, so busy—

Tom winked to his audience. "No one deserves to be on their own."

"How many times have I told you, Ken! Mommy's gone to heaven."

Kenzie wheezed. He turned back. Clap, clap, clap went the audience, then the music was cranked up. The party-goers clambered for their turn on the stage.

Hands in his hair, Kenzie blinked over and over. His vision was blurring. All the figures were merging, looking like the jelly at the birthday parties Kenzie had never had…

What the *heck* was going on? Kenzie couldn't see as he stepped back, bumped into people, and tried to escape the mess of bodies. On edge of the crowd now, he was shaking so badly he was near *weeping*. Jesus Christ, why was he breathing so damn hard?

Blundering into the corridor, Kenzie leant back on the walls. Slowly, his vision came back.

People were lying on the floor. Stoners sat with their knees up. Drunks lay over the stairs, hands draping through the railing, clutching bottles of beer, vodka, or whatever kept them from staring at Kenzie and judging him—

Kenzie smacked his hand on the wall.

It was okay. *He* was okay. From the wall, alcohol seeped into his fingers. Great! More mess for Callum to clean in the morning.

Tom was raving at the back of the room in front of the fireplace, having the time of his life. Coming back into the party, and disregarding the crowd of people, Kenzie ducked past strays and toward the only dog he deemed as worthy.

Squeaking, the girl onstage jumped down, completely naked now. Apparently, she'd lost her knickers in her stripping performance.

"Kenzie, what's up?" asked Tom. "Where you been?"

"Come on, man," Kenzie urged. "*Freedom*! No more cameras, no more Doug!"

Kenzie slung his arm over Tom's shoulders. Their favourite song was on, and the summer break was the best time of the year.

The boys raved well into the night, not even the break of dawn stopping them.

There was little point to Melinda taking a bath; she was simply bathing in the misery she felt. She leant back. The bubbles soaked her shoulders; the bathroom smelt like flowers. Melinda let the water's warmth in, because she needed something, anything... kind words, sincere smiles, just *basic company*.

Melinda sniffed. Her eyes were sore... how was she still crying? Resting her head on the bath, she glanced at the ceiling. Then, she took her phone from the washing basket, again.

"I hate you, Kenzie," she whispered. "I hate you so much..."

Melinda glowered at the man's Facebook page, and the actual face that had caused everything to turn blacker than soot. However, she felt no anger, no rage toward the blond responsible. Instead, she just felt a gut-wrenching sorrow as she scrolled through the page, reading paragraph after paragraph of sympathy directed at him, and abuse directed at her.

How could one person be so evil? He was the star of a children's TV show. He donated to charities. He visited dying fans in hospital!

Upon checking her own Facebook page, Melinda had decided she was going to deactivate it; there was another video circulating, the one Dana had filmed of her drunk. In her inbox, people she'd gone to school with, people she'd raced around the block with on her tricycle, were calling her a bitch, a liar, and a slut. Fifty-one messages down, she saw a message from Cassidy:

No wonder you were asking me all them dumb questions. You wanted me in on it, didn't you? I may be a hater of that stupid band, Melinda, but I'm not a liar. You're the reason people get raped, and then don't get believed.

Oh, Melinda was going to drown herself, or hang herself with the dressing gown cord on the door-hook. Her poor sister, father, Jack, even her mother—

Melinda put her phone behind her, on top of the washing basket. Her legs looked like doormats. She coated her legs with suds, then, she selected a razor from the windowsill on her right, and tugged it along her thighs.

"Shit!"

It was small, the cut on her leg, caused by lack of concentration. Yet...

At the appealing thought, Melinda shook her head, however, she kept watching. She kept watching the blood trickle into the bath, thinking about how she didn't deserve to be liked, to be loved, or to live. Then, with the curl of her lips, she snapped the razor, and took the blade out.

Holding the shiny blade, she stared at it with a deep burning hatred, then back at her thigh with a deep burning hatred.

She didn't hate Kenzie. She hated *herself.*

Melinda dragged the blade side-ways across her thigh, and groaned with the release, and the beautiful, beautiful marring. The tap dripped. Jack howled in the kitchen. The scar grew longer, bigger, *bloodier*, while Jack kept howling, howling, and howling. She did it again, and again, then—

"For god's sake," she cried.

She threw the blade across the room, and scrambled to a stand. She yanked the plug, and drained the water. Outside the door, Jack scatted excitedly.

Melinda hugged the towel close, gazed at the blood trickling down her leg, and trembled.

"Ashley," said Julie.

Ashley kept stirring, and stirring. The cake mixture was one of the batches that just hadn't gone to plan, but Ashley kept stirring, her head cocked to one side.

"I won't ask you again, Ash. This is important."

The spoon sunk slowly into the mixture.

"Sorry, Mom."

"It's all right," Julie replied. "Just go through."

Ashley stared at her for a minute. Did she really have to do this? She hadn't even gotten changed from her school uniform yet, instead choosing to 'help' her mother clear the morning cake mess... surely she should be allowed to go and change first?

Her mother's expression took away the need to ask. Ashley made her way into the living room.

Brad was sat in the armchair, reading a magazine. Although, it was obvious he wasn't reading it, because it was upside-down. Ashley felt body heat behind her as her mother skirted around her and stood in front of the coffee table. Ashley swallowed.

The coffee table was cracked in the middle.

Folding her arms, her mother nodded at the sofa, Brad flicked a page, and Ashley sat sullenly on the sofa's edge, on the opposite side to her sister.

"Right." Brad put his magazine down. "Ash, we know you wanna get changed, but like your mother said, this is important."

Melinda's dressing gown, despite the heat, was wrapped right around her. Her fingers were tense, and her face... her face was paler than Ashley had ever seen it.

Brown eyes teaming with sorrow, Melinda met her gaze. "Hi."

"Hi," replied Ashley.

Julie curled her lip. "Tell her, Melinda."

Her sister rubbed her hands over her knee. "I'm moving out."

"What? But... you can't!"

"She can, Ash," said her father. "And she will. We gave your sister chance after chance Ashley, please understand that. But after what happened last night, we simply can't have her in the house anymore."

Don't look at Melinda, Ashley told herself. She focused on her father, and how greasy his wavy brown locks were, because he hadn't showered in three days.

"There are a few arrangements we've made." Julie picked up a wad of paper, and tossed it carelessly onto the table. "Have a look, Melinda, and decide what you think's best."

"Here?" said Melinda hoarsely. "In front of everyone?"

"Yes, Melinda, in front of everyone."

Was she flicking through the papers? Was she crying? Was she trying to rip them up? Ashley wouldn't allow herself to look.

She looked at her father. "Dad." No one to open presents with. "Dad, please, maybe we can..." No one to stay up all night with, eating midnight feasts and giggling. Inching further forward in her seat, Ashley tried her request once more. "I-I'll sleep down here if you want, if you don't want us in the same room?"

"I don't think she's getting the point, Jules." Brad nudged the woman. "I think we should just let her get changed—"

"It's fine."

To that curt reply, Melinda gasped tearfully.

"Mel," Ashley clasped her sister close "I didn't mean it when I said I hated you! I love you, and I don't want you to go. Mel, please, don't go, I don't want—"

"Ashley!" said Julie.

"No, wait a minute, Jules, let them sort it."

Still holding the papers, Melinda prised her Ashley's hand away. "I'm sorry, Ash, I'm really sorry—"

"Oh, Mel!"

Melinda caught her hand mid-air. "No, don't." She smiled again, then looped her fingers through hers. "It's fine. There are two rooms to rent available, but Aunt Flo has a room free, so I'm gonna go there."

Ashley shook her head.

"No Ash, I am. I need to. I'm sick, and I'm a danger, not just to you but to everyone."

"No, you're not, you're—"

"I'm gonna pack my things later." Melinda pushed her gently away. "I *know,* Aunt Flo's a pain, but I'd rather let someone else have the rooms, 'cause there are people out there who need it more than me."

"No, you won't, cause you're not going. You don't have to, you don't—"

Melinda whimpered. "I've got to."

"Ashley." Their mother stepped in. "Get away from your sister, now."

Ashley shrunk back to her own side, while Melinda pulled her dressing gown in, and ducked her head to their mother's verdict:

"Mel, that's fine. We'll ring her, and she can come around tonight, to sort things out. Then, Ashley, you can go back with her and stay there the night. Melinda can stop on her own. Me and Brad need a night to ourselves anyway."

Melinda allowed the heartless separation, but Ashley had other ideas:

"How could you? She's my sister! I need her, I—"

"You don't, Ashley!" Julie retorted. "You don't need someone who treats you like shit."

Ashley, desperate now, made to interrupt, but her mother was quicker:

"Go back upstairs. I'm sorry you're upset, but it's just the way it has to be."

Ashley fled from the room. From the corridor, she briefly heard her father sitting on the sofa to comfort Melinda. Julie simply scoffed at her to be quiet, because it was her own fault.

Ashley stopped at the staircase. Jack whimpered as he met her stare. "Jackie…"

Ashley hugged him close, and let her own tears flow.

Chapter Thirty-Seven

As the BMW pulled up, Tom felt a lump in his throat, one so big not even swallowing could get rid of it.

"Thanks, mate," Tom said, peering out of the window to the semi-detached house that awaited. "It would have taken ages to get here by taxi."

"No worries, man." Kenzie wiped his hand over the dashboard. "It's a pain getting the taxis, with Aston asking the driver a billion and one questions."

Kenzie was styling his spiked hair. God, Tom could pick him out from a crowd of *thousands*. They could have blond hair. They could be tall, muscular, tanned. They could even have a smile to rival the smuggest villain, but Tom could still stand at the top of the podium, point into the crowd, and shout 'there!'. There was the one who made him laugh, and who was always there to burst space hoppers with, and break desks.

"Can I see your ID please, driver?" mimicked Tom.

"Don't let no fans in the car."

"And check all coffee before he drinks it just in case it's tainted. No, wait, screw that, just make him drink his own piss, cause that'll be safer!"

Smirking, Kenzie finished his hair, while Tom clenched the handle of the bulky suitcase that was crushing his thighs. At the house, the birds continued to peak near the plant pots; his mother had fed them again.

Kenzie tapped the steering wheel. "Well, sod off then, Landsby."

Clumsily, Tom left the BMW with his suitcase, and made sure not to turn back and thank Kenzie again, because if he had—

"Have a good holiday," called Kenzie. "Dipshit!"

"You too, dickhead!"

Kenzie didn't wait. Tom had been halfway up toward his house, when he heard the blue BMW skid around the corner. From the plant pots, the birds scarpered, while Tom paused on the prickly doormat.

The house hadn't changed a bit. Tom moved away the ivy that hung from the porch roof, as it was tickling his head. White pillars towered up, from each side of the door. Flowers with lanky stems brushed the windowsills. The curtains needed washing, and there was a flurry of children's squeals from inside. Feeling a wave of nostalgia should have kept the smile on Tom's face, but as he rang the doorbell, all he did was plonk his suitcase on the ground, and think of Kenzie as he drove away from him until the end of August.

There was a storm of thudding footsteps. The door was opened, then: "Tom!"

Immediately, he was embraced by the spindly arms of his mother. He near inhaled a lungful of the black curls that tumbled all the way down her back.

"All right, all right, Mom!"

As she pulled away, her green eyes sparkled, contrasting exotically against her pale, freckled skin. "Oh Tom, I'm so proud of you. But you're still so *skinny*!"

"And where d'you think I got that from?"

"Cheeky!" Nose-to-nose with him, the woman ruffled his head.

"I have been trying to eat more, you know—"

"Tommy, Tommy, *Tommy!*"

Tom was nearly bowled over by his twin brothers, two five-year-olds who between them packed a bulldozer's weight and a set of identical grins.

"Whoa, hey guys."

Stepping back wisely, Tom's mother smiled as she readjusted the elastic band that was wound around her ponytail. Tom acted enthusiastic. Slipping one arm around each of the boys that clung to his hips, he gazed down at their sleek, black bowl-cuts, and marvelled at how tanned each twin had gotten.

"All right lads, which one of you nicked Mom's fake tan?"

"Oh no!" said David (or Kyle), at the exact same moment as a lolloping thud, a chorus of barks, and a bang came from the corridor.

"Retreat, retreat!" The twins screeched, jumping back.

"Oh god," his mother said. "Here's the cavalry."

Down the corridor came three yapping, slobbering, over-excited dogs. The German Shepherd leapt up, his paws whacking Tom's shoulders, his tongue smothering his face with wetness and rotten meat. Tom puffed as he struggled to get in the house:

"Aw, Matty, guys, chill, just... ah!"

Betty, the ginger chihuahua, growled playfully, tugging at the bottoms of his jeans, while Hetty, the Yorkshire Terrier, simply sat in front, barking.

His mother snapped her fingers. "Right, boys, grab Tom's suitcase."

An alarm went off.

"Oh shit, the pizzas!" Tom's mother cried. "Be right back!"

David (or Kyle) darted to the suitcase. The other brother took on the stairs, shouting as he went:

"Craig, Craig, Tom's here. Tom's back!"

Tom was set free. Wagging their tails, Matty and Betty followed his mother into the kitchen. His brother charged past him with the suitcase, yelling about pizza.

Tom ruffled the patient Hetty. "You doggos, what are you like, ay?"

What was everyone like, Tom mused as his mother opened the oven and released the tomato sauce, and the oozing cheese.

They certainly weren't like his best friend, who had driven off.

In Hereford, a timid, mixed-race boy waited outside his old cottage. The sky was cloudy; for summer, the air was quite cool. Next to his suitcase, Callum stood on his tiptoes, and peered through the door's glass window of Jesus.

Where were they? He'd rung the bell...

Callum prodded the suitcase with his foot, and picked at the wool on his thin brown jumper. Around him, the expanse of trees and grass between other cottages rustled in the breeze, while a group of ducks quacked overhead. He hadn't seen them for a while, the couple that waited behind those neat, cream bricks.

Callum rung the bell again.

Shuffle, shuffle, click.

Picking up his case, Callum waited with anticipation as the door gradually creaked open, and a short, plump, hunched African man peered around the flimsy wood.

"Who is it? What do you want?"

Putting down his suitcase, Callum mumbled.

"What?" The old man cupped his ear. "Speak up lad, for Pete's sake, I can't hear what you're saying."

"I said stop messing around." Callum grinned. "You know what I've come for."

The joke no one else would fully understand was over; the man opened the door fully and they embraced.

"Ah, Callum." His eyes were welling up. "I'm so glad you could make it. All those trains, just to see us."

"I always come back, don't I?"

"Like Lassie."

Sniffing, Callum was near overcome as he inhaled that warm, musky scent that could only be known as his grandfather. Looking down the blue corridor, he took it in: the framed photos, the homely classics playing from the phonograph, the tiny shelves that bore those trophies that always, always shone, and the grandmother that was padding down the hall in her slippers, her head shaven now, and the skin that matched Callum's heaving with tiny freckles. In her shaking fingers, she carried the savoury pastry that took Callum right back to childhood.

"Callum, dearie," she said. His grandfather hobbled away, then stood, proudly, by her side. "I knew you'd come, so I made your favourite rhubarb pie."

After dragging his suitcase in and closing the door, Callum took the pie from her hands; it was unlikely her Parkinson's would allow her to hold it much longer.

"Gran, t-this is…"

The top layer of crumbly pastry was cracked, yet it was a labour of true love. His grandparents were politely apologising for not answering straight away. The carrots in the back garden had needed to be free of weeds, all in time for the next gardening competition. Callum glanced out to the garden.

He nearly dropped the pie.

"He didn't want to tell you," his grandmother explained. "He got delayed. Even then, he wasn't if his flight would be on time."

Tears were tricking down Callum's cheeks.

Outside, waving from in front of a vegetable patch in the garden, was his father.

As the sky outside was patterned with exotic oranges and baby-pinks, Tom held up his phone, and snapped a photo of himself pouting in front of the sunset. His single bed, shaped like a race car, creaked as he leapt back onto it. Smiling, he posted the photo to his Twitter.

He was finally home, in his childhood bedroom. He was so happy to at last have a break. He propped his head on the bed board, and his legs in front of him, then watched the comments from those wonderful, wonderful Beamers pour in.

The dogs yapped downstairs, and the twins fought over the remote. Tom began to type replies, just as another set of wails sounded downstairs.

A shadow filtered in through the doorway.

Tom sat up abruptly. "All right?"

"Yeah." Kicking away stray HotWheels cars, Craig paused in front of him. "You?"

Tom stared. His older brother's lips were so thin, his smile was barely visible, and his skin so pale it was near translucence. Dead-straight, his greasy black hair hung in his eyes, and shielded the bottle-green colouring.

Tom put his phone down. As always, Craig looked shifty. He scanned the hallway, then reached into the pocket of his faded blue jeans.

Suddenly, Tom's stomach did a flip so strong it rivalled an Olympian acrobat.

"So," Craig near sung at him. "You enjoyed the family pizza then?"

"Yeah."

"Good, good."

Tom picked at his nails. "You should have come down. David and Kyle miss you."

How was he going to tell Craig that he'd gotten too thin, and that he needed to wash?

"Oh, do they? Which one said that then?"

Downstairs, one twin crowed, while the other whined. Their mother had firmly told them just who would have the remote, and as usual, one wasn't pleased.

Tom frowned. "Erm…"

"David's the one with the freckle on his nose, and Kyle has the higher voice."

'"Of course. It was probably Kyle who nicked the fake tan too. He's always been the naughtier one. It's been a while, hasn't it?"

"Yeah." Tauntingly, Craig shook the bag. "It has."

"I thought you'd given up," Tom said.

'"Aw come on, Tom, where's your fun gone?" His knees bumped against the bed. "Has that pretty-boy run off with your sense of humour?"

"It's crack, Craig. You know Mom don't like it."

Craig winked. "Especially the strong stuff. Right, yeah, I forgot. Since you've turned into a big pop-star, you're too good for your druggie brother."

"I never said I was too good for drugs. I just said that I didn't think it was a good idea anymore. You know what the press are like."

"Actually, Tom, unlike you and that little prick you auditioned with, I don't. I know what rehab's like, though."

"You had to go there, Craig."

"Not really. I only went 'cause you guys wanted me to. They don't do no good. They don't ask you why you do it. They just tell you to put the roll-ups down, cause life's 'so much better out there'. Bullshit, man." Craig turned his back. "I may as well just sod off out of here. I'm better off in a cardboard box."

"No, wait—"

"Do me a favour." Pausing in the doorway, Craig threw another bag to Tom. "Use some of these up. There's roll-ups and LSD in there. I went off LSD ages ago, but as for the roll-ups, I near busted my ass trying to get hold of them. But then again, you' like having your ass busted, don't you, *Thomas?*"

The door closing was the only sign Craig had left.

Tom tossed the bag onto his pillow. Standing, he raked his fingers through his hair, and faced the window. He quivered, in the glare of the sun, and the smell of BO Craig had left behind.

"Fuck it."

Tom reached for his draws. He tugged open the top one, and took out the lighter Kenzie had brought him from Alton Towers, but decided to pop a pill instead.

Half an hour later, or something like that, maybe, Tom's heart was racing. Why was it so *dark?* Where had his shirt gone, and why was it so damn *hot?* Down his pale skin, sweat poured.

Vroom, Vroom!

"What the *fuck?*"

The HotWheels cars that had once been his treasured collection, were racing!

Tom was trapped in the centre of the track, not that there was any need for a track, because—vroom! Screech! The cars were aiming for him! Yelping, scrambling back, Tom hit his bare back painfully against the bed, no, the *crowd* that cheered in the docks.

Thomas....

A tiny man sank his teeth into his shoulder. Tom yowled. Another did the same to his ears, his neck. Shouting, Tom veered around, and spun in a half-circle. Frantically, Tom dusted the people off his body. But then, the cars sped toward him, all in a line, every colour of the rainbow—

"No, no!"

Squealing, Tom finally made it to the wardrobe.

The only thing that confronted Tom as he closed the doors to those leering headlights, was the silence that followed.

Knees-up, Tom rested his head against the shirts. What a beautiful thing silence was.

What a brilliant thing the next *vision* was.

The wardrobe peeled away, and the scene changed.

"Hey, you okay?" He questioned the towering blond that stood in front of him.

"Yep." Kenzie simply smirked back. "Now shut up, Landsby."

Tom shut his eyes, and whimpered.

Kenzie whispered: "Shush. Don't let them hear, don't let them come in." Then, he captured his lips with his own, and the elevator plummeted. It landed, in a pool of pink and orange happiness, only to be complimented by the sun that shone above...

Tom awoke. In the wardrobe, he had stiff knees, a stiff neck, and a stiff—Kenzie! He had to thank Kenzie for allowing him to open up, and be who he truly was!

Tom dug his phone from his pocket. 'Oh, he had to text him!

I love you.

Thankfully, Tom blacked out before he got the chance to hit send.

Chapter Thirty-Eight

"All right, Ashley," smiley, cheerful Aunt Flo said as if the girl was two, not seven. "Your turn now."

Ashley reluctantly made to pull the next brick from the Jenga block, while Melinda nearly vomited her stomach contents of chocolate and sadness all over her silly aunt—*lodger*.

Flo was obsessed with hygiene and safety; she had dyed her black bob *far* too black, then made it worse with a red fringe. Plus, she had glasses that made her eyes rival a hooting owl, yet Melinda had to pack her bags, and leave with her on the weekend.

Kenzie had promised to 'fuck her life up', and fuck her life up he had.

The tower of bricks collapsed.

Aunt Flo began to laugh. Ashley wriggled uncomfortably on the living room floor, and Melinda's lips wobbled as she firmly told herself that she would not cry.

Ashley nudged her. "Mel, are you okay?"

Melinda nodded.'

Jack snoring softly in the kitchen, and that leak in the pipe outside that was still dripping were sounds that soon, Melinda would never hear again.

Aunt Flo began hurriedly re-building the castle. "Well, looks like I've won that one, girlies. I bet you can't beat my score, Mel!"

"I'm not playing, remember?"

If only she could have said that weeks ago, to Kenzie.

The sound of the doorbell ringing was a saving grace. Melinda jumped up. "I'll get it."

"Oh," Flo said. "But I can—"

"I said I'll get it!"

The self-harm scars still hurt. Self-consciously, Melinda smoothed down her nightgown, aka her father's black t-shirt, as she hurried from the living room.

Aunt Flo echoed behind her:

"Who on earth? At this time of night?"

"It's only eight o clock," grumbled Melinda resentfully. "Moron."

The knocking was getting more frantic, more urgent, and so was the voice that shouted her name.

Melinda yanked the door open.

Hands linked, face downturned, Jay immediately made Melinda angry. "Mel, I'm sorry to bug you, I know you don't wanna speak to me, but—"

Melinda went to slam the door, but Jay caught it.

"Wait!" he said. "Please, why haven't you been answering my texts?"

Melinda leant on the doorframe, and admired her bitten nails. "Cause I don't wanna speak to you, dumbass."

Being as foolish as he was, Jay squeezed his index finger, and tried again. "I'm really sorry. I honestly didn't mean for things to happen like that. You know what I mean, don't you? I really did think I'd sent it on private! I've deleted Facebook now, and I'll never go on it again till I learn. Sophie said she'd teach me, but please, I don't wanna fall out with you and be on my own at college—"

Melinda slammed the door in his face.

When Aunt Flo asked who was at the door, she'd simply tell her she the person had got the wrong house.'

The mansion was so quiet, and the furniture so immaculate… black sofas blended into the darkness, while the red carpet mirrored a bloodbath beneath. The main living room was huge, with ornaments and statues standing proudly on the white-marble fireplace, various photos framed in gold on the walls, and a plasma screen TV. To the left, the kitchen waited to be used, but of course, the owner hardly ever came here, so the mansion just seemed to wait, in perpetual darkness, until…

The door opened. The light was switched on.

Kenzie Hudgson peered around the room.

Of course, the room was how he'd left it. The walls were still white. There were no stains of pesky children, or litter of messy teenagers. It had taken him forever to finish driving Tom around, and sorting last minute arrangements, but finally, he was home, and he was relieved.

He wasn't scared. He switched the TV on with a sigh. He wasn't intimidated, or inwardly panicking. He slumped on a sofa, and flicked through the channels, sitting alone under the glare of the black chandelier. Behind him, the fireplace loomed, ready to char the ashes of any trespassers to hell. Kenzie twitched. This was his home—

"Do you have to go out again, Daddy?"

He didn't need anyone else.

"Just cause your mother's fucked off," the bald, fat man replied. *"Doesn't mean I can't too."*

Kenzie ground his jaw, clenched the remote, and turned the TV up louder.

"But you said you'd stay home tonight."

The crowd cheered; their cameras flashed, to which the models struck that pose of perfection. There was no slam of a door, because Kenzie was alone in his mansion, and he was happy…

"Yeah, well looks like I lied, didn't I?"

He lasted seconds before he bolted. 'Scaling the stairs was beyond easy, with the pent-up emotion rampaging in his head. Growling, he shoved open the bedroom door with a bang.

Immediately, he remembered his knuckles creating that huge, gaping hole. Other than that, the room was the same as always. The bed was still that same ruby-red, and the desks and draws still in the same place. Everything had stayed the same since he'd changed bedrooms, everything except…

"Yes…"

The wardrobe.

Kenzie was consumed with an overpowering sense of glee, one that brought a smile to his face, and his panic right down. He opened the door. He looked in, and flicked through the various dresses, long shirts and leggings… it was all there, and it had all been so, so, wonderfully worth it.

Every moment had been calculated, every memory of her savoured and stored in his head to twirl round and round, then manifest into what was now the best idea Kenzie had ever had.

Touring her room had been... fun. Terrifying her had been absolutely delicious. Yet now, the holidays had arrived, and she was home alone. Since had there a better time?

His dove underneath the bed, and pulled out an old shoebox. As he slid it open, he was grateful of the fact that when someone lived alone, there was no need to padlock every damn thing. But of course—he pushed the golden tissue paper aside, and ran his hand over that cold, metal exterior—that would soon change.

In preparation for his plan, he'd had to screw bolts on the bedroom door.

Kenzie pulled out the handgun.

Kenzie checked for the bullets. They were all still there, ready and waiting, like the text on his phone he'd read half an hour ago:

Mom's kicking me out. She's having drinks with Dad, probably slagging me off rotten. Whatever. I've finally managed to get my aunt and Ash to leave. Now's the perfect time for you to call me and have this out, instead of texting. If you have the balls, that is. Anyway, stay away from my house. After the weekend, I won't be there anymore.

Kenzie hadn't replied to that', because sometimes—Kenzie slid the gun into the waistband of his jeans—actions really did speak louder than words.

What's going on? Everything's just... white.

"H-Hello?"

Where is her house? Where are her family? She's trapped in this land of white. There are no sounds, and no smells. Peering around once more, she calls out again, louder this time:

"Hello, please, is anyone there?"

Tap, tap.

The girl squeals.

Tap, tap.

Someone's coming! Her lungs are caving in; she can't breathe, because coming toward her, despite her shaking her head and stepping backwards, is the smirk of... of...

Kenzie reaches out his hands, poison swirling beyond his chocolate-

brown eyes. Melinda opens her mouth, and screams a long, echoing scream:

"*No!*"

Melinda threw back the bedcovers, gasping. Flossie landed with a bump on the floor, and Melinda's nerves gradually eased.

She was in her bedroom. It wasn't white, but black with darkness, and there was no Kenzie. Palm on her chest, Melinda shut her eyes, calmed herself... and then held her head.

For some bizarre reason, Jack was barking his head off by the bed. In her dress still, Melinda had fallen asleep in Ashley's bed; her own was littered with empty cans she'd thrown at the wall.

Fuck! She'd drank far too much. Swiping thirty quid from her mother's purse, she'd got changed, then gone out after Flo and Ashley had left. She'd come home with a big bottle of Bacardi and several cans of fruit cider.

"Jack, shut it! My head's banging."

Bark, bark, bark!

"Jack!" Melinda reached over, and switched on the desk lamp. "Jack seriously, what the hell is the matter with you?"

Rolling her eyes, Melinda swung her legs out of bed, and rubbed her tired eyes.

Jack blocked her way to the door.

"Fucks sake, Jack."

Bark, bark, bark!

"*Jack*, shift, I need some water."

Frantic, Jack grabbed the back of Melinda's dress.

"No! Bad dog! Let go! Jack, I'm going. No, you're not coming with me." Annoyed, Melinda dumped him on Ashley's bed. "Now *stay there.*"

Ever since he'd got his cast taken off, he'd been a bloody pain! He was scratching at the door, whining to be let out. Ignoring him, Melinda went to the bathroom to get a drink. She caught sight of her phone in the toilet.

Damn it! So drunk she'd been swaying, she'd been sending another 'I'm sorry' text to Ashley, and she'd accidentally dropped it.

Nothing could describe her irritation when she realised it was completely fucked, or when she realised she didn't have a glass on her, so she'd have to go downstairs.

So what if her parents noticed the missing money? What else could they possibly do to her? They were staying the night at Karen's anyway, and coming back in the morning. her mother had texted her right after she'd texted Kenzie.

Texting Kenzie was another regret.

Hang on…why was the TV on, Melinda thought when she got downstairs.

To make matters worse, it was a DVD of the Three Beams show; she could hear whoever was watching it mumbling. Ugh, it was probably Ashley! She'd probably begged Aunt Flo to take her home, the baby.

"Ashley," Melinda moaned, several glasses of water later. "Ash, turn that shit off and go to bed. And don't tell Mom about the Bacardi upstairs. I only drank half anyway."

From the living room, the Three Beams Show went on. Kenzie said some ridiculous, cheesy line.

Melinda raked back her hair, and called Ashley's name again when she reached the living room.

In the episode, Kenzie was on the phone. She could hear him saying goodbye to someone.

"Okay," Melinda huffed. She was getting really, really annoyed now. If the fool didn't come to the door right now, she'd drag her out by her hair. As a chuckle onscreen sounded from the arrogant lead singer, Melinda silently opened the door just a tiny bit more, and peered inside, ready to yell at Ashley.

What she got in return was the blood draining from her face, and her entire body turning dangerously, bitterly, *cold.*

"Sorry, Roy, I really gotta go now."

The fear had frozen Melinda in the corridor; she was gaping in disbelief.

There was no wondering how he'd gotten in, or why he was there. Just the fact that he was sitting on *her* sofa in front of the TV was enough to drive the steak of insanity into Melinda's heart.

"Yeah yeah, no worries," he said. "Bye, Roy, catch ya later."

Melinda made for the kitchen. Her footsteps were sneaky, and noiseless. Taking big, lurching strides, she skirted around the table, and headed straight for the utensil drawer.

Power, resolution, control… Melinda held the biggest knife in front of her face, and it reflected, eight inches long, in her eyes with a silver glint.

Grateful, she was, of Jack's barks upstairs. She got back to the living room door without Kenzie noticing. She hovered, for a moment, her heartbeat drumming in her ears. Then, she struck:

"Get out!"

Kenzie jumped up, taken by surprise. He wasn't wearing his costume, just a black t-shirt, and grey faded jeans that were ripped and smothered in chains. His hair was gelled; odd strands fell in his eyes. It had been in a while since Melinda had seen him, but she could take him; it was easy, now she was armed.

"I said *get out!*"

"Whoa now, Mel, easy—"

"I'm not gonna ask you a-fucking-gain!"

"All right, Mel," Kenzie said, taking a step forward. "Just calm down. We know how this'll end." He winked. "I only wanna help you."

"No. *You* are trespassing. Now take your cocky little ass, turn around, and get the fuck out, 'cause this is my house! I said get out! Get out before I—"

Kenzie reached into his jeans, and pulled out a handgun.

Melinda stiffened, her courage gone.

His fingers were etched around the trigger, his lips curling as he prepared to blow her brains out.

"I'm in a very, very good mood tonight, Mellbell. So, I'm gonna give you a five second head-start. On your marks, get set… go!"

Melinda did just that.

She banged the door shut, attempting to slow him down. It was no use; he barged through, just as her fingers connected with the front door. She only just made it out in time. Gasping, she stumbled out into the night, the knife in her hand. She charged for the only safe place she could think of: the wood.

She didn't look back, so didn't spot his BMW in the driveway, or check to see if he was following her, or scream out for help. Instead, she vanished into the trees, terror firing a million questions all at once.

Where was he? Was he behind her? What the *hell* was she going to do?

"F-Fucking hell…"

The leaves crunched under her feet. The twigs scratched her bare legs. It was only her final question she received an answer to.

The tree ahead was same one that she'd climbed up many times as a child. Through her whimpering, she dived for the trunk, and climbed up it like a squirrel fleeing from a hungry, hungry fox.

Somewhere along the way, she lost the knife.

Curling into a ball, Melinda sat in the tree, and choked back a sob. She listened out, into the silence of the night. The silence, silence, silence—

Jangle, jangle, jangle.

"Wanna hear a fact, Mellbell?"

Craning her neck, Melinda spotted him from the mass of leaves that covered her. He was standing below where she sat, shining a torch round and round, his voice high and his smile wide.

"I know you're here, so I'm gonna presume you said yes."

Melinda didn't move an inch.

"Basically, running from me" —he paused, and shook his head—"is like fighting an illogical war."

Kenzie began walking upwards, the jangling of his chains getting quieter and quieter. Shining the torch, he was calling her name, singing it in that melody that had become so, so haunting. And as that melody played, Melinda remembered:

The house phone.

He'd hadn't had his gun with him; he'd probably tucked it away again. But, Melinda was taking no chances. Shivering, she waited until he was completely out of sight. Only then did she timidly climb from the tree, and head straight into that illogical war.

Chapter Thirty-Nine

Bursting into the house, Melinda panted as she hurried for the kitchen; the house phone was a beacon in the dark.

"Nine," she said into it. "Nine, nine…"

The phone didn't ring.

"What the hell?"

He'd cut the wire. With the gutting realisation, Melinda hopelessly slammed the phone back down.

There had to be another phone! Surely, somewhere…

Melinda's phone was in the toilet. Her mother had taken hers; so had her father. Ashley had been texting her, so she definitely had hers.

"Fuck!"

Unhelpfully, Melinda kicked at the dining room table. Her hands meeting her head, she gasped:

"Come on, come on… plan B, plan B…"

Plan B was to just *run,* and hope there was a shop open somewhere, or a house she could bang the door of. It was risky, because Kenzie was still out there, but what choice did she have now? Reluctantly, she headed outside.

The second Melinda saw those headlights, she knew 'she'd fucked up, big time. Thrum, thrum… the lights were shining on the left of the house, outlining her shadow on the wall.

Briefly, Melinda remembered running with Jack, running for her *life.* She clenched her hands. Then, she stared right at Kenzie Hudgson, mentally telling him that she would run no more.

The car horn beeped.

Melinda ran.

Back to the wood, back to the wood! Melinda cursed at the grass as it weaved between her toes and tried to trip her up. She had no knife, and the further up the hill she ran, the thicker the grass was.

Fuck, the *car.*

It was following her; terror, panic, oh god! He wasn't beeping the horn, or playing the music, but he was getting closer. Melinda shrieked. She kept running, her chest heaving, her entire body almost *buckling*.

Melinda looked at the trees ahead, and willed them to uproot from the ground and come to her. She could feel the heat of the car lights on her bare legs. The grass wasn't long enough! He was going to *mow her down*.

"Fuck off!"

Snarling at him was one of the many things Melinda would live to regret. The car accelerated, and it got so, so damn close, that above the sound of the grass being mowed down, Melinda heard him tell her to 'bring it on'.

Out of nowhere, the trees seemed to rush to her rescue. The car screeched. She turned back; she caught a glimpse of it halt drastically, and steam rise from the wheels, but then she was in the wood. She felt leaves, not grass, and twigs, not warm night air.

She bent over, a stitch in her side. The only way now, was downhill.

"No..." she told herself. "You can do this. Move."

Several times, she nearly fell and broke her neck on the way down the hill that was steeper than Everest. '

At the base of the hill, was the lake. And, past the lake, past that terrifying stretch of water, was the twenty-four-hour off license she'd been to.

A burst of pain shot up Melinda's foot. She yelped... then, she tumbled.

Crying out, her head met the floor, just as she heard a set of footsteps charge through the grass. She felt the fear that she was completely screwed, that it was over, but she had no time to contemplate the consequences of tripping over the rock, because her fall didn't stop. She screamed as her body rolled over, and continued rolling, all the way down the slope.

Eventually, she rolled to a stop.

Melinda groaned. Face down in the dirt, she struggled against the exhaustion. She was hurting. She had a stitch in her side. Dizzy, her head was still throbbing, and her stomach still lurching. Where was Kenzie?

Swallowing, Melinda placed her hands on the leaves, dragged her knees in, and pushed herself up. Twigs in her hair, she looked back at the hill.

Framed in-between two trees, was the predator himself.

Melinda didn't have to actually see it, but she knew he bore that grin, the one that showed every one of his teeth, as he tauntingly shined the torch over every inch of the ground.

Spluttering dirt, Melinda looked ahead to where she was about to run. And she didn't move her hands, or her knees. She just stared at the shining water, frightened as it shone in the moonlight.

Kenzie… a quick check revealed the light nearing her, turning the meters to inches; it would damn devour her if she didn't move. But *water…*

Oh, fuck it.

The torch nipped at her heels. Sliding all the way, she neared the edge of the lake. She winced; mud was oozing onto her feet. The cold was lapping at her skin. However, she could sense his hands on her in her memories, roaming her body while he sucked on her neck, and that was enough:

She dived in.

The water swamped her. She headed for the grassy end. It smelt. It was cold. Her feet touched the bottom; she shrieked, water going into her lungs and making her splutter.

Finally, she got there. She ducked her head under. She tried, oh, she tried, to hold it under, but she ended up with even more water in her lungs; she gasped, clutching at the long grass.

She had no idea where he was; she could see no light, no grin. Nevertheless, she parted the grass, flinching as droplets splattered her cheeks, and ducked into the makeshift house. Thankfully, the water was now under her waist.

Melinda hovered in the grass for a good while. She held her hands above the water, and willed not to touch, think about, or look at it. She focused only on the warmth of her silent tears, the drumming of her heart, then the quiet of the wood as the leaves rustled in the breeze.

Was he gone?

Melinda exhaled. She just had to wait it out, wait everything out. She couldn't ask herself what the heck she was thinking her drunk self-texted Kenzie, or if she would even get out of there with her life. She just had to concentrate, wait, and then rush for the off-licence. Yes… it was the perfect plan, the perfect—

They were there for a few moments only, his arms, but they were like a vice. She saw them wrap around her waist. After that, she had no time for anything else. A cruel, taunting whisper was delivered into her ear:

"Gotcha."

Melinda was lifted out of the water.

She screeched. She struggled. She kicked the fronts of his legs, wailing desperately as her body met the air, and the lake was taken further away from her.

"No, no, no! Get off! Kenzie, please!"

He dragged her backwards, laughing to himself, while she pleaded:

"Don't kill me! My sister needs me, she—"

Kenzie put her down.

Immediately, Melinda tried to escape.

Kenzie grabbed her arm, and spun her to face him.

"No!" she yelped. "Let's just talk this out, let's—"

Kenzie plunged his fist into her stomach.

The pain was so intense, her entire body doubled over. Kenzie did it again, furious.

Melinda heaved.

"So, you thought I weren't gonna come back? Damn, Mel." Kenzie stepped toward her. "You're stupider than I thought. You know, I even turned down a fit bird to come here, but ah well." Melinda whined as his hands met her waist again. "She'd have been nowhere near as good a fuck as you."

Kenzie picked her up and slung her over his shoulder, as if she were simply a bag of potatoes.

She could see the ground; the leaves were becoming grass. They were going back to her house. She could see the back of his black trainers; every jangle of the chains on his jeans made her flinch. She was going to die, right there, in her own back garden.

"We're gonna have a lot of fun together, you and me," Kenzie said teasingly. "Here we are." He opened the car. "Now get in here, and don't make a sound, or I may just have to put a bullet in your mouth."

Kenzie tilted his shoulder, and disposed of Melinda on the backseat.

"K-Kenzie—"

He yanked on her ankle and pulled her toward him.

"Ah!" Melinda struggled to sit up.

Okay, this was a nightmare! Surely, she'd wake up?

Kenzie cocked his head to one side, and she *heard* him lick his lips as he reached down, and fumbled with his jeans...

"Kenzie, please... d-don't—"

He ignored her. He removed the thin metal chains from his jeans, then, reached for her hands.

"*Please*. D-Don't do this," Melinda whimpered; he grasped her hands. "Don't hurt me, *please*!"

He smirked. "Oh Mel. What I plan to do to *you* will be much worse than hurting."

Melinda tried to pull back.

"Ah, ah, ah, Mel."

Instantly, Melinda stopped, at both his words, and her own fear.

Shaking his head, Kenzie pointed his finger, scolding her. "Don't do that, that's naughty."

Please—he' wrapped the chains round and round her hands, then her feet—please let Ashley be okay. Please don't let him hurt her.

Shoving her to make her lie down, Kenzie winked. "Try and get some rest, Mellbell. You'll need it for later."

Melinda felt a throw falling on top of her. She looked out of the window, and watched him... leave?

Maybe someone was around? Maybe someone could save her?

Of course, that wouldn't happen. She had to get out of this on her own. Her body ached. Her limbs were tightly bound. She was stuck in his car, trapped underneath a leopard-print throw. Yet somehow, fight him off. She'd escape.

When Kenzie opened the front car door and got inside, she was reduced once more to a statue.

"You left the front door wide open, dummy," he said. "God job I locked it, ay?" He jingled her house keys at her. "Oh, and thanks for the booze, too! Oh, relax, Mel." He locked the doors... all of them. "We're just going for a drive... just me, and you."

Melinda bit the inside of her cheeks. She must have pulled on the chains, because they jangled, and he glared at her in the review mirror.

A tiny sob came from Melinda's lips. The man that had bolted that dressing room door, kept her awake all night with texts, stolen her dog, then ruined her life was looking at her, and she couldn't stand to look back in case he *shot* her.

Curling into a ball, Melinda hid herself under the throw; she no longer allowed herself to see anything, because as Kenzie started the car, and began to reverse, turn around, then *take her away,* she didn't want her last memory of her house to be her leaving it behind.

"Didn't you ever do PE at school?" Kenzie quipped casually. "You run so *slow,* babe. I was trailing you the whole way. And when you fell over, my god, that was hilarious."

Callum should have been sleeping; from his bedroom, he could hear his grandparents, snoozing peacefully.

'His father had gone home now, but he'd brought the laptop over himself, along with hugs and smiles, all the way from New York.

Twitter hummed with the usual traffic. Callum hummed as he scrolled down the page, and again he asked himself:

What was he doing?

The fans wouldn't want him. He opened a new page, one that swallowed the view of his personal Twitter, and started recording. He was doing this once, and once only. If he screwed it up, it was getting deleted, and that was that.

Callum cleared his throat when the recording button blinked red.

"Hey guys—"

He sneezed.

"Sorry, didn't mean to do that. Let's start again. It's me Callum, and yeah, I'm posting a video for once. It's just a quick question. Sorry about the timing, what, with what's happened with Kenzie. But I've been planning this for a while. Videos stand out more, and I wanted to ask…"

He paused.

Callum bent his index finger. Eyes roaming, he clocked his childhood drawings, pinned to the wall. Courage came back when he saw his favourite, his grandparents' favourite, *everyone's* favourite. It was the one where he was playing a guitar at a children's party, *alone.*

"Sorry, got distracted. Anyway, I wanted to ask… if I did a meet-up, by myself, how many of you would come?"

Thousands of fans sat awake, still posting on Twitter. Mainly, they listened to Tom.

Tom had blogged about how he had a major headache, couldn't sleep, and had gotten so 'drunk' he'd nearly sent a bogus text… how exciting. Most of the fans had been pouring over him, however, a small percentage were staying awake with Callum, and for him, that was enough. He thought of Faye, of his band mates, and then, of what *he* wanted for a change.

Callum nodded a quick thank you, stopped the recording, and posted it without checking it.

Determined, he waited for the response. What he didn't expect, however, was for it to be a positive one.

Chapter Forty

"Melinda," her mother warns from her hospital bed, sweat still a mask on her face. "I'm telling you now, be careful."

Melinda's 'mind groans at the idea of a squealing, messy toddler mucking up her room. She shifts, trying to at least look happy, as the short, brunette nurse approaches.

"Hi, Melinda," she says. "Time to say hello to your baby sister."

As the woman kneels to her height, Melinda meets her with a pout, and at the squirming, wrinkled alien in her arms, she directs her highest resentment. With an excited wink, the nurse hands her the baby.

Melinda's hatred vanishes. The baby... her first smile, locked behind those caramel eyes, lands on her.

"Oh! Oh, hello little one... you're beautiful."

The baby coos. It stretches. It clasps her little finger in her hand, and all of a sudden-

"Aw," Brad says, "Look at them!"

She's not just a baby; she's Ashley, her little sister.

What had become of her now, the girl Baby Ashley had stared at with such wonder?

In the scorching heat of the throw, Melinda listened. On the road, the car was still gently driving; not once had it slowed, or braked suddenly, or even sped up. Pulling her knees in further, she bit the chain to stop herself howling. She had no clue where they were going.

He'd tie her up. He'd rape her, beat her, and carve his initials into her body... if he didn't shoot a bullet through her head first.

Melinda popped her head out from under the throw. Her hair, dry now, hung in mats over her eyes. Startled, she blinked at the light they drove past, and put her *every* focus on reading the signs. They were on a motorway. They were nearing Worcester, and Kenzie was eyeing her in the review mirror.

As Ashley's bright eyes called to her from the back of her

subconscious, Melinda spoke to him:

"Where are you taking me?"

And he didn't answer.

The dog is perfect. Yapping, bouncing, licking the sisters all over, the puppy is the life and soul of the breeder's house.

Melinda, at sixteen, has fallen in love. Ashley's trying to grab his tail from behind, while the Jack Russell licks Melinda's fingers, and wrestles with her hand. Nervously, the other puppies hover by their mother in the corner of the room.

"I see your girls have taken to him," the breeder says. "I'm glad, to be honest. Out of all of them, he's had the least interest. I will warn you though, he's very, very hyperactive."

Brad snickers. "It's pointless warning us. They've clearly made their mind up."

Julie, who is with him, and holding her preferred puppy, sighs:

"Girls, does it have to be this *one?"*

'The sisters look at their mother, and call out a united yes.

They'd stopped. Melinda opened her eyes. Determination, along with Ashley's night-time whispers, Jack's barks, and her parents' cuddles, persuaded her to lift her head. Her hands were useless; she had to strain her back to rise high enough to see him.

Craned around in the seat, he had a glass of straight Bacardi. "All right, Mel? Fancy a drink?"

What the *fuck* was wrong with him?

"Fine, suit yourself. Now, you've gotta hold still for this next bit."

Melinda flinched. He was coming. His foot connected with the car floor, and Melinda tried to retreat backwards, but the chains—

"Aw, I'm sorry about this, truly I am," he purred, reaching into his pocket. "But I can't have you trying to escape."

They'd came off the motorway! There were no other cars around, and he was lifting a wet rag, all traces of amusement gone. His gun was in the glove compartment. The road was dirt now, and there was a petrol station ahead!

Pointlessly, Melinda attempted to plead with him.

Kenzie grumbled. "Oh, just shut up, you fucking pain."

Melinda squealed. She was going to die! He was going to smother

her, he was going to—

He straddled her. Gasping, Melinda tried to swing at him, but the chains were too strong and she *could not reach*.

"Oh, so you're gonna try and fight me now, are you?" asked Kenzie smugly.

Melinda choked. "N-No, no." She shook her head, desperate. "I'm not, I—"

"Sweet dreams." Kenzie jeered, rising the cloth. "Don't think about me too much."

"Kenzie!"

Melinda 'screamed into the cloth as he clamped it over her mouth. She wriggled. She screamed some more, thinking of Ashley, thinking of her parents, thinking of escape. Yet suddenly... she felt woozy, and numb.

She couldn't fight; she couldn't... yell any more. The sight of Kenzie above her, laughing, was becoming *black*.

"Dad," The upset four-year-old leans further into her father. "Why does Mom hate me?"

Melinda gazes at him, the truth evident in the way his eyes seem to dim. The TV plays in the background. The cartoon bunnies dance around the golden carrot, and instead of watching them, the little girl simply awaits the answer to her question.'

Her father sighs. "She doesn't hate you, silly."

"But, Dad—"

"She's just stressed. Please, Mel, believe me. The baking drains her sometimes. She doesn't mean what she says."

Melinda looks away. Resting her head on her father's chest, she vows to never again ask that question.

The first word that left Melinda's lips was a curse. Hatefully, she pushed back her hair. Her hand stuck in a mix of dirt and algae. Hang on, when had her bed gotten so... *wide?*

Melinda moaned with an odd pain, and near crawled to her bedside table. Opening her eyes, she allowed the strangely deep, groggy sleep to leave her subconscious, in exchange for a brush that would be painful against her scalp.

She gasped.

She wasn't in her room. She was in… in…

Melinda bolted to a sit, peering around the room wildly. She didn't know where she was!

Slowly, bit by bit, she began to remember, and her surroundings started to make sense. The sheets she was sitting on were ruby-red. They felt like silk, and contrasted flawlessly against the sunlight that streaked through the window on her right—

Sunlight? *Sunlight?*

Melinda began to hyperventilate. How long had it been? Cream walls, dark wooden floors… there was a bathroom, straight ahead, and a wardrobe next to it. From somewhere, she could hear heavy rock music playing.

Devastated, she slumped into her hands.

Kenzie had 'taken her.

Melinda headed straight for the door.

Locked.

She tried to yank it open, every memory from the previous night haunting her.

"Help! 'Let me out, please!" She kicked the door. "Damn it!" The pain ravaged her bare foot, and she retreated with a whimper. "P-Please…"

Why had he taken her? What did he want? And why *her?*

Of course, she'd ruined his life; he wanted revenge. A small, black chandelier hung from the ceiling, with a threat to drop its spikes down on the girl, the one that stood behind the door and started to weep with hopelessness because she was going to *die*—

Scrape.

Melinda was 'already nearly screaming at the thought of seeing him again. But she dived straight to the pale-green envelope that lay on the floor. She shredded the seal. She took the paper out, and scanned the handwriting she'd never seen up until then, her eyes frantic.

Melinda,

I know what you're thinking: What? No hello, or asking if you slept well? Nah, this is more important. We're going to play a game, you and me. If you win, I'll let you go. But if I win? You're staying

here.

That's right, darling, you'll keep your master's company, just like a good little slut should.

Here's the rules:

You've got half an hour to find the key to the big gates. If you find it, you can unlock them, you can leave, and we'll never speak again. I'll be hovering around, to make sure you don't cheat, though. I'm kinda frustrated right now, if you catch my drift.

One problem though: if you run out of the time, you're mine.

Of course, you can deny this. You can just give up. I could do with a sex slave, after all, and paying for one just isn't the same, you know?

Your time starts, darling, when I open the door.

Good luck.

Good luck? Oh, Melinda would give him good luck.

It was a risk, her freedom against his desires, but not one she wasn't prepared to take.

"All right." She crumpled the paper, and threw it behind her. "Come on then, Kenzie."

Ashley, her parents, and Jack were cheering her on as she sneered, calling for him. Neither fear nor logic were allowed to speak to her anymore; the door handle was turning.

Kenzie was a coward, and it was time to beat him at his own pathetic little game.

When the door opened, she bolted out as if she were about to start a race. Her surroundings became a blur as she moved across the red carpet, then swung a right and darted down the first staircase she saw. She had half an hour...

She peered around, caught her breath, and took in what was obviously his living room, with a sense of pure dread.

It was so *big!* She couldn't do this!

Yes! Yes, she *could*. Quick, she had to *move*, now, else she'd be stuck at the mansion forever!

Melinda lunged for the fireplace. She picked up the ornaments, and tossed them to the floor. Where was this damn key? She lifted the guard, then bent down and riffled through the coal. Tipping out umbrella stands,

charging back on herself and throwing up the sofa cushions, she shouted:
"Damn it, Kenzie!"

Jumping to the floor, she thrust her hand under the sofa, and found nothing. Anger seared in her scream; she flipped the table over, sent the papers scattering, and then clawed them to pieces. Nothing, again. The DVD case behind the TV had a collection of DVDs; Melinda hurled them around the room, opening every box. She even checked inside the DVD player, because damn, she was *not* staying here a moment longer.

Sometime later, the entire floor was littered with debris. In the middle of the wreckage stood Melinda, her hands in her hair.

According to the clock on the wall, it was 10.20 a.m. She'd started at ten. How the *hell* had she spent twenty minutes searching the *living room*? As if he'd make it that easy! It was probably in the kitchen!

Going into the kitchen, Melinda had learnt now that there was no time to scrape every surface, and peel away every layer.

She dashed cutlery, bowls, and plates from the cupboards to the floor. She uprooted tins, tore open cereal boxes, and riffled through the dishwasher. Even the bin was a victim. Feral with *lack of time,* Melinda made tipping the thing over her final effort. Then, she chose the stairs as her next target, because it was probably up there.

Creak.

Melinda stilled on the middle of the staircase. She tilted her head to the noise she heard upstairs.

It was footsteps.

"Shit..."

Doubling back again, Melinda fled the stairs, then ran across the living room to the white-painted door. Opening it, she rammed it closed again, hoped he wouldn't come through, and was confronted with a hallway so wide, so vast, it rivalled the field outside her house.

The entire area was gleaming white. At the top of a marble staircase, she looked down at the indoor fountain on the tiled floor's centre. She looked up, and saw yet another black chandelier, this time with crystals and diamonds, hanging over her threatening to drop.

To each of her sides were so many different rooms, she felt her adrenalin start to leave. There was no way, no—

Double doors leading to the garden! Maybe she could... just climb the gate?

Melinda had had no idea what she was *going* to do, but the second she heard the door behind her begin to open, she changed direction. Going to the right took her into a room with a pool table. She slammed the door. Leaning on it, she stopped, and tried to get her breath back.

What? How stupid of her! She was wasting time! If she didn't find the key, then—

A lack of creaks was a bomb to Melinda's already scattered brain. Suddenly, she was hyperventilating, and running down back to where those double doors were. She had to run, run, *run!*

Wait!

There was a glint from the fountain! Melinda clattered down the staircase. The statue, on closer view, was an eagle, and on the end of its beak...

"Ha!" Yanking the key free, Melinda then bashed through the front doors. "Fuck you!"

She couldn't believe it! She was laughing manically, as she rushed down the concrete path on her way up. The path cut through a rainbow-like flower bed; apple trees surrounded it, with a cropped grass lawn, all of which went unnoticed.

Clattering to a stop, Melinda paused for a moment to take in the metal, towering gates with the metal, square padlock *she* was about to unlock. Then, she sucked in that breath of power, that feeling of utter, utter triumph.

She shoved the key into the lock, turned it, then...

"What?"

Melinda tried again, and again, and again.

The gates... they wouldn't open! The key wouldn't work!

Melinda cried out, bewildered. Kicking the gate, she tried to climb it, but fell straight back down.

Turning back revealed a jingling sound, then, a figure that could only emerge from Evil itself.

Coming right toward her, in a red t-shirt and blue jeans, Kenzie sported a grin which said everything he didn't. Slowly, he held a second key higher, and jingled it again on the keyring.

Melinda backed against the gates.

It was when he was mere inches away, that he stopped jingling the *correct* key, the one Melinda now realized he'd had the whole time. It was when he was within touching distance, and Melinda had nowhere else to run to, nowhere else to go, that she gasped:

"No... Y-You bastard, you... you..."

The ground seemed to open up beneath her feet. He said nothing, choosing only to smile when Melinda began to tremble. He lunged for her suddenly, pinned her to the gate, and jeered in her ear:

"Game over, Mel."

Melinda saw the flash of his hand in front of her; she screeched when that wet rag was thrust over her mouth and nose again.

Bucking against the gate, the girl was wrecked with a suction-like sensation that tugged all life from her, and the last thing she heard before her world went dark, was the man responsible chuckling:

"I win."

Afterword

This book may be work of fiction, however, the themes within are very real in society.

Part of the reason Melinda felt like she could not come forward, was due to Kenzie's high-profile celebrity status. When Jay's accusation surfaced on the internet, she was trolled horrendously online, and victim blamed, which only silenced her further.

Unfortunately, trolling and/or victim blaming happens a lot, when a stalking/assault case hits the open air (especially in cases concerning a celebrity). It prevents victims coming forward and needs to stop.

This is not the end of Melinda's story. I plan to release the second book in this series very soon, where we will see Melinda fight for her survival. We will also see how deeply everyone is affected by Melinda's disappearance, and how they realise that maybe, they could have done something to help.

If you, or anyone you know has been affected by any of the themes raised in this book, please reach out to the below:

RAINN Sexual Assault Helpline
Website: www.rainn.org

Black Country Womens Aid (BCWA)
Website: www.blackcountrywomensaid.co.uk

Rape Crisis (England and Wales)
Website: www.rapecrisis.org

Victim Support:
Website: www.victimsupport.org.uk

The Survivors Trust
Website: www.thesurvivorstrust.org

Male Survivors Partnership
Website: www.malesurvivor.co.uk

The National Stalking Helpline Website:
www.suzylamplugh.org/Pages/Category/national-stalking-helpline

Other places you can get help include:
- Freephone National Domestic Abuse Helpline: 24-hour on 0808 2000 247
- a hospital A&E department
- a genitourinary medicine (GUM), a contraceptive clinic, or sexual health clinic
- NHS 111
- the police, or dial 101 (in an emergency, dial 999)